SURE OF ONE

ARROW TACTICAL SECURITY

BOOK 2

ISABEL JOLIE

Choose love.
xo
Isabel Jolie

ISABEL Jolie

Editor: Lori Whitwam

Proofreading: Karen Cimms.

Cover Design: Damonza.com

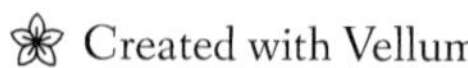

A hungry wolf at all the herd will run, in hopes, through many, to make sure of one.

WILLIAM CONGREVE

PROLOGUE

JACK

"What brings you to San Diego?"

"Business. As always." It's my standard answer. "What about you?" I glance one last time at my phone, slip it into my briefcase, and give Chuck Strand, the president of our industry association and an old family friend, my full attention.

"Oh, have some friends a little north of here. They've been after us to spend some time on their boat, travel along the coast. Judy's been looking forward to it."

"Sounds nice. It's a gorgeous coastline." The menu set before me catches my attention.

"Perks of the job, you could say." Chuck lifts his menu.

A low, vibrating hum emanates from my briefcase.

"I'd imagine so." It's Chuck's job to befriend everyone. "You know, I have a house here in San Diego. On the beach. Hardly ever use it. Fully staffed. You and Judy are welcome to it whenever you want."

"Thank you, Jack. Appreciate that. Might take you up on it."

Chuck sips his water and sets the glass down. He fidgets with the handle of the knife.

The hum from the briefcase continues, and I bend down and zip it closed.

"You said you're here on business, but your daughter lives here, too, right?"

"She does. Hence the house." I lift my eyebrows and give him a conversational smile. I bought the San Diego property after the divorce, after my ex-wife relocated here.

"She must be a teenager by now. You got a picture?"

"Sir, um, are you Mr. Sullivan?" A young hostess stands before me. She can't be more than nineteen. Her skin is flushed, and she's holding her hands together in front of her stomach.

"Yes. What can I do for you?"

"Um, sir. You received a phone call. Patricia Jones, she works with you?" I nod as my gut grows uneasy. "She needs you to call her. It's urgent. You can use our phone or–"

"I'll call her. Thank you." The vibrating hum grows louder as I unzip the briefcase. "I'm going to take this–"

"Go, go." Chuck waves me off as I press Patricia's name. He pours his brand of southern-style attention on the hostess.

"Patricia. What's going on?"

"Jack." I still, standing in a hall near the restrooms. "I don't quite know how to tell you this." A restroom door opens, and I nod at the exiting patron. "There's been an accident."

"At the office?" She's back in Houston. "At one of the plants?"

"Oh, Jack." Her grandmotherly voice waffles.

"Patricia. Speak."

"Cassandra was in a car accident this morning."

My fingers ice over. The phone slips, and I clench my hands and press it hard against the side of my face.

"Taking Sophia to school?"

"I don't know."

"Was Sophia in the car?"

"No. No. It was just her. Sophia's safe."

"What hospital?" I charge toward the outside of the restaurant.

"No, Jack."

"Is she at home?" An attendant approaches, and I give him my name to retrieve my car.

"Jack. She didn't make it. Um...she's...Jack, Cassie died."

"What the..." I saw her yesterday. "That doesn't make any sense. Where is she?"

"Jack. Her car is still registered in your name. The police called trying to reach you. It happened this morning. An investigation is ongoing."

"An investi–"

"Jack. I need you to listen. Her name hasn't been released yet, but it will be. You need to get to Sophia. You need to be the one to tell Sophia."

Oh, my god. This can't be happening. Did I cause this with everything going on?

"Jack, I told the police she was an immediate relative, and you would be the one to let her know."

"Right. Of course." I'm numb. I can't. *What the hell?* "Are you sure? I just saw her yesterday." She asked me for a second chance. And what did I say? Did I even...oh, my god, what were my last words to her?

"Jack, I know this is hard. But Sophia needs you. You've got to get to Sophia."

Right. Sophia. Her mom is her everything, and god knows we're not exactly close since the divorce. How the hell will I tell her?

"Jack? Are you there? You've got to get to Sophia. She's at school. I've been in touch with them. She's in class. But they said when you arrive to go to the front desk. They'll have a private room available, and they'll get her from class."

This can't be right. Cassie. *She can't be.*

"Jack? Listen. I know this is hard, but you've got to get to the school."

"Are you sure it's Cassie? Did you see photos?"

"Jack. Listen to me. It's Cassandra. And your daughter needs you."

"How?"

"She was hit at an intersection. The car apparently didn't stop at a stop sign. The police officer didn't tell me more. The person who hit her died in transit to the hospital."

"And Cassie?"

"She was...they think it was instantaneous. She didn't suffer. Jack? Are you okay?"

A weight slams down on my shoulder.

"Jack? I'm gonna drive you. Okay, son?" A car pulls up, and Chuck opens the back seat door. There's a driver behind the wheel.

"Jack?" Patricia's concern pulls me back to the curb.

"What do I tell Sophia?"

"Jack, you tell her that you love her. And that you'll be there for her."

Oh, my god. I can't.

Chuck approaches. His arm extends, and I shove his hand away. *How the fuck does he know? What's going on?*

"Jack, just tell her. And be there for her."

I will. I will be there for her. God, I haven't been there for her in years. Not really. But I will be there for my daughter now. I don't know how, but I will.

CHAPTER 1

Three years later

Ava

A mechanical beep sounds at the gated driveway entrance. One solitary seagull swoops below the terracotta tile eves of the white stucco mansion, touches upon a palm frond, and soars away with one shrill cry. I press the black button again, listen, and wait.

A tall, imposing man in dark green cargo pants and a black V-neck t-shirt appears out of nowhere. He's got a short buzz cut hairstyle, reflective sunglasses, a healthy tan, and holy mother, he's wearing a gun holster.

I should not be here.

The armed man stands to the side of my car and motions. I don't comprehend the gesture, and then it clicks. I roll down my car window.

"Hi." No response. "I'm here to see, ah..." My mind draws a complete blank.

I've interacted with a lot of different people in my life and walked on the side of life most would refer to as wild, but guns and I don't mix. I search the cupholder for the scrap of paper with the names. This is what I deserve for doing this off-the-wall favor. I should never have agreed to a house call.

"Ma'am. This is a private residence."

"I know. I'm sorry. It's just... Oh, here it is." I hold up an envelope from an old credit card bill with scribbled names on the back. "Sophia. Sullivan. And her dad's name is Jack. Mark Sullivan asked that I come by." The man's face remains blank. His lips are frozen. "They're expecting me."

"And your name is?"

"Oh. Ah. Ava Amara. I'm..." I don't know who this man is or if I can share why I'm here. "They're expecting me, but I'm early. I added in more time to the Google estimate, expecting more traffic, but..." I trail off. His fingers cover one ear, and those lips finally move, but I can't make out what he's saying.

The iron gate slides open noiselessly. Before me, clear, crisp water spills over a marble sculpture into a fountain base that could double as a swimming pool. The driveway circles the magnificent feature, and the armed man directs me to drive around the fountain and to park to the side. My car's wheels rasp over the smooth pavers as I inch around the circular bend.

The lawn sports thick green grass. Bougainvillea vines loaded with fiery pink blooms sprout out of enormous deep blue pots. Palm trees sway, and tropical greenery fills perfectly manicured beds. A roughhewn marble pathway leads to a massive glass and iron front door.

The expanse of glass reveals a breathtaking view through an imposing marble foyer to a glass back wall and the vast blue ocean beyond.

"Ma'am? Are you ready?"

Wow. I reach over the front seat, grab my cell phone, and slam the car door shut.

"Do you work for the Sullivans?" I ask the armed man as we step through the white stucco arch into the picturesque courtyard.

"I'm part of the security team."

Security.

Mark Sullivan has been my number one donor for years, but I've never been to his home in Texas. Does he have security, too? Is that what billionaires do? But, if he did, surely Patrick would have mentioned it. I mean, I guess I knew the Sullivans were wealthy. There'd been news coverage when his daughter went missing. But this level of wealth is incomprehensible.

Patrick is my compadre, my equal. He didn't prep me at all. After this is over, I'm so calling him and giving him a piece of my mind for not warning me.

"Would you mind waiting here? I'll let Mr. Sullivan know you've arrived."

The man's shoes rasp against the polished marble floor in harsh succession. High above, an opulent crystal chandelier hangs from a domed ceiling some thirty feet above my head. An enormous white potted orchid sits atop an ornate round table centered below the chandelier. There's a simple, straight staircase off to my left, and a showstopping curved one toward the front. The entire back wall is glass, but the center glass is thick, and up close it registers that the thick glass is an elevator. *Holy mother.*

I halfway expect a table with a check-in sign and uniformed employees asking for my credit card. The style is both austere and pompous. The excessive use of gold and veined marble belongs on the cover of *Traditional Home* or *Architectural Digest* or possibly *Hotel Lobby Design*, if such a publication exists.

A whooshing sound fills the otherwise silent cavity. Two dark haired men accompany the armed man. The automatic floor-to-ceiling sliding glass doors close behind them.

One man is enormous and stands nearly a head taller than the others. All three of them are over six feet tall, so the one man intimidates with his height alone. The other man stares at me with a laser focus.

I attempt to return his stare, and my nostrils flare as I force air in and out of my lungs. The skin along my cheeks and throat heats in direct contrast to the harsh air conditioning. The crisp lines of the collar on his golf shirt and his gleaming silver Rolex watch match his intense perusal. There is absolutely no doubt. He's judging me. Scrutinizing me. What did Mark tell him? Is he familiar with my sordid past? Is he disappointed I'm wearing a turtleneck with long sleeves so he can't scan for fresh track marks?

I'm here as a favor to a friend. And the jerk is judging me. He's a rich, clueless prick.

There's not a single strand of hair out of place on his immaculate head. It's Saturday, and the jerk's shirt is tucked into ironed shorts. Instead of bare feet in leather loafers, I'd half expect black dress socks pulled straight up to his calves.

Even in shorts, he exudes a powerful and dominating persona. He's not as tall as the enormous man who is off to the side, speaking to the armed man in a hushed private conversation. But the intense man is taller than I am and has no issue looking down on me. Those sternly set lips brook no room for kindness. The dark brown hair, thick eyebrows, and dark eyes combine to create a menacing persona. I could envision him with a whip in hand, a woman in a collar kneeling at his feet. He's that kind of dominant.

The armed man exits through the front door. The click as it closes resonates through the formal space.

"Hi." My voice sounds small. I glance between the two remaining men, and my nerves slip into overdrive, something that is not at all helped by the intense man with the scowl.

"Hi," the towering man says as he slides his sunglasses up onto his head, exposing crystal blue irises. "I'm Ryan Wolfgang. A friend of Jack's in town for the weekend."

The other man, presumably Jack Sullivan, stares at me with a borderline inappropriate intensity. *Jerk.*

But there's something about that name. Wolfgang. It's unusual, and I've heard it before. Recently.

"Do you have a sister, by chance?" I ask the only man evidently capable of speech.

"I do." His answer calms my nerves with the impact of a quaalude. We have a commonality.

"Indie?" I ask. He and his sister don't look alike, but there's an intangible quality about him that reminds me of Indie.

"Indigo Wolfgang. Her friends call her Indie."

"She may come to stay with us."

"Us?"

Ah, shit. Indie hasn't told him. "Well, I met with her two days ago." Mr. Wolfgang doesn't look pleased. "She mentioned she needed to speak to her family."

That's a total lie. The whole point of our program is to provide a path to independence, but soothing his ego might make him go easier on Indie if he confronts her. I shouldn't have said anything.

"We have a small community of condos and apartments. Mark Sullivan, ah, your uncle," I look over to the wordless glaring man, "has been incredible. We wouldn't have been able to build our center without his help."

"Nueva Vida." Jack Sullivan grumbles the name of the center I helped to found. So, the judgmental jerk can speak and he's familiar with my center. What else did Mark tell him?

"What's Nueva Vida?" Mr. Wolfgang asks.

He's asking for his sister, but I hesitate out of consideration for Indie. But he can look us up online. I can give him the answer he will find online.

"A secure place for recovering addicts to adjust to real life. We help with job training skills and placement and strive to provide a clean, safe environment because transitioning back to life is hard enough without worrying about your next meal or living in a dangerous place." Jack Sullivan's heated stare and expressionless face crack my stream of consciousness, and I shove hair behind an ear and refocus my gaze on the polished marble floor before my thirty-second elevator pitch comes to mind. "We subsidize rent payments until each person can afford the full rent. We let them live with us until they're ready, financially and emotionally, to fully re-enter the world. Rushing to return to normal can be a trigger for relapse."

"How do you know my uncle?"

"Patrick."

Jack Sullivan crosses his arms and looks like he wants to eject me from his castle. "And Patrick is?"

Holy shit. Fucking Mark. Mark warned me that he was closeted, but the idea that his family doesn't even know Patrick is insane. The two men have been in a committed relationship for fifteen years. I cross my arms, mirroring Jack Sullivan's posture. As much as I would like to, I won't out Mark to his nephew.

"A mutual friend."

Mark told me his niece has been rejecting therapy. Returning to normal life after her abduction has been a struggle. He asked me to come by and meet with her, so I sat in slow traffic for nearly two hours to get my ass here on a weekend and do my biggest donor and longtime friend a favor.

"My uncle said you're the best." Jack Sullivan's gaze runs up and down my casual dress and I can't shake the feeling that, based on my appearance, he distinctly disagrees with his uncle. But, as it happens, I disagree with his uncle, too.

"I'm not the best." Typical Mark. He oversells. "I don't force any one methodology. I support as much as I can. Ultimately, it's the individual who has to choose recovery." I tilt my head, matching Jack's questioning head tilt. This is such a waste of time. "If you don't want me here..."

"I'll go check on Alex." Mr. Wolfgang's voice reminds me that Jack Sullivan and I aren't alone.

"Ask Sophia to come up," Jack says to Ryan in a tone heavy with resignation.

"Mark," I say, causing Jack's eyebrow to shoot up, so I adjust my phrasing, "your uncle mentioned that Sophia has been resistant to meeting with therapists."

"If Sophia agrees to meet with you, we'll need you to sign a nondisclosure agreement."

On the bright side, it sounds like he's giving her a choice. Sure, plenty of addicts have rehab forced on them, but based on what I've gathered from the newspaper, this man's daughter isn't an addict. She was kidnapped. She's suffering from trauma. And if she's not ready for therapy, Mr. Dominant may need to locate some patience.

I can't take the stare off, so while he continues to glare, I peruse his palatial residence. The furniture and fancy art and sculptures probably cost a fortune, but it's all gaudy and cold. The design elicits the same kind of feeling as when you walk into an uptight church and feel underdressed.

Footfalls on marble echo through the chamber. We both turn toward the distant sound. A waif-like girl enters. She's wearing a pink swimsuit cover-up that's wet from the waist down. Her blonde hair sits in a twisted messy bun on the top of her head. She looks nothing at all like her father. Her too-thin arms and knobby knees have me questioning if the articles in the newspaper were at all accurate, because she's got the body of someone who did heroin more than just once or twice. Coral nail polish glistens on short nails, hiding her nail beds.

She approaches us, crosses her arms over her flat chest, and her loud yell cracks through the silence with the force of a bull whip.

"Seriously?"

Her dad blinks.

"You're bringing in grunge queens now? Are you growing that desperate? You don't get it. You'll never get it because you'll never go through what I went through. Give it a rest. So what if I'm not ready to hang out with my friends? Don't punish me for not being the perfect little girl. This is..." She waves her slim hand in my general direction with a dramatic flair worthy of an entitled teen. "Why won't you listen to me?"

Whoa. I hold up my palm.

"Look. If she doesn't want to do this, I shouldn't be here. It doesn't mean she'll never get therapy. It just means she's not ready right now."

The girl blinks, and her stance softens.

The power is in her hands. With recovery, her father can't force her to do squat.

"That's it?" her dad asks, hands on his hips, anger directed at me.

"Listen to your daughter. Like, actually hear her and process what she's saying."

"See?" Sophia interjects. "I don't need a therapist."

"I didn't say that." I address the young girl with a soft smile, letting some of the annoyance with her jerk of a father dissipate. "Therapy is good for anyone. As I understand it, you experienced trauma. Every person experiences trauma differently. Different emotions, conflicting emotions, can bubble up at the damnedest times. It's good to talk through those emotions. Give them names. Naming emotions can be healing. But only when you're ready." I look between father and daughter. They don't want me here, and that's not a formula for success. I'll let Patrick and Mark know I showed up as a favor to them, but there's nothing for me to do here. "Best of luck to you both."

Sophia's aqua eyes swim in her pale skin. The newspaper stories described her as fifteen, but her thin frame would have me guessing she's twelve. Assuming she's not getting high regularly. Her lips soften. Not into a smile, exactly, but I suspect it's appreciation I'm seeing. This poor girl has been through so much. She needs someone to listen, but she's not ready to talk. She may never be ready to relive it. Some aren't. Recovery takes time, and the process is unique for all.

There are many things in this world I do not know and do not understand. But as a recovering addict, I do know there is no magical pill to swallow and no yellow brick recovery road. It's a climb up from hell, and each person has to find her own foothold, over and over and over again.

"Sophia. Take care of yourself." I offer her a soft smile, and she dips her chin in a way that indicates a timid nature, quite the contrast to the defiance when she entered.

A shiver climbs my spine as my boots click across the marble and his gaze heats my back. Intimidation? Fear? I refuse to glance over my shoulder as I pull the heavy glass and iron front door handle and step into the bright sunshine.

CHAPTER 2

Jack

My gaze trails the woman in black. She's leaving. With no fight at all, she's leaving what could have been a lucrative client. I'll give it to Uncle Mark. The man possesses unique friends.

The heavy front door closes. Through the glass, I watch as Arrow security greets her near her car. He'll ensure she leaves the premises without wandering around. It's good that she's leaving. There was something about her that unsettled me. The heavy makeup offset those enormous eyes and made it difficult to do anything but stare. She held herself in a way that denoted strength. Shoulders back, spine straight, and something I can't quite define. Maybe that's why I can't stop staring?

"I like her." My daughter's soft-spoken words tear me away from the scene outside.

"You just turned her away?" The sixth therapist we've met. The first to arrive at our house.

"I didn't say I want therapy. I just said I liked her. She listened. And she wasn't ninety."

Be patient. I stifle my exhale, hoping Sophia doesn't pick up how incredibly challenging it is to remain calm when I want to throttle sense into her. "All of us listen. I listen."

"No. You don't." A touch of her mother's defiance flits through her expression, ever so briefly, before she spins and heads off to her bedroom.

I give up.

Fuck.

My hands ball into fists. My head falls back, and I gaze up at the ceiling.

No, I don't give up. I will never give up. She's my daughter.

My drink is still on the terrace, and I could go sit outside. But I expect Ryan and Alexandria will go for a walk on the beach, and I'd prefer to give them privacy. Ironically, Ryan and Alexandria began dating while working to find Sophia. Ryan, or Wolf as we used to call him, is an old friend from my Navy days, and Alexandria was a close friend of Sophia's mother.

As one of the founders of Arrow Tactical Security, he's visiting this weekend to review security measures with me, and Alex is here to spend time with Sophia. But that doesn't mean they shouldn't also enjoy time together. Sure, I'm paying him and investing in Arrow Tactical, but it's their weekend, too. Seeing them together, how their faces soften when they look into each other's eyes and seemingly communicate wordlessly, reminds me of me and Cassie. At least, how we were in the beginning. So many years ago.

I push the door of my office open. Out of habit, I scan the shelves and my desk, searching for any new item or for anything out of place. Paranoia, it seems, is the price I pay for the discovery that a greedy son of a bitch placed listening devices in my home.

In my office, I push the chair away from the desk and stare out over the Pacific. A motorboat in the distance sails over waves. Farther out, a large cargo ship passes, but it's so far away it looks more like a toy boat than the massive rig it is.

This morning, a layer of smog coated the sky, but the afternoon sun burned it away. As I stare out across the bright blue horizon, those outsized brown eyes and shaggy black hair overlay the sky. The woman didn't waste time. I'll give her that. One brief assessment and she left. No need to linger. No need to pitch herself.

I should head outside. Go for a run or a swim. Something to clear my head. But first, I owe Uncle Mark a call. I'll let him know his recommendation crashed and burned, and express gratitude for sending her out.

As I pick up my cell from the charger, a name flashes on the screen. FBI Agent Ryland.

"Ryland," I answer.

"Jack. I have some updates for you. Am I catching you at a time you can talk?"

"Yep."

"Wayne Killington has a bail hearing set for Monday."

"Okay." The bastard can't possibly..."You don't think he'll be released on bail, do you?"

"District attorney thinks it's likely."

"No."

"He's got a good defense attorney and—"

"That is not acceptable—"

"I know. I hear you."

"Clearly, you don't."

"We aren't happy about it either. But he's not deemed a flight risk. No priors. High standing in the community."

"He lives in my fucking neighborhood."

"I know."

"I can't leave my neighborhood without passing that bastard's house."

"I understand. The district attorney will request denial of bail, but he gave us the heads up that he's not hopeful."

That bastard not only slept with my wife when we were married, he arranged for my daughter to be abducted. The men he hired plugged her up with heroin and raped her. And they want to let the fucker out on bail? My teeth grind. Rage and a sense of helplessness battle deep within. *This is fucking bullshit.*

"If he's released, we recommend you file for a protective order."

"He kidnapped my daughter. Do you really think he's going to care about violating a protective order?"

"Probably not. But it's always a good idea to file one."

Our justice system is beyond fucked up. Everyone knows a protective order doesn't do jack shit, but yes, let's all dance around and pretend it works.

When I end the call, I find my way to the other end of the house. Sophia's bedroom door is closed, and my knuckles rap softly against the solid wood.

"Come in."

Sophia's freshly showered. She's changed into a pair of loose pajama pants and a long sleeve sweatshirt, and her hair is wrapped in a towel on the top of her head. She crosses her arms over her chest and waits.

I sit on the edge of the bed and pat the area near me, gesturing for her to join me. Her eyes narrow, questioning what's going on. Her newfound defiance is good to see. For so many weeks, she did little more than cry, piece puzzles together, or attempt to sleep. Hearing about Wayne might uncover the buried rage, the anger she must feel at having had her innocence torn from her. A healthy dose of fury might be a good thing for Sophia.

"Agent Ryland called."

She's stoic. I want to pull her into my arms and hold her, but she'll stiffen. When she stiffens, it absolutely kills me because I can only imagine what she's gone through. So, I face her, leaving my arms open on the off chance she wants to be held and comforted.

"They set a bail hearing for Monday."

She says nothing. She doesn't move.

"They expect he'll be released after paying bail." She's completely unreadable. Eyelashes fluttering and her chest rising and falling as she breathes are the only discernible signs of life. "We won't know until Monday."

Still, nothing. No reaction. My chest aches.

"He won't come near you. We have security. I probably shouldn't have told you. There's nothing to worry about. I don't mean to scare you."

Thoughtful, clear blue eyes, so much like her mother's, study me. "You did the right thing. I need to know. Thank you. Can I... I'm going to take a nap now."

With a nod, I reach for her knee and squeeze. She stiffens. My chest throbs.

When I reach her bedroom door, I glance over my shoulder. She's lying on her bed, on her side, knees drawn up to her chest with her arms wrapped around them. Her eyes are closed. There's a light blanket draped over a chair in the corner of her room, and I lay it over her.

My baby daughter, so frail and hurt. My heart shatters for the umpteenth time. I want to take her pain away and make her whole. I want my happy, carefree Sophia to return. And I don't know how to make any of that happen.

"How did things go with the therapist?"

Alex's voice breaks my trance. I've been sitting outside on the veranda for god knows how long.

Alex, or Alexandria as my late ex-wife called her, is the closest thing Sophia has to an aunt. Cassandra, Sophia's mother, considered Alexandria to be a little sister. She lived with Cassie and her dad as an exchange student before we were married. Alex lives in Santa Barbara now, but since the abduction and recovery last month, she's visited twice. Sophia loves her, and I'm beyond thankful she's been coming around because I suck at handling this. Sophia needs a woman. Hell, what she really needs is her mother.

"Sophia liked her." I rest my temple on the tips of my fingers. My head aches.

"That's good."

"She also says she doesn't want to talk to anyone." I hate this helpless feeling.

"She needs to, though."

Alex isn't wrong. My daughter is currently curled up on her bed in the fetal position and there's nothing I can say or do to make it better. Therapy is my last resort. The last sane option I have at my disposal.

"What's wrong?" Ryan comes into view. He pulls Alex into his side, and for a moment, seeing the two of them together burns. I get up and lean over the railing, ensuring they aren't a part of my view.

"Wayne Killington will very likely be released on bail." An audible gasp confirms Sophia and I are not alone in being disturbed by this prospect.

"We'll increase security. We can set up surveillance over his property. If he leaves, we'll know." Ryan aims to reassure me, and I have confidence in his abilities.

I don't have to tell Ryan that they should spare no expense. I paid a one-hundred-million-dollar reward to get my daughter back. And in the past month, I've earned nearly that sum back from interest and growth on investments. Ryan knows I'll do whatever it takes to keep her safe.

I also want her healthy. I want my happy, smiling, carefree daughter back.

"If she liked the therapist, maybe you can convince her to meet with her." Alex is remarkably good at reading people. I don't have to say much, and she seems to know what I'm thinking. Ryan is a lucky man. If Cassie were a mind reader, she and I might have worked out.

"She lives pretty far away," Ryan says. "I can have my team research alternatives. Find someone who lives closer."

"My uncle recommended her." Ryan doesn't need to waste his team's time. A long commute isn't insurmountable. We didn't get off to a great start, but she'll come around. At least, it's worth an offer. "If she doesn't work out, then I'll check in with you."

Ryan Wolfgang isn't a man I would expect to be knowledgeable about San Diego therapists. But then again, I didn't know he had a sister.

"So, your sister." Alex rubs Ryan's arm in a consoling manner. "She knows the therapist?"

"When we visit Indie tomorrow, I'll ask. I did some top line research on her facility, Nueva Vida, and Ava Amara has earned a wealth of local accolades. I can see why your uncle recommended her. But your uncle isn't from here. He doesn't understand the hellish drive she'd have across town, or you'd have to get to her out in the Valley. I mean, I suppose you could take your helicopter."

My phone vibrates, and I check the screen. "Speak of the devil. It's my uncle. Probably wants to know how it went. I'm gonna take this inside."

Out of habit, I meander into my home office. "Uncle Mark."

"Jack. How'd it go?"

"Not sure. Sophia may not be ready to talk to anyone."

"That's not an option. And you know it."

Ever since my father died, Uncle Mark has stepped in with his version of a fatherly role. He likes to manage me like I'm an employee, but given he doesn't have any kids of his own, one can't blame him. Plus, I've worked for him for years. He mentored me and prepared me for the CEO position within our family company, Sullivan Arms. As chairman of the board, once each quarter, I present to him. He's my biggest supporter, and given my brother wants nothing to do with him or the family business, for all practical purposes, I'm the only family he has.

"Jack, you need to trust me on this. Ava's good. She's good with people. She'll help Sophia get her feet back on the ground."

"I'm going to look into other therapists who are closer to home. I'm told her commute would be undesirable." She also left without being asked to leave.

"Jack. Listen. Go with someone we know. That we trust. Someone you can trust to not share Sophia's experience with the media."

"Any therapist would lose their license if they talked."

"And make a ton selling the story to the press, even as an anonymous source. The tabloids would pay a mint for Sophia's story. Why risk trusting a stranger?" Would a therapist really do that? I can't blame my uncle for being cautious, but his concern sounds extreme. Then again, I'm the one who thought a security system from the nineties combined with a gated community would keep my daughter safe.

"You trust this woman that much?"

"I do. I wouldn't recommend her to my family if I didn't."

If Uncle Mark is this certain, I'll pay her a visit. She didn't offer her services, but that doesn't mean she won't work with Sophia.

Everyone has a price.

CHAPTER 3

Ava

"We got the estimates in." Juliette drops a manila folder on my desk, and I don't miss the unspoken "I told you so" emanating from her.

She plops down on the sofa and immediately sits forward, readjusting the pillows. I designed my office with the explicit purpose of creating a comforting space. The seven cutesy throw pillows work within the comfort goal, but it's also telling to observe how a person sits on the sofa. Some will sit and won't adjust a single pillow. Some will so intently focus on adjusting the pillows that they delay the start of a session. One man picked up all the pillows and placed them on the floor. Juliette picks her favorite pillow out of the lineup, stacks it in front of another pillow, and crosses one leg over the other.

Her straight, blonde hair skims a thick pearl necklace. The outline of her bra straps shows under the cream silk, something she probably didn't notice this morning because she left the house in a suit coat. Every day, she hangs her suit jacket on the back of her desk chair until it's time to leave, when she'll put it on again.

"How bad?" I could open the folder and read the answer, but I'd prefer to hear it. I don't know why. Hearing it, reading it, if someone came in and sang the numbers, no matter the delivery, it's going to be bad news.

"Seventy-five thousand. That's the lowest bid. But that's an estimate."

"If we go with them, can they start work today?"

"Where are you going to get that money?"

"We could do a fundraiser. Or raise money online through Kickstarter or a similar service."

"They want fifty percent upfront."

Of course they do.

When Patrick and I joined forces to create Nueva Vida, we did it because we understood firsthand how difficult it is to transition after going through rehab. What we failed to comprehend is how difficult our lives would become, constantly raising money to keep this nonprofit afloat. Many people just don't care about drug addicts, making us a much tougher donation story than, say, cancer.

"Every. Single. Year. Something goes wrong." I say this to the ceiling with my eyes closed, letting frustration and annoyance and a sense of defeat swirl. And that's it.

I slam my palm down over the folder. That's all I'll give the negative. I open my eyes and meet Juliette's skeptical expression head on. "Can you do me a favor? It's July now. Can you please review our financials for the rest of the year? Tell me how much we need?"

We always try to avoid peppering Mark Sullivan for additional funding beyond his annual donation. Patrick especially hates it and generally refuses to do so. But Mark understands unexpected events happen, especially when one buys apartment buildings originally built in the seventies.

"The forecast is useless if you don't follow it."

"Jules." My fingers clasp the end of the armrests. She's jabbing at me. But it's not because I'm asking for updated financial projections. She's annoyed with me. We've worked together for years, and I can see through her attitude. "Are you still upset that I gave that apartment to Reid?"

"He wasn't next on the list." She crosses her arms. "You let him jump nearly fifteen spots."

I exhale. She's correct. I broke policy for Reid, and I shouldn't have. But if you can't help those you care about, what's the point in doing something like this, anyway?

"I hear you." I look her directly in the eye. "I promise. I won't do it again."

I hope I won't do it again. I shouldn't have done this for Reid, but I couldn't help it. Juliette has been working with me for a long time, but she doesn't know my dirt. She knows the glossed over website version. The cleaned-up version one shares with women who don pearl necklaces.

"You should follow the process," she says with a softer tone. When she stands, she repositions my sofa pillows. "All decisions should be up to the admissions coordinator. They'll follow the process, and you won't have to say no."

A hard rap on the doorframe nabs our attention. Jack Sullivan strolls into my office. I peer past him, searching for Sarah, our receptionist.

Juliette backs up into my desk. Any trace of confidence and determination is lost in his presence.

Of course, Jack's bespoke suit puts hers to shame. The navy material sculpts his broad shoulders in a way only a custom suit could. He's undeniably handsome with thick, dark hair and tanned skin. His countenance speaks of power, his suit money, and the way the dress shirt binds to his chest and neatly tucks into his slacks, it's clear he's fit. If memory serves, he used to be in the Navy. He has the look of an athlete, the kind of man who has prioritized health for decades.

His gaze wanders around my office, no doubt reading the affirmations and positive thoughts hanging on wooden boards and in frames all over the room. We don't get many put-together clients in our offices. The successful businessman might find my affirmations silly, but the people who come through my door are often crawling on life's rock bottom, and you never know which positive thought will click.

The set of Jack's angular, shaved jaw reveals a determined mindset. It doesn't matter that Sarah isn't sitting at her desk. He would have bypassed her and entered unannounced, anyway. A man like Jack Sullivan does not ask permission.

"After you get those numbers, please come back in." My voice jolts Juliette out of her startled trance.

"Right. Ah, can...do you want to go over the project bids?" She glances at the manila folder on my desk.

"When you come back with the numbers."

Time is of essence, something she reinforces with a harrowed glance at the folder. She needs to award the job, so work can be scheduled. We have people in two apartment units without running water, and we had to identify alternative accommodations. I could let one of the tenants move into my apartment and stay on Patrick's sofa. I could sell my car, but the couple grand I might make wouldn't come close to meeting the initial payment. What is half of seventy-five?

"Ava?" Juliette's question pulls me back into the room. "Call me?" From behind Jack, she gives him an inquisitive look. "Should I close the door?"

"No," I answer as Jack commands, "Yes."

She closes the door.

"Mr. Sullivan. How may I help you?" I stand behind my desk and fold my hands in front of my waist. "Would you care to have a seat?"

The sofa is low, considerably lower than my desk chair. As expected, he stands.

"This is where you work?"

"Yes. These are our offices. We took one apartment in the first building we purchased and converted it into a series of offices plus one larger meeting room for group therapy. Would you like for me to show you around? We have a small community—"

"No, thank you." He walks to the window and peers outside. There's a street that runs below the window, but a broadleaf tree partially conceals the asphalt. "Sophia likes you."

I sit down in my desk chair and wait. A man like Jack Sullivan doesn't drive through city traffic without a reason. He wants something. There's no need to guess because a man like Jack will tell me exactly what he wants.

"Things have changed since we saw you on Saturday." I gesture to the chair across from my desk for him to sit. He folds his arms across his chest. He's so tall I have to lean my head back to direct my gaze at his face. "I'd like for you to meet with Sophia."

"Jack. Sit." I push out the most cordial tone I can, but the words don't particularly convey softness. Still, I'm exhausted, I need to do math, and he should be sitting for this conversation. "Tell me more about what Sophia needs. I'm familiar with the case, but only through the news. If you tell me more about what you are looking for, what she needs, and your expectations, I can recommend a qualified therapist. I have connections all over the city."

"My uncle swears by you. He says there are a lot of bad therapists out there."

I stifle the grin that wants to break out. Mark Sullivan is a jaded man. I can totally see him not only saying that, but fully believing it. I snuck into his circle of trust through my friendship with Patrick.

"I promise to recommend only the good ones. The absolute best." Jack Sullivan is a man who only wants the best. He and his uncle are the same.

"The man who arranged for Sophia's abduction has been released on bail."

My eyes widen, and he nods, silently agreeing with my nonverbal reaction.

"There's no need for her to be afraid. She's secure. I have significantly expanded our home security since her abduction. She is safe. But she's...I can't get through to her."

"What is she doing?" If she's endangering herself, she might need to be hospitalized.

"She's barely eating. She won't speak to friends. I struggle to get her out of her room. She's depressed. Or anxious. Or maybe she's going through withdrawals. I don't know."

I remember the articles in my news stream. I only skimmed them, but Patrick told me that men who do both drug and human trafficking had taken her.

"Did they give her heroin?"

He nods, and his lips tighten into a straight line.

Heroin and I are old friends. But they didn't have her that long. Could she be addicted? Certainly. But what he's describing to me sounds more like trauma. He wants her to bounce back, but sometimes recovery takes years. "If she's in withdrawal, there are drugs to soften the withdrawal, but they only had her for a week, right?"

"The doctors said she doesn't need methadone. Look, Sophia won't talk to anyone. For whatever reason, she decided she likes you." I can only imagine the aged experts he has paraded in front of her that make me seem appealing. "Come down for a week. Stay with us. I'll make it worth your while."

This man is so sure of himself. I applaud his confidence. But this is one case where flashing a credit card won't solve his problems. One week of nonstop therapy won't buy him a cured daughter.

"You think I have a magic pill? I'll fix her in one week? What are you? An insurance company?" I can't help but throw that dig in. I hate insurance companies. The hatred comes with my line of work.

"How long would you need?"

"For what? Your daughter is going through recovery. It's a process. It will be a long process." I could go on and explain more, but he strikes me as someone who wants the pill and doesn't want to hear why a pill to solve this issue doesn't exist. He's the kind of man who would tell an employee to just get the job done without acknowledging any obstacles.

A part of me would very much like to throw him out of my office. As the founder of Nueva Vida, my role is mostly administrative. Other than some group therapy sessions, I mostly focus on the running of our center. I am not the person he seeks. But this center wouldn't exist without Mark Sullivan's funding, so of course I will sit and listen.

"I'm low on trust these days," he says.

The admission has me searching his features, and all I see is bare honesty.

"I don't know how much Uncle Mark told you." His gaze falls to a spot on the carpet. "Wayne Killington wasn't just an employee. He was a friend. A family friend. They raped Sophia. Multiple times. I don't know if Wayne raped her, or if it was only the men he hired. She was drugged, and her memory is... The police couldn't get much out of her. Killington lives in our neighborhood. Sophia is—"

"Terrified." The word rushes out before I can stop it. I should never complete sentences for him.

"He eliminated one person who could testify against him." Jack turns to the window, arms crossed, hands balled into fists.

"And he got out on bail?" I need to go back and read more of those articles about this case.

"There's nothing to connect him to the death. It looks like suicide. But we all believe he's behind it."

This case is unusual, but unfortunately, a raped woman is all too common. She needs a practicing therapist. My skill set is drug addiction, and my passion is growing the capabilities of this much needed center. Hell, if I don't focus, we'll close down before the end of the year unless Patrick agrees to ask Mark for more money.

"She won't talk to anyone. Not really. But she likes you."

I follow his gaze to my forearm and the string of wildflowers coloring my inner arm.

"I'm touched that Mark believes in me. But I'm not nearly as qualified—"

"Qualifications are not my biggest concern. Mark says he would trust you with his life. If my uncle trusts you, I do, too. Get Sophia to talk. To start the process. Then we'll bring in whoever you say or do whatever... I just need her to begin. She won't talk to me. And she said she liked you." She spent two minutes with me. And I wore long sleeves. "Come stay with us. A week isn't long enough? One month then. I'll pay you..." He scans my office as if looking for a number sign on one of my affirmations. "One hundred thousand dollars. For one month. That has to be more than you are making now."

One hundred thousand dollars is more than twice what I make in a year. Nueva Vida is a nonprofit. But my salary is not an issue. I didn't start this to accumulate wealth. However, with one hundred thousand dollars, my plumbing issues disappear. We wouldn't need to go to Mark asking for another donation. My head feels light, and I clasp the edge of my desk.

"My uncle said you do a lot of administrative work. You were the founder of this place?"

"Yes."

"You can do administrative work remotely."

"I have group therapy—"

"In the evening, twice a week."

What the hell?

He leans forward, arms resting on his thighs. The white of his dress shirt and gold cufflinks show near his wrists. Short, well-manicured nails adorn rugged, suntanned fingers.

"We'll make arrangements for you to continue those sessions."

"You know, we won't have sessions every day. That would be... if you think you are going to expedite her recovery with my living in the house with you, that's not... Therapy requires time. Think of it as an open wound. Healing requires time."

"It's fine. She'll get to know you. Trust you. You can observe her. Even if she never opens up to you, you'll be in a better position to make recommendations to me. And I can't be at the house all the time. I need someone other than security to be in that house with her."

Finally, the truth. He sees me as an expensive babysitter.

"It doesn't work like that."

"One hundred thousand dollars."

The manila folder on my desk taunts me. Why am I arguing? He's offering rescue.

"One month." He leans forward over the desk, and I breathe in his musky scent. When his cologne mingles with the conversation, it doesn't feel like we're still talking about Sophia. He's so close, leaning into me, as if this discussion is about us. "For my uncle. He said you would do this for him."

Everything I have, I owe to Mark and Patrick. Without Mark Sullivan, there would be no Nueva Vida.

This doesn't make any sense at all, and from a therapeutic perspective it is an unorthodox solution. But if Mark Sullivan wants me to spend time with his niece, I will. Besides, what choice do I have? My alternative is to beg Mark for more money after denying this request.

"Okay. In exchange for an upfront payment of one hundred thousand dollars, I'll live in your home for one month and spend time with Sophia. I will work remotely during the day. But, you understand, she may not want to ever talk about what happened to her. You may not see progress. Recovery requires time."

"I understand."

CHAPTER 4

JACK

"Do not let him put you in a table by the window." Fisher's eyes meet mine in the rearview.

"Got it."

Fisher doesn't like that I'm taking this meeting when he's the lone security detail. But we are meeting in an upscale public restaurant. No one will try anything.

A valet holds up a finger, letting Fisher know we're next.

"When we get back, we'll need to discuss updated security needs." Fisher rests an arm over the passenger seat and rotates slightly. "You have one more meeting after this, right?"

The valet opens the driver's door before I can answer, but after the car drives away and Fisher and I stand before the steps to Juniper & Ivy, the restaurant my lunch appointment requested, I confirm. "We should be back no later than six this evening. Now, in here—"

"I'll sit at the bar. I called ahead. They have a place for me."

"Should I act like I don't know you?" The whole security detail is new to me. It's not that I was against it before, but it didn't feel necessary. Nothing proves necessity like having your daughter abducted from your home.

"No. We can walk in together. I'm wearing a visible earpiece and a gun holster. I want them to know you arrived with security. His security will be in the restaurant. Possibly dining with you."

"Would you like to dine with us?"

"No. I have a better view from the bar. Just remember, don't sit near a window. My view outside is limited."

Juniper & Ivy is in a newly renovated, previously abandoned warehouse. Soaring ceilings with exposed pipes combine with dark wood beams, bright, open sliding doors, and an expansive open kitchen to create a warm, vibrant space. The polished concrete floors and stacked concrete walls blend into the background against a bustling restaurant. One word to the hostess, and she leads me to the back wall with three curved semicircular leather booths with curtains hanging along the sides.

In the corner booth, the farthest from the windows, my appointment awaits with a smile. Victor Morales stands as I approach, his smile wide and augmented by a thick mustache. His pink plaid dress shirt and navy suit jacket tender a friendly facade. He holds out a pudgy hand, but before I take it, I glance back at Fisher settling onto his barstool.

Get it done.

"Jackson. So good to see you again."

"You too, Victor." His sweaty hand leaves a hint of moisture on my palm. I refrain from swiping it on my pants leg until I'm seated across from him at the table and can surreptitiously remove the film of Victor Morales's touch.

We dispense with the standard cordial greetings. One man in a dark suit stands to the side of the booth. He blends in with the restaurant, and waitstaff bump into him occasionally, given his proximity to a kitchen door. There's another similarly dressed man sitting at the bar near Fisher, and one more stands outside on the perimeter of the patio. None of the restaurant patrons appear to be giving the men a second thought, although it occurs to me Fisher was correct about expanding the security detail. Is a three-man security detail standard?

It's not until they have served cocktails that Morales leans back against the plush leather and gets down to business.

"Mark suggested we have this meeting. He says you plan to hire a replacement head of sales."

Given our current head of sales is under house arrest and awaiting trial, a fact well-known by all, I can't exactly deny this truth.

"I'm evaluating my team. Promoting from within is preferable, but there is a possibility we will hire from outside. Given we lost two high-ranking executives, it may prove unavoidable."

"Shocking about Reyes." Victor places his palm over his heart.

"Yes." It's the only response I can muster.

It's well-known Victor Morales, an American, has family ties to the Morales cartel in Mexico. It is conceivable he had something to do with my daughter's abduction. But this is the way the game is played.

I sip my bourbon and let the burn ease my constricted throat. His dark eyes narrow as he evaluates me and my reaction. "Did you have someone you wanted to suggest for the role?"

"No, not specifically." Victor is a distributor, and his company is an important wholesale client. He smiles again, wide and friendly. "I knew Wayne well. I'm heartbroken, for you and your family. Betrayal. It's something that cannot be tolerated."

I swallow and nod. "Well, his day in court is coming."

I wait, wondering if he'll mention that Larry already paid his dues. Officially, he committed suicide, but there's plenty of speculation someone backing Wayne had him murdered.

"If you need recommendations, I'd be happy to send some referrals your way. My primary interest is in seeing that our current arrangement continues. Sullivan Arms is an important partner for DeCampo Distribution. Your uncle assures me you want to continue our relationship."

"DeCampo Distribution is an important partner. We rely on your distribution channels. Of course we want to continue our relationship." He's relaxed and friendly. He requested this lunch. Given his primary business contact is awaiting trial, I agreed to meet with him in a client service capacity.

"And you plan to continue with the yachts? As I understand it, the El Capitan is currently under federal possession."

Prior training kicks in. The yacht in question was privately owned by Wayne Killington, but Victor must assume it was a company vessel. I wish I was wearing a wire to capture this conversation.

"Given my role in the company, as Chief Executive Officer, I wasn't aware of the details of the arrangement. But obviously, we wish to continue to grow all aspects of our business."

"Excellent." He smiles and rubs his hand over his stomach.

Conversation between us halts when the waitstaff approaches with our lunch. I have no appetite but force enough down to fake a nonplussed disposition.

"Now, you and I, we won't get into the weeds." He waves an arm around the open-air restaurant, and I understand him implicitly. This meets my expectations and is why I didn't bother with a recording device. "When you have your man appointed, I'll have him talk to Enrique."

"Enrique?"

"Enrique Morales. Yes, if you can't remember our last names, if you guess Morales, you've got a good chance of being correct." He rolls his r's with an impressive fluidity that deepens his accent.

"Right. Enrique."

"We have five yachts. I assume you'll replace El Capitan?"

"Certainly."

I have a pretty good idea we were running guns into Mexico and drugs into the US. DeCampo Distribution is one of our largest wholesale accounts, and it seems they were also our smuggling partner. This covert agreement is one I suspected but didn't have proof of until this lunch. I imagine my uncle, the old guard, has no idea how low our leading sales team sank to continue our growth trajectory. But he and the board are partially to blame for a slip in ethics, as they've been demanding sales growth for years despite a saturated US market.

I'll play this game to uncover all the players, but there's one thing that must be clear, or else there's no point to what I'm doing.

"If we continue working together, I need your guarantee that nothing will happen to my daughter."

Victor's eyes widen and his palm returns to his heart. "My friend. The Morales clan values family above all else. We would never. Let me reassure you." He reaches across the table and clutches my forearm. "We had nothing to do with your daughter. We had some personnel who assisted, but they faced a swift reprimand. I do not operate in that manner. If someone went after one of my children, I would end them. You have my word. I wouldn't do that to you. If you double-crossed me on a deal," he releases my forearm, and his lower lip protrudes in an expressive gesture, "that might change." He pauses and stares directly into my eyes. "We understand each other?"

"Yes."

He lifts his glass in toast.

"We can't control everyone, Jack. Remember that. But our actions teach. And family comes first. Always."

He clinks his glass against mine.

I summon the expected words, taught to me by my uncle and mentor, "To a long and profitable partnership."

CHAPTER 5

Ava

Patrick dwarfs the plastic chair in the coffee shop. His knees rub the top of the table, and his large, ebony hands transform the coffee mug into more of a teacup. When he smiles, his white teeth gleam, and it's hard to look anywhere other than those pearly whites. He passes me my coffee and squeezes my shoulder with a gentle, friendly touch that is achingly familiar. I miss the days when we had coffee every day, when we worked together day in and day out.

Years ago, he up and left for Los Angeles. He says he prefers the vibe, but I know the real reason. He loves having a place where he and Mark can be freer together. Mark doesn't feel like he'll run into anyone from his world in Los Angeles, whereas several within his family's company and within the industry apparently live in San Diego.

Now Patrick sells ads for a variety of publications, and he assists when needed at Nueva Vida. Mark hooked him up with his media sales job and a swank home in West Hollywood.

The man with all the connections currently paces the sidewalk outside the coffee shop with a phone to his ear. As always, the silver fox wears a suit and tie. Patrick, my friend, is in dark jeans, pointy dress shoes, and a pressed button-down splashed with vibrant color.

"While he's outside," I jerk my head toward his lover, "how's living together going?"

After years of long distance, Mark finally moved from Houston to Los Angeles.

"Eh," His gaze passes over me and through the glass doors, "it's not much different. Still spends a lot of time in Houston. Still works a lot."

"And you're a secret?" I get Mark loves the city he's called home for six or seven decades. What I don't have patience for is his keeping my best friend in the shadows. Patrick deserves so much more.

I can't get over that he hasn't even introduced Patrick to his nephew. It's one thing to keep your sexuality closeted. Quite another to not even introduce the most significant person in your life as a friend.

"You don't have any idea what it's like to be a gay man in that world," Patrick admonishes me, like he always does when I criticize the love of his life.

"You're right. I don't understand how he could give his life to the gun industry."

"It's his family business." Patrick doesn't like guns. Refuses to have one in the house. Or at least he did. It wouldn't surprise me if a condition of Mark moving in meant they have guns somewhere, in the bedside dresser or wherever one stores guns. "Look. I'm happy. Be happy for me."

I give him a thoughtful smile, one that says I am happy, but god, I hope he's strong enough to continue handling this half-love.

"Not to change the subject, but imagine my surprise when I saw a list of Nueva Vida tenants." Patrick still reviews the financials for Nueva Vida, and he gets regular reports. "Is that a good idea?"

"He needs help." I meet his eyes. We've been there, and we help others find their way out. That's what we do.

"He's your kryptonite." The weight of his gaze pours over me like the gaze of a compassionate priest, judgmental with a touch of kindness.

"Was. Past tense." I push my shoulders back and center my coffee mug in front of me. I will not kick Reid out. Patrick can't force me.

"Did he just want a place to stay, or does he need money?" My gaze falls to the sugar packs crammed in a crystal dish, color coordinated sections separated into pink, green, and white. "How much?"

Reid needs more than I have, and I haven't promised to give him anything. But that's Reid's business, not Patrick's.

Patrick's dark hand falls over mine. The stark contrast in our skin color serves as a focal point, and Patrick's soothing deep tone wraps me in tenderness. "Ava, hun, you are worthy of love. I worry sometimes when you let people treat you like trash that you don't believe that."

"He hasn't treated me like anything." My gaze lifts, and I bounce his caring thought right back to him. "What about you? You are worthy of love. Why don't you expect more?"

The glass door to the coffee shop swings open, and Mark enters, bringing a swift end to our discussion.

"Sorry about that. Now, come here, beauty, and give me a hug."

Mark wraps his arms around me in a bear hug. At times, I've really wanted to hate this man, but I can't help but love him. Sure, he's flawed, but he's also the most generous man I've ever known. He cares deeply for everyone within his circle. The man met me at my absolute worst, and he supported me through rehab. His firm hold warms me from the inside. After stepping back from our hug, his brows come together, and he tugs on a piece of wayward hair.

"Did you get more earrings?"

I laugh. He's not really asking. He loves to tease. I went through a phase where it seemed I couldn't get enough piercings. I've also got my fair share of tattoos, although I cover them a lot these days. When I get into something, I go all in.

He pulls out the chair, and the metal legs scrape the tile. Patrick pushes Mark's hot mint tea over to him, as well as the honey bottle.

"Ava, you can't possibly know how much it means to me that you have agreed to help Sophia."

That's another thing about Mark. He's direct. His hand covers mine, where Patrick's once was, and he squeezes to the point of discomfort.

"Of course." I look him in his eyes and offer a reassuring smile. I am here for him, just as he has been for me. "But I have to tell you, I am not the best choice."

"That's just you being modest."

"No. It's not. You know I spend little time as a therapist."

Patrick holds up his mammoth hand. "You helped me."

I roll my eyes, and he snaps his fingers in my direction. Patrick and I went through rehab together, but he's had a few relapses. I've been there for him during his relapses, but he pulled himself out.

"I'm not sure I understand why he wants you to live with them," Patrick says, his gaze flitting back and forth between Mark and me.

My eyes widen, and I jerk my hand out from under Mark's. "I know." I cross my arms and look directly at Mark. "That's ridiculous."

"But," Mark's baritone voice bears attention-grabbing authority, "there are extenuating circumstances. I've given it some consideration, and I understand Jack's point of view." Of course he does. He's blood family, a distinction Mark weighs heavily. "Can you do me a favor?"

His question tames the swirl of ire circling my emotions.

"Of course. I'll do anything for you."

He briefly nods. "Good. As you know, I'm chairman of the board. Several board members at Sullivan Arms are concerned Jack's not ready to return to work."

"Return? Because he took time off?" I vaguely remember articles mentioning he had stepped down during his daughter's abduction.

"Understandably, he needed to be home. He wouldn't normally come back so soon after the whole..." He flails his hand in the air chaotically. "But we have a big vacancy right now. Two big vacancies within the company. Our head of marketing and head of sales. That's why I've had to step in more, even though I should be retiring." Now his gaze drifts to Patrick, and he softly smiles back at him. "Several board members are concerned that he's not ready to return to work. There's concern he's not ready to step into such a demanding role. If he isn't ready to take it back onto his shoulders, I need to know. If he seems unstable, or unduly stressed... can you keep me updated?"

"I can't spy on him, Mark." His eyes flash to mine. "And he's not my patient. Even if he was, I wouldn't... that would breach doctor-patient confidentiality."

"And I would never ask you to do something that compromises your principles. But just... I'm his uncle. I have two nephews. Before he died, I promised my brother I'd look out for his sons. For our family. Can you just let me know if I need to be concerned? Or more involved? If there's anything I should do?"

"Of course."

He reaches inside his suit jacket pocket and pulls out a narrow gift box wrapped in Tiffany blue paper and sets it in front of me.

"What's this?"

"A little something to thank you." Patrick beams at him with so much love I can almost envision it as glittery stars shooting across the small round table. "Open it."

I tear at the wrapping. For the last however many years, all my gifts have been from Patrick. We exchange birthday and holiday gifts. This one, on a nothing day, and completely unnecessary, drums up both excitement and anticipation. Mark gives mind-blowing gifts to Patrick, but this is my first wrapped gift from him.

A velvet jewelry box rests inside. I lift it out and use the edge of my nail to forge the opening. The Tiffany logo adorns the inside of the fabric top, and a long silver charm bracelet stretches against sky blue velvet.

"A charm bracelet?"

"I thought you might like it. You can, of course, exchange it. But each of those charms represent a special time with us. Most of these are from Tiffany's, but I had some custom made." Mark's finger hovers over the first charm. "This one is a star, because I remember how clear the night sky was when I discovered you in the park."

Patrick had descended into a binge. We were both homeless and strung out. Mark hadn't heard from Patrick in weeks, and he'd come to find us. Then he had a police officer arrest us, so we'd wake up in jail. In the morning, he gave us both a choice. Jail or rehab. I've never known why he took us both in. He could have easily only looked after Patrick. One addict in your life is quite enough. But he took me in as one would a stray.

And maybe because Reid had been arrested the week before, it was enough of a wakeup call. I made it through rehab, and I haven't relapsed since.

"This charm is a house, because you helped Patrick find his home. I couldn't be there for him. He had to find his own way, and you gave him what he needed to transition." My fingers tremble, and I tighten my grip on my coffee mug. "This charm is a heart, because you possess our hearts, and we hold yours close to ours." My lower lip quivers, and when I chance a glance at Patrick, I lose it because the big softie has tears streaming down his face. "And this charm is an airplane. You can pick whichever trip you want to fill in for that."

I absolutely love flying on Mark's private plane. He's taken me on the most extraordinary trips of my life.

"And last, this charm is a present, to signify the gift you are to us. Thank you, Ava, for being there for Patrick all these years. For being strong and choosing life."

Patrick gets up and wraps his arms around Mark and places a kiss on the top of his nearly bald head. He gives me a teary, hard look that says, "I told you he's amazing."

Mark gets up the second Patrick releases him from his hug. Patrick and I both watch as he strides to the restroom in the back of the shop, head down. He's not comfortable with emotion. And as much as I hate to admit it, I understand why Patrick loves him.

When Mark returns to the table, all eyes are dry. The bracelet charms tinkle on my wrist, and it fits in well with my stacked bands of twisted silver and beads. Mark looks from my wrist, to Patrick, and then into his mug.

"You should know, once I retire, and I am no longer in the gun industry or so tightly associated with my family business, I will tell my nephews that I am gay. I will introduce Patrick to my family, when it's not a risk to my family." When he lifts his eyes from his mug, his shame hits me front and center.

Dammit, it's the twenty-first century. I understand he's older, and he's lived his life half-full, but he shouldn't. It's not fair to Patrick, but not it's fair to Mark either. I consider the man I met earlier. Jack Sullivan is a conservative, suit-wearing, rich jackass for sure, but homophobic? I doubt it. Mark should give his nephew more credit.

"Maybe you should—"

"No. You don't understand." He's quick to cut me off before I can plead my case. "And even if Jack is okay with it, I don't want to place the burden of my relationship on his shoulders. He has enough going on. Enough battles within our company, with the board, with our industry. He doesn't need this." His finger motions between him and Patrick.

The pain in his expression, in those dark eyes surrounded by salt and pepper brows and wrinkled skin, keeps me from pushing my case too hard.

"I don't like it. But you both know that. I think if someone doesn't like the two of you together, they can fuck off. But I'd never out someone. That's your decision. For what it's worth, I think you're doing a disservice to yourself, to Patrick, and even to Jack and Sophia by not being honest with them."

My words, like always, are disregarded. With a shiny new

clinking bracelet, probably worth more than my beat-up Subaru, I head home to pack. Because of course I will do Mark a favor. I can be a glorified babysitter, and who knows, maybe I will actually be able to help Sophia. Sometimes an impartial, nonjudgmental set of ears goes a long way to assisting with the healing process.

CHAPTER 6

JACK

In the back seat of the Range Rover, I lean forward to pass Fisher a slip of paper with the address for my next appointment.

"I'm going to need to work in an additional stop this afternoon."

The Juniper & Ivy passes by the window, as Fisher's eyes meet mine in the rearview.

"I'll need you to stay outside for this next meeting. Preferably unnoticed in the car, but if anyone is watching, it's not the end of the world if they see you."

As we pass the San Diego shops and restaurants, I cross one leg over the other. The back seat in the Range Rover is plenty spacious, but I prefer to drive myself. Fisher scans the side mirrors, the rearview, and the road ahead with the same level of attention taught at Langley. He turns left multiple times as we crisscross through town, headed in our direction, but with care to ensure we are not followed.

Until recently, I refused security, believing I didn't need it. I don't give a damn about myself, but I sure as hell care about my daughter. If I'd had any idea she would be a target, we would've had an entire platoon surrounding our home.

And now? I hire the best for protection. We didn't catch everyone responsible for Sophia's abduction. But no matter how long it takes me, or how much I need to spend, we will. And I won't allow Sophia to be left without any parent, so now I have security too.

When we hit I-15, traffic slows. Fisher's thumb raps against the steering wheel. "We could walk faster than this."

It's true. Gridlock is an issue on the freeways.

"I'm sure you didn't take the job at Arrow to be a driver." Fisher didn't pass BUD/S, the SEAL training course. There's no shame in that. From what Ryan told me, if he tried again, he would pass. A torn rotator cuff and pneumonia combined with a candidate's death one month prior had the normally unresponsive medic team pulling him out with twenty-eight hours remaining in his week of hell. How, or why, he found his way to Arrow is a piece of information Ryan didn't share.

"Part of the job." Fisher glances over his shoulder and shoots me a relaxed smile. "This is the most secure arrangement for transport. I'm in the best seat in the vehicle to determine if we're being followed or if there's an ambush up ahead. If something happens, you're in the best seat in the vehicle to hit the floor and take cover."

Right. It's not like I'm defenseless. I whip out my phone and dig through email. As CEO, I get cc'd on an endless amount of email. Patricia, my assistant, is pretty good at flagging what I need to pay attention to, but if she misses something, it's on me.

Shortly after pulling off the freeway, the Range Rover slows.

"Is this it?" I peer through the back window at a Holiday Inn Motel that's seen better days. The parking lot spans the length of the two-story motel, allowing convenient parking for any guest. Rusted gold room numbers hang along each door. I catch sight of 219 and point.

"That's where I'm going."

Fisher doesn't say a word. He parks directly in front of the room, two rows back, and scans the area.

I leave him to his work and climb the stairs that lead to the second floor. A door to a room opens, and a shirtless man covered in tattoos burps and announces he's going to get ice. As I pass him, I see a nude woman lying on the bed with a cigarette in her hand.

When I reach 219, I rap my knuckle below the numbers. The door opens a few inches, and the brass chain pulls tight. My gaze rests on a deep décolletage covered in freckles, bound by a lacy tank top beneath an unbuttoned white blouse. A gold necklace with a rose charm hangs just above her bountiful breasts.

The chain rustles, and the door opens wider. Elsie greets me with a hand on my neck and kiss on my cheek. She backs away, and I take in her heavily painted lips and the thick coat of blush inexpertly applied to her cheeks. Her tight skirt hits just below the knee, and the sky-high heels lift the top of her head to my chin.

"Do I look the part?"

I glance over my shoulder and step to the side, ensuring Fisher and any other person looking can see my friend. Then I push the door closed.

"I don't think I've ever seen you in shoes quite like that." Black leather strips crisscross and ride up her ankles.

"Well, if you're meeting a lover at a motel, I figured my normal scuffed black office flats wouldn't fit the cover. Pulled these out of my closet when I got the message we needed to meet as soon as possible."

"I appreciate the quick response."

"You've never made this request before. We take it seriously."

"You know that, huh?"

I've worked with the CIA as an informant ever since my departure from the Naval Academy. They were primarily interested in my international meetings. Elsie has been my contact for the better part of the last year. We typically meet in secure locations designed to fit within my routine. This is definitely an exception. I admire her ingenuity, but given I'm not married and money is not an issue for me, I can't help but wonder who would believe I'd ever bring a woman to a dump like this.

She's already closed the blinds and has assumed a seat on the edge of the bed.

"Did you notice anyone following you?" she asks.

"No. My security detail didn't notice anyone either."

"Is your phone in the car with him?"

"Yes." Her gaze floats over my body. She's looking to see if there's any other potential listening device on me. But there's not. Arrow routinely checks my home, watch, and clothes. Before, I didn't believe risks applied to me. I learned my lesson.

I lean against the wall opposite the bed, next to the dresser and television set.

"I met with Victor Morales today."

"Of the Morales Cartel?"

"The one and only. He admitted men from his family held Sophia."

She narrows her eyes. "We knew that."

"Sounds like he punished them. Maybe eliminated them. He asked me to continue a business arrangement. The same one he had with Wayne Killington."

"The Morales Cartel is one of Sullivan Arms international clients?"

"No." I tug on my chin, considering. It's not clear how Wayne concocted the deal on the ledger side. Every gun we manufacture shows up somewhere on a sales record. The parts we sell aren't as trackable. But wholesale distributors, like DeCampo, are responsible for their own ledgers. "More is going on than merely funneling guns to a cartel, as we could have done that legally by selling to DeCampo and remaining uninvolved in where the inventory actually ended up. Victor assumed I was aware of the deal specifics, and I played along."

"Why would he assume you were aware?"

"With Killington out of the picture, my uncle told him to talk to me. But I can guarantee you he didn't know what kind of arrangement Wayne Killington had with Victor. Wayne was gunning for greater distribution to Mexico. It angered him when Sullivan Arms was deemed too small of a manufacturer to be included in Mexico's lawsuit against US gun manufacturers. My uncle agreed with him. Said not being seen as one of the top players was bad for business."

The lawsuit claims US gun manufacturers have contributed to elevated crime within Mexico and are responsible for countless deaths. The suit implies that gun manufacturers are indirectly responsible for the expansion of the illegal drug trade by providing arms to drug growers and traffickers.

Most would consider exclusion from the suit to be an advantage for Sullivan Arms. But, to someone who has dedicated his life to growing the company, exclusion feels like an insult.

"So, your uncle believes it's just another sales account?"

"DeCampo Distribution, Victor's business, has grown to about ten percent of our sales. It's a significant wholesale account. Mark probably met Victor at a lunch or dinner. It's not unusual to wine and dine big accounts. He's American. Native English speaker. If you met Victor, you wouldn't immediately think he's a cartel crime boss."

"I've seen his profile."

"He dresses like any other *Fortune* 500 CEO. Acts like any of them too." But since she's already seen his profile, it sounds like he's already on the CIA's radar. "If I understand Victor correctly, the high-end yachts are used to send guns down to Mexico and bring drugs back in."

"Heroin?"

"He didn't specify, but given that's what they drugged Sophia with, that's my bet. He offered to recommend replacements for Wayne and Larry. I assume those replacements would handle everything. Continue the operation."

"Do you think there's anyone else within Sullivan Arms involved?"

"Others have to be involved. Our CFO. An accountant who

worked for him. Someone in compliance. There have to be a handful of people in on this deal, at all different levels within the company."

"Do you suspect human trafficking? Or only drugs and guns?"

I meet her deep blue eyes across the room. She takes a band off her wrist and pulls her hair back into it. Her breasts bulge from the movement.

"He didn't say anything that led me to suspect human trafficking. But he didn't get into details. He wants me to replace the yacht that's currently under federal possession. Did you guys find anything on that yacht?"

The feds apprehended Wayne Killington on his yacht. The vessel was owned by him personally and valued at around twenty-five million. As part of an ongoing criminal investigation, the vessel remains in federal possession.

"FBI and ATF are running the show on that one. I'll get an update." She purses her lips. "Are you planning on playing along? Replacing the yacht? Hiring his recommendations?"

"Why not?" If she disagrees, now is the time to tell me. My commitment to the CIA cost me greatly. For years, I served as more than an informant. It's time they help me. "I want to figure out who's involved. I told you guys from the get-go. My company produces high-quality guns. The people in our company are a lot like me. They love the sport. They appreciate the craftmanship. The last thing any of us wants is for our guns to get into the wrong hands. That's why I agreed to inform you on all of our international dealings. I've even infiltrated meetings at your request. I don't want to source arms to the wrong people. That's not the world I want to foster. Help me on this. I want to figure out exactly what's going on and who is involved."

"What are you requesting?"

"A full-scale operation. This is bigger than the feds realize."

"Smuggling contraband on boats is done all the time."

"But these are expensive boats that require financial backing. My gut tells me this reaches well beyond Sullivan Arms."

"Let me run this up the chain. You're an informant. Not an operative."

"I've spent more hours on the range than any CIA officer. Plus, I have Navy training, and I'm skilled in hand-to-hand combat. I can't imagine a better partner for the CIA. And Arrow already works with the CIA, NSA, and FBI. I'm a partner in Arrow Security." If she runs it up the chain, someone will recognize my name.

"I'll bring it all back." She crosses her arms, pushing her breasts high. It's disconcerting seeing my liaison in anything other than standard office apparel.

"I know you have at least one undercover ATF officer within our company. It would be beneficial for me to know who he or she is."

"It's highly unlikely there's an undercover ATF officer in Sullivan Arms."

"But—"

"You may be under the impression I know everything, but I don't. There could be an undercover operative within Sullivan Arms, but knowing what I know about the ATF and the DEA, I'd say it's more likely any undercover operative works for Morales in some capacity."

After Sophia's abduction, the FBI backed off the case because of an ongoing operation. They never shared the details, but Arrow's FBI contact definitely mentioned an ATF undercover operative that they'd been worried about exposing.

Wayne Killington had been like family to me. He'd run both marketing and sales for Sullivan Arms. When I stepped away from the company after my ex-wife's death, he'd expected to become CEO.

Only, he didn't get to remain CEO. I returned to lead my family's company. I never comprehended Wayne's anger. Had no idea he so desperately wanted the CEO role that he would attempt to create another distraction to pull me away from the company once again. He will go to jail for arranging my daughter's abduction.

Prosecution is busy building their case and preparing for their day in court. And we're still trying to understand his relationship with the people he hired. Those people ultimately turned against him, and in doing so, exposed a gun and drug trafficking scheme. A scheme that, based on my lunch with Victor Morales, continues.

"Has your security team found any more listening devices within your home?"

"No. But we still haven't figured out who Wayne hired for his tech." He had someone in his corner who was adept at hacking into security cameras and splicing video. My bet is that same person provided him with the listening devices to plant within my home.

"You need to exercise caution. These people won't hesitate to kill." I hear her, but there's no choice. These people are working within my family company. The company my grandfather started and my father and his brother grew into a billion-dollar international company.

"Elsie, if the CIA doesn't want to work with me on this, or doesn't want to refer me to a government agency that will work with me, I'll do it all on my own."

There's no reason to explain why I'm committed to tracking down every single person in this scheme. It involves my family company, my product, and my daughter. Wayne and his partners fucked with the wrong man. And every time I look at my little girl and think about what those greedy, sick bastards did to her, I become more determined to uncover every single participant and to serve justice.

Back in the car, Fisher pulls out of the Holiday Inn parking lot. "Everything go okay?"

"We'll see. I didn't meet with a decision maker."

Fisher nods. He's former military. He understands.

"While you were inside, I was notified that Ms. Amara arrived at your home. Are there any instructions I need to relay?"

The San Diego buildings whiz by as Fisher prepares for another left turn. The familiar methods of checking for tails almost make me smile. But a vision of the therapist settling into my home has me pressing against my sternum. I'm not sure what it is about her. All that dark eye makeup, but yet there's a rawness to her. A contradiction I sense more than see. Or maybe the pull stems from something as elementary as I am not exposed to individuals with edges as rough as hers. She's nothing like my circle. I don't particularly trust her. But I do hope she helps Sophia. I haven't been able to.

"Just keep an eye on her," I say to the front seat. Fisher's right eyebrow raises above the line of his sunglasses. "She's a therapist. I don't think she's a threat. But if you see any signs she might be trying to sell her story or something..."

"We can monitor her phone calls and texts."

"Do that." I pull out my phone and open the email app. "While she's living in my home, do that."

CHAPTER 7

Ava

The top windows lining one side of the basement room let in light but are high enough to provide privacy. A host of low-light plants sit in raised planters. Small cacti in cream ceramic pots are scattered about on shelves. To create my office, the designer brought in a comfortable sofa, two inviting armchairs, a small corner desk with a chair, plus colorful abstract artwork hanging on the walls.

When I texted Jack Sullivan asking if there was a room in his house that I could use for meeting with Sophia, he first suggested her bedroom. I had to explain that's not a good idea. She needs a safe space to share, but it needs to be one she can leave and return to at will. Not one she must sleep in every night.

Of course, this whole idea is insanity. I am a licensed therapist, but I'm out of practice. It didn't take me long after meeting with patients to realize I carry too much of their burden. In psychology, we call it identification. I identify too closely with my patients; I feel too much of their burden. Keeping my emotions in check during sessions proved to be too challenging. And yes, maybe it's because almost all of my patients were addicts and I, too, am an addict. They wanted me to tell them how to kick it, how to stay away from the drug, but it's not that simple. There's no special sauce to share. I'm lucky. I kicked it, and I don't know why I was able to, but some others can't. I wish I had the sauce, the words, the magic. I wish I could save everyone.

I'm far enough away from those dark days that my yearning isn't nearly as strong. I love my life too much to throw it away. Shoving a needle in my neck holds no appeal. But how did I get here? What gives me the strength to sidestep temptation?

Determination? A self-hatred for who I was? A night inside a prison cell? Living in the back seat of my car? Living on the streets after they towed my car, and I didn't have the money to get it back? And any time I got my hands on money, I spent it on my all-consuming priority.

There are several things I know after years of meeting addicts. One, I'm shit at predicting who will make it and who won't. Two, there are a lot of factors that tie into success. We founded Nueva Vida on this premise, and we do everything we can to promote a successful re-entry to real life after rehabilitation. But so much is up to the individual and the universe.

That's a hard concept for loved ones to grasp. Which is part of the reason I'm sitting in this freshly painted room with brand-spanking-new furniture and a thick, lush rug that probably cost more than all of the secondhand furniture in my apartment. Jackson Sullivan wants to do it all for his daughter.

I can't blame him. From what I understand, unlike many addicts, she didn't make any bad choices. Someone kidnapped her and shoved a needle in her arm to gain control. From what I've read, they didn't intend to sell her, but they were human traffickers, and they applied their techniques to subdue her.

I'm not at all sure I'll be able to help her. I tried to explain this to Patrick. On the drive over, we had a long conversation that mostly entailed me reiterating how I was not the best choice and Patrick refusing to listen.

It doesn't take a rocket scientist to know that Sophia liked me because I dress more like a teen than an adult. With all my earrings and jet-black nail polish, at least, I imagine that's how she'd see me. I bet every doctor she met in her ultra-elite private hospital setting was over the age of sixty and wore a business suit. And if a person was younger, I bet she had conservative and judgmental written all over her. I know, because I've been there. I've seen it. The more expensive you go, the more expensive the degrees and the air of superiority suffocates.

He could find someone like me, but better. Someone who currently practices and has fine-tuned her skills over years of helping patients. But, as Patrick said, why not take the money? It's a month at a beachfront mansion and one patient to meet with a couple of times a week.

Once Patrick and I got the idea to create Nueva Vida, I quickly discovered I get much more out of building a safe environment than meeting with patients. Or I should say, Nueva Vida fulfills me much more than counseling did.

But, as Patrick reinforced, in exchange for working remotely for one month, I get paid one hundred thousand dollars. Working remotely won't be an issue. He does it almost year-round. I'm free to go back each week for my two group therapy sessions. Those are the only two counseling sessions I currently do. This arrangement is only for a month, and the center's current financial crisis goes away.

And there is always a chance I will be able to help Mark's niece. My hunch is she's not truly an addict. Even if she suffered withdrawal symptoms, her risk of relapse is likely small, as she doesn't have any idea how to acquire drugs on her own. She doesn't have that circle of friends pulling her down. She will not walk into a party, judgment impaired with alcohol, and have someone offer her a syringe. At least not for years, not until there's even more time between her and the drug.

No, my hunch is she's dealing with shame. And shame is a mighty cross. It's my understanding no one really knows everything that happened to her. She doesn't want to talk about it. And she might not be ready to relive it.

That, I can understand. I can offer a non-judgmental ear to let some of whatever's inside her come out. If she wants help. Can't force it. No matter how much Daddy Gazillionaire pays, you can't force it. Recovery must come from within.

A shadow falls against the hallway wall. It becomes so still I wonder if the light out the front doors has changed, and something outside has cast a shadow. I call out, "Hello?"

Today is my first day in the Sullivan house. One of the security guards greeted me at the gate. After instructing me to park in front of the fountain, he took me to a guest room at the front of the house, gave me a tour, and left me in this temporary office.

The armed guard took my car keys and said he'd park it in the garage, because of course there's extra space in the garage for my car. Most people have six-car garages.

Sophia Sullivan edges into view in the hall. She's wearing shorts, a long sleeve t-shirt, and socks. Like before, her blonde hair is pulled back. There's not a wisp of makeup on her youthful skin, no earrings or necklaces. Her shoulders hunch forward.

"Sophia. Hi."

Her gaze takes in the room, roaming from the sofa to the art on the wall to the plants. I'll need to rotate these plants outside for sunlight, as otherwise they'll die here, but I'm a big believer that plants make a space habitable.

"You think you can decorate the rest of the house?"

"Not a fan of your father's style?" I smirk and bottle up the urge to wave a hand and urge her to sit. She hasn't crossed the threshold yet.

"What style?" She crosses her arms over her chest and rests her back against the doorframe, angling her body so I'm directly in her sight path.

"Your bedroom's quite gorgeous." When Resnick, the armed security guard assigned to give me a tour, took me to her room, I'd been blown away. But it also hadn't felt like a teen's room. It felt like a hotel room, or a photograph from a high-end magazine.

"My mom picked out that furniture."

"She had good taste. She did a good job with your room. Did she decorate the rest of this house?" The house has a traditional decor befitting someone with a royalty fetish.

"No." Sophia's posture hasn't altered, but her tone has.

Something about my question bothers her. Her mother died years ago, but it could still be painful. I choose a therapeutic silence. It's an uncomfortable quiet, but it will allow Sophia to choose our conversational path.

"I hate the furniture in this house."

All right. Immaterial objects are as good of a place to start as any.

"I get that." Agreeing with her will allow us to bond. And she's right. The structure of the home is breathtaking, but the decor is nauseating. She resumes taking in the decor of this room. "You know, your dad put me in touch with the woman who decorated this room. Evie Cole. Do you know her?"

She shakes her head.

"I bet if you asked him, your dad would let you redecorate any room you wanted. Evie told me this room was storage before. She said she's done a few of the rooms in this house."

Her eyes narrow thoughtfully. I'm saying this without knowing the man at all. He might actually like the formal vibe. Evie could have designed some of the rooms Sophia hates. But her dad is paying me one-hundred grand to be around should she want to talk to someone. He infamously paid one-hundred million for information leading to her safe return. I'm pretty sure if I tell him giving her a project, like redesigning a room or two in the house, will help her recovery, he'll readily agree.

"You think so?"

I nod and push out my lower lip for emphasis. "Absolutely."

"I'd like to get rid of a lot of the mirrors upstairs. They're freaky."

"Not a fan of the gilded age?" In the dining room, enormous

tapestries hang beside massive mirrors framed with baroque gold. The room is an odd room to me anyway because this house is chock full of ocean views and that room is toward the front of the house with a view of the courtyard.

She stands in the hallway, arms crossed, shifting weight from foot to foot.

"Do you want to come in?"

"No."

I laugh. She's acting like I'm going to bite.

"Aren't we supposed to follow a schedule?"

"We can. I was just thinking that you could come in and sit."

"Come in and sit." She practically spits out the words.

"Have you heard that before?"

"Like every therapist says it."

"Right." I am careful not to cross my arms, and my hands fall limp at my sides because I'm wearing a long black skirt that doesn't have pockets. "Well, I'm gonna sit."

I stride over to one of the plush armchairs.

"Dad says you specialize in addiction and trauma."

I scrunch up my face. "Eh, yes and no."

"I'm not an addict."

"I doubted you are."

She strides into the room and props herself up on the wide armrest of the sofa. My mom would have yelled at me for sitting on a piece of furniture like that, but this furniture is hers, so she can sit on it however she likes. Besides, a lot of those life rules are complete crap.

"Someone drugged me. But I don't crave it. I cringe when I think of needles. The only alcohol I've ever had to drink was wine with my family. You don't need to be here."

I tilt my head, sifting through the battery of information she unloaded. I hear anger and frustration. But Jack shared her medical records with me. She went through withdrawal. When I went through withdrawal, I sure as fuck knew what I craved. How did it work with her?

"No cravings at all?"

"It's not like I want to jab a needle in my arm." She purses her lips and squints. "Do I wish I could return to that? The feeling of weightlessness? Where nothing matters? Nothing at all? Yeah." Her voice falls to barely a whisper. "I'd give anything to have that. But that doesn't make me an addict. I wouldn't ever poison myself."

"I understand."

"Do you?"

"Yes. I am a heroin addict." I correct myself, because while that verbiage is coming under fire, it's a habit that's hard for me to break. "Recovered," I amend. "But I'll consider myself an addict until the day I die."

"And you're okay with that?" She looks disgusted by me. I'm familiar with the look. Way too familiar.

"What's the alternative?" There. That defensive response is why I'm better at administration. I exhale. "Yes, I'm okay with it." I look her in the eye. I could go on and tell her it took me a really long time to find self-acceptance, but this isn't about me.

"Well, I'm not like you. I'm not an addict. My dad needs to get a grip."

This girl's got blue eyes, and damn if they aren't dark and stormy. But, in all fairness, she came out of a terrible experience with people tossing an undeserved adjective at her. And her father crossed the brink of insanity and bought a therapist to live with her.

"He likes control, huh?"

"Oh. My. God. Does he ever." I don't even have to prompt her. The next half hour flies by. I mentally catalog his list of offenses and silently curse myself for not having a recording going.

To begin with, she's got the earliest curfew of all her friends. This point really offends her. He has crazy rules about the length of her skirts, and she's not allowed to wear anything that shows her stomach even though all her friends wear clothes like that. He doesn't allow her to wear heels, nor is she allowed to date, not that that's been an issue, but he finds it necessary to remind her at random times. She's not allowed on the phone after ten p.m. on school nights. As evidence of his overbearing tendencies, she shares that he monitors everything on her electronics and has certain sites blocked. The tyrant reads all of her texts. And, as if all that wasn't enough, he still forces her to access only YouTube Kids. A combination of exasperation and disbelief mixes in her expression when she shares he wouldn't let her on TikTok or Snapchat until she turned fourteen. Fourteen!

She's so animated I don't want to stop her. From what I've been told, she hasn't spoken to any friends since the kidnapping. It's like someone allowed the teen girl in her to speak, and there's an explosion of bottled-up words laced with emotion. Linking back to that thing which I was so guilty of in my practice, countertransference occurs.

Countertransference is when the therapist comes to feel for the patient. I always feel too much for my patients. And I can tell you, if I'd been living with all the rules he imposes, I would've rebelled like nobody's business. Hell, I did rebel like nobody's business, and I had a fraction of her rules. Her dad does need to get a grip.

Bonding is the universal tendency for animals and humans to attach. This, right here, what's going on between Sophia and me, is bonding. And it happened suspiciously easily. She needed this.

Fisher taps on the doorframe. We never closed the door. I didn't get up to do it because I didn't want to interrupt our flow. And to my knowledge, we were the only ones down in the basement, anyway.

"Dinner is ready. Chef asked that I come tell you."

"Chef?" I ask with a raised eyebrow.

"Yeah. For now," Sophia says, her conspiratorial tone fully present. "Dad goes through them like water. This one's lasted about two weeks. Food is..." She waffles her hand.

Fisher disappears.

"Well, we had a good session. You think you'll be up for more?"

Her eyes widen. "That was a session?"

"Sure." I shrug. "You did good." I get her surprise, since I, too, have experienced sessions in a clinical hospital setting. "Sessions don't have to be painful. I mean, sure. It can be painful digging through uncomfortable emotions." That's the hope. "But it can be what we just did."

She grows quiet. She transforms from open friend to suspicious girl. It fully hits me at this moment what a bad idea this is. I'm crossing lines by living with her. I shouldn't eat dinner with her. Where will I draw the line between therapist and friend? But the idea isn't that I will be her therapist. The idea is that by sharing with me, she'll take those first steps, and be open to a therapeutic relationship with a therapist in the future.

"I'll do more sessions. Twice a week. No more."

She flits down the hall, her noiseless footsteps leaving me full of second guesses. One hour of listening, and she's open to two therapy sessions a week. It's been a long time since I joined in on a peer supervision group, but this is a situation where I could benefit from pointers from others.

Who am I kidding? Any rational therapist would tell me to end this arrangement immediately.

My phone rings, and I fish it out of my tote bag. Reid's photo shows on the screen. It's a photo from our early twenties. In hindsight, it's the era that marked our slide downhill. I should update his profile photo. I slide to answer.

"Hey. I need to run up to dinner. Can I call you back?"

"Did you go home?"

"No, I'm... at someone else's house. What's up?"

"Will you be home later? I'll swing by."

"No, I'm...it's a long story. I'm out of town. Everything okay?"

I glance at the doorway, cognizant I'm expected for dinner. At least, I think I am.

"I just...you know that money I mentioned?" I close my eyes and breathe deeply. "It's not what you think. I owe someone. And he's not really giving a shit that I'm making crap washing dishes."

I pinch the bridge of my nose. Fucking dealers.

"How much do you owe?"

"Ten."

"Thousand? Were you dealing?"

"No. Yes. I don't know. You know what it's like. He wants to be reimbursed for what they seized when I was arrested."

"Ava, you coming?" Sophia's distant voice echoes through the house.

"I've got to run."

"Ava, he's not messing around."

"Reid. I'll get it to you on Tuesday. Stop by my group session."

I end the call, drop my phone in the tote bag, and jog up the stairs.

CHAPTER 8

JACK

The salt-tinged sea breeze blows against my skin as I sit back, swirling the golden amber in the crystal glass. The crescent moon overhead casts shadows over the back yard. Along the beachfront, a man crosses the perimeter. It's unfathomable there was a time I didn't hire security. Seeing the interloper, and knowing he's one of ours, sets me at ease. Sophia is safe.

"Sir." The deep tenor belongs to one of the security men, and with reluctance, I shift from facing the misty shoreline to face whichever employee found me.

Mansfield stands in the doorway. Like me, he's former military. He's physically fit, alert, and trustworthy. He shaves his head but wears a full dark beard. As the only one in the security detail with a shiny scalp, he's easy for me to remember. If memory serves, he left the military after losing hearing in one ear from a nearby explosion.

I speak more loudly than I would for others as I raise my glass. "Care for a drink?"

He's night shift. He'll say no, but it feels inhospitable not to offer.

"No, thank you. Came to let you know I'll be on shift for the night. It's me and Evans."

"Thank you."

He gives a curt nod in response, then rotates to his side. "Goodnight, ma'am."

I swivel the chair to see into the shadows. Sophia?

No. It's Ava Amara. Her long bangs cascade over her eyebrows, and her full pouty lips gleam red. In the moonlight, her pale skin nearly glows against that black mane. Her skintight black tank top molds to her breasts and highlights a narrow waist. There's a sliver of pale skin between the bottom of her tank and her weathered jeans. I let out a sigh of exasperation. Everything the woman wears draws the eye. I should look away.

"Hi." Her timid tone doesn't fit with the heavy combat boots. Of course, she's not wearing real combat boots. Hers are for fashion.

"Do you wear any colors?"

She doesn't glance down. The corners of her full lips lift into a semblance of amusement.

"I like black."

"Dark soul, huh?"

"Very."

Ava Amara is a kindred spirit.

"Would you care for a drink?"

"Sure."

I blink away surprise. I'm accustomed to offering drinks and being turned down.

"Sophia's asleep. I hope you don't mind. I was just kind of wandering around."

She must think I'm a lunatic for having security roaming twenty-four-seven and demanding she stay here in the house. It probably is overly protective. But given what's going down, limiting the number of people entering and exiting the premises is smart. Plus, Uncle Mark may trust her, but he trusted the same men I did. The men who burned us.

"What's your poison?"

"What are you drinking?"

"Oban." I hold it up, and the moonlight cuts through the amber liquid. "Scotch from the Scottish Highlands." The woman has unnaturally enormous eyes, and out here in the dark, they almost appear black. Bewitching. "But of course, we have wine. Full bar. Anything you like." I refrain from mentioning the fruity mixers. She might be a woman, but I expect her tastes aren't traditionally feminine.

"Do you have soda?" She's not asking if I have a mixer.

"Right this way."

We step back inside, and I refill my glass and she grabs a can of Diet Coke. I put ice in a glass and slide it to her.

"Are you an alcoholic?" I have a fully stocked bar on every floor in this house. Two on the main floor if you include the small bar near the dining room. There are also four different wine refrigerators in the back of the basement and a fully stocked cellar.

"No." She pours the soda over the blocks of ice, taking care the fizz doesn't cascade over the side. "But I don't drink."

"Ever?" A stiff drink is one of the few things I look forward to each day.

"No." She answers with a soft expression, unafraid to meet my gaze.

"But you're not an alcoholic?"

"Alcohol was never my poison." She smiles a friendly enough smile as she replays my word choice back at me. "But that doesn't mean it might not weaken my resolve or lead to bad choices. So, I stay away from it."

I knock back another long swallow and relish the burn in my throat and the subtle heat in my limbs.

"How much have you had of that?"

The Oban bottle is about half empty. I might have opened it this evening. "Let's go back outside."

I like it outside. I breathe easier out here. The pool glitters in the moonlight, and the sound of crashing waves compliments the soft sound of trickling water from the hot tub overflowing into the pool.

I sit in one of the chairs, and she chooses the other one. When I purchased outdoor furniture, my designer told me a lone chair feels lonely, so I ordered chairs in pairs. On every deck, near the pool, there are only pairs. Since it's so damn hard to get my daughter to come sit with me, I sit in them alone. Until tonight.

I hold my scotch up to her in a silent toast. My gaze glides down her curves.

She pulls one leg up against herself and wraps her arms around it.

She might be cold. I could ask her. Go inside and dig up one of the outdoor throws Janet, the house manager, insists we keep on hand for guests.

Those doe-like eyes take me in. She leans against the arm of her chair, closer to me. Her thick, heavy bangs obscure the sides of her face, and a desire to brush the black locks away from her pale skin swells.

I need to get hold of myself. She's here for Sophia. I swivel my chair to angle it toward the ocean.

"Thank you for coming here. I appreciate it."

"I'm doing a favor for a friend. And..." She raises her hand in the air, palm side up, and shifts it around as if presenting evidence. Silver bracelets shine in the light, emitting a light clink as charms and inches of silver slide against each other on her slim wrist. "Living here is hardly a hardship. Your fee is generous." She sips her soda and sets it down on the small table between us. "I would have agreed to live here for much less."

My head hits the back of the chair, and I focus my gaze on the pool, away from her. Everything she wears shows off a voluptuous, tempting silhouette. Even her ripped jeans.

"Are you always so generous?"

She's questioning my negotiation skills. As she should. Most people negotiate with the goal of spending as little money as possible. I negotiate to acquire my end goal as efficiently as possible.

"It all comes down to money." If I needed money, I would be a better negotiator. If she didn't need money, she couldn't be bought as easily.

"Hmmm?" Either she didn't hear me, or she doesn't understand.

"I suspect that's true about humanity. Every. Single. Person." I lift my glass for emphasis and stare at her through the amber liquid, treating the crystal as a diffuser so I don't stare at her chest. "Has a price."

"Are you drunk?" There's the amusement I heard earlier. Hell, maybe I have had too much to drink.

"It's been one of those days."

"I get that." She pulls her other leg up onto the chair, so both legs squeeze against her, hiding her curves.

"Are you making any headway with Sophia?"

She shrugs.

The waves crashing nearby are the only sound.

"It's only been a few days."

I am adequately admonished. She did tell me it would take time. Her short black nails press against her shins just below her knees.

"You wear black nail polish."

She holds out one hand, splaying her fingers, inspecting them as if she doesn't know what color she wears.

"Do you like?"

I don't, actually. I find it quite morbid. But... I like it on her. I'm not a fan of silver jewelry, but I find hers appealing. Everything about her is appealing, and I'm not sure why. Heavy eyeliner, a mass of untamed hair, thick bangs, and earrings that claim all the space on her earlobes. "What other piercings do you have?"

"You're a funny drunk."

"That's not an answer."

She drops her boots and kicks the ground, spinning her chair in a circle like a child.

Only there's nothing childlike about her. I want to explore her. I want to fuck her.

A dark shadow crosses the fence, and I follow the man with my eyes. It's not Mansfield. His head doesn't shine. I knock back the rest of my glass. Swallow. The burn flows down my esophagus and sears deep within.

"Ava Amara," I say as she spins. "Do you have nipple piercings?"

"Now I know you're drunk." She stands, picks up her glass, wipes the table with her palm, and leaves me sitting alone in my chair.

What the hell is wrong with me? Why would I say that to her? Why do I want to fuck her? She's not my type. She's here to help my daughter. And Sophia seems to like her. I've ruined too much for Sophia. I won't fuck this up too.

The sky spins. Shadowy gray clouds shift, obscuring the stars. I want more scotch, but if I give in, I'll pay for it in the morning. So, when I head back inside, I bypass the scotch and head straight up the stairs to my shower. Steaming hot water pours down on me, and I close my eyes and envision her doe-like eyes and rounded breasts. She bends before me, and those full cherry lips wrap around my cock. My grip tightens, and the vision shifts to the top of her head and my fingers intertwined with her hair, directing her. In record time, my milky release flows down the drain.

CHAPTER 9

Jack

The back of my hand swipes the strands of vomit from my mouth. My stomach curls in on itself as I wipe the nasty on my shorts. An older woman near the water line scowls my way. Two children, likely her grandchildren, pay me no mind as they scurry around seeking seashells.

Fuck, I'm a mess. My head throbs and sweat oozes from my pores. I reek. A filthy, disgusting, hungover drunk. Jesus, I haven't vomited on my morning run since my twenties. My Oakleys are doing a piss-poor job of minimizing the sun's glare, and I ache everywhere. But I've got about a quarter mile to go, so I raise one thigh, my standing ankle sinks into the sand, and I push forward.

There was a time when I could have finished the entire bottle and not paid this much of a price.

Back at the house, the arid, cool air conditioning chills my sweaty skin. After downing a bottle of water and four aspirin, I pad down the hallway to Sophia's room. Her door remains closed. She's slept late this whole summer. I've no idea if that's just normal fifteen-year-old behavior, or if it's a sign of depression. My brother, Liam, says my nephew never wakes before noon and that sleeping late started at thirteen. But my nephew is hardly a shining example. I hear he's regularly in the tabloids and a favorite among celebrity gossip sites. Liam says he seeks the limelight to bolster his fledgling acting career. For my part, I keep Sophia away from her cousin.

On the way to shower, I stop by my office. I scan the subject lines in my email for anything requiring immediate attention. One subject line catches my eye: Yachts for Sale.

The email is from a sales rep with a Miami dealer. Victor must have referred him. The man is serious about getting his distribution line back up and running. He mentioned five yachts. Are they his? Are there more partners?

It's almost eleven in the morning on the east coast, so I shoot off a response, asking the dealer about new options. The ones in his list appear to be in good condition, but I have no desire to fly to Miami. My preference is for a new model to be delivered to San Diego. And since I'm not in the yacht business, I email my brother to ask if he knows how crews work. Will this mean more people on my payroll? I assume so. Janet, my house manager, might be knowledgeable. One thing I can count on is if she's not aware, she'll get me the information.

Of course, if I need a crew, I should probably have Morales refer them. If I'm using this vessel strictly to transport contraband, I'll need a crew that won't turn me in to the feds. And there's no reason to involve innocent people.

I slowly spin the chair like Ava did last night, thinking about Morales putting his cards on the table. He had little to lose. He didn't give me enough information to prosecute him. I already know our books are clean. I've had the FBI pouring through our finances searching for ways to prosecute Wayne Killington, our CMO and Interim CEO of Sullivan Arms, and they have found nothing.

I stare out the window overlooking the Pacific. It'll be another gorgeous day. Blue skies, chance of a passing storm in the afternoon, but the system will likely blow on by. A swarm of seagulls circle over the waves. One gull dips, disappears, and reappears. The school of fish below the waves gets taken out, one by one.

Here I am, in a similar position. Trusted by a criminal organization. Why do they trust me? The only reason I can surmise is they find it too unbelievable that as the leader of our company, I didn't know what was going on. Which is fine. With the resources of the CIA, I can dig in and see exactly what kind of operation is occurring, and one by one, I can pick out the players. I won't even have to act as the predator picking them out of the sea, because the CIA, ATF, or DEA will capture them. All I need to do is play the game and funnel information back to the good guys.

I need to alert Ryan. He can handle informing those who need to know within Arrow Tactical. On every undercover operation, there's a need-to-know basis for sharing information, but those men are in charge of Sophia's safety. They'll need to be aware.

Arrow completes a background check on every person who enters this house—house cleaners, pool cleaners, gardening and kitchen staff. They keep an eye out for any weaknesses that might be exploited. They look for connections between visitors and employees. I just added a new circle for Arrow to monitor.

Footfalls break me out of my thoughts. I glimpse a flowing black dress. Ava Amara.

Fuck. I owe her an apology. Or do I? She's already here because I'm paying her. I shouldn't have asked about nipple piercings. I was definitely out of line, but she brings it out in me.

Ryan sent me her background check. She's got a sordid past. I wouldn't be surprised if she turned tricks for drugs or cash. The arresting officer noted on her arrest report that she was a suspected prostitute. But they charged her with possession of heroin. A long time ago.

When I enter the kitchen, she's pouring herself coffee. She glances over her shoulder at me and asks, "Would you like some?"

Her tone is friendly. The dress I glimpsed is a long, sheer, black swim coverup. The outline of a black two-piece bathing suit shows through the fabric, as does the curve of her waist and alluring backside.

Jesus. I need a shower. "No, thank you."

Those enormous eyes scan me, questioning. Perhaps expecting an apology for my behavior.

"As you're aware, I had too much to drink last night. Caffeine the morning after an overindulgence doesn't sit well with me."

"More of the hair of the dog kind of guy?" One thick, lush eyebrow lifts and disappears beneath her bangs. She's mocking me. Or maybe she is truly inquisitive. She might wonder what kind of living environment I provide for my daughter. It's a fair question.

"No," I answer. Silence fills the space between us. I turn to leave, to get that shower. I am such an ass. Past experience aside, I owe this woman an apology for my behavior, so I stop and just get it out. "Last night, I may have been out of line."

I should probably face her so I appear apologetic, but I don't. I glance over my shoulder to see if she heard me.

"No worries. I'm not one to judge someone for their actions when inebriated."

Right. If she's willing to say that in front of me, she must know I'm aware of her past. Which makes sense, given most would assume Uncle Mark wouldn't send someone into my home without updating me. Of course, he didn't tell me as much as one would expect. He said she'd struggled with addiction and trauma. But he only offered the top line, whitewashed summary. I discovered the gritty details from Ryan's research.

"Dad?" Sophia enters, clearly surprised to see me, based on her tone, although why, I'm not sure. For all she knows, I always hang out in the kitchen in the morning. She's normally locked in her bedroom. She's wearing a navy one-piece bathing suit and flip-flops.

"Morning," I say to her. "Can I fix you breakfast?"

She steps closer to me and her nose crinkles.

"You stink."

"Haven't showered since my run."

"I'm good." She opens the refrigerator and takes out two bottles of water. "You about ready to go down?"

She directs her question to Ava. This is what I wanted. For Sophia to grow to trust Ava. To spend time with her, and when she feels like it, to share what happened with someone who has the experience and wherewithal to know how best to respond.

"Sure." Ava thrusts her mug out. "Can I take this down to the beach? Or is there a to-go cup I should use?"

"You can take it," Sophia and I answer simultaneously. Sophia smiles at me. It's not one of her full-on, bright, radiant smiles, but it's undeniably a smile. "You need to go shower. I can smell you from here."

Right.

"But if I were you, I'd grab a different cup with a top," Sophia says to Ava. "We're going to haul chairs and boards out...you might need to set it in the sand."

"You're going paddleboarding?" I like that she'll be going with someone. I never worried much before, but when she went missing, there was a period of time that we feared she'd gone out on the water by herself and something had happened. That's obviously not what happened, but now an ocean mishap is just one more fear on top of all the others I harbor.

"Yeah. I'm going to teach Ava." She glances at Ava, who is gulping her coffee. "We could maybe give your coverup to the security guy on the beach."

"That's not what they're there for," I interject.

Ava's mug clinks the marble countertop. The black fabric rises up her body, revealing first her calves, then her thighs, that shapely ass, the curve of her hips and waist, the band of her bikini top, her shoulders, and then it's over her head. She hangs the garment over the back of one of the kitchen chairs.

"Let's go." Sophia has already passed me, headed to the stairs that will take her down to the lower level and the side door. "Dad. Go shower," she demands before disappearing.

Ava glances over her shoulder with a soft smirk. There's a sway to her full hips as she leaves that floods me with a vision of my hands clamped on her, holding her in place as I drive into her. I step to the window and watch as she and Sophia disappear down the side path.

My uncle claims she's a reliable therapist. A close friend of his I can trust. A woman who will be good for Sophia. Yet I wonder if my uncle realizes she's also divine temptation. My bet is the woman is all kinds of naughty. An absolute joy to fuck. And she didn't hold my comment against me.

What the hell is wrong with me? I should go get a shower. I should get my day started. But no, I stand by the window and watch Ava in a bikini that leaves little to the imagination wade into the water. It's not until she looks back at the house that I break away.

CHAPTER 10

Ava

Goosebumps spread the second the side door opens. A lot of beachside homes don't run air conditioning constantly, but apparently when you're rich as fuck and don't give a damn about money, you crank it.

Sophia waves a hand in a goodbye motion and scurries up the stairs. "Meet you for lunch?" she calls out. "Around noon?"

"Sure."

Since my swim coverup is upstairs where I left it earlier, I dash straight to my bedroom suite. I crank on the shower and stand to the side until steam fills the space, then drop my sand covered suit and let the hot water pour over me until my skin blazes red.

As the water thaws my frozen limbs, I try to remember the last time I had so much fun outdoors. Sophia and I laughed so hard at my struggle to maintain balance. My biceps burned as I pulled the paddle through the salty water. There were others out on the beach, but for a long stretch, it felt like the ocean was ours.

Zero therapy occurred during our paddleboarding session.

Twenty feet remained between us during most of the outing. I struggled to keep up with her, and occasionally lost my balance and fell sideways into the chilly surf. We laughed plenty, but there wasn't much conversation. Still, physical exercise and the sun can do wonders for mental health. I'll paddleboard every morning if she wants.

Why didn't he go out with her on the waves this morning? Did she ask him, or did she only ask me? Will he join us at lunch?

The basement bedroom he's set me up in is almost as luxurious as Sophia's magnificent suite. The bedroom has an enormous window with a view out to the ocean, only it's on the ground floor, so there's a shadow from the overhang of the main floor's wrap-around deck. I rather like it, because it makes my room darker and cozier. A shadow crosses the grass, and I press a button on a remote to lower the shade.

Armed security personnel continually roam the property. It's a constant reminder that Jack perceives danger lurks. He doesn't want Sophia transported anywhere. He wants her on lockdown. And for now, she seems willing to play along. She still refuses all contacts with friends, and, according to Jack, this has been the case since the abduction.

She'll get there. He described her as morose and locked in her room. But she seems to be coming out of that easily. So easily, it makes me wonder how hard he tried. Did he try at all, or did he just issue demands, and when she didn't comply, he went and spent a hundred grand on some cockamamie scheme since there wasn't a pill or drug doctors could prescribe to solve the issue?

After getting dressed and towel drying my hair, I stare out over the grassy lawn and swimming pool. From the ground level, you can't see the sand. Large pampas grass mounds completely hide the fence barrier between the Sullivan property and the public beach. But over the tops of the grasses, crests of white pop among the navy blue.

My phone rings, pulling me out of my reverie.

"Ava? You there?" Patrick's voice calls to me through the phone line.

"Yeah. Hey."

"How's it going?"

"It's...going."

"That bad?"

The light blue sky and gently swaying tall grasses mock the dilemma I face.

"On one hand, it's like a vacation in paradise. On the other hand, I shouldn't be here. Patrick, you and I both know that. This isn't how therapy is done."

"Hey, you're the one who always said theological purity is an academic extravagance."

"Because no one theory applies to any one person. It doesn't mean I should live here, for god's sake."

"Same theory applies. Besides, he wants her to be ready to return to school in the fall. Is that going to happen with once or twice weekly sessions?"

"You can't rush recovery. And who the hell cares if she misses some school?" Sophia has been making up course work this summer from what she missed last spring. She can do that in the fall. School is really not the point.

"Yeah, well, wrap your head around spending a month with her, because the center needs the money. I've spent the day going over the last quarter's bills." Patrick used to be our bookkeeper. We hire someone now, but he reviews everything periodically. "Expenses are high."

"Because of those damn pipes."

"We've got more freeloaders than we forecast."

"Would you stop calling them freeloaders? You've been there. Just like me." He makes a noise of indifference, but it's etched in annoyance, and everything clicks. "You're still pissed about Reid."

"I worry about you. You know that. I love you, sweetie."

"I love you, too." I make a smooching sound and then pull my legs up to my chest. "So, how bad is it? Do I need to go to the office?"

"If you come in, will the bills disappear? 'Cause if they do, I have to tell ya, that's some magic act. But no, we'll be fine. I saw you deposited Jack's entire check into the business account. You're not paying yourself at all?"

"Well, I get paid by Nueva Vida. I had Jack make the check out to Nueva Vida."

"You are dedicated to this place. I'll give ya that."

"I believe in it. I think we're doing a good thing. There aren't enough resources to help people transition. But Patrick...I do need some of that money for personal use. Can the center pay me a bonus, or does that get really weird with taxes and stuff?"

"Taxes and stuff. Yeah, you will never be our accountant." He smacks his lips. "How much do you need?"

Shit. It would have been so helpful if Reid reached out before I electronically deposited the check.

"Ten thousand."

"What the–"

"I got an estimate for redoing my bathroom. If it's a big deal, I won't..." Guilt strikes hard and fast, square on my shoulders. I'm a natural born liar, but I hate lying to Patrick.

"Thank god. I don't know how you shower there."

"While I'm here, it's the perfect time to renovate."

"Hey, no worries. I'll handle it. I'll get the money transferred." I hear him mumbling and can visualize him writing a note on his to-do list to confirm with the accountant how to handle it. "So, tell me, what's it like there?"

His question reminds me that while he's been with Mark for ages, he's never met his family.

"Jack's home is gorgeous. Sophia hasn't truly opened up to me yet, so I don't really know how much she's suffering, but if you met her, you'd probably think she's a normal teen. You wouldn't suspect anything is wrong, necessarily. Jack... he's not... I was going to say he's not a warm and fuzzy dad, but that's a judgment I haven't been around long enough to make. He's different."

"Yeah?" Now Patrick sounds completely amused, but that's just Patrick and his nonsense. "Exactly how is he different?"

"He's just..." I search for the words. Sure, he's a man who wears a suit but... "He's serious. Bossy. I can't decide if he's an asshole or if he's a decent guy with a shield."

"A shield?"

"Yeah. Remember how Mark treated me initially? Like, impersonal? But you told me he was actually not a hard-ass at all. That there was a softer side? And you had to earn his trust before you saw that side?"

"Jack's like that?"

"Maybe. He scowls a shit-ton. I haven't seen the softer side yet."

Patrick chuckles. "My girl wants to see the softer side. Or maybe that came out wrong...maybe that's not the side you want to see at all."

"Patrick, would you!" I jump off the bed and tighten my towel with the phone scrunched between my ear and shoulder. "Hey, I'm coming in tonight for a group lesson. Do you think I'd have the money by tonight?"

"There will be a hold on it if I transfer the money. What did you do? Are you using one of those subcontractors who wants payment up front to cover materials?"

"I save money that way." Damn, I'm a good liar.

"Yeah. You do. Just take the money out of the safe. There should be enough. I'll replace it next week. That gives me some flexibility for how I handle it on the ledger."

We keep cash on hand in the safe. It's a practice Mark recommended, as he said it's always a good idea to have a cash reserve for emergencies. Patrick says Mark also keeps gold bars in a safe, just in case everything goes to shit.

In over ten years of business, this will be my first time digging into the cash reserves in the safe.

After we say our goodbyes, the guilt gnaws at my stomach. I barely touched lunch and hid away in my office all afternoon. I struggle to listen in the group session, which isn't like me. But it's doubly hard, because Reid isn't at the session.

It's not until the end, when we're shaking hands and saying goodbyes, that he enters the meeting room. He's thin. His pants hang below his hipbones. His shaggy hair looks tangled but clean. His nails are cut short, and the nail beds look healthy. One small hole on the shoulder of his smudged Texaco t-shirt hints at the age of his threads.

"Sorry," he says sheepishly to me as he nods to Natalie. She smiles at him and nods goodbye to me before heading out the door. "They kept me late. Had a no-show. Overtime," he says, eyebrows raised with an expression that says it's good but it's not good.

"You caught me."

"I really appreciate you doing this. I'll pay you back."

"I know you will." I lift the strap of my tote back onto my shoulder, and the keys jangle from my finger. "Let's go."

His brow wrinkles. "Wait."

I pause at the door, studying him. Searching for any signs at all. "Did you think I'd give you the cash? No way, man. Who do you owe? I'm paying him directly."

"You don't want to do that." Reid's firm. His head shakes back and forth. Steady. Insistent.

"Reid. I do it this way, or you don't get the cash."

"This guy is bad news."

"Aren't they all?" I step through the doorway, hand on the knob.

Inside my tote bag, I have a switchblade. I don't carry guns. Not because I don't like them, which I don't, but because I don't have the skills for them to be useful. But with ten thousand dollars bound by a rubber band sitting at the bottom of my tote, I long for a pistol to hold.

I follow Reid's lead. He goes on and on as we walk about how I don't know what I'm doing. It's better if the guy never meets me. He's the kind of guy who will come after me for money whether I owe it or not. I only half-listen, as I watch every person we pass with suspicion, my hand clenched around the strap of my tote as if I'm hanging off a cliff and it's my lifeline.

I don't need Reid's explanation. He got arrested with a small amount on him. Which means he probably hid a larger amount somewhere and the rightful owner wants repayment. Only Reid doesn't have it to give because someone, a bad cop, another junkie—the who doesn't matter—nabbed it after the arrest. Reid's fresh out of rehab, and these fuckers know it and they heard he has a job. Doesn't matter if a dishwasher makes shit. They want their cut. Same shit, different street corner.

We pass a homeless man kneeling on the sidewalk. I look directly into his eyes. I always do that, because I want them to know I see them. I didn't spend ages on the street, but I spent long enough that I know it sucks to become invisible. I dig into my jeans pocket and hand him a five. His hand shakes as he takes it, and I hope he spends it on food.

Reid pauses outside a Subway sandwich shop. "This is a bad idea."

I reach past him and push the door open. This location is a shithole. Two uniformed guys behind the counter look up at us when we enter. There's a row of booths on one side with green topped tables. Sitting in one of the booths is a nondescript guy. White male, dark hair, buzz cut, in a button-down oxford and a lot of rings on his fingers. He's muscular and fit, nowhere near as skinny as Reid. Which tells me he's not doing drugs. He's smarter than that. The guys behind the counter head into the back.

Reid gives me one last shake of his head that tells me he is full-on against this. He's trying to protect me, and for that, I love him a little bit more. I slide into the booth beside Reid and face this guy who, upon closer inspection, looks more like a kid than a man. It wouldn't shock me to learn he's under twenty-one. He looks me over and spreads one arm out along the booth. A toothpick extends from the corner of his mouth.

"You're the chick who helps the kids."

I search his face for anything familiar. But I get nothing. I'm pretty positive he hasn't entered our center. "And what do you do?"

The toothpick shifts up and down. Then a smile spreads and the guy looks even younger. "I help 'em, too."

"That's rich," I say. I don't take my eyes off him because if his hands go under the table, I'm moving.

"Man's gotta eat." He shrugs. "Man's gotta party."

I reach into my tote, and he practically leaps up out of the booth. His hand goes to his back pocket.

"Just getting the money," I say as Reid waves his palms in the air. I only see him out of my peripheral vision, but I assume he's doing some hand signal for *calm the fuck down*. I toss the stack of money onto the table and slide out of the booth. The guy's ass is now sitting on the edge of the booth and his feet are on the seat.

I can't help but think this guy isn't nearly as scary as Reid made him out to be. But looking again at those muscles and the rings on his fist, I have to acknowledge he could beat me up. And it would hurt.

"Are we all good now?" I ask.

"You paying for him?"

"I am. And I need you to leave him alone." He picks up the stack of bills and thumbs through it.

"So, am I going to see you next month?"

"What do you mean?" My stomach sinks. *What the fuck, Reid?*

"He's on a payment plan."

"How much does he owe?"

Reid lurks in the corner, eyes cast down.

"Another $40K. But we cut him a deal. Payment plan."

"You think he can cough up ten a month as a dishwasher?"

The guy grins wide, and that's when I notice how jacked the guy's teeth are. They twist every which way. "He's got options."

Fuck. I hate this world. He's probably been asked to do deliveries. Sales are pretty much done online these days, but deliveries are dangerous. Always a risk it's a sting. Reid's ideal personnel. Theoretically off the stuff and street smart.

My head spins, and I turn and charge out of the place. Reid calls out behind me. "Wait."

Fisher blocks my path. Reid slams into my back. My gaze falls to Fisher's holstered handgun.

"Let's go," he says, arm stretched, indicating he wants me to lead the way while he follows.

"What are you doing here?"

"Protecting Sophia. Before I let you back in that house, I need to know everything."

CHAPTER 11

Jack

The view on my monitor shows two talking heads in front of a whiteboard. After the upheaval within Sullivan Arms, it's a good sign that Cliff Hartman, the head of compliance, and Phillip Moore, my interim head of sales, like each other well enough to convene in the same office for our meeting.

Cliff is a balding man with a few random long gray wisps of hair that cross a freckled scalp. He's a good guy and was one of my dad's close friends and confidantes. He's also good friends with Uncle Mark. They're about the same age, but my uncle makes noises about stepping aside whereas Cliff plans to die at his desk. Of course, Mark Sullivan has been talking about stepping back for at least ten years. I doubt it will ever happen.

Phillip is in his late thirties, just a few years younger than I am. He's a go-getter and has great relationships with the dealers. His weakness, as my uncle points out regularly, is his strained relationship with distributors. But that's only because Larry Reyes dominated all distributor relationships, a fact that led him into alliances with questionable characters.

Larry Reyes is dead. Suicide in his prison cell. But we all know it wasn't suicide.

Cliff and Phillip converse back and forth discussing a mailing we're planning for the dealers. Compliance and legal review every piece of marketing material that goes out the door. The ad agency included suggestions for a rewards system for the distributors as incentive for them to push Sullivan Arms products. Cliff isn't necessarily against it, but he doesn't like the idea of doing anything that might encourage bending laws to sell more guns.

The conversation bores me, but also soothes me. Hearing them argue over advertising leads me to believe neither have it in them to push illegal shipments on the side.

"Jack," Phillip says, turning in the direction of the computer monitor but probably looking at the video reflection of himself, "you've heard both sides. What do you think?"

"You want me to overrule compliance?" *What a fucking waste of time.*

"Well, we're at an impasse. I understand what Cliff is saying, but we've done similar programs in the past. He's taking an extremely risk-averse view."

"Phillip, you're new to this role. You've taken on a lot, and you're doing a good job with it. Let me make things easier for you. We don't override compliance and legal. Ever. You got that?" The glare from an overhead light reflects off Phillip's glasses, preventing me from getting a good read on how he's accepting this reality. "I understand that Wayne did things differently. But I'd like to remind you he's currently awaiting trial." I refrain from adding that I hope he rots in prison. "That event alone has put Sullivan Arms in the news and most likely under regulatory scrutiny. Plus, let me remind you — we sell guns. We should always work within the confines of the law."

Cliff gives me one solid, approving, almost fatherly nod.

The men within Sullivan Arms are what I think of as good ol' boys. They come by their love for guns honestly, having grown up developing their shooting skills with a love for hunting. We have employees who come from all over, but there's a core demographic that's southern strong, so I always ramp up my southern dialect when interacting with my team.

"What else ya got?"

"The annual NRA banquet is coming up," Phillip says.

Damn if it doesn't feel like we have fundraising banquets every month. But he's right. The grand doozy is around the corner.

"Yeah?"

"What level donation are you giving? Do we need to do an ad around it?"

He's asking if I'm going to give over a million dollars. If I do, then I get an obnoxious jacket. It's good industry PR. But if I can get out of going, I will.

"Right now, you're our interim sales. Why don't you make the grand donation? It'll make a splash, and it'll open up introductions for you to key accounts at the banquet."

"You know I believe in the NRA, but I don't have that kind of money to—"

"You donate it and expense it. Sullivan Arms pays, but it'll look like it's you."

"I can help you with that," Cliff offers. He's perfected our political donation system over the years.

"Anything else?" I ask.

"No. Thanks, Jack. How's Sophia doing?" A lot of men ask me that question, but Phillip has a way of doing it that comes across as genuine. Maybe it's not so much how he asks, but the knowledge that he has kids of similar ages.

"She's recovering." The statement is more than I want to share. It's not like I'm going to tell my colleagues that she still refuses to talk to her friends. I won't share with them my biggest fears. The obvious fear that she's going to ask for tutors in the fall to avoid returning to school. My deeper fear that she's suffering more than I can comprehend. And perhaps my darkest secret, my fear that my daughter will never open up to me. I will never be a suitable replacement for her mother.

Cliff and Phillip offer a series of grim nods and grunts of understanding and I end the online meeting.

My phone rings thirty seconds before my scheduled call.

"Ryan." I spin my chair to face the ocean. "How's it going?"

"Good. It's just me on the line. I'll update the team after we speak."

"Thanks. I know you prefer everyone joins in, but I need you to hear this, and only you. You're still checking the property for listening devices, right?"

"We do a daily sweep."

"Good. I need to meet with you in person."

"When?"

"Today? Tomorrow?"

"Let me check with Alex. If she's working this evening, I'll fly down end of day."

"Thanks." My thumb hovers over the red button. He's in charge of my security, so I ask, "Fisher told you about Ava's run-in last night?"

"Yeah. He trusts her. Did you learn more?"

"Ran the photos Fisher took through the database. No arrest record. Yet. Now, Ava's friend? Reid Miller? He's got a rap sheet a mile long."

"You think I should ask her to leave?"

"She's clean. She hasn't done anything wrong. But–"

"She's got a weakness." I know where he's going. My exhale is louder than intended.

"Yes, but Fisher's read is that she would never do anything to harm you or your daughter." There's a pause. "My sister is moving into Nueva Vida in two weeks."

"Okay." He never talks about his sister. I'd been surprised to learn he had one.

"She's an addict." He says it like that explains everything. "Was. Is. I don't know. She's in rehab. Ava's center is highly recommended, but it's hard as hell to get a spot. She gave her one."

As if talking about Ava's center compels her to appear, there's a rap on my office door and she peeks her head inside.

"Lunch?" she mouths.

"I've got to run. I'll share my schedule with you. Pick the time you want to meet, and we'll discuss specifics then."

Ava pushes the door open. She's wearing black leggings, black running shoes, and a loose black sweater that hangs seductively off one shoulder. It does, mercifully, conceal her breasts much better than the skintight tank tops she likes to wear. The heavy eyeliner fails to hide her nervousness, and I gesture to a chair. She hesitates, resting her hand on the back of the wooden frame.

"Chef is making lunch for Sophia and me. Sandwiches and soup. Thought I'd see if you want to join us. Get your order."

Both Chef and Sophia text me regarding meals. Ava has something other than my lunch on her mind.

"I'll text my order to the chef." I go for cordial. "Thank you for thinking of me." Her skin flushes, and those chipped fingernails tap against the back of the chair. The line of silver bracelets jingle, glimmering in the sunlight through the window. "Is there something else?"

"Do you have a minute?"

I hold my hand out, gesturing to the empty room. She's in here. I clearly have a minute, or she would not have been allowed to enter.

"Sit."

She continues standing, and my cheek muscles involuntarily flex.

"I've been here for four days now."

"Yes."

"And I'm building Sophia's trust. Trust is important. And I've been thinking about that a lot." Those long lashes flutter. "On one hand, seeing her so much, in a casual setting, has sped up the development of that trust. But this is not an advisable situation."

"Have you made any headway?"

"Tomorrow will be our second session."

"Only your second?" What the hell has she been doing?

"These things take time. She's been through a lot. And you need to realize that the trauma she experienced doesn't magically go away. It'll never truly go away. But she will learn how to manage it."

"Do you think she's... has she mentioned cravings?"

"No. But if she does, you know there are options for managing cravings."

"I don't want her on methadone."

"I don't think she needs it. But if I change my mind, I'll go to bat with you on that unfounded judgment." She's no longer holding on to the chair for balance. Lines form around her lips as she glares at me. This woman really would fight for my daughter. She and I are more alike than I originally thought.

"What she's craving right now isn't the drug as much as the release. She wants to forget."

A meeting reminder flashes on my screen. The meeting is with our CFO to prep for an upcoming board meeting. I can't miss it.

"Well, that's not an option," I say. "Earn your money and help her through this."

I read through the meeting participants on my phone, and as much as I might like to continue talking with Ms. Amara, I cannot reschedule this meeting.

"I can't make lunch. Ask Chef to bring my lunch in. Smoked salmon over a kale salad."

I click on a link to review the material before the meeting. Sales are down, which is as expected, given our internal shake-up. But we can't miss revenue projections. It's too likely someone out there will spin it to say we took a hit when we blocked illegal sales. Of course, that's exactly what is happening, but I need to find solutions.

Not only do I miss lunch with Sophia, but I also miss dinner. I am shit at managing my schedule. Cassandra hated me for that. Work destroyed our marriage. My daughter needs me, and I'm letting work impede being there for her. My eyes burn, and a dull headache throbs mercilessly. My behavior is not acceptable. I should be a better father. I should be a better man.

Ryan flew down. I met him at the helicopter landing pad while Sophia ate dinner with Ava. I told him everything about my role with the CIA. I explained that I'm hoping they clear an undercover op, but if they don't, I'll continue working with Victor Morales, and I want Arrow to have my back.

Ryan agreed, but one question he asked plays on repeat. "How do you know you're not being played?"

The troubling answer is, I don't. But working with the CIA has honed my instincts. And my instincts tell me Morales trusts me. If I play along, I'll learn a lot more about this scheme than Sophia's abduction revealed.

Moving forward, we agree to a weekly meeting at a nearby gun range.

It's late when I tap on Sophia's bedroom door and peek my head in. She's asleep. Her golden hair spills over the pillow. With care, I step over and press my lips against her temple, just like I used to do when she was a toddler.

She stirs, rolling away from me, and I whisper, "Love you, sweetheart."

The house is dark and quiet. I make my way to the basement bar, then to my evening chair. Outside on the lower patio, I swirl the golden liquid in my glass. There's a quiet to the night I enjoy. A subtle whooshing sounds signaling the opening of the sliding door. Without turning, I sense the woman behind me.

"Ava," I say, then sip, letting the burn down the back of my throat bring me into the present. "Does it bother you when I drink?"

"No."

"Then come join me. Sit here." She chooses to stand near the chair, and damn if I don't find her resistance appealing. "Thank you for having dinner with Sophia." An explanation for my absence from dinner is on the tip of my tongue, but I bite it back. Cassandra would have demanded one, but I don't owe Ava anything.

"She needs you, you know?"

"I'll do better." I hate the words as I say them. I never do better. I side-eye her. Her deep brown eyes look almost like dark pools out here at night. "What about you?"

"What about me?"

"Fisher updated me. Are you going to break ties with..." I can't think of his name. His background report sits on my desk. "Your friend?"

She lets out a sigh and sinks into the seat beside me. "Would you give up on Sophia?"

She's out of her mind. "Is this friend your son?"

"No. But he's like family. We've been through a lot together."

I consider that. There's a short list of people I would do anything for. Sophia. My brother Liam. Uncle Mark. Cassandra made the list before a car collided with hers. My nephew doesn't make the cut. He's an idiot. Ryan, of course. He's a business partner now. He helped me find my daughter.

"If his life was in danger, what would you do to save it?" That's really the crux of the matter. That's the security risk this questionable friendship of hers represents.

She's silent. Her hands wrap around her stomach, below her breasts. She looks sad, and that's not my goal.

"Would you lie? Steal?" The men who held Sophia, as far as I know, did it for straight cash. Like a job. But it's conceivable they had someone in their lives they needed the money for. Or an addiction to feed.

"I would lie. And steal. But if you're asking me if I would harm anyone else, the answer is no. I would never." She sits up straighter. "But I wouldn't steal from you."

I hold up a hand while staring straight ahead into the darkness. "You can steal anything. Just nothing of Sophia's and no photographs." I don't give a crap about anything in this house. I bought it mostly furnished and had no part in my designer's selections, with the exception of select rooms. "How much more money do you need?"

"You already paid me. Overpaid."

"Are there any others like your friend?"

"Huh?"

"Anyone else you would do anything for? Who might need money in the future?"

She can't save them all. But there's no point in arguing with someone like her. If she'll stick her neck out for a guy willing to bring her along to meet his drug dealer, she'll stick her neck out for almost anyone.

"I'm okay for money."

"What if I gave you your financial independence?"

"I'm not sure I understand what you mean."

I temple my fingers as I rest my elbows on my thighs. "If you are financially stable, there are lower risks." I have more money than I'll ever need. More than Sophia will ever need. More than her children will ever need. "How much more do you need?"

"I don't. I'm...you and your uncle have been extremely generous. I don't need more." It's the way she bites the corner of her lip and looks down to the corner of the seat cushion that I know she's lying. She needs more than what I gave her. Of that, I feel certain. Probably for her ex. I've been respectfully calling him her friend. But one call to my uncle, and I learned the truth.

"I don't want you going to those group sessions anymore." She needs to cut off contact with her so-called friend.

"I'll find someone to fill in for me." Her easy agreement surprises me.

I study her in the dim light. She has an underlying sexuality that intrigues me. But I don't have the time or the inclination to woo her. And more than that, if I entered into a relationship with anyone, not just Ava, that would be one more person I would disappoint.

"Ava Amara." Her arms mirror mine on the arm rests. "What if we arrived at an additional arrangement?" Her head angles slightly to the right, the only indication she heard me and is listening. "What if we expanded your services? And in return, I paid you enough to be financially sound?"

Those short black nails curl under her palm.

A sliver of guilt for the heartless proposal has me spinning my chair so I am no longer facing those doe-like eyes, and I speak to the shoreline.

"The arrangement would need to be private. Sophia could never know. Obviously. Only while you are here." I tap my left fingers. "What's your price, Ava Amara? One. Million. Dollars?"

I close my eyelids and wait. Does she get the Austin Powers spoof reference with the over pronunciation of "one million dollars?" A piddly amount of money for me, but it's a life changer for someone like her.

She could scream at me. Slap me. But, based on what I understand about her past, I doubt I'm the first person to proposition her.

Will she say yes? Will she counter? Ask for ten million? If she says yes, will she crawl to me on her knees, pull out my dick and suck me off? My dick twitches, coming to life at the vision. That would be good. I'd like that.

I've had arrangements before. At a Houston club where Liam and I are members. For a period of time, here in San Diego. I've never been so blatantly transactional, but she works for me. A payment ensures feelings do not enter the equation. I can't risk her becoming emotional near Sophia. My last arrangement did become emotional. I ended things shortly after Sophia moved into my house.

I wait for the answer. And wait. The secret to a good negotiation is to not appear too eager. To not rush the opponent. Let them mull it over. But she's taking too damn long. So, I open my eyes and look at her chair. It's empty.

She's gone.

CHAPTER 12

Ava

The crisp air conditioning blends with the salt-tinged summer night.

Holy fuck.

Jack Sullivan is out of his mind. He has more money than the gods, so I suppose in his world, spending a million is comparable to me shelling out two hundred bucks for a pair of jeans. Insanity, but something I once rationalized as a splurge. Only I buy jeans, and he buys a person.

No. He wants to buy a service. An exchange of goods. It's an exchange I've made before. Sex for drugs. Not necessarily spelled out so callously. But men would offer to share their stash, and there was an implied understanding. It's not something I'm proud of, and it's something I've put behind me. But it's there. And he must sense it.

The automatic door slides to a close, and I wave a hand over the threshold to keep it open. I'm wasting air conditioning, but that's a nonsensical consideration, given the dollar amount he just threw out there.

Life changing.

One million is nice, but it's not life changing. Or is it? But even if it is, at what cost?

I've worked too damn hard to put the past behind me. Could I feel good about myself if I agreed? Sure, it's tempting. The idea that when a pipe bursts or a donation falls through, I won't have to go into a tailspin, sure, it's tempting. But would I feel good about myself?

I push open my bedroom door and fall onto the bed. I sit up and kick off my shoes. This is insane. How much did he have to drink? He didn't sound drunk.

Is this what it's like to have an incomprehensible amount of money? He could burn it in the fire pit by the pool, all night long, and he'd still be immeasurably wealthy. It's too much to wrap one's head around.

I can't believe he asked me that. So calm. The funny thing is, if I met him randomly in a bar, well, first, I'd assume he wasn't interested. He's refined and businesslike. Patrick refers to my style as bohemian. I think of it as cobbled together from secondhand stores and sales racks. Whatever you call it, it's not Rolex and fine leather.

But if he did hit on me, I'd probably go for it. Maybe. He's handsome. Gorgeous, really, when his lips aren't deadlocked in a scowl. If the light hits his eyes right, it's clear the color is closer to topaz than brown. Under the right conditions, they appear luminescent. He reeks of power and wealth. The man could walk into any bar, anywhere, and have anyone he wanted.

It's been so long since I've played the single scene, what do I know? I close my eyes and run my hand vigorously over my face. But when I stop, I check, and no, all that shit really happened. Story of my life.

I'll just ignore it. He'll regret asking in the morning.

Footfalls against the wooden floors outside my bedroom freeze my lungs. I strain to listen. The click of shoes grows louder.

"Ten million."

Ten? Did I hear him right?

"Did you hear me?"

Holy fuck.

"You are out of your mind."

"Do you require more?"

I sit up on the bed and open my eyes. It takes a minute for my sight to adjust to the dimly lit room. The hall light glows behind his shadowy form.

"Are you high?" It's the obvious question. I can't really see his pupils. What would be a billionaire's drug of choice? Opioids? Coke?

"I'm negotiating. Not particularly well, it would seem." He seems almost amused, and yes, he's drunk or high on something.

"You need to get out. Think of your daughter."

"I am thinking of my daughter. This would be a contractual agreement. One she would never find out about. The contract outlines expectations and ensures a mutual understanding of the parameters of the arrangement."

"You're thinking with your dick. And you've taken something that is screwing with your logic. You need to leave, and if you're lucky, you won't remember this in the morning."

"Are you saying no to my offer?"

I roll over onto my stomach and reach for a pillow to pull under me. I need something to cling to. This is unreal. "You need to go."

"One hundred million. That's my final offer. You can give me your answer in the morning. And Ava?"

I am fairly certain my mouth is wide open, given air flows through it.

"I'm not high. I'm not drunk. I offered a hundred million reward for information leading to my daughter's safe return. That money ended up back in my bank account. It's nothing for me to give it to you. I trust you'll do good things with it." He slips his hands into his pockets and his shoulders shrug, like we're having a perfectly normal late-night conversation. "Think of all the people you can help."

"Why?"

"That's what you do, right? Help people?"

"Why me?"

"Why not? You're living in my house. I'm attracted to you. Enthralled. Inexplicably, I'll admit. You enter a room, and I want to touch you. Fuck you. But I can't offer more. One, there's Sophia. She's my priority. And two, as you've already noted, I'm not enough for Sophia as it is. But that doesn't mean I don't have needs and desires. I don't care about the money. When you have as much as I do, money doesn't matter. It's simple. I want you. For a specified period of time. You set the terms. Your hard limits. Your soft limits. It won't be every night. But I don't sleep well." Another nonchalant lift of those shoulders. "You can help me with that. For the rest of your stay here. And my money will help you for the rest of your life. It can be a donation to Nueva Vida, if you prefer."

He steps to leave, but pauses in the doorway, casting his gaze over my body. Goose bumps rise across every inch of my skin.

"Sleep on it."

CHAPTER 13

Jack

Twenty-five unread emails. That's not too bad for a Saturday morning. Weekends are my time to catch up. Sophia gets moving late in the morning, so I can get through quite a bit before she's looking for a breakfast companion.

Saturday mornings are also my long runs. The only sounds are my breathing, the waves, and the occasional seagull squawk. But this morning, my offer played on a loop.

Liam would tell me I'm out of my mind. Ryan would too. Maybe I am. But I like the idea of a no-strings arrangement. There would be no guilt because I am paying her extraordinarily well. And she'll do something good with the money. She'll help people. Teach them coping skills. Build a supportive community. Do job training and help them find housing once they are ready. I visited her website.

In a financial arrangement, there are no expectations or risk of emotional attachment. She won't try to hold hands in front of Sophia. She'll keep it professional during the day, and what happens behind a closed door will be between us. No one will be able to bribe her. She'll have no reason to choose to harm Sophia out of greed or desperation. At the end of her agreement, she will leave.

She'll be financially independent and have the resources to grow her nonprofit as she desires. Sophia will, with the grace of gods, be farther down the road to recovery and closer to a return to normal. And I'll get to fuck the woman I've been craving since the day she walked in my house. With any luck, after I have her once or twice, I'll be sated. We can continue as if she's a fellow club member for the duration of her stay. A clean, straightforward, mutually beneficial arrangement.

Ava hasn't yet agreed. But she will. Everyone has a price, and I made her an offer no sane person would refuse.

Objectively, this arrangement reeks of anemic morals and ethics. Instead of asking her on a date, I paid for what I wanted. And it felt so damn easy and natural. What is wrong with me? When did I become this person?

There was a time when I wasn't like this. A lifetime ago.

The dull headache returns, and I pop a couple of aspirin, then scroll through the emails, scanning subject lines. My assistant will comb through any I leave her to handle.

Patricia, my assistant for the last eight years, works well with me. Our system works. Even when I took time away, I kept her on as my assistant. She's completely virtual these days, as she still resides in Houston, but we've worked together so long, proximity doesn't matter.

One subject line from Cliff garners my attention. In a nutshell, he's concerned about the agency's latest ad campaign. It has yet to run. I stare at the image of a fit man in camouflage and his grip on one of our rifles equipped with a scope. He looks like he's going to war, but soldiers are not our target market. This ad targets our core US market, the couch commandos. These men don't buy guns to hunt animals. These men buy guns to exercise our second amendment rights to form a militia and protect our democracy. The marketer's insight is that our core market wishes they had what it takes to go to war, and they spend billions in pursuit of the fantasy.

Couch commando is a common gun industry term used by ad execs to describe one target market segment. This ad will sell guns. Our competitors run ads like this. The focus group feedback on this campaign is overwhelmingly positive.

My father and grandfather had it easy. Back in their day, it was all about marketing to hunters and sportsmen. But there's a limit to the number of guns a hunter needs. Those out-of-shape dads can only carry so much iron into the woods. And a quality gun can be passed down for generations. For our industry to grow, for our businesses to thrive, we must seek additional target markets. And grow, we have. There are now more guns in the US than there are people.

Personally, I agree with Cliff. The moral ground is mired in muck. But aside from morals and ethics, this campaign doesn't align with our high-end brand.

Sullivan Arms is known for its craftsmanship and innovative scopes. Of course, our technical advancements have attracted the couch commandos. After all, we've secured hundreds of millions worth of military contracts, and that doesn't go unnoticed by the military wannabes. Should our campaign shift from a hunting focus to a military focus? Which campaign will drive the most sales?

I click out of Cliff's email. I'll have to give the campaign consideration before weighing in. From a marketing perspective, the biggest issue with that new campaign is that you can't tell any difference between us and any leading gun manufacturer. We all use fear to rationalize additional gun purchases by men who probably already own dozens of guns. If I kill the new ad campaign, I won't be doing anything good for society, because everybody else is doing it. But what will I be doing to our sales?

Ethics aside, it's bad branding. We need to stand out. I've always wanted to focus on craftsmanship and technical advancements over fear-based mongering. If we want to be perceived as a high-end product, we need to focus on the reasons we're worth the extra money. Earn the distinction of being best in class.

But if I kill it, I'll raise enemies within the ranks. Somewhere within my company, there are skeptics. They question my commitment to the gun industry and to Sullivan Arms' growth strategy. I'm selling myself as someone willing to go to the extreme of questionable international arms sales. Killing this campaign might lead some to distrust me.

No, I've got enough going on without bringing critical attention. I'd prefer they think I'm playing along. It's just one damn print campaign for next year.

And, with the right adjustments to additional emphasis on innovation in the body copy, maybe next year we can shift into the new product we have in covert development. Fingerprint recognition so a gun can only be fired by the owner was in development thirty years ago. The industry revolted at the idea that a gun manufacturer, Smith & Wesson, would do anything that might show gun manufacturers held responsibility on their shoulders. The NRA orchestrated an unofficial blackball. Distributors dropped them. Gun stores dropped them. The CEO lost his job. And research halted. But I've picked it back up and have been working on it for years.

The team I have working on it is based in Israel. They also develop our scopes. They owe me an update, but with the time difference, and given it's the weekend, I add a note to call them on Monday.

My phone vibrates, and Ryan Wolfgang's name flashes.

"Hey, man."

"How's it going?"

"Can't complain. Alex is meeting a friend for brunch, and Trevor and I are about to head up to the hills for mountain biking."

"Nice." I click to close out of my email.

"Someone was trying to hack into your server."

"Sullivan Arms?"

"No. Your home system. When we took over your security, we set up your home system on a protected server. Before, what you were using had minimal protections. Fine for the average Joe, but..."

"Yeah." He'll never let me live down being so lax in my personal security. In retrospect, I don't know why I thought using a system from the early nineties would be sufficient. I didn't want cameras at all the entrances to my home. I still don't.

Ryan and his team will know more about my personal life than I would choose to share. But at least Ryan is a friend, and I'm a silent partner in his firm.

"Erik's team is all over it. Whoever it was didn't get in, but my gut tells me someone is trying to get access to your email. Maybe your phone."

"One of these days, I'm going to need to meet Erik." Erik Lai is one of the Arrow partners, but he lives up north in Napa. He and another partner, a woman by the name of Kairi, oversee all things Internet. My unofficial role is weapon development, something I wish I had more time to pursue.

"He's not the friendliest guy," Ryan says. "But we're planning an offsite. Think you could get away?"

"Maybe not right now."

"Didn't think so. Just in case, I'll let you know when we get something on the calendar. The reason for my call is to warn you to proceed with caution. Consider switching out phones for important calls. Be on the lookout for a package from Erik. He's sending you alternate government issued phones and trackers."

Who would try to hack into my phone? The Morales Cartel? I've opened a door into working with them, and they are notorious for monitoring potential employees and partners.

"Dad?" Sophia's voice has me spinning my chair to find her standing feet away.

"Hey, sweetheart." A sadness overtakes her facial expression that slices me to the quick. "What's up?"

"It's Saturday." She levels the statement and leaves it there. A bomb to be handled with care. She watched her mom plant the same bomb over and over. And I promised…

"Hey, Ryan, my daughter is awake, and she and I are spending the day together. Can we touch base on this later?"

"Sure thing. Just wanted you to know. Also, if they get in your server, Erik will take it down. So, if you don't have access at some point, you know…"

"You can't stop them?"

"We can and will. But taking the server down is an effective route if it's being attacked. Right now, Erik is following the trail to figure out who is doing this. Could be nothing."

I'd like to get more information, find out if he's raising on-site security, ask him why I need a tracker, but for now, he's got a team working, and I have a daughter who needs me.

"Let's talk later," I say and don't miss the flash of something in Sophia's eyes. What was that? Surprise?

I push up from my chair and pointedly leave my phone on the desk. My hand falls to her back, and I lead her out of my home office. She's wearing multicolored pajama pants that skim the floor and a giant Gap t-shirt she bought at a secondhand store last summer. Apparently, secondhand stores are all the rage. Her blonde curls are pulled up into a band on the top of her head, and I want to pick her up and throw her in the air like I used to do, but she's no longer that little girl, so I stymie that desire.

"How does an omelet bar sound to you?" she asks.

"Delicious."

We round the corner, and my feet halt. Ava stands behind the kitchen counter with a big ceramic bowl pressed against her hip. She's wearing a formfitting tank that molds to her curves. Tattoos line her arms. The silver bracelets are mostly gone. Her arms flex from holding the bowl and spinning the whisk in the eggs.

Her eyes meet mine, and a dash of color rises in her cheeks. Waves and half curls claim her bangs and thick mane, giving her a just-out-of-bed look. Her fresh, makeup free face lends an innocence I suspect doesn't exist. I hope it doesn't exist, or I'm complete dirt.

I stare. I should look away, but I don't. She's living in the house, and I asked her not to leave, so of course she's here. But it feels different. And I know why. Without all that dark eye makeup, the thick eyeliner and dark shadow, she stuns. My lungs contract.

"Dad?" Sophia's hand touches my wrist. "Are you okay?"

"Yeah. Of course." I reach out and tug on her earlobe. She swats my hand away and shoots me a look that says, *Stop it, Dad.*

"You spaced out." Sophia leaves me standing at the kitchen entrance. "Check the bowls and see if there's anything else you want in your omelet. I put out everything I could think of."

"No, this looks great."

"We were thinking after breakfast we would go paddleboarding, but there's so many people out there already. So, what do you think about playing a game?"

"A game. Like what? Sequence?"

"Yeah. The three of us."

I glance at Ava, and she offers a slight smile.

"Sure," I mumble.

"Oh, and Dad, I wanted to ask..." Sophia looks to Ava, and Ava offers a supportive smile. An uneasiness stirs in my gut. "Would you mind if I changed some things in my bedroom?"

Relief fills every pore. I don't know what I expected my teenage daughter to ask, but this is easy.

"Not at all. You know, I have that designer. Cheri... no, Evie." I snap my fingers. "Evie is her name."

"She's the one who did my room, right?"

"Yep." I pop a sliver of red bell pepper into my mouth. I thought Sophia loved her bedroom. "If you want someone else, feel free. Show her what you want, and she can make it happen. You can direct the show."

I pointedly look at my daughter's sea-blue eyes, eyes that make me think of Cassandra pretty much every time I look into them. I've got brown eyes, but apparently a recessive blue gene too, and somehow she lucked out with her mother's gorgeous blues.

She bounces up and down on her heels and claps her hands, looking happier than I've seen her look since everything happened.

"You can redesign anything you want to in this house."

"Really?" Sophia is looking between me and Ava, a genuine smile lighting her lips.

"Of course." For her smile, she can do anything she wants. As long as she stays safe. "What would you change?"

"Well, the weird marble statues for one. This entire house feels like an old lady's house with all the gold and scrolls." My eyes meet Ava's. Does she agree?

"Whatever you want." It's not like I picked any of it out. I moved in with it furnished. Cassandra and I had divorced, and I needed a place for my daughter to spend time with me here in San Diego. After Cassandra died, I should have made it more of a home, but she died so unexpectedly. My grief had been nearly debilitating. It was all I could do to step up and adapt to being a single father overnight.

"Why don't you treat this like a design project?" Ava asks as she sets out three omelet pans and pours the whisked eggs into them. "You know, go around and think about what you'd like to change. Create a presentation board for your dad. It could be a fun project."

Sophia's cheeks glow. She looks more alive this morning, and I have to admit, Ava's suggestion is solid. It'll give Sophia something to focus on. A way to fill her time and build her confidence. It bothers me to no end that she won't spend time with friends. I miss my carefree, happy kid. But maybe this little project is a step forward.

"I'll go get her contact information for you."

Back in my office, I pick up my phone. I can't remember the woman's last name, so I text Janet and ask her to send me the designer's contact information.

There's a light rap on the doorframe. Ava stands in the doorway.

"I told Sophia I'd make sure you didn't get stuck in here. But, um, real quick..." Her gaze falls to the floor.

"You accept my offer."

She blinks. Once. Twice. "You were serious?"

"I'm not a particularly jocular man."

"Right." She peers down the hall. She stretches her fingers out, then balls them up, then stretches them out. "Okay. I'll do it."

Of course she will.

"But I need to return to Nueva Vida this afternoon." She shifts from one bare foot to another and understanding dawns.

"Is it smart to give a recently rehabilitated man a load of cash?"

Those long eyelashes flutter. Her lips purse. She swallows. "I wouldn't." She shakes her head back and forth in quick jerks. "I'm going to pay the person he owes."

I pinch the bridge of my nose and exhale. She's out of her mind. "Tell me how much he owes, and we'll send Fisher."

"I need to go."

"No. You don't." I cross my arms, wondering what her logic could possibly be.

"I need to see Reid. He'll tell me where to find him."

"Dad? Ava?" Sophia's voice is distant. She's still in the kitchen. But time is short.

"Fisher will know where to make payment."

"I just..." Her eyes plead.

Annoyance simmers, but it's not my place to be annoyed. I assume she wants to tell Reid she's saved him.

"Fine. Go with Fisher." We can't have her getting murdered this afternoon. The last thing I want is to have to tell Sophia someone else in her life died unexpectedly. "Let's get back to the kitchen."

"I'll be back after dinner." She whispers the words in the hallway.

I give the briefest of nods, and understanding for her meaning sinks in. Anticipation for tonight swells.

I smile at Sophia when we re-enter the kitchen and get out the blender to prepare a protein shake. Omelets are fine, but I'm going to need the extra protein.

"Ava's going back to her clinic this afternoon, so it'll just be the two of us. Sound good?"

"A game. Just the two of us?" She frowns.

"Paddleboarding is still on the table. Or we could take the Jet Skis instead?"

Sophia debates options with me, and Ava listens. When she's done with her plate, she quietly clears it and leaves. She's almost out of the kitchen when I remind her. "Don't forget Fisher."

CHAPTER 14

Ava

A sense of freedom soars the second I pass through the Sullivans' driveway gate. The grill of a Range Rover blocks my rear view, and I press the accelerator.

I stretch my neck, left and right, accelerating past perfectly manicured lawns leading up to palatial estates. The surreal situation has my head spinning. It's like I'm trapped in a weird dream. I bite the corner of my lip to confirm I am indeed sober. Pain sears beneath my tooth. It's real.

I pick up my phone and dial Patrick, setting it to speaker so I can let the phone rest while driving.

Ring. Ring. Ring.

"There she is. How's beach life treating you?"

"Patrick. What the hell have you gotten me into?"

"Whoa. What happened?"

"Nothing." I exhale and press my head against the headrest. "How are things there?"

"Fine. Mark's arriving this afternoon. So, if you need to tell me something..."

"No. Or..." My head is swimming. I can't come out and tell him. Why did I call him? What do I want him to tell me? "Patrick? Do you ever think of yourself as a kept man?"

There's a long pause. I click the blinker to turn onto the freeway.

"Well, let's see. My lifestyle far exceeds what an ad sales rep moonlighting at a nonprofit could support. I live in Malibu. I haven't flown less than first class in at least ten years. There's a Ferrari in my garage. If you are asking if I feel bad about it, which is what the judgmental word 'kept' implies, no. I'm with the love of my life. We've been together for fifteen years. He plans to retire, and soon we'll live together full time. Hell, we practically do now. His business trips have dwindled to practically nothing. If anything, I've had to adjust to him being around so much. Where the hell is this coming from? I'm getting worked up just answering your question."

"Sorry. I don't mean anything bad by it. I know you and Mark are together. Just–"

"Is something going on with you and Jack?"

I curl my lips together and check my rearview. The Range Rover is about one car length behind me.

"If you could make a lot of money for having sex with someone, would you do it?"

"In this scenario, do I want to have sex with him?"

"He's a good-looking man. Fit. Brooding. Extremely attractive."

"Six or eight pack?"

"You don't know that yet."

"Holy shit balls. It's Jack. How much did he offer?"

I laugh out loud. I can't help it. Patrick is so damn dramatic.

"Mark's always worried his nephew is too soft. Like he'll do something for the good of humanity, like support gun control laws, and the whole gun industry will blackball them. But damn. Look at that. The boy has kink."

I roll my eyes, not that he can see me.

"How much did he offer?"

"You won't believe me."

"Try me. I've been with his uncle for a long-ass time. You seem to forget that."

"One hundred million."

"Dollars?"

"Donkeys. Yes, dollars." An uncontrollable grin spreads across my face. I check the rearview again. Yep, there's a Range Rover.

"Are you shitting me? Ask him if he's bi. I'm game."

I laugh so hard it hurts. Maybe this is exactly what I needed to crack the surreal shell. Laughter with my friend.

"He's out of his mind," I say.

"Who cares? Go for it. I know you're freaking out. I hear it. But why?"

"Well, it's unethical, for one. And if his daughter found out, it could derail any trust I build. And let's be honest. Me living here isn't at all recommended by any ethics board as it is. But it is a lot of money. He's truly out of his mind." It's just unbelievable. I mean, we didn't discuss his kinks. I'm not naive. I know there are some whacked men out there, but he can't want anything that would be too horrible. One hundred million is a lot of money.

"Well, it's not that surprising, I guess. He is a man who offered one hundred million for his daughter. And they asked for twenty-five. Money means nothing to that man. This will set you up for life. Hell, you won't even need Mark's donations for Nueva Vida. No more charity events if you don't wanna. And he's gonna have a vested interest to keep it private. I bet you've already signed an NDA."

"He requires anyone working on his property to sign an NDA."

"See. Mark does the same. Take advantage of the rich fool. And if he's anything like his uncle, the sex will blow your mind."

"I'm not sure what I expected you would say when I called you, but it's not that."

A shrill horn blares next to my car. The driver flashes the finger at another driver on the highway. I stay in my lane and check my rearview. There's still a Range Rover.

"Are you in the car?"

"Yeah. Going back to Nueva Vida. Part of my agreement includes no more group sessions."

"Why?"

I have no desire to hear Patrick chew me out for giving Reid money. "He's controlling, I guess."

"That could bode well for the bedroom."

I roll my eyes. "Nah. It's more to do with safety."

"I bet. Publicly offered up a hundred million reward. I bet there are tons of people wanting to be the next one to nab his daughter. If he publicized his going rate for lady friends, there'd be a parade of women walking by his house every day."

"No shit." I giggle. And it's completely inappropriate. That's me. Gallows humor all day long.

Sometime after ending my call with Patrick, I parallel park in a questionably legal parking spot near Nueva Vida. Street parking can be tough to come by, and there's no place for Fisher to ditch his gas guzzler.

I wave goodbye as he shouts out the window, "Wait for me."

He wanted to drive me, but I refused. He can deal with paying off Reid's debt. The kid didn't look particularly scary to me, but my perspective differs from the average Joe's. But I'll be damned if I'm going to let Fisher join me with Reid.

If I could call Reid, I would. But he doesn't yet have phone service in his apartment. That's not always a bad thing. Severing connections from the past can be very helpful when building a bridge to the future.

I rap on his apartment door. He's on the second floor, and it's an outside wraparound deck. Around the corner of the building, I see Fisher charging my way. The door opens, and I push inside.

"Hey. What's up? You okay?" Reid peers outside.

"Close the door." He obeys but rests his back on the door, arms crossed. "Are you in trouble?"

"No. Nothing like that. I just...I wanted to speak to you alone. Is anyone else here?"

He's got a studio apartment, but there's a half wall up between the kitchen and the rest of the apartment, and an en suite bathroom.

"Just me." He sniffs. "Gotta leave in a few for my fabulous dishwashing job. Dream job USA."

"Right." I cross my arms and study him. The whites of his eyes are clear. His nail beds look healthy. He's still underweight, but that takes time. "I'm paying off the shithead today."

He tilts his head like he didn't hear me. "Martin? How?"

"I got some extra money, and I'm paying him off. I don't want him coming around here. I don't want him messing up things for you. But that means you can't have anything to do with him. You understand that, right? Like, you get that, right?"

So-called friends are Reid's sticking point. In and out of rehab for years, and every time, it's his friends who pull him down. He's got shitty friends.

He nods, and that's when I catch it.

"What did you do to your face?"

His hand goes up to his temple. "Had the cabinet open, bent down and the open door popped my head."

The lights aren't on in the apartment, and I can't really see. I step forward to flip the light switch, but he blocks me.

"What is this about? Why are you paying off my debt?"

"Because I can." And because you don't need this hanging over your head. "Do you remember our senior song?"

"High school?" He grins. Our class had all kinds of shitty songs in the vote. *I Hope You Dance* from some country singer had been the rage, and we'd been scarily close to that winning, but Reid corralled the band and even the jocks, and *Steal My Sunshine* won out. The lyrics don't quite match the upbeat song, which when I think about it, might be why Reid loves it so much and fought so hard for it. That, and he said a sappy country wedding song would suck.

"Don't steal my sunshine. You hear me? I'm not going to be around for the next couple of weeks, but I need to know you're going to be okay this time."

His brow wrinkles. "Where are you going?"

"I have a client. It's..."

"That Patrick guy? He's trying to get you away from here, isn't he? He doesn't trust me. Or you and me."

He takes a step forward, and his gaze has more heat than I've seen from him in years. He's definitely sober. Which is good to see. I hold my index finger out and shake my head.

"Nope. That's the last thing you need right now."

He grins his naughty-boy grin. "You sure about that?"

"Reid." I laugh. "Yes, I am. Get your feet under you."

When I open the door, I expect to see Fisher hovering. But he's resting against the railing about two doors down, arms crossed. There's a seriously large earbud in his ear.

After giving Reid a hug goodbye, I turn the opposite direction from Fisher and head down the corridor to the steps. Fisher's feet shuffle along the concrete behind me.

When I reach my car, I wait for him. "I'm gonna swing by my apartment and then head back to the Sullivans'. You want to come with me there? Or is this where we split?"

"Will you text me when you're headed back?"

"Sure."

He holds his hand out for my phone and promptly enters his number into it.

"This is weird, you know?" This is the feeling of the week, not just the moment, but Fisher doesn't get that. "I don't need security."

"I'm about to pay off a gang member for your ex-boyfriend. You sure about that?"

He slides his sunglasses down on his nose and swaggers away like he's a cop on one of those reality television shows.

"Be careful," I shout after him. Fisher's cocky, and I'm not sure I like him, but I don't want him getting hurt.

As I crank my car, I shake my head for the umpteenth time. This is all unreal.

CHAPTER 15

JACK

"Dad, I'm going to go get a shower."

"Be sure to put some moisturizer on. Your nose is red. Did you use sunblock?"

"Yes, Dad." She rolls her eyes as she turns away from me. Like I'm the idiot. Maybe I am. I forgot to mention sunblock when we went out. My skin is darker, and I never burn. Her pale skin easily burns. When she was little, Cassie would coat her in the white stuff.

Now she's fifteen. Am I supposed to remind her or trust her to apply it? I don't think I ever mentioned it when she first came to live with me full-time. But we were both so shell-shocked, my memory of that whole first year is hazy.

I stretch my shoulders as I meander through the house. We paddleboarded for hours. If my muscles are sore, I'm sure hers are, too. I need to have more days like this with her. I need to spend more quality time with her, not simply time in the same house with both of us in different rooms.

After we shower, I'll see if I can interest her in ordering a pizza and watching a movie.

My phone rings as I pass by my office. I step in and pick it up, bracing for a barrage of missed emails and texts. Ryan Wolfgang's photo and name flashes on screen.

"Hey." I check the time. Fisher followed Ava. He should've paid the guy already. Did something happen? Is that why Ryan's calling?

"Are you out of your mind?"

I glance down the empty hall and step inside my office, closing the door. "What do you mean?"

"One hundred million dollars? Seriously?"

With a deep inhale I sit down on the front of my desk and cross one bare foot over the other. How would he know?

"She told someone?"

"Yeah, first thing as she drove away from your house. But that's not the point. I mean, if I knew you were that hard up–"

"Stop." I don't like being called out, but I'm still grinning. I can't expect a Navy bud to not give me hell for this. "It's not like that."

"What's it like?" Ryan's not a guy I would ever call a jokester, but yeah, this is him giving me shit. And I must admit, I deserve it.

"Does the whole team know?" Shit. I really didn't think about my request for them to listen to her conversations. I should've known she'd mention it to someone. "She wasn't talking to the press or anything, was she?" *Fuck.* I didn't think about that at all. I mean, I'd go full denial and fire her ass, but–

"No. Just a friend. Your uncle's partner, actually."

"Which partner? A board member?"

"His boyfriend? Sounded like they've been together a long time."

Look at that. Liam was right. Our uncle is gay. Or bi. He almost married a woman decades ago. "Let me guess. A guy named Patrick?"

"Yep."

I exhale. "You think he's going to tell my uncle?"

"Sullivan, you don't pay me to play that game."

I do sound like a woman. "It's fine. If he tells him, I'll explain."

"I'd like to hear that explanation."

"It's a good use of money."

"Really?"

Fucker. "Really. She'll put the money to good use at her nonprofit. I don't need the money."

"Well, tell me what you do need."

"I'm not having this conversation with you."

He laughs. Ryan never laughs.

"Glad I could entertain you. The whole team knows?" *Fuck*. This is one of the reasons I hate security.

"No. The person monitoring the feed this afternoon brought it straight to me."

"Why?"

"Because she's Gen Z with a twisted sense of humor. The official reason was she wanted to know if we should continue listening in her bedroom."

"You've got bugs in her bedroom?"

"We didn't know if we could trust her. You asked us to monitor her."

"Because I wanted to know if she was making any arrangements–" I stop myself from saying more and push off the desk. "Kill any devices in her bedroom."

The fucker laughs.

"And that's not because of me. That's wrong."

"But her phone?"

I just gave her enough money so that she could never be blackmailed or threatened or connived into doing harm to Sophia. "Nah. Stop it. She's only here for three weeks."

"What happens after three weeks?"

"Her contract ends."

"Right."

There's a tease to his tone I don't like, but I drop it and end the call. If I can get out of this with that limited amount of razzing, it'll be remarkable. To someone like Ryan, I've lost my mind.

He's wealthy in his own right, but he can't comprehend a billion-dollar net worth. I earn more money in interest each day than I can possibly spend. My daughter will never have to work. Her children won't either. Giving away this money is nothing. And it's money I already gave away once that never left my bank account.

As the water streams over my head, I visualize Ryan's eyes bugging out when he heard that tape. And I can't help but chuckle.

Sophia falls asleep on the sofa about twenty minutes into the movie. A full day outside will do that to anyone. But this summer, ever since the abduction, she sleeps so much. She wakes as I lift her off the sofa and tells me she's good to get herself to bed.

After she goes upstairs, I flick off the movie. It's one she picked. Some kind of take on the Addams Family. Maybe more of a television show than a movie.

I pick up my phone and catch up on email. I'm in the middle of an industry report when steps click down the stairs. I rarely sit in the basement den, but Ava's bedroom opens into the den, and I didn't want to miss her return home.

The clicks grow louder, and the temptress herself appears. What is it about her? She's not my type at all.

"How'd it go?"

"Fine." She crosses her arms. "How does Fisher know where to find Martin?"

"He's good at what he does. Plus, he's with Arrow. They have connections."

"With the police?"

"If needed." I was going to say feds, but there's no point in explaining further. "Do you need to freshen up?"

Her bracelets jingle. She's applied all her dark eye makeup. She rubs one thumb over the other thumb's nail repeatedly. Those doe eyes look at me with a mix of trepidation and interest. She's curious. She doesn't know what to expect. Maybe she's nervous. I can set her mind at ease.

I want this to be enjoyable for us both. A sexual release. Money aside, I won't force her. If she's not willing, we'll call it a night. Like Sophia, I'm tired from a day beneath the sun. But anticipation pulses through my veins. If she backs down, I'll be disappointed. Because I am very much looking forward to losing myself inside a woman tonight.

"If I'm okay like this...I don't really have anything to change into."

I let out a sigh of relief. This is going to happen. We'll do this now. I'll make her feel good. I'll release some of this tension that sits in my shoulders and pulses in my temples. And then we'll both retire to our respective bedrooms.

I'm a member of a club in Houston. At TMPT, we do this kind of thing all the time. It's the purpose of the club. Not exactly this kind of arrangement, but close enough.

"Straight back."

CHAPTER 16

Ava

"Straight back," he says. "Last door."

The central room that opens onto the ground deck area is set up much like a living area. It's more casual than the rest of the home, and a flat-screen television hangs over an unlit fireplace. My guest suite is off to the left. In front of us is a long hallway. To the right is another hallway that leads to a well-equipped home gym and the office the security team uses.

A series of closed doors line the hallway to the back. The tip of Jack's finger brushes my arm, and a fission of energy, much like an electric shock, zaps me. My knees wobble under the weight of my body as I shift forward.

The white painted walls, ten-foot doors, and substantial curvy molding intimidate. Underfoot, the glistening marble floor shines. White with black streaks cross irregularly in an erratic lightning pattern. The bright white elicits a heavenly glow, but the ebony strikes an ominous chord.

Somehow, I manage to traverse the hall without tumbling to my knees.

My feet stop where directed. It's on the right side of the hallway, and there's a lock. He presses his thumb to a black glass square.

Click.

He twists the knob. The door opens.

Across the threshold, the white marble transitions to polished black. Warm black velvet dresses the walls. A thick, black, furry carpet spreads across the floor. Faux flames flicker in spots along the walls, giving the room a seductive warmth. The room itself is gorgeous, but it's the furniture that steals my breath.

I step across the threshold, marveling at the lush design. To my right is a glass cabinet held together by roughhewn welded metal. A series of glass butt plugs sparkle under the shelf lighting. Small whips and threaded tassels lay in a disordered pile on the bottom shelf. Silky black material, fuzzy handcuffs, and masks are piled haphazardly on the eye level shelf.

An inviting silky bed claims the back corner of the room. Bindings hang from all four posts. A large hook gleams from the ceiling near the center. Silver hooks hang along the wall to the far corner, and rope dangles from the hooks. And to the right, floor to ceiling glass panes held together by the same welded metal as the shelf surround an oversized walk-in shower with gold overhead shower faucets and handheld sprayers. An oddly shaped curved leather bench occupies the area in front of the shower and folded black towels rest on top of it.

Between the shower and the wall hooks stands a blood red leather St. Andrew's cross.

"I should ask if there is anything you don't do." His words send goosebumps scattering up my arms.

I should tell him that for what he paid me, I would think he didn't care, but I'm speechless. Patrick said that if Jack was anything like his uncle, the sex would be fantastic. Is the entire family into kink?

"If there's something you aren't comfortable with, I want you to tell me. Don't let the dollar amount sway you. I won't do anything you don't want me to do."

I've had a wild past, but I've never been in a room like this. Even so, I'm aware I need to be careful what I say. I am not naïve. There are definitely BDSM elements I'm not open to. This room is unexpected.

"I'm not sure I can answer that." I step out of my sandals. The cool marble tingles the pads of my feet. I step onto the rug, and the moment my toes hit the silky fur, I suspect that it's mink. I've never owned a fur coat, but I did once touch the sleeve of a mink coat, and there's a smoothness and luxury to it I've never forgotten.

"What do you mean?"

"I don't have an extensive knowledge of kink. I don't know all the words. Pain does not excite me."

Overhead candelabras flicker, and I'm close enough to discern the exaggerated plastic rivulets mimicking candle wax. My heels dig into the fur rug as I slowly twist to face him.

He's tugging on his chin, and there's an infuriating smirk playing across those handsome lips. To this wealthy playboy, I'm his toy.

"Anal?" he asks.

I don't think I've ever done anal, but my reality is I'm not quite certain about that. When segments of time are forgotten, it's impossible to say what one has or hasn't done.

"I've read about it. If it's done right." I look at him pointedly, because *right* is an important word. Owning a room like this doesn't guarantee he knows what he's doing, or that he's good at it, or that he doesn't get off on causing pain. "It's probably fine. Pain doesn't turn me on." I glare, ensuring he understands. "I'm also not into golden showers or anything crazy."

"Good. We're similar. How do you feel about being tied up?"

One glance around the room, and it's clear he's into it. My bet is we're in a soundproof room. I've already placed my trust in him. If I go missing, Patrick will come looking.

"It's fine."

"Blindfold?"

"Fine." No one has ever blindfolded me but given the size of some of those glass butt plugs, and the metal configurations on one shelf, a blindfold feels benign.

"Take off your clothes."

He turns and steps to the wall. A loud click sounds, and I'm pretty positive he locked the door. My pulse quickens and my hands grow cold.

"Should we sign a contract?"

"A contract?"

The lift of his eyebrow and the quirk in his lip smacks of derision. Who am I, this lowly purchased person, to question his greatness? My gaze falls to the fur on the floor.

"A written document that outlines what we are agreeing to." I've read about them. He doesn't need to act like it's unheard of.

"We can write one up if you like. But it would be unenforceable in court." He pauses. He toes off his shoes and steps closer. Dark, unreadable eyes lord over me. An invisible vice constricts my ribcage. "Therefore pointless."

He's correct, of course. But other people have those agreements, and my understanding is that it sets expectations.

"If you wish to draft a contract, I'll sign it." Black socked feet protrude from the bottom of his slacks. His dress shirt remains pressed, but he rolls his sleeves halfway up his forearms. It's Saturday night, and he's in business casual.

This is insane. I should tell him I need time to think about this. I should go call Patrick and tell him what's going on. Double-check that he still thinks this is a good idea.

"Ava, do you need some time?"

His facial expression remains unreadable. His dark hair is ruffled at the top, and I envision stepping closer to run my fingers along his shoulders, and higher to feel the rough end-of-day growth that shadows his jaw, to inhale his cologne. In this room, in this lighting, his eyes are dark. There's no amber, no hint of light.

In the rest of the house, he's stern. Intimidating. Out of my league. Hell, beyond my galaxy.

Yet here we are in the same playroom. And he's a dream. Frenetic energy pulses between us. At least, I feel it. The current warms my skin and sends my heart racing. Is it attraction, or unruly nerves? Or some combination?

He's attractive, and I'm not pure. Sex isn't new to me. I find it to be both enjoyable and fulfilling. He's offering me money for something I enjoy. I don't like how that makes me feel, but he's offering me enough money I can get over it. He's the one who is being taken for a ride. And I'll do good things with his money. Life-changing things.

I lift the hem of my tank over my head and let it fall to the floor. Cool air circles my exposed breasts. I'm not wearing a bra. His sharp intake of air loans me the courage to raise my gaze from his socks up to his face. His gaze remains fixed on my bare breasts.

I wiggle my hips and let my loose, ripped jeans fall. They slide over my butt, down my thighs, and pool at my ankles. I stand before him in only my panties, tattoos and jewelry. The tattoos tell the tale of my sins while cleverly covering scars.

"Step to the wall."

There are four walls in this room. He points ahead. A silver metal hook protrudes from the ceiling. I glance to the St. Andrew's cross.

"Not tonight." His smirk deepens. "Tonight, I'm going to get to know you."

I face the wall, showing him my backside, knowing full well my thong bares my buttocks. My feet pad across the fur, projecting a strength I don't feel. I'm not scared. I do not fear this man. A part of me wants very much to partake in the pleasures he offers. But nerves fire ruthlessly, betraying my facade of calm. A yearning grows, chipping away at those troublesome nerves. Cool air circles my nipples. The audacity of standing nude in a sensual room, surrounded by pleasurable toys, turns me on. With my back to him, it's easy to imagine this is an erotic fantasy.

I stop below the hook and glance over my shoulder, silently asking if this will do. The sight of his heated dark gaze elicits shivers.

"Your eyes are enormous."

I blink.

"Has anyone told you that?"

Surely this man is not looking at my eyes. "One kid said I looked weird."

"What was his name?"

"I don't remember." He wasn't a nice boy. I remember the clothes he wore. The collared polo shirt and the pleated shorts. But oddly enough, all I remember is that his name started with a T. I haven't thought about him in ages.

The glass door to the artisan cabinet clicks when he opens it and then clicks closed. Jack lifts black silk from the cabinet.

"Look to the wall."

I do as told. Anticipation mounts. Will he tie my hands? What is his kink? What turns the billionaire madman on?

Smooth, cool fabric brushes across my temple. His hot breath warms my ear.

"Don't lie to me. In this room, we do not lie. Ever. Do you understand?"

I nod.

"Use your words."

"I really don't remember."

The tip of his nose touches near my ear. He bows his head until we are temple to temple.

"I'm going to blindfold you. Are you ready?"

"Yes."

Silk covers my eyes, and the room goes dark. The sensual material blocks light and caresses my skin. I inhale a light, clean scent. Strands of hair pull as he knots the fold. I push back against the mild discomfort. My nostrils flare as I breathe in, reassuring myself that the fold does not constrict my airways.

"Put your hands together." I automatically do as told, and silk encircles my wrists, then he raises my joined arms.

"I'm going to leave your arms tied high. How's that?"

I tug and discover he's somehow tied my arms to an object, most likely the hook hanging from the ceiling.

"You can pull down. It's secure." His fingers light along my back, and my core clenches. "That okay?"

"Fine." My arms might go numb, but at the moment, being displayed, control removed, is decidedly erotic. "Do I need a safe word?"

"Not today. Besides, we already determined you and I are alike, remember?"

My mind goes blank. I want to feel his touch. My nipples ache. My eager core throbs expectantly. I am so ready.

"Neither of us gets turned on by pain. Any screaming in this room will be screams of pleasure."

The cool air whips around my nipples, my arms tingle as the blood flow diminishes, and I spread my legs to allow the coolness to circulate near my heated, pulsing core. With my eyes covered, a hyperawareness of physical sensations surges, all the while reminders of the implications of sex and the fear of relapse surface.

I didn't allow myself to have sex for a year after rehab. I treated it like a nuanced drug.

No amount of money is worth a relapse.

I feel his presence behind me. He's not touching me, but there's an energy coursing between us. The energy vibrates and lights my skin. I can't see him, but if I could, I would bet his hand hovers over me, inches from my shoulder blade, shifting down the curve of my spine, along my hip. Close enough for sensory impact, but without physical touch.

Cool air replaces warmth, and I hear movement. A click of a cabinet.

"Do you like sensory play?"

"I, ah, wouldn't know." I'm hardly innocent, but my sexual

encounters are more of the wham-bam variety. Oral is about as much foreplay as I ever expect. Reid, my only committed partner since rehab, preferred sex fast and rough.

Something soft brushes down my spine and swipes across the top of my ass. My muscles clench at the sensual touch.

"Do you like that?"

"Yes."

The softness sweeps across the side of my right breast, with tendrils cascading down the breast, over the nipples, across my chest, continuing on to caress my left breast. A vibrating energy awakens my left side, alerting me to his physical proximity.

"You have a beautiful body. But you know that, don't you?"

Sometimes I know, and sometimes I don't. There are moments when I love my body for all it can do and all it has survived. And there are others when I get lost in comparisons and envious wishing. But these are realities he doesn't want to hear. This man bought me for sex.

My shoulder muscles heat, and I push my ass out, pulling down on my arms, stretching. The muscular burn transcends from my arms to my shoulders and down my lower back. My thighs take part in the deep stretch, and soft, ticklish threads coax the divide between the globes of my ass and back up my spine.

Hot warmth and wetness encapsulate my right nipple, and I gasp. His tongue circles. There's a pinch and suction. My core aches, and I squeeze my inner muscles, coaxing my need in the only way I can while tied.

He leaves my right nipple, and cold air freezes the tender tissue as his mouth claims my other one. The contrarian sensations of cool and warm send chills down my spine as my thigh muscles flex. A soft touch, as light as a feather, skirts my knee, up my thigh, and through my labia. I whimper.

And then warmth replaces the feather.

Holy shit.

It's his tongue.

My knees go weak, and I let my weight hang against the bindings. The silk tightens against my wrists, and my fingers tingle.

"Spread your legs."

I comply immediately, without hesitation.

"Ava." The way he says my name is simultaneously commanding and sultry. "I like the way you taste. Would you like for me to continue?"

"Yes."

He doesn't chuckle, but I imagine he smiles. I imagine he likes this. God, I hope he likes this, because I fucking love this.

And then the rough growth of his chin and jaw rub hard against my sensitive flesh, a mild distress softened by the forceful laps of his warm tongue and the mix of suction. When he plunges inside me, it takes me by surprise, and I jerk forward, my almost numb arms springing to life. It's his finger or maybe an object, I'm really not sure, but whatever it is soothes the ache that's been building since the moment I shed my clothes.

My orgasm strikes hot and fast, and behind the blindfold flashes of bright orange and yellow dot the black. Warmth caresses my inner thigh, passing to the front of my leg as I come down from the rapid escalation. He lifts my arms, and I stretch. He unravels the bindings, lowers my arms, and briskly rubs my wrists and along my arms. A million pins and needles light my arms as blood returns and the sensations override the glory of what just happened.

He places my hands against the wall.

"Press here."

The velvet fabric warms my chilled palms. I flutter my fingers, encouraging blood flow and exploring the divine texture. Pressure on my spine instructs me to bend, and I do so until I'm bent over from my hips, ass out. The fabric of his pants leg brushes against my ankle.

"Spread your legs."

A zipper unzips. A mental visual of him grabbing his cock and stroking himself hits me hard, and my throat tightens. I swallow and anticipation mounts. A protruding object slides along my ass crack.

The intruder is warm and smooth. I squeeze my muscles, tightening around what I know must be his erection. He grunts. The warm, almost-silky object moves lower, between my thighs. My clit contracts. My breathing is hollow and rapid.

With one powerful thrust, he enters me, and I push back against the intrusion. He stills, balls deep, and grips my hips. His fingers dig into me. My knees tremble. A hushed exhale tickles my ears.

And then he pummels me, in and out, over and over. Fabric buffs my ass as I push with all my strength against the wall, thrusting against him, and it hits me. He's still clothed. It's like he's the man from a porno with his dick sticking out of his zipper. He hasn't even bothered to let his pants fall.

His left hand abandons my hip. Cold air replaces his hot skin. A whirring mechanical noise mixes in with his heavy breathing and my panting and guttural moans.

A cool, hard, vibrating object presses against my clit, and I cry out in surprise. His hips slow, and he pulses within me. I whimper as a slow, winding orgasm meanders through me. I push out against him, seeking more touch, wanting a more intense vibration on my clit. He collapses over me, and a soft warmth presses against the nape of my neck. His clothes create a welcome tactile experience. The vibrations end.

Cold air replaces the fabricated warmth. His dick slips out from between my legs. The zipper zips. I feel his presence, a pressure on my lower legs, and I'm in the air. I let out a small squeal in surprise. My head lolls as the back of my neck rests against what I believe must be his arm.

With care, he sets me down on silk. Soft, thick padding. It's the bed. His fingers tousle with the blindfold, and it's gone. I blink. The room remains dark, lit only by flickering faux fire and candles.

He's at the cabinet, arranging things, his back to me, fully dressed except for his shoes.

"I used a condom." He announces it in a way that makes me feel like I should respond. Like maybe it's a test. I'm sprawled out, limp and naked. "Are you on birth control?"

"The pill."

"Good. I'll have someone stop by the house to test you. I'll get tested too. I don't like condoms."

Various responses to his assumptions come to mind. There's a part of me that wants to fight. Another part just wants to close her eyes and go to sleep.

"Smart to get a druggie tested," is what I say. And then I cringe. I've gone years teaching myself to be better. To have healthier internal thought processes. An hour into this arrangement, and I'm slipping.

His head bows. The cabinet clicks closed. He pads to the door and slips on his shoes. His hand rests on the doorknob.

"You can sleep in here tonight or in your room. When you leave, the door will automatically lock, and you can't re-enter."

The knob turns, the door opens, and he exits.

CHAPTER 17

JACK

It's Monday morning, and my focus is laser-locked on hitting my six-minute mile goal. Sweat pours down my temples, and if I swiped it away three seconds later, I would have missed the signal. The Joey's Pizza box hangs off the metal trash can, half in, half out. We've got to come up with a better fucking system.

I slow and stretch, sticking one ankle out at a time. My lungs burn, and I revel in the familiar sensation. I've got three miles on the return trip. This pause in my schedule had better be quick.

My contact sits on a bench about twenty yards from the trash can. She has a dog on a leash, and she's reading a paperback with a coffee in her hand.

My head stretches left, then right. There's a runner about a quarter mile up the beach. In the nearby alley, a garbage truck beeps. All the beachfront, shops are dark, given the early morning hour. My foot props on the edge of the bench, and I stretch out my quads. I give a quick nod to my contact and drop my gaze to my ankle.

"Mike Ventola was killed last night in a Texas prison riot."

I continue stretching while stifling the urge to demand what exactly Mike Ventola, a stranger, has to do with my case. Red flag warnings are out thanks to a system coming in off the Pacific, and my gaze centers on the monster swells.

"Claimed he worked for Killington." My neck cracks as I stretch it to the side. The feds are building the case against Killington for smuggling guns. Sources claim the evidence is piss poor. The evidence for abducting my daughter is irrefutable.

I scan the area. There's no one near, and the winds are strong enough no one could hear us unless they were close.

"Never heard the name."

"The FBI meeting was scheduled for this coming Wednesday."

"Who knew?" It's pretty fucking clear we're dealing with high-powered people. Maybe even someone within the FBI.

"Not many. But he ran his mouth all over. Too many knew his story."

Fuck. "Is the FBI meeting with his cellmate?"

"Today." She says behind her paperback book. If anyone were to watch us, it wouldn't be clear at all we're speaking to each other, but I'd imagine she looks like someone in desperate need of reading glasses the way she's holding her book so close to the front of her face.

"Anything else?" I ask as I hold my left arm straight across my chest, cupping my elbow, pulling it tight as I twist my torso to the right.

"Homeland says he has ties to some far right-wing groups. He may've been blowing smoke."

Or he might have ties to far-right groups, and he also worked for Killington. The two are not mutually exclusive. And the death in the prison riot might have had nothing to do with his upcoming meeting. As always, there are too many possibilities.

"Your undercover op proposal is still under consideration. FBI will likely take the lead in a cross-agency task force. We'll be in touch."

I don't have a response to that. Our government is slow to

respond, as expected. And there's no surprise to hear about a turf war.

"Have a good run." She drops her paperback into a small tote bag, signifying her little update is over.

Back home, I shower and dress. Then shoot a text to Ryan.

Range this afternoon?

As I sip my coffee, I peer out the window. I picked this house solely because of the proximity to my daughter's home with her mother, but there are things about it I've grown to appreciate. The panoramic ocean view is one aspect I value. But this morning, the view in the swimming pool is more riveting than the Pacific.

Ava climbs out of the pool, and her pale skin shimmers in the morning sun. She's wearing a black one-piece swimsuit. I am growing accustomed to seeing her in black. Her one-piece hides the tattoo scroll that traverses her ribs, and her hair covers the forest on the nape of her neck. From this distance, I can barely make out the inked flower tattoo on her right arm, and I can't see the one on her left wrist at all.

Ava watches Sophia continue with her laps. From what I can tell, Ava believes in the power of natural endorphins. Sophia has never been a slouch, but she's never been disciplined with her exercise. Since Ava moved in, Sophia's attitude is brighter. But she still refuses to see friends. She's still tight-lipped and claims she remembers nothing from her abduction. I don't believe her, but how much can a father push? I wish her mother was alive. Sophia needs her, and I hate that she's not here for her. I am a subpar substitute.

Ava glances back at the house. She covers her eyes, as if she's trying to see if I'm behind the glass. Or maybe she sees me.

All I see is an incredibly sensuous woman. She's beautiful. Raw. Real. She's risen above her sins. Maybe that's what appeals to me. There's beauty in being shattered and possessing the power to heal.

The mythical Phoenix transfixes humanity with the elusive ability to regenerate. Her story is that of the Phoenix.

To say she's not a part of my circle, or my world, would be a gargantuan understatement. Yet from that first day, she's lured me in. I crave her. She's only here two more weeks. The deadline to fuck her out of my system looms.

Underlying guilt gnaws at me. What I offered is wrong. I am twisted and disturbing. Perhaps what is most disturbing is my pull to her, because in this moment of introspection, I recognize her appeal extends beyond physical attraction.

But what, exactly? What about her past appeals to me? Is it a power trip? No, I don't want to tear her down. I admire her strength. But there's something about being with someone who has made questionable choices. She's less likely to judge me for my past. She doesn't even seem to judge me for buying her.

WOLF

2?

The text comes in, and I tear myself away from the view, refill my coffee, and enter my office to double-check my schedule.

Perfect. I'll pick you up at the helipad.

Ryan and I agreed to meet out at the range because the noises all around us ensure no device can catch everything we say. He's a busy man in his own right, and it's unfortunate he has to waste time flying down to talk with me. For years, I rolled my eyes at CIA precautions. But given everything that's happened, there is no safeguard too great.

If needed, we will write out anything that is sensitive and burn the pages. One week ago, I would carry on a conversation with him in my vehicle. Or in my home office. But now I won't. I hoped Killington's arrest would lead us back to normalcy, but it seems it's stirring the enemies.

But I'm not stopping. I will continue to figure this out. I will take down every single person responsible for what happened to my daughter, no matter how wealthy or powerful.

Fisher taps on the door. I update him with our afternoon plans and then my morning meetings begin. During my first meeting, I email Patricia to let her know she'll need to reschedule a few meetings this afternoon.

On the way to the range, Ryan hands me an iPad with a presentation loaded onto it filled with potential yachts. All the yachts his team has located are currently available and can be outfitted according to my needs. I select the one he recommends.

We have a private area on the range. My security team hovers nearby, ensuring no one approaches us. Even with everything going through my head, I achieve a near perfect score. Skill comes with practice, and I have practiced most of my life. Ryan and I agreed that we would use this time for practice, in case anyone is watching. And, like any skill, practice aids precision.

Out of ammunition, I move to leave the privacy of our hutch. A battery of firepower surrounds us. Ryan grips my elbow, holding me in place. He taps my headset. I shift it back, exposing my ear.

"We've been looking at the entire staff of the Texas prison. Still searching."

"You're not going to find anything in financial records. These guys are too smart."

"Maybe," he concurs. "But we found that the warden and the senator appear friendly. We've located photos that show them at events together going back ten years."

"Is that unusual?" I've long suspected elected officials were involved somehow, if only through bribes to assist with cover-ups or looking the other way. A senator would fit, but a warden in a maximum-security prison very well might be friends with a senator. Hell, those are often appointed positions.

"We're researching that." Ryan keeps emotion close to the vest, and to any observer, he remains unreadable. "But the senator also has extremely close ties to the NRA."

"Now that, I can confirm, is completely normal. You can't get elected in Texas without close ties to the NRA."

"We're just connecting dots."

"Let's get this boat operational. That's going to give us players we can track and follow."

I don't give a damn about the little guys, the ones who are paid to smuggle guns and drugs. I want to climb my way up the food chain and take out the source.

"I don't like this. My bet is they're playing you. Looking to see who you involve."

"I've given that consideration. But that wouldn't make sense. If they don't trust me, it would be a much smarter plan to keep me in the dark. To continue to work around me."

"Maybe so." He scans the area. There's one man in a vest at the far end. His headset covers his ears, and he concentrates on his target. "Any word about your ops request?"

"Still under consideration."

"So, we're moving forward as if they aren't involved?"

"Yep."

"I'd feel better if they were read in on this yacht. You don't even know what they're smuggling."

"We've got a good idea." Ryan does not look happy with my decision. "Sounds like they'll authorize it, but it'll be FBI taking the lead."

"That's good."

I slap him on the back. "You've got a lotta love for the CIA, huh?"

He grunts. And I chuckle loud enough that Fisher glances our way.

After returning Ryan to his helicopter, I join in a few more meetings, then rush to a business dinner. My goal is to limit myself to two business dinners a week.

Ava isn't a babysitter, but I have to admit, it's nice knowing Sophia isn't having dinner alone. Before this whole mess, I didn't worry as much because she'd have friends over or she'd go out with friends. Hell, Sophia loved the independence of a night at home alone. It'll be a long damn time before that happens again. If ever, because I'll have security around her for life.

When I pull into the drive, the night shift greets me at the gate. Yes, I had gates installed. Before the incident, I fell for the misguided notion that security gates at the entrance to the neighborhood were sufficient. I park in my garage, enter through the side door, and check on Sophia. A light shines over the threshold. I tap lightly on the door, then twist the knob.

She's asleep with a book on her chest. Her fat little dog lifts his head, but he lowers it back onto her leg after recognizing me. I press my lips to her forehead, lift the book, careful to mark her page, and read the cover. *My Life as an FBI Agent*. Interesting. After turning her light off, I quietly pull her door closed.

Downstairs, a shower runs. It's the only sound filtering through the darkened hallways. A shadow crosses the outside patio, and I recognize the outline of another nighttime Arrow employee. Three shifts, twenty-four hours a day, seven days a week, we have a security staff on-site. A dull pain throbs across my brow, and I consider going upstairs for water and bed.

But as if pulled by an invisible force, I find myself in front of her bedroom door. I turn the knob and push the door open. I toe off my shoes and pad quietly to the bathroom door. Steam curls out the opening. Condensation coats the bathroom mirror. The subdued sound of water pouring onto tile is the only noise. My heart rate increases, as if I'm at a jog, yet my pace is remarkably slow.

Her eyes are closed, her head tilted up, as if worshipping the rain. Those thick bangs of hers are off her face, soaking wet, and her forehead gleams under the overhead light. Without makeup and bands of jewelry, her natural beauty stuns. Chipped black nail polish partially covers short nails, but her toenails are bare. A single silver band wraps around one toe.

We all wear armor. Armor can come in many forms. But here, with those magnetic brown orbs closed, I see her with her shields set aside. She backs away from the waterfall. As if she senses me, she turns, glancing over her shoulder, her dark hair coursing down her back, soaked. A thick stream of water travels from the ends of her hair, down her spine, to her delectable, full backside.

I didn't think it was possible, but her eyes widen, and my cock, already at full attention, begs for release. My fingers work the buttons on my shirt.

"Should I meet you in the room?" Her question bears an echo effect against the tile, muffled by the shower and draining water.

I throw my jacket into the nearby soaking tub as I give a quick shake of my head. My shirt follows. I undo my belt, unbutton and unzip my pants, and remove them, along with my socks. She remains facing the water, her head turned to watch me.

With two steps, I'm behind her. Her skin is warm and wet. Pliable. My dick presses against her back, and my hands glide along her watery waist until I capture both her breasts. She looks up at me, and I'm so close, she's forced to press her back against my chest. I tweak her nipples, and they peak, begging to be sucked. My gaze falls to her lips, red and full. Billows of steam suffuse the shower.

"Should I put my palms flat against the shower wall?"

I palm her ass, then slap it. All I hear in her question is insolence.

Her tongue slips out over her lower lip as the globes of her butt press against my groin. Before I can push her forward and tell her to spread her legs, she twists in my arms and falls to her knees. Cool air shocks my front, and then her tongue licks up my shaft.

My palms fall flat against the tile. I groan. Dark pinpoint pricks flash as she takes me in her mouth. Holy fuck, her hot mouth feels good.

She kneads my balls as she takes me, fucking me with her mouth. It's unexpected and mind-numbing. All too soon, my balls tighten, as does my lower back.

"Wait," I pant. But the vixen ignores me.

I snatch her up by her armpit and claim her disobedient mouth. My tongue plunders her. Some part of my brain tells me to back down, to let her breathe, but she counters my kiss as if she's starved, and I give in, pressing her against the wall. My erection presses into her stomach, and her hot, wet skin feels incredible. I find her center, and she whimpers as my finger invades her slick slit. Her hips buck against me, riding my hand while I lose control, sucking on her neck, pinching her nipple, rocking my hips against her.

She twists once again, breaking away from me, and confusion stalls action until she rises on tiptoes, securing my cock between the velvety smoothness of her butt cheeks, her forearms pressed against the shower wall.

"This is how you like it, right? You don't want to face me when we have sex?" Her eyelashes flutter, and the water roars in my ears. "You can pretend I'm someone else. I'm okay with that. But I need you. Inside me. Please."

My mind blanks. She's so fucking wrong. No other woman enters my mind when I'm inside her. I twist her around and lift her.

"Put your legs around me." She obediently lifts her thighs, and I move us away from the shower spray. "Arms around my shoulders."

She does as I command, her dark eyes locked on me. I rest her back against the tile, using the wall for leverage, and I impale her, thrusting deep inside her warm cunt, the place I've wanted to be all fucking day. I freeze for a moment and get one hand solidly below her ass, and then take everything. All the bullshit of the day pours out of me as I pound into her. Her nails scrape my back. We both groan and grunt like wild animals. And the only thing I know for sure is that deep inside her is where my dick needs to be. She's tight, and warm, and she fits me. She quivers around me, milking me, and I falter, on the edge, and then she squeezes and it's like a vise grip around my cock. My forehead hits the tile as my release pulses out.

We both slide to the ground. She turns, so she's beside me, and the water pours over her legs. Our chests rise and plunge, as if we've run a marathon. A part of me wants to pull her up against me, to press kisses to her forehead, to hold her with the intimacy of lovers. But that's not what this is.

With a deep sigh, I push up off the floor and offer her my hand. There's a soapy washcloth hanging on a peg, and after letting the stream of water warm it, I reapply soap, and clean every inch of her, allowing myself extra time over her perfect, full, gorgeous breasts.

"I like this." She raises a questioning eyebrow as I gently caress between her legs. "I like it bare."

She takes the washcloth from me and returns the favor, only when she reaches my junk, she swipes it all over, soaping up my balls and cock, and looks up at me with hooded eyes. "I like this. It doesn't have to be bare."

Manscaping is something I believe in, but I'm not bare. I'm not that into grooming. "It's good that you don't need it to be bare."

She laughs. I did not design my comment to be a joke, but her laughter lightens the room, and I grin harder than I've grinned in years.

She turns off the water, and I wrap her in a plush towel. There's only one towel on the nearby hook, so I leave puddles of water across the bathroom floor as I search for a second. When I find one and wrap it around my waist, I catch her watching me.

"You didn't have to turn me around there, you know. You can do whatever is most comfortable for you."

"You don't need to play therapist with me." That's what she attempted. She wants to decipher me. We've only been in the playroom a couple of times. I don't like to face the people I fuck because it's too personal. But in the shower, I chose a different way.

"Trying to figure you out isn't playing therapist. At first, I assumed you had a fetish, but you have yet to try any of those anal toys in the cabinet. Then someone told me you're still not over your ex."

"Who told you that?" I reach for a hand towel and scrub my head furiously.

"Sophia."

I back up to the counter and rest against it. "Shit. That's what she thinks?"

"She says it completely tore you up when she died."

I cross my arms over my chest, thinking about the implications of this. Should I talk to Sophia?

"But she says you know she cheated on you. Or she's pretty sure you figured it out when it came out Wayne abducted her."

"She told you all that?" I knew they'd been spending a lot of time together, but I expected her to talk about herself, not me.

Ava's skin glows almost red, and the white towel wrapped around her sets off her dark hair and those large brown eyes and swollen lips. I close my eyes and attempt to focus on what's important.

"Should I talk to Sophia about all of this?" I exhale and spin around. I grip the counter, lean forward, and peer down into the sink. "Cassie and I…"

"After she told me that, I suspected you turned me around so you could pretend it was Cassie you were fucking."

I bark out a laugh but then choke it back. My uncle might have been wrong about Ava's strength as a therapist if that's what she deduced.

"I knew Cassie was cheating on me. But, in her defense, she believed I was cheating on her." I let out a sigh. "And in some ways, I was, but not with a person." That one throws Ava for a loop, but that's all she's gonna get out of me. "Our marriage dissolved years before she cheated."

I thought I could save our marriage once I had the time. I thought… I'd have the time. There's no point in baring my soul to Ava. She's leaving in two weeks. "Let me ask your professional opinion." Her dark orbs flash to mine, and I'm struck once again by how gorgeous she is without all that heavy makeup. "Is it better for Sophia to believe I'm over her mother, or better for her to believe I still mourn her?" Ava's brows come together, and an adorable line creases over her nose. "Which scenario gives Sophia the best foundation? Which will help her the most?"

"I don't think..." Ava stutters and stops. "You and her mother gave her a good foundation with your love. My professional opinion is that the truth... that's what your daughter deserves. Anything else is manipulative."

Maybe I am manipulative. I bend down to pick up my clothes.

"But I think you're doing a good job."

"You do?" I'm not certain I heard her correctly.

"Yeah. I do. She loves you. She's been through the wringer, but all things considered, she's doing okay."

"That's your professional opinion?"

"Yes."

My chest feels lighter as I exit her bathroom with my clothes balled up and a towel wrapped around my waist.

Sexual release and a pep talk. I don't care what Ryan says. She's worth the money.

What a despicable thing to think.

CHAPTER 18

Ava

Sophia sits on the sofa without adjusting any of the throw pillows and pulls her knees up to her chest, bringing her sandy sandals onto the sofa cushion. "I wish Dad would stop this."

This is a good start. I press record on my phone. This is our fourth session, so she's familiar with how I work and that I don't like to sit and take notes while she's talking.

"Stop what, exactly?"

"Forcing this." She splays her hand out. "I don't have a problem with you. I like you. You're worlds better than the geezers from the hospital."

Jack shared her medical records with me, and I saw the list of well-respected therapists who struck out with Sophia. All of them highly trained and well-respected professionals with decades of experience. One of the side effects of decades of experience is age, and I suspect Sophia might suffer from a bit of ageism. But, truthfully, it's hard to blame a fifteen-year-old girl for not wanting to discuss sexual trauma with someone she might see as more of a grandparent. In our society, sex isn't a grandparent-safe topic.

Sophia chews at the corner of her lip. We've already been over the benefits of therapy, and instead of rehashing the basics, I employ a valued therapist's technique, and wait silently to see if she moves on from this original point of contention.

"But I do like you." Her gaze lifts from the spot on the carpet to me.

"I like you, too. Your opinions about therapy don't insult me. Nothing you say in here will hurt me or offend me. And, like we discussed, this is an unorthodox situation. First, I rarely handle cases like yours. And I'm a family friend." Her gaze has fallen to the carpet again, but based on the tilt of her head, with her right ear angled in my direction, I am fairly certain she's listening to every word. "Our goal in these talking sessions isn't to complete your therapy, but to get you to where you are ready to talk to a therapist. Your father is hoping—"

"He wants to cure me. But unless you have some magic pill that eliminates my memory, he can't just swipe his credit card and cure me."

This is more than she's said before. It's an acknowledgement that something horrible happened and it changed her. She doesn't move. She's frozen, maybe from the realization that she's shared more than she wanted.

"Did you ever see the movie *Eternal Sunshine of the Spotless Mind?*"

Her gaze lifts and her shoulders relax. "No."

"I saw it years ago. Maybe we could watch it in your fab media room sometime?" She studies me. She might be suspicious of my abrupt change of conversation. "I can't remember the specifics of the movie, but if I recall correctly, the basic premise is that the magic pill you speak of exists. So people have the option of never living with terrible memories." Her gaze falls to the floor. "Or pain. Or heartbreak."

"The pill doesn't exist, so it's not worth talking about."

"Well, I don't remember specifically, but I think the moral of the film is that we wouldn't want the pill even if it existed."

"I would."

"Would you?"

Her eyelashes flutter, and her blue gaze fills with scorn.

"I've had bad things happen to me." I pointedly look her straight in the eye, letting her see my truth. "If I could wipe out those horrific experiences, I don't think I would." I mirror her position, pulling my legs up onto the sofa, shoes and all, aiming for conversational. "I'm a big believer that I'm stronger because of my past."

"That's ridiculous." Lines around her eyes form as she squints. Her fingernails dig into the polish on one of her toenails.

"Maybe. The notion might feel ridiculous at the darkest moment. When the pain is so intense, the body sometimes becomes numb to create a protective cocoon. But..." I let my feet fall to the floor and lean forward, arms resting on my thighs. "Once a woman finds her inner strength, and mends, she discovers the power of recovery."

"You say it like glue or tape is all you need."

"I don't mean to imply it's easy. But when you look back in history, over some of humanity's darkest times, during wars or famines, women soldier on. And we do so because after recovering from a tragedy, we learn." She inserts her thumb into her mouth, and I pause until her nail finds its way between her teeth. "We learn we possess the power to survive. Anything. No matter what gets thrown our way, we can buckle down, dig in, and survive. There is no might like a woman mended."

"You don't know what happened to me."

"No," I agree. She's made it clear to a litany of law enforcement and medical professionals that she doesn't wish to relive it. I don't blame her. I understand. And that's probably a reason I sit here in this chair, agreeing to this unorthodox approach. There's a terrified child inside Sophia.

Those bastards drugged her with heroin, and I suspect what

she's most terrified of is that the flashes of memory haunting her really happened. Having been a heroin addict, I have a good idea of what those flashes of memory might be like. How there's a haze and a long expanse of black with no memory at all. But a sliver of experience strikes the forefront, like a far too vivid film flickering in one's mind.

Silence prevails. Through the glass, the distant sound of waves breaking on the shore filters into the room, lifting the weighted silence.

"Dad should back off," she says quietly with an undertone of frustration.

"Your father is concerned," I say. She closes her eyes and tilts her head back. I halfway expect her to place her palms over her ears. "As any parent would be. You've been through something horrific, something no woman or child should have to endure."

Jack carries a fierce love for his daughter. Her pain renders him helpless. He's desperate to cure her. To protect her. One day, she'll appreciate his love and love him for it.

"I'm fine," she says in a whiny, small voice, and I suspect she intended her defense to come out differently.

"You will be." Her body falls against the back of the chair, and she curls into a fetal position. "Can you tell me why you don't want to visit with any of your friends? Lauren, Celeste, Zane... they've all come by checking on you."

I suspect if she'd simply spent time with her friends, her dad wouldn't have pushed so hard for therapy. He might have willfully bought into her claim of being fine.

"I'm not ready."

Her eyes are closed and at a glance, she could be mistaken as sleeping. I wait. If we sit here in silence for the rest of our hour, that's okay. If she's not ready to share, then she's simply not ready. Rehabilitation, like so much in our universe, doesn't happen in one day.

The second hand on the clock on the wall ticks the seconds. I pick the minute marker that will end our session and wait. *Tick. Tick. Tick.*

Two minutes remaining. *Tick. Tick. Tick.*

One minute remaining. *Tick.*

She lifts her head, but her eyes remain closed.

"My friends will want to know." She swipes the side of her cheek, eyes closed, lips puckered.

"You don't have to tell anyone anything. 'I don't want to talk about it' is a perfectly acceptable statement."

"They know I was raped." Her head falls to her knees, and blonde waves fall around her like a damaged halo.

My first instinct is to argue with her, but I stop myself. She's read the news articles.

I've been raped before, too, but I always viewed it as my fault, because I put myself in a precarious situation by getting drunk or doing drugs. I'd always thought it would be worlds better to not be responsible for my shitty experiences. But maybe there's just no good way to be assaulted.

"The rape wasn't your fault." Her shoulders quiver and the most incredible urge to get up and hug her befalls on me. But right now, she needs more than a hug. "It's nothing to be ashamed of."

"It's gross."

"The men who assaulted you are gross. What happened is horrific. But you, Sophia, are not gross. You, Sophia, are as beautiful as ever. Inside and out. What those men did to you, their actions didn't take away your beauty. Yes, it's true. They stole your innocence. You saw firsthand the horrible, ugly things men can do. But they did not steal your beauty. They did not steal your soul. If anything, your soul shines brighter."

She raises her head. Golden strands cling to the side of her damp, splotched face. She glances at the clock.

"I don't want to talk anymore." When her feet hit the ground, she bends, stretching, shakes one foot, sniffles, and exits the room without looking my way again.

After she leaves, I close the door and return to my desk. The session audio plays, and I type away, taking notes. I screwed that up. I should have asked her to tell me how she felt. A good therapist doesn't talk over a person or attempt to tell them how to feel.

But still, even so, she made progress. A step forward is a good thing.

My phone vibrates with a text.

MR. SULLIVAN

The chef doesn't work on Saturday. We're ordering in. Any preference?

The two of them should eat dinner together, without me. And I've been in this house all week. I need to get out.

You two eat. I'll get my own dinner.

MR. SULLIVAN

If you're going out, Fisher's on duty. He can join you.

Thanks, but that's unnecessary.

MR. SULLIVAN

I insist.

I toss my phone down. I don't have it in me to argue. All things considered, it's been a good day, and I want to leave it there.

A handful of beachfront restaurants exist about a mile down the beach. The fresh air will do me good. If I'm lucky, I can get a small table outside in the sand and watch the sunset.

I'm halfway down the side path when a deep, masculine voice asks, "Where are you going?"

"For a walk on the beach. I'll probably pick up some fish tacos from the Baja Taco stand." Jack narrows his eyes. Somehow, even in board shorts, a black t-shirt, and leather flip-flops, the man intimidates with a boardroom stance. Or maybe it's just that he bought me, and the idea makes me uneasy. He crosses his arms over his chest. It's a powerful position, but it's also defensive. This isn't personal, so I explain. "You should have dinner with Sophia. She may need you. It will be good for the two of you to have dinner together."

The man obviously loves his daughter. Eating dinner with her should be a part of his daily routine.

His stern expression softens, and he angles one foot in the house's direction and gives a quick nod of agreement.

My foot sinks into the sand, and I place one hand on the gate.

"I'll see you later. Let me know when you're back."

Yes, sir is on the tip of my tongue, but I stop myself. He might miss the sarcasm. So, I simply open the gate.

I'm about half a mile down the beach when my senses pique. I scan the beach behind me. Fisher, identifiable by his crew cut and trimmed beard, follows from a distance.

Un-fucking-believable.

CHAPTER 19

Ava

With tacos and a Diet Coke in hand, I snag a table and whip out my phone. There's a man at a nearby table drinking a golden pale ale. Condensation gathers on the glass. I remember the way a cold golden pale ale tastes on a warm day. How my muscles relaxed with half a beer's worth of alcohol swirling through my veins. But that's not for me.

The waves breaking in the distance divert my attention, and I count them crash. The salty ocean breeze calms me, and with deep inhales, I suck it in and let it go. After the fifth wave, I press his name.

Patrick answers on the first ring.

"What have you gotten me into?"

"Wait a minute, now." Patrick chuckles. "You're a grown-ass woman. You chose this. What's happening? Do I need to go down there and kick Jack's ass?"

"Like you'd do that." Patrick's a lover, not a fighter, but his offer means a lot to someone like me. I'm short on people who look out for me.

"If he's being an ass, I most certainly would. Or Mark would. Mark's always going on about keeping Jack in line."

Fisher stands off to the edge of the patio. He has his hands folded in front of him in a feeble attempt to blend in. The piece in his ear might be mistaken for a hearing aid, but if anyone studies him, it's clear he's scanning the area, searching.

"Is it his kink that's getting to you, or his charming personality?" Patrick asks. "Give me some sense of what we're dealing with here."

I lower my head, letting my hair fall around my face, and speak with a low voice. No one's sitting close to my table, and everyone out here is a stranger, but this conversation is personal.

"He's not an asshole," I admit. If I'm totally honest, the mad billionaire possesses some positive traits, as exemplified by his love for his daughter. Observing him, living in his house, it's probable he's lonely. "I mean, he's definitely uptight. Untrusting. He had security follow me down the beach."

"Where are you?"

"I went out to grab tacos."

"Well, you can't really blame the guy. Not after what he's been through."

Patrick is right. You can't call it paranoia or even overprotectiveness, given they kidnapped his daughter.

"That's actually kind of sweet he's worried about you."

"I don't think that's why." My gaze locks with Fisher's from across the sandy stone patio. "I think he's worried I might sell out to someone."

"What do you mean?" Patrick sounds truly stumped.

"Isn't that how they do it? Kidnappers learn the routine first. Is there any chance someone is still after Sophia?" It might just be the constant presence of armed security, but I can't help but feel there's an omnipresent risk.

"From what I know from Mark, they got the guys responsible. Except, his crazy high reward got a lot of publicity. That's like lotto money. I guess... maybe some random could come after them." He clicks his tongue. "Hey, now, I know what this is. You don't feel good about taking the money, and so now you're assuming he thinks the worst of you. And in your little head, the worst you could do is take money to sell out his daughter."

"My head's not little." There is absolutely no reason for him to use diminutive adjectives to belittle me. I exhale. "But yes, I hate I took his money." It's a crappy feeling.

"How's the sex?"

A flash of the powerful orgasm ripping through my body heats my skin.

"Enjoyable."

"Heh. So, Mark's nephew isn't as skilled as he is. Sorry about that."

"I didn't say—"

Patrick's deep laughter interrupts my defense. *Whatever*.

"I don't know, Patrick. I don't feel good about this. It's been a long time since I did something I didn't feel good about."

"You're doing what anyone else would do. If I were in your shoes, I'd do it. Hell, one could argue I *am* in your shoes."

It's not the same thing, and he knows it, but I douse my taco with spicy sauce instead of arguing with him about the merits of his clandestine relationship with Mark.

"I think I might be in your neck of the woods next week. Want to meet for lunch?"

"Really? Why are you coming here?" I sit up straighter and speak louder. "Is something wrong at the center? I haven't gotten any emails—"

"Girlfriend. Everything is fine. Mark has some meetings down that way, and he suggested we spend a night in Laguna."

"Oh. That's sweet. I love Laguna." Laguna Beach is one of my favorite California beaches. The coastline is staggering, but it's the small artist town that really makes it memorable. It's between Los Angeles and San Diego, and it's a perfect spot for a romantic getaway.

"You want to join us for a night?"

"Thanks for the offer, but you know I'm not into that." I grin as he chuckles.

"You know damn well neither are we. Nah, I just meant if you need a break…"

"If I spend a night away from the compound, it'll be back in my apartment and at Nueva Vida. And my master has made it clear that's not permitted."

A text comes through, and I squint to read it. One of these days, I'm going to break down and increase the font size on my phone.

REID

Where are you? Call me.

"Patrick, let me eat my tacos before they get cold."

We end the call, and minutes later, after devouring my meal, I call Reid.

Reid and I aren't as close as we used to be. But he doesn't have many people to lean on. Ideally, he will develop some connections while at Nueva Vida. He needs positive influences in his life. He needs a Patrick.

The phone rings and rings. I sit up straighter, preparing to leave an upbeat message.

"Ava?" Reid's voice sounds distant, and I smash the phone against my ear.

"Reid? Is everything okay?"

"Where are you? You've been gone forever."

"I told you I have a project. I'll be back in a couple of weeks." He breathes heavily into the phone. "Reid, are you okay?"

"Yeah. I just miss you." He sounds sad, possibly borderline

depressed. It's a good thing I am far away, because it would be nearly impossible for me not to go straight to his apartment and offer him a hug, and I can't be his crutch. "Do you want me to water your plants?"

"That's really sweet, but someone else is doing that for me. How's job hunting going?"

"Juliette has a few leads for me. She's been pretty helpful. Maybe this time I won't screw it up."

"Hey. You're doing good. You've got a job. You're just looking for something better. This is all part of the process." He knows that. He's been through it more than once. I so much want to ask him how the group sessions are going, but I don't want to push. "What are you doing tonight?"

"Well, I'd hoped I could talk you into picking a show with me."

"I can do that from here."

"Yeah, but you won't be on the sofa with me. It's not the same."

I smile in spite of myself. Yeah, it's a good thing I'm more than a couple of blocks away. "What kind of shows are you into these days? I spend a lot of time watching shows lately, too."

"Really? Your project doesn't keep you busy around the clock?"

My gaze meets Fisher's. *Oh, Reid. You have no idea.*

"You always were this big workaholic girl. Leave it to you to build apartment buildings."

I laugh. "I haven't built any apartment buildings."

"When you come home, come see me."

"I will. You take care of yourself, okay?"

"Ava? Thanks for everything. You know, for paying and shit. Don't know how you did it, but thanks."

"No problem. I just want you to get better."

After I end the call, I stand and clear my table. Reid sounded better at the end of our call. He's going to get through this. I feel it in my gut. This time, he's going to stay clean. And I helped that happen. Doing what I'm doing, getting him the money, alleviated a stress he didn't need.

Fisher nods and gives me a smile. I wave in his direction, since we're apparently not pretending we don't know each other.

I press Juliette's name. We cover off on life's minutiae while I make my way slowly back down the beach.

"Are you making any headway with our investors?" She believes I'm here working with our primary backer on revised financials and securing additional funding. It's not entirely a lie.

Jack leans over the balcony as I approach the house. The sun set long ago. Somewhere behind me, Fisher trails my path.

"I'm working on it. A few more weeks." Two weeks, to be exact, but who's counting?

The gate clicks closed, and I slip my phone into my pocket. The temperature has dropped, and goosebumps grow along my bare arms. I rush up the path to the side door and sling it open. A high-pitched beep sounds. The alarm system beeps every single time an outside door opens.

I glance behind me for any sign of Fisher before closing the door. I'm not sure what etiquette is when security trails you. Should I have held the gate for him? This door? There's no sign of him, so I close the door and squeal in surprise.

An enormous shadow looms in the hall.

"Sophia has retired for the night."

There's a hunger in Jack's eyes, or maybe it's not exactly hunger. It's an expectation. No, a demand. He wants me. He wants his release. His nightcap, if you will.

"Did you two have a good dinner?"

"You're cold." His gaze travels down my arms.

"The temperature—"

"You should have taken a jacket."

I briskly rub my arms, attempting to eradicate the telltale bumps. But they're not going away, probably because it's not the temperature that's bringing them about. Not anymore.

Jack's hair is unkempt, like he's run his fingers through it a million times. The movement of his chest, rising and falling, draws my attention to the curves of his pecs, and the thick blood vessels that traverse his lower arms. His expensive gold watch glitters under the overhead light. It's the only thing about Jack that shines. His hair, his eyes, his tanned skin, his angular jaw, and take-no-bullshit expression all hint of darkness.

"Are you ready?" It's a question and a demand. Everything about him screams demand. Everything except the meaning of his words. His tone belies a hint of uncertainty. Even though he's paying me an obscene amount of money, if I say no, he will acquiesce.

He's the billionaire. But I have the power. For now. In this moment.

Outside of these walls, he'd never look my way. And the kind of men I go for, well, they're nothing like him. But none of those men looked at me quite the way Jack is looking at me in this moment.

Lust fogs my thought processes. It must be the dim hall light skewing my sight and reality. Because I yearn to touch him. To run my fingers through his unruly strands and trace his firm chest. To feel him, filling me, pulsing inside me. I have always loved sex. But I haven't craved it, not like this. Not in a very long time.

"Ava?" There's a question again.

"Yes." My unwavering answer leaves no room for questions.

"Down the hall, to the right." This time, the words are a demand.

I pass him in the hall, inches of space between us, triggering an energetic pulse. Without touching, I feel him. My breath quickens, my pulse races, and a touch of dizziness impacts me.

"You have the most gorgeous eyes."

My eyes are freakishly large. But if he wants to keep going on with that line, I'll let him get away with it.

I am the first one to reach the door, and I twist the knob. It's unlocked.

"You aren't afraid of Sophia wandering in here?"

"After Sophia went to bed, I prepared it."

The door opens, and half a dozen candles flicker. Against the backdrop of velvet walls and leather adornments, the warmth of fire engenders erotic passion. I turn to tease him for doing something borderline romantic, but he presses me up against the wall and his tongue plunders my mouth. He shoves his thigh between my legs, and his hard erection presses into my stomach.

Rough hands comb my body, grabbing at clothes. He tastes of sugary sweet bourbon, and I kiss him back like I'm starved, craving the forbidden liquor. Buttons snap. My clothes hit the floor. His teeth graze my nipple. I reach into his boxers, and my fingers wrap around his length, rewarding me with his uncontrolled groan.

He flips me around.

"Hands on the wall."

I obey, but as if he doesn't trust me, his palms cover the back of my hands, ensuring secure placement.

"Keep them here," he insists.

Rough, warm skin presses along my ribs, over my hip bones, and lower. One finger finds my slit, and it's my turn to groan. But it's only for a second. His palm flattens against my spine, directing me to bend.

His soft tip presses between my ass cheeks, then farther down until he's rubbing my entrance. With one thrust, he fills me. He pauses, and I suck in air.

It feels good. He feels good. And then he thrusts, over and over, pounding into me. A claiming, a possession. All I can do is moan and gasp and grip the wall for purchase as my leg muscles quiver and my knees weaken. He slows and reaches for something, still inside me, slowly rocking into me. There's a whirring sound, and the next thing I know, a heated metal vibrating object cups my mound and his hips slow.

The warmth and the vibration under the glow of candles lifts me to a surreal place. Sensations overwhelm my body.

"So good," is all I can get out as I writhe, squeezing my thighs, groaning and moaning. I pull my hand, wanting to twist my nipple, but they're locked in place under his one hand. All I can do is close my eyes and revel in the whirlwind of sensations.

His thrusts pick up speed. With each drive, his skin slaps mine. I stretch, pushing my weight into my hands, pressing against the wall, pushing my ass back, meeting him thrust for thrust. He hits me deep, in just the right spot.

"Yes." I am not entirely positive if the word leaves my mouth, or maybe I chant it. My legs tremble and my muscles tighten. My toes curl. The slow building frisson of energy rips through me, unleashing a powerful mind-altering orgasm. My head falls forward as I come to, bearing witness to the pulse within me. The vibrating device clatters to the floor, and his head falls to my shoulder.

He presses his lips to my back, and his hand cups my breast. The unexpectedly intimate sensation has me pushing up, but I hit his chest. His arm wraps around me, squeezes once, then he pulls out.

"I'll get a warm washcloth to clean you up."

That's when it hits me. He didn't use a condom.

"I guess you got the results back?"

He nods as he steps away and opens a cabinet door. The sound of running water replaces the thrum of my pounding blood reverberating in my ears.

Apparently, the rich have doctors who make house calls. His arrived, and Fisher delivered her to my office. I assumed she also tested Jack, although I hadn't asked.

"That was quick." I lift my skirt and tank off the floor and search for my panties.

He steps forward, holding out a black washcloth, and I reach for it, but he brushes past my hand and places the warm, wet cloth between my legs with an unexpected gentleness. His tenderness touches me more than it should, and the second he pulls away, I slip my tank top on and step into my skirt.

I wonder if he designed this room, or if his ex-wife did. But, then again, his wife never lived in this house. After Sophia's abduction, publications republished photos of him at his wife's funeral. I don't remember everything from those articles. I mostly skimmed them, but

I still remember the photograph of Jack standing beside Sophia near a grave.

He washes his hands at the sink as I pull my panties on.

"Did you design this room?"

He smiles. It's a subtle smile. A borderline smirk. Entertained more than smug.

"I hired a designer. Different than the one I sent Sophia to. She specializes in rooms like this. Told her what I wanted. She did her thing. Equipped it with what she called the luxe package."

I think about the style of the furniture upstairs and even in the kitchen. He apparently didn't bother to touch that, but yet he prioritized a sex dungeon of sorts.

"Do you use this room a lot?"

"Don't worry. All the toys in here are new."

That's not where I was going. "Did you go shopping?" It's difficult to imagine this businessman entering a sex store, but I guess they do it all the time. Or online. He can buy anything online.

"I have a house manager. She takes care of everything. Like making sure this room is cleaned with complete discretion. Restocking."

"A house manager. How have I not met her yet?"

"She's good at her job and stays out of the way. She keeps everything running."

"And she knows about this room." I say it more to myself than to him. It's all so bizarre to me.

"I don't like to bring women into my bedroom. To answer your original question, since Sophia has moved in, no, I don't have women over often. None at all since..." His words trail, but I guess he means since her abduction. The event altered his universe.

One by one, he blows out the candles and opens the door.

"Thank you."

I almost miss his hushed remark. I stop in the hall as he closes the door. The lock clicks, and he double-checks the lock. Satisfied, he turns and heads down the hall, leaving me standing there, awash in a variety of emotions I do not wish to define.

CHAPTER 20

Ava

Outside my quote-unquote therapy room, a gardener tends the beds. Fuchsia blooms sway in the ocean breeze. A vacuum runs in a distant room. And one of the armed security men strolls by.

Those men don't really need to walk the perimeter. There are cameras in a back room which allow someone to watch the grounds at all times. I've seen them in there, watching the monitors. However, that room has no view, and I suspect they take turns walking to preserve their sanity. Or maybe it's a strategy to ward off anyone considering anything nefarious.

Upstairs, Sophia is meeting with the designer Jack hired. The woman is gorgeous. Tall, blonde, and immaculate. I'd guess she's in her mid-thirties. Jack wasn't here to greet her, but she clearly knows him, given the first thing out of her mouth was, "Where's Jack?"

She wore a tight pencil skirt, five-inch heels, and a silk tank top that practically draped over her perfect D-cup breasts and tucked into her skirt, highlighting a narrow waist and toned stomach. Maybe

Jack paid her too. Hell, maybe she's on his payroll and arrived expecting to fulfill some additional duties.

Sophia asked me to stay to meet with her, but I ducked out, saying I had work to do. And, I do have work to do. We have a team status meeting starting in forty-five minutes. But I left because this is something Sophia should do on her own. With her father's unlimited funds, she's redesigning her bedroom and most of the living areas upstairs. She's going to explore updating the kitchen too.

On one hand, it's obnoxious to give a fifteen-year-old girl carte blanche over the house design. But on the other hand, the place is stuffy, and her dad should have redesigned it when he moved in. And she's still refusing to meet with friends. Maybe this will be the extra diversion and ultimate confidence boost she needs to transition back to school life.

My screen saver pops on, a sign that I've been staring out the window for too long rather than doing the work I should be doing. The second my fingers touch the mouse, my phone vibrates.

Patrick's name shows, and I pick up the phone and move to step outside. There are many sitting areas in the back yard, and I plan to find one and sit in the salt-tinged air.

"Morning," I say to him as I step through the automatic sliding door.

"There she is," Patrick says. He's one of those people who carries a smile in his tone.

"Are you in San Diego?"

"I am. Arrived yesterday."

"So, are we going to lunch?"

"No. I need to spend the day here." His tone drops, and my stomach falls.

"Uh oh. What's going on?"

"Your one and only is what's going on. He's breaking the rules, Ava. I told you, he's bad news."

I roll my eyes. There are people who would say every single

addict is bad news. Many would say I'm bad news and so is Patrick. Once an addict, always an addict, and all that.

"What rule did he break?" I locate an Adirondack chair below the overhang of the deck. The grasses along the beach perimeter break, allowing a view of the ocean, and I claim the spot.

"Hitting on a newcomer. Not even here for a week."

My grip on the edge of the armrest intensifies. Reid knows better. He knows the rules and understands my views on men preying on women when they are in a vulnerable state. At one point in time, I explored a women-only center, but Patrick was my partner, and so that didn't totally make sense. And as he pointed out to me, women-only doesn't mean sex-free.

Rehabilitation centers are notorious for housing sex-craved men and women. Sex is a natural drug that lifts the spirits. But, if the activity brings on feelings of shame or self-hatred, it can be as slippery a slope as alcohol or pot.

Our compromise is that the apartments at Nueva Vida are not co-ed. Of course, this doesn't prevent same sex interaction, but it helps protect women who might be preyed upon by sexually-starved men.

"Someone saw him practically fucking her against the side of a building. We can't have that."

"I'll talk to him."

"You're going to talk to him?" His deep elongated words mock me. "His ex is going to call him and tell him to stop messing around with other women, and you think somehow that's going to work? It's too complicated."

"Things ended between us years ago." He relapsed. The third time since we'd been together, and I finally ended our relationship.

"Doesn't matter. It's not your place to warn him off other women. He'll misunderstand the warning. Think it's jealousy."

"He's smarter than that."

"Is he? Or is he doing this to get your attention?"

"He's just horny. That's all." Still, I can't believe Reid would do this. I stuck my neck out for him by moving him up on our waiting list. I paid his debt.

"I'll handle him. He's not at his apartment right now. But when he returns, I'll give him the warning."

I hate it, but Patrick is right. There's too much history between Reid and me. Anger goads me, and I probably couldn't suppress it. And Reid could misconstrue a warning from me.

Patrick suspects I'm not over Reid. But he's wrong. I bend for Reid because I so much want him to recover, but bending is a bad thing, and I am smart enough to know that.

"How're things otherwise?"

"Fine." I lean my head back against the chair, and my gaze falls upon spiderwebs in the corner. Even in a house with a full staff, the spiders find a way. "Are you sure I shouldn't come back?"

"So you can see Reid? Hell no. You stay where you are. You making any headway with Mark's niece?"

"Some. You know what it's like when you're not ready to talk."

"Yeah, I do. We both do. How's the sex?"

Humor has returned to his tone, and I roll my eyes again and grin. "Can't complain."

"So, it's not all about him then?"

"No. He's got talents." I smile and wish I could see Patrick's eyes. I'm sure he's lighting up at the prospect of hearing about good sex.

"I like to hear that." He chuckles, and a door closes in the background. "Just remember, my friend, *Pretty Woman* is fiction."

His comment hits like a gut punch. *Jesus.* He's the one who encouraged me to do this.

"Thanks for that, Patrick."

"Hey, don't take it the wrong way. You've got two more weeks. I just don't want you to get your heart broken."

And then there's the unstated, "I don't want you to relapse." It's been ten years. Ten years clean. There's no fucking way I'll relapse. And I'm not giving my heart to a guy who bought me, either.

"This is one fucked up world you live in, Patrick." And yes, that's my passive aggressive way of reminding him he's not much different than me.

"Tell me about it, kid."

Back in my bathroom, I check myself out in the mirror and pull out my makeup. More mascara, more eyeshadow, and more eyeliner make me look more like me. I add my jewelry, stacking all the bracelets and filling every single ear hole, then return to my desk for my Zoom call.

Hours later, when it's time for my session with Jack, I'm mentally prepared.

CHAPTER 21

Jack

It requires every ounce of self-control to relax my facial muscles and conceal my disgust. The advertising guys in the room watch me, the CEO, sitting at the end of a long conference room table. Uncle Mark sits to my right, staring at the ad displayed on the overhead projector.

"Don't Let Them Take Your Guns and Leave You with Only a Phone for Protection." The headline is straight out of the NRA playbook.

I steeple my fingers and direct my question to Cliff Hartman, the compliance officer. "Are we stealing NRA ad copy now?"

Uncle Mark breaks his attention from the ad on the wall. His expression is unreadable, but I sense he's observing me to judge if I'm up to the task of CEO.

As a board member, he shouldn't be here, but he's been more involved since I returned to work after Sophia's abduction, wanting to help me out where possible so I can spend more time at home. I appreciate the sentiment, but I don't appreciate the job performance appraisal.

Cliff exchanges glances with Phillip, our interim head of sales. Phillip looks to Roberto, the head of marketing under Phillip. I watch them all, wondering who is going to catch the ball and answer my question.

"It's part of an industry campaign to build support for an expanded version of the Protection of Lawful Arms in Commerce Act."

"Does this fall under our NRA quota for supportive marketing efforts?"

Roberto curls the end of his notepad with this thumb and says, "We have to talk to them about that."

Elizabeth, the ad agency's head account person, senses that she needs to take control. "We have additional ads to show you."

"Excellent. Because this one doesn't do a damn thing to sell our guns."

Normally, I wouldn't participate in the initial ad agency presentations. But Uncle Mark had me fly out for lunch today with Senator Talbot and Chuck Strand, the NRA president. I had some extra time, so they pulled me into this half-cocked dog and pony show.

Elizabeth clicks the clicker in her hand, and a different print ad covers the screen. This one features a Sullivan product. The prestige hand carved walnut base will earn its place as a family heirloom. The headline reads, "The Only Thing That Stops a Bad Guy with a Gun is a Good Guy with a Gun."

The overused headline does not remotely entertain me. Once again, I look to Cliff, my compliance officer, and he remains silent. Of course he does, because there's no reputable point of dissension for him to take on this.

"That headline targets the self-defense market, but the rifle you are featuring targets the hunters and the shooting competition market."

Elizabeth is the only woman in the room. I don't want to bury her in front of the men who report to her, but I can't help but wonder if she doesn't understand our product line and the target markets.

I hired a new agency after Wayne's arrest, mainly because I have enough to worry about without wondering if there are bad apples, or guys, as this print ad states, in my ad agency.

"We can feature any of your pistols too. This is the NRA fall campaign, aimed at buttressing support going into the mid-terms." She passes a printout to me. "We followed this brief."

I glance down the document, and sure enough, Sullivan Arms provided a sample selection of headlines to be used and a list of products to feature. To my agency's credit, they didn't feature a high-capacity magazine, a folding stock, or a flash suppressor, products which for some inexplicable reason are listed on the brief. With the addition of any two of these products, you create what is widely considered to be an assault rifle.

A click sounds, and the next ad is of a family in camouflage brandishing rifles. The headline reads "The Family That Hunts Together Stays Together." The ad is fine except for the fact that a four-year-old boy is holding a rifle with a military-grade scope.

I pinch the bridge of my nose. Killington is a bastard, and I hope he goes to jail for life, but one thing I will say for him, he shielded me from this kind of rampant ignorance.

"Is this stock photography or did you hold a photoshoot?"

"This is from the photoshoot last month in Montana."

Mother of god.

"In the future, please make a note to use age-appropriate guns." It might be my imagination, but I could swear everyone is looking at me like I am speaking an unfamiliar language. "This kid is way too young to have a rifle. He should hold a BB gun, and even that would be eyebrow raising in some circles."

Elizabeth looks directly to Roberto. Cliff's gaze falls to his phone.

Uncle Mark says, "Why on Earth do you have a child in this photo?"

Thank fuck. For once my uncle and I agree.

Roberto speaks up, "He focus-grouped well. We wanted a likable family."

"Roberto, we create top tier, high-quality guns. All made right here in the US of A. We aren't one of those brands that resell shoddy iron at low prices. Our campaign needs to be product-oriented. If you want likeable, add a dog." I breathe out and hope my words sink in.

"The campaign presented today is strictly to align with NRA goals as we head into the mid-terms."

"Find a way to make our ad dollars serve both Sullivan Arms and the NRA."

With that, my uncle and I stand and leave the room.

Lunch with the senator goes about as one would expect. Cordial, swapping of a lot of hot air, and concluding with handshakes and expectations to meet again at a fundraiser his friends are throwing for him. Thankfully, my uncle covers for the Sullivan family on Texas politics. Well, except for the NRA. Chuck Strand pushed me on the upcoming NRA fundraiser, and with reluctance, I confirmed my attendance.

After lunch, as the senator drives away, my uncle turns to me. From his paternal expression, I expect some kind of good job speech.

"I'm going to head home," he says.

Skin sags below my uncle's eyes, and the outside light reveals a deep bluish skin tone I haven't noticed before. The collar around his neck doesn't fit tightly. It's actually, as I look closer, too loose.

"Are you feeling okay?"

We took his car here. I had every expectation he would remain attached to my side throughout the afternoon, especially since I have a marketing meeting. He fears I am not aggressive enough with marketing and business decisions. I believe we can be both aggressive and brand-focused.

"Didn't sleep well last night. Besides, I'm semi-retired. Remember?" He gives my shoulder a fatherly pat.

The valet pulls up with his custom Rolls Royce convertible. He never rides with the top down when I'm with him, but he's driven convertibles for as long as I can remember. He slips on his sunglasses, steps out of the shade and into the sun, and when he turns around, he looks like himself. It must have been the light we were under, but under the sun, he's the powerhouse I've always known.

"How are things going with Ava Amara?" His tone strikes me as disapproving, and my spine straightens, lifting me to my full height, slightly taller than Uncle Mark.

"Good. Sophia seems to like her."

One of his eyebrows raises above the frame of his sunglasses. "From what I hear, she's not the only one."

"What is that supposed to mean?"

"Look, I'm not trying to intrude. But I remember how easily you get attached. I remember what your father went through when you fell for Cassie. I didn't think Ava would appeal to you, or I wouldn't have recommended her. But since she has, just–"

"What exactly do you think is going on?"

"Cut the crap, Jack. We have friends in common. I know exactly what's going on. I don't like it. But I'm trying to focus on what's important. Unfortunately, I'm not sure you've got what it takes for the kind of arrangement you've structured. To keep her at arm's length. You're too sensitive. Soft."

I can't believe what I am hearing.

"Just be careful. She's a friend of mine. I care for her, but she's not another Cassie. She won't rise to the occasion by your side. She's not someone you can bring in public. It'll take the media a nanosecond to dig up her past. She doesn't try to hide it. As CEO of a gun manufacturer, you can't be dating an addict. Much less anything else." Again, he does the fatherly thing with a soft pat on my shoulder.

He's talking out his ass. What the hell does he mean by "she's not another Cassie?" Another wife? No shit. I'm not looking for a wife. I'm not even looking for a relationship. The old man is becoming nonsensical with age. Ava and I have an agreement.

Stunned, I watch as my uncle tips the valet and awkwardly sinks down into his low convertible.

Fisher approaches as the engine of the pearl white convertible revs. There's an earpiece in his ear, and he's wearing a black suit. Gone is his beach casual outfit from home, and in its place an outfit that any passerby would automatically assume is security apparel.

"Sir. We have a car here. Would you like to ride with us, or would you prefer we call you a driver?"

"I'll ride with you." I follow Fisher to a rented SUV, and my phone vibrates.

It's an unknown number, but only authorized individuals can access this line, so I answer.

"This is Jackson Sullivan," I say by greeting.

"Jack." The familiar voice rubs me the wrong way. "Heard you're in town. So am I. Any chance we can meet?"

"Who is this?"

"Ah, forgive me. How presumptuous of me. It's Victor."

I scan the street. Traffic slows as the stoplight on the nearby intersection turns red. Business professionals cross the sidewalk, and a young woman pushes a baby carriage into a store on the opposite side of the street. Nothing stands out as out of place.

With a nod at Ryder, the Texas based Arrow employee who is working with Fisher today, I climb into the back of the SUV.

"I have—"

"Already spoke to your assistant. She said you have an opening, and she can push your two o'clock to three."

Since when is Patricia agreeing to scheduling changes without talking to me first?

"Where would you like for me to meet you?"

Fisher's eyes meet mine in the rearview. I lift a finger to my lips, indicating for him to be silent.

"We're at The Gold Standard. Swing by."

There's a click, and I check the phone to confirm that, yes, he did just end the call.

"Well, boys, looks like we've got an unexpected stop."

Fisher checks the side view and pulls out into the traffic.

The Gold Standard is a high-end strip club. My dad used to tell stories about how all the gunrunners used to have after-work parties at strip clubs. Or, sometimes, they'd just have parties at home and invite strippers. That stripper life kind of died out as the revenue continued to climb and lawyers began weighing in about scrupulous behavior as some of the bigger players went public.

We park in the parking garage and agree that both Fisher and Ryder will join me. They're dressed similarly, and as I walk in with two armed suits behind me, I look the part of a CEO who won't take any bullshit.

A woman in a tiny tight black skirt, heels, a bow tie, and a black vest that bounces with her steps revealing perky breasts leads us through a dark room with a stage and tables off to the side. She takes the stairs, and we head up to a balcony with sofas and private sitting areas. The music pulses. It's lunch hour, and I'd guess the place is about half full, filled mostly with men, but there are some women mixed in with the men who lunch.

Victor holds court in a back corner. He's sitting in a semicircular leather booth, and there's a scantily clad woman leaning into his side. Her dark hair and voluptuous curves remind me of Ava. Ava is more attractive than this woman, especially with those haunting, hypnotic eyes of hers, but she'd fit in here with her eclectic assortment of tattoos. She might fit in, but she'd never step foot inside a place like this. She'll never need to, given my sizable payment.

The tightness in my chest intensifies, and I hold out my hand in a professional courtesy. Victor leans forward, and the woman at his side slides out of the booth and saunters away into the crowd. Fisher positions himself on the back wall lining one side of the sitting area, and Ryder flanks the opposite wall.

"I hear you purchased the boat."

This is curious, because I do not know how he would know I've done any such thing. Wolf's team will need to figure that one out.

"Yes. I did." I pull out a chair across from him and sit.

There's a candle on the table and dimmed overhead lights. He leans forward and motions for me to do the same with the twist of an index finger. Music blasts through the space, offering a level of privacy. Curtains hang on each side of the booth, providing an additional level of discretion, should we choose. On stage, a dancer twists around a brass pole.

"An underground tunnel was discovered last weekend." He speaks in a low voice which requires me to shift my chair and come even closer to his side. "I've got product I need to move. Your boat, it'll be stored in San Diego?"

"That's the plan."

"How long before it's operational?"

"I need to hire a crew." I cross one ankle over my thigh, sitting back.

I've never hired a crew before and am uncertain what is involved, but my gut tells me it's better to not let him know that. The only thing I can figure is that Killington let him assume I'd been aware of the smuggling operation. It's possible Victor wouldn't have done business with him if he'd known he was dealing with a rogue employee. He let me know from the get-go he thought Sophia's abduction was unconscionable.

He holds a finger up and motions for one of his men to come over. A man in a suit, with a shaved head, tattoos covering his neck, and one large silver hoop earring bends to hear his boss. Morales says something to him, but with the deep bass vibrating across the floor, I don't stand a chance of hearing their conversation.

The bald man stands straight and backs into his darkened corner.

"I can provide crew."

"It's a hundred-and twenty-five-million-dollar super yacht. Are your men qualified?"

His expression says that I have clearly pissed him off.

"You think I don't own a yacht? You just can't have too many. The feds these days, they are vicious. The Coast Guard... they check registry. Doesn't do to own more than one super yacht unless you've got a couple halfway around the world."

His eyes narrow, and I have the urge to adjust my position in the seat. I might have let him in on my ignorance. But he snaps his fingers and leans forward.

"I'll send my order to Phillip." It takes a tremendous amount of effort to keep my expression neutral. I wanted to find out who within my organization he worked with, but I did not expect it would be Phillip. *Motherfucker*.

"Twenty million for your product," he says, looking at me. "Wholesale pricing. It's fair." He slides a hand into his jacket and pulls out a cigarette pack. Directs the pack to me, offering one, and I decline with a shake of my head. He lifts one, and the bald man leans over with a lighter. He drags on the cigarette, blows out, then leans forward. "We reload in Mexico. When we unload stateside, I'll transfer you a five-million bonus. Same arrangement we had with Wayne. *Bueno*?" He sucks on his cigarette.

"*Bueno*," I say.

A topless waitress appears, and I glance at my watch.

"I need to head out," I say, shaking my head to decline a drink.

"Stay," he says. "Enjoy a lap dance. Go into one of the private rooms."

"Thank you, but I need to stay on schedule."

He grows serious. "How is your Sophia?"

This man might be a gun and drug smuggler, and possibly even a human smuggler, but to his credit, he is a family man.

"She's still recovering." I move to stand, and his hand clasps my wrist. "What he did to your daughter." His lips purse, and he shakes his head tightly. "Unforgivable. Should you decide you want something to happen," he shrugs and gestures, "let me know. I have ways."

"Like Mike Ventola?"

His eyebrows nearly meet over his nose. "I do not know that name."

"No worries. *Gracias*, Victor." I remove my hand from under his grip, offer a brief nod, and depart.

Victor has connections to prisons. But if he's not the connection eliminating informants, then who is? And damn. Phillip. Who else? One thing is certain. My list building has begun.

CHAPTER 22

Ava

SOPHIA SULLIVAN

Any interest in Chinese? Dad's working late.

I stare at the text. She's upstairs, and I'm in my temporary office downstairs. I'm more than happy to eat dinner with her, but she's still refusing to meet up with her friends.

Recovery is a marathon. It doesn't happen overnight. But school is just over a month away.

The grant form I'm working on is a never-ending series of questions, and I need a break from it, so I push away from the desk and head upstairs.

When I tap on her door, there's a meek, "Come in."

She's sitting back on stacked pillows with a blanket over her legs and a book in her lap. From what I can tell, other than the mornings when she goes out with me, she holes up in this room. Based on my experience as a teenager, I'd categorize this as completely normal behavior, except that her phone still sits charging in her dad's office, untouched.

"Whatcha reading?"

She holds up a Sarah J. Maas book, *The Court of Thorn and Roses*. I haven't read it, but again, it strikes me as normal, healthy reading.

"Is it good?"

She nods. Okay, then.

"Your dad's got a business dinner tonight?"

"He's in Houston today. Something about he got stuck with some extra meetings." She rolls her eyes. "Happens all the time. Or at least, it used to." She closes the book on her lap, like she's resigned to the interruption. "Chinese okay?"

"Sure, but isn't your chef making dinner?"

There's a chef who keeps a variety of meals stocked in the refrigerator with simple instructions for reheating. I've only laid eyes on the chef twice. The cleaning service comes daily during the week, yet mostly I'll hear them vacuuming but never see them. It's as if the Sullivans have instructed the staff to steer clear of the house occupants as much as possible. I see the Arrow employees far more than the employees who serve Jack's every need.

"I'm so sick of that food. Aren't you? I mean, don't say anything... Janet would replace him in a heartbeat."

"Who's Janet?"

"The house manager. She runs everything around here."

"Have I seen her?"

"No. She manages a lot of the houses in the neighborhood. I think she comes by in the morning when we're outside."

"Huh."

"So, is Chinese good? I could do Mexican."

"I mean, yeah." I drag my thoughts away from house staff I rarely see to the question of food. It's around five o'clock, but I'm not at all hungry. "It might be nice to invite a friend over," I prompt. "Or friends. Your dad isn't home."

When I was her age, my friends would have jumped at the chance for a parentless place. We craved independence, even though at fifteen we didn't do anything bad. It was just that idea of being parentless that appealed so much.

She frowns. "If you don't want to eat dinner with me—"

"Sophia, that's not what I'm saying. I'd love to order Chinese. I just thought—"

"There's no one I want to see." She opens the book on her lap, dismissing me.

I study her as I close the door, wondering if maybe her reticence has nothing to do with traumatic recent events and more to do with her going to a private school filled with nasty mean girls. That's not what I've been told, but until she opens up and shares, anything is conceivable.

We order Chinese and eat it while watching episodes of *Law & Order SVU*. It's interesting to me she watches a television show about trauma victims. There have been studies done that show that reading novels about abuse can be therapeutic and empowering. I wonder if these little bursts of well-plotted shows have the same empowerment effect. It's conceivable that seeing these people suffer and survive strengthens her.

After hours of *SVU*, we say goodnight at close to midnight. Downstairs, the moonlight shines through my window. I don't bother turning on a light as I prepare for bed. Once in bed, I can't seem to fall asleep, so I count stars.

Footsteps fall in the hall outside. I pull the comforter up to my shoulders and watch the door.

Two security guys cover the third shift. Their offices are down the back hall, so it's not unusual to hear them. But they would never enter my bedroom. Or at least, I assume they wouldn't.

My breath stills as the doorknob twists. The door opens, scraping the thick carpet fibers.

Jack fills the doorway. He's in a suit and tie, but his tie is partially undone, as is the top button on his dress shirt. The door closes behind him, and he clicks the lock. The moonlight reveals the direction of his gaze, but I can barely make out his eyes. In the dim light, they are dark and hooded.

I remain frozen, watching. He toes off his shoes as he tugs on his tie. My breath returns, and the comforter rises and falls.

"Ava?" he whispers as he shrugs off his suit coat. He drops his jacket and tie on a chair.

One by one, he unbuttons the buttons on his dress shirt. He removes cufflinks and sets them on the armrest. The shirt falls onto the chair, and then his undershirt.

"You asleep?" His fingers work his belt buckle.

There's no point in feigning sleep. His trousers fall to the floor, and he steps out of them. I sit up in bed.

He steps to me, naked except for boxers and black dress socks. Under normal conditions, it's a look that would have me snickering. But in the dim light, the socks are barely distinguishable. And his muscular, tanned chest and firm abdomen are nothing to laugh at. Nor are his tented boxers.

He fingers the collar on the old t-shirt I'm wearing. His hand glides down to my waist, lightly brushing over my breasts, and lifts the fabric up and over my head.

"Better."

I swallow and reach for him, letting my legs fall over the side of the bed. My fingers lightly touch the band of his briefs, and his fingers tousle with my hair. When I look up, into his eyes, his gaze singes every fiber of my being, as if he's a live wire and I've touched it with my feet planted on the ground.

I lower his briefs, and once they are over the curves of his muscular ass and his ample erection, they fall to his ankles. I grip his shaft and squeeze. Watching him, I lick up his protruding veins and take him in my mouth. His eyelids close.

He likes my mouth on him. There hasn't been a night since our agreement that we haven't fucked. Maybe that's why I couldn't go to sleep. Some part of me expected him to walk through that door with expectations.

I take him deep, to the back of my throat. Tears spring at the corners of my eyes. He grunts and groans. His hips rock forward. His hand guides, but he's gentle. I wish for him to be rough. To demand. To treat me like shit. But he doesn't.

So I choke myself on him. Saliva drips down his cock. My fingers use it as I work his base and his testicles. He expands in my mouth. I suck harder. An urgent desire—no, need—builds. He pulls a chunk of my hair, forcing me off his cock.

"No," he commands. He lifts me below my armpits and tosses me back across the bed sideways. In a flash, my panties are down my legs and over my ankles.

He spreads my thighs, and I steel myself. He's fucked me with his mouth many times, but always when I'm standing. Tied to the cross or back against a wall. When I stand, my legs nearly fold when the orgasm rips through me.

He places his arms below my thighs, and my center clenches. Anticipation and desire blend.

"Yes." Regret for speaking hits me, and I clamp my mouth shut.

My ass brushes against the comforter as he tugs my whole body down to the edge of the bed.

His tongue slips between my folds, and I shudder. It feels so fucking good. His tongue laps at me, working my sensitive areas, fondling my clit. My fingers twist my nipples as he plunders me with his fingers and his mouth.

My muscles clench. The sensations are almost too much. All kinds of noises escape.

Just enjoy it.

Let go.

Fuck this feels good.

My spine curves as my orgasm begins. I let out an animalistic sound. His head snaps up, and I reach for his hair, aiming to shove him back down. But he's up, rising off his knees. He maneuvers my legs, limp like noodles, so they are up against his body, one foot at each side of his face, and he thrusts his cock inside me.

My back arches at the sudden intrusion, and my muscles clamp around him. My spine flattens against the bed as his hips thrust. I suck in oxygen. His muscles strain. A blood vessel in his neck pulses, highlighted under the moonlight.

He's like an unleashed animal. He holds me in place as he takes me exactly as he wants. Every time he thrusts, he hits deep, sending shockwaves through my pelvis and to the outer perimeters of my limbs. My toes and fingers tingle. I shout as the impending orgasm unleashes. Every muscle trembles. My eyelids close and tiny, brilliant lights dot the backs of my eyelids. He stills and groans.

"Damn, Ava." He pulls out, and one glance at his hard dick and it's clear he didn't let himself come.

He rolls me onto my side and slides me up farther on the bed and climbs on behind me. He lifts my thigh and reenters me from behind. His movements are slower this time. His breath is in my ear. And fuck if he doesn't feel even better than he did before.

"Touch yourself," he commands. "Rub that sensitive clit."

Sensitive would be the correct word. My skin pulses with sensations. All I have to do is press the pads of my fingers against my mound, and the pressure coaxes my clit. I close my eyes, reveling in how damn good it feels.

He pulls out and rolls me onto my back. My pliant muscles allow him to maneuver me like a rag doll. I'm breathing deeply, nearly gasping, and he's damp with perspiration. I reach up and wipe a bead of sweat from his brow, and he dips his head, his lips falling on mine, and his tongue enters my mouth as his dick drives inside, stretching me, filling me.

I taste myself as he kisses me, and I tug his head closer, demanding a deeper kiss. He breaks the kiss, gasping for air, and he trails kisses, sucking skin as he goes, down to my breasts, and the rhythm of his hips slows.

I reach between us, and we both watch as he pulls out and slides back in. The tips of my fingers find my apex, and I press and pull and play.

"Fuuuck." He groans.

I'm not sure if it's his fingers, or his cock pulsing within me, or the weight of his body over me, or the pressure of his thighs against mine, or the combination of it all, but my muscles quiver with the onset of another orgasmic release.

He collapses on top of me, and my arms rest on his back. Holding him like this feels remarkably awkward, given all we have done. But I ignore the awkward and hold him as his heartbeat and breathing regulate.

Since we're on the bed sideways, our feet hang off the edge. He rolls off me, onto his side, and his right hand claims my breast, gently massaging it, the pad of his thumb brushing over the nipple, as he places wet kisses against my shoulder. I'm too spent to move away, and I don't want to. But this level of intimacy isn't our normal. It's not what I expected he would want when I agreed to do this.

"I needed you," he shares. "I came home." He swallows. "And I needed you."

"Tough day?" I want to know who he was with. I want to know if he's sleeping with other people. How often does he do this? Make these arrangements with women like me?

"A shit day," he says and falls onto his back. He's staring at the ceiling, but his hand remains clamped possessively on my breast. I allow myself to roll a little on my side so I can explore the rivets of his chest. His heartbeat thumps beneath his ribcage, solid and strong. He closes his eyes and lets my breast go to rub his eyes. "Sophia said you ate dinner with her. Are you making any headway?"

"She's not ready." It's my most honest assessment.

"How much more time do you need?" The frustration he's feeling comes through in his tone.

That's an impossible question to answer, so I don't. Instead, I roll farther onto my side, suck his nipple into my mouth, and bite.

"What the...?" He laughs. It's more of a chuckle, but I like it. I push up off the bed, and he claims my breast again with a light, tender touch.

"Don't ask me impossible questions."

We scowl at each other, but the slight grins on our faces counteract the standoff. He's concerned for his daughter, and I empathize. I also admire his fierce love. Beneath his cold exterior pounds a passionate heart. My fingers flatten over his chest, memorizing his rhythm.

He lets out a sigh and closes his eyes. "Patrick told my uncle about our arrangement."

"Oh. I'm sorry. I...can't believe–"

"It's okay."

"That's why you had a bad day?" I try to envision what Mark would do. What he would say.

"No. There are things going on. Things I can't really share. But let's just say that I'm still worried about Sophia's safety. I'm glad she has you here."

In the moonlight, my stack of silver bracelets and beads glimmers. I rest my ear against his chest and listen to the soothing beat.

"When you work late...it's not just business, is it? You're doing something...it's all about keeping her safe?"

His fingers work through tangles in my hair, and my arm tightens around his waist.

"It's always about family. Or country. One of the two."

"Sophia's going to be okay."

"Yes. She will be. Just...for now, while you are with us...be aware, okay?"

"Is something going on?"

"Always."

An urge to rise up and press my lips over his almost overpowers me, but I gain control. He's paying me. My heart can't get involved. This is sex. Just sex.

I hop off the bed and stroll naked into the bathroom, perhaps with some extra hip sway, just in case he's watching.

When I finish in the bathroom, he's gone, as are all his clothes. The rumpled, stained bed cover offers the only evidence of his midnight visit. It's a good thing there is evidence. Otherwise, I might suspect I suffered from one helluva vivid erotic fantasy.

CHAPTER 23

JACK

"Dad, are you going to the shooting range today?"

Sophia comes into my office wearing incredibly short shorts and a Cage the Elephant concert t-shirt that's so long you can barely see the hem of those short shorts. Her golden hair is wet and based on the extensive wet areas on the cotton shirt, she didn't bother to towel dry her hair. Her blue eyes sparkle, so much like her mom's that sometimes I feel like I'm looking at the reincarnation of Cassandra.

"I am." My fingers hover over the mouse, closing the website I had been visiting. "What are you planning on doing today?"

My gaze travels to my bookcase and the shelf with her phone sitting unused. There was a time when I would have loved for her to refuse a phone. But now it's just a blatant reminder that something is wrong. My daughter still hurts, and she hasn't yet fully recovered. I have more money than I can spend, yet I can't fix this for her.

She stands behind one of my chairs. Her fingers graze the curved walnut back. That's when I notice her black nail polish. Ava wears dark nail polish. Is she styling herself like Ava? That will not do.

"I'd like to go to the gun range with you." Sophia's statement snaps me back into the moment.

"You want..." Those blue eyes are tentative. And it hits me like a tsunami. She doesn't feel safe. "Sophia, I promise you, you are safe in this house." I push up out of my office chair and come around to her. "I know, before... I was ridiculous to not have a better security system in place. And I will never forgive myself." Sitting on the edge of my desk, I lean toward her, reaching for her slight hand. "But we are like Fort Knox secure. No one is coming here uninvited."

"Dad," she takes my hand in both of hers, "the person who..." She falters, and I still, holding my breath. She has yet to say out loud what happened. Her gaze falls, but her grasp on my hand tightens. "We knew him. He was one of your closest friends." My eyes close because I can't look at her while hearing her. The pain batters me because she's only speaking the truth. "I don't blame you, Dad. It's not your fault."

My eyes sting, and I grit my teeth. She lets my hand go and approaches the bookcase. Her back is to me, and I gather myself. My fingers find the knot on my tie, and I straighten it and tighten the noose.

"I want to learn how to shoot." She turns and presses her back against the bookcase. She lifts her chin, defiant, and once again I am blown away by how similar she is to her mother. "I want the ability to defend myself. But more than that, I come from a gun manufacturing family. Shouldn't I know how to use a gun?"

She should. Cassandra hated guns. That was something she and I argued over, but it was one of about five hundred things we argued over, and I didn't fight hard for my daughter's gun skill development. Given what happened, I probably should have.

"You want to learn how to shoot?"

"I want to compete."

"Competitions, huh?"

She nods.

Uncle Mark must have filled her head with family legend, telling her how the Sullivans used to win all the shooting competitions. I certainly never told her.

She's fifteen. She's a little old to be jumping into competition, but she can do anything she sets her mind to.

"Then come with me." I check my watch. "I leave in fifty minutes." Her body twists, heading out the door. "But you can't wear that." I point at her bare legs.

If her mother were alive, there's no way she'd let her leave the house like that. Her butt practically hangs out of those short shorts. Her nose crinkles in the way she does when she thinks I'm making zero sense.

"Jeans. Or pants. Boots would be good. Make sure your toes are covered."

I'd like to tell her to change her nail polish, but I recognize that's overreaching. After she leaves my office, I send a text to my house manager asking her to send a selection of light pink nail polishes to the house.

And then I think about the woman behind the black polish. Ava wears dark, poorly made clothes. She has money now and can afford to buy whatever clothes she wants, but maybe she could use some prodding. I type out a text asking the house manager to buy Ava clothes, but I flounder with the request, as I'm unsure what direction to give.

I search for women's clothing. An ad for Nordstrom pops up, and in under ten minutes I have a selection of clothes ordered. If Sophia is going to model herself after Ava, then Ava should wear the right kinds of clothes.

Then I call Ryan.

"Jack. Was about to call you. Your boat will be in transit to San Diego by the end of the day."

"Excellent."

"There's a lot of interest in the boat crew that's hired for this initial trip."

"No doubt."

The work I've done with the CIA has centered on international partners. They've had tremendous interest in countries buying weapons and in gaining insight on the individuals showing up to meetings to negotiate volume purchases. For the most part, my CIA career has centered around truly benign information sharing. But now, we're dealing with smuggling. Crimes on US soil.

"I meant to ask you. Who did you say you had lunch with yesterday?" On the flight home from Houston, I gave Ryan top line updates.

"Senator Talbot, Chuck Strand, and my uncle."

He says nothing. I wait patiently. In theory, we're on a secure line. In theory, they sweep my office for listening devices daily. But technical capabilities have increased to the point I'm not sure anyone is safe from surveillance.

"Are you close to the senator?"

"He's a seventy-five-year-old politician." I spin my office chair so I can take in the Pacific. "I think he and my dad were friends back in the day. He's friendly with my uncle. He's big shit in Texas."

"He's an investor in several private prisons."

He's a wealthy man. If he's like me, that's not surprising. "You realize he probably doesn't know everything he's invested in, right?"

"I'm not talking about stock. These aren't publicly traded."

"Which ones?" I ask, but I suspect I know the answer.

"Two big companies own one hundred and seventy private correctional facilities. He's a significant investor in both companies. They own five prisons in Texas."

"Interesting." But being a financial investor doesn't necessarily mean one can pull strings. "But somewhat meaningless. You remember what I told you about Morales, right?"

Morales basically offered to eliminate the man. My guess is Morales has some of his men currently serving time and technically still on his payroll in multiple prisons. It's my understanding that's how things get done in prisons. Criminal organizations have men serving time and readily available to do as-needed work.

"I remember. See you shortly."

"Sophia is going to the range with me today."

A silent beat crosses the line.

"Good for her," he says.

I roll my eyes. Part of me agrees with Ryan. Part of me is proud of her effort. But there's another part of me that absolutely hates that she feels the need to hold a gun. I am doing everything I can to make her feel safe. "Should we plan to meet somewhere else?"

"No. I'll hire someone for private lessons."

"You won't teach her?"

"Sophia doesn't listen to me as well as she listens to others. I'll step aside during her lesson."

"Sounds good."

"Thanks, Wolf." I don't use his old nickname often, but it feels more personable, and it rolls off my tongue.

"Jack?"

"Yeah."

"You know it's a good idea that she learns to shoot, right? It's just smart. She'll be a target for the rest of her life."

He's referencing the one hundred million reward I offered for information leading me to her alive. Desperation beat common sense. The FBI agents on the case had been furious with me. And in calmer moments, after that press conference, I recognized the lunacy. But dammit, I did what I had to do.

"Gotta run."

There's a quiet that envelops the house when Sophia falls asleep. When I close the draft of the meeting documents for our upcoming board meeting, I check the time, and awareness of the late-night quiet peaks. Outside my window, a dark shadow crosses the lawn. The third shift at work.

Sophia didn't do too bad with the handguns. The rifles hurt her shoulder, but she had a steely determination. I picked an older, grandfatherly man for her instructor. He will be patient with her as she learns the ropes and refines her skills.

It'll be nice to spend time with her at the range. There's not much I can bond with her on, but guns, if she's into those, at the very least, are a way to spend time with my daughter.

Ryan and I also shot several rounds. And he let me know the undercover operation has been approved and the FBI will lead. Since the operation is somewhat underway, the FBI will be working with Arrow as a contractor on the project. The CIA will be looped in. As well as various groups who monitor things like firearms and drugs. It's a logistical fucking nightmare, and I'm glad I'm not involved in all the politics that will no doubt circle the covert operation.

Sophia and I ate dinner together alone. I didn't ask where Ava was. Sophia said she had another session with her, but she didn't share more.

The door creaks as I push it open. Sophia lies on the bed, eyes closed, sleeping like a peaceful princess. Her little dog doesn't even lift his head.

When that dog dies, Sophia's next dog will be a German shepherd or some sort of protection dog. I blame myself for what happened to Sophia, but that little dog is complicit too. She probably licked the men who took Sophia.

I carefully pull her door shut and silently cross the house, heading down the stairs to find Ava.

A golden light projects beneath her bedroom door, and I rap my knuckles against the wood. As I wait for her to open her door, I'm torn over where I want her tonight. The room with all the toys is down the hall and readily available. But I can't deny the silky bed cover felt fucking great against my skin. Maybe I should ask Janet to add more silks in the playroom.

The door cracks open. Ava stands before me in a black lace bra and a black thong. Always in black. She's wearing a garter with black thigh highs and black five-inch heels with silk threads that wrap around her ankles. My cock instantly hardens.

Those captivating eyes observe me with a trace of amusement. She absolutely knows what she does to me. She's fully aware I will show up at her door every single night. And tonight, she dressed for play. So, the playroom it is.

With one quick glance along the hallway to ensure we are alone, I hold my arm out, gesturing for her to pass before me down the hall. She's wearing a black transparent mesh robe that seemingly floats behind her. The globes of her ass flex with each step, the skin bare thanks to the strip of fabric covering her crack and nothing else.

A desire to rip that fabric apart makes my fingers itch. I will take her from behind tonight. I might even try some of those anal toys to stretch her out.

When she reaches the door, she turns to the side, creating room for me to press my thumb on the keypad. Tonight, there are no candles. I didn't prepare the room. I don't have a plan. Tonight will be about improvisation.

I turn on the light and quickly lower the dimmer, watching as the golden light paints the velvet patterned walls in sultry warmth.

My gaze falls first on the leather cross, then on the massive black bed. So much in this room is black, as if designed with Ava's taste in mind. The door lock clicks behind me, and Ava approaches. Tonight, she draped her eyes in heavy makeup, and her dark, luscious lips seem to soften her pale skin. She loosens my tie, and my blood quickens in my veins. I stand in the middle of the room, watching as her fingers adeptly remove my clothes. They pause on my belt buckle.

"Remove your shoes."

I bend to obey. If she wants to take control, I'll let her. Hell, I'll revel in it.

"And the socks." I can't beat down the smirk. So, she's not into old men in black dress socks. Duly noted.

After removing the offending items and setting them to the side near the door, I return to the vixen. This time, she falls to her knees. She removes my dress slacks and boxers, and fuck, as she licks up my shaft, those magnetic dark eyes look up at me with a mix of desire and hunger that almost sets me off.

I twist a strand of her jet-black hair around my finger and, with a rough tug, pull her deeper. She gags and her eyes water.

"I think you're gonna need a safe word." Power pulses through my veins. Oh, the things I will do to her. She's going to have to take control another night.

Her head pushes back on my hand, and I let her back off my cock. She swipes her palm against her chin, cleaning it up, while one hand grips my shaft with a pleasurable firmness. Her breasts glow in the dim light and her cheeks flush, those lips swollen from sucking. She's a sex dream, on her knees. My erection throbs, but I welcome the break from her mouth, because she was pushing me too close to the brink too quickly.

"Safe word," I repeat. She blinks, and her tongue licks that plump lower lip.

"Norway."

Her unexpected word throws me, and I half-laugh.

"Interesting." I pull her up off her knees and guide her to a leather bench. The bench vibrates, but I don't plan on using that feature. "Care to enlighten me?"

My palm slaps her ass, and the sound blends in with the low, pulsing music. Tenderly, I smooth the skin, then slap it again. She twists her head to gaze up at me, and she smiles. So, she likes that.

I step away and open a drawer, searching the contents.

"It's a place I want to go."

I lift a tube of lubricant and an anal plug.

"Do you like anal play?"

"I'm not sure."

"Have you had anal sex?"

"Maybe." She turns her head so she's facing the ground, and I remember her history.

"You're not sure?" I hold the anal plug out for her to see so she can object if she doesn't want this.

"I don't remember all the times I've had sex. Drug addict. Remember?"

It's a taunt. But her perfect ass resting high in the air distracts me from the conversation. I apply a generous amount of lube to the plug, then some to my finger. Gently, I push into the tight opening with a finger, spreading the warming liquid. Her ass clenches.

"If I do anything you don't like, you've got your safe word."

"It's fine. Do what you want."

I insert the plug. There's a nice sized base to prevent it from going higher. Even if she has had anal sex before, she needs stretching. Pain isn't the goal. I want to bring her pleasure. I crave her pleasure.

"Can you walk?" I ask as I lift her off the bench.

There's a sloping leather chaise designed to accommodate a variety of creative positions that I'd like to try, but it's across the room. Those sinful eyes blink, so enormous a person could fall right into them and never climb out.

She doesn't answer me but takes a careful step. She glances over her shoulder, and in a seductive tone, asks, "Where to?"

"The chaise. Straddle it, one leg on each side."

She does as I instruct, and I take a moment to take her in. Dark hair spills over the back of the narrow chaise. Her back arches, lying against the curve of the frame, pushing her full breasts up like an offering. Her legs are spread open, displaying her bare, tantalizing pussy.

Damn. She's fucking gorgeous.

I taste those breasts, sucking her delectable nipples and swirling my tongue until she squirms beneath my touch. Of course, each time she squirms, she's moving the plug. The jerky movements of her hips let me know she's adjusting.

I suck my way down her belly, sucking hard enough to leave marks, all the way down to her core. She remains transfixed as I stretch across the chaise and lower my chin. My tongue licks up her slit.

She sucks in air and gasps as my tongue delves deeper.

The pulse of the music quickens, and my tongue fucks her to the same beat. Her fingers tug on my hair, and I raise my head with a *tsk*.

"Arms down. If I need to tie you, I will."

Her chest rises and falls rapidly. My cock is so fucking hard it's borderline painful.

"Do I need to tie you?"

Slowly, she shakes her head.

I dip my head and twirl my tongue around her little exposed nub.

She tastes good, but it's the way she trembles beneath my touch, seeing her muscles flex and quiver as I thrust two fingers inside her without warning, how she squirms with my mouth on her sex that really gets me. And then that scream as she pulses her release, tightening hard on my fingers. My cock leaks with need.

"Please," she whimpers.

"Please what?"

"Fuck me."

"Oh, trust me. I will."

I slide her up the curve of the chaise and climb on, straddling it, facing her. Then I lift her over me, my cock straight up at attention, wanting and needy, just like the vixen I'm holding.

I position her over my tip. She plants her feet on each side of the chaise, recognizing that I am letting her take control. Slowly, she lowers herself, taking me. Inch by inch, her tight warmth pulses around me. She feels fucking divine. Her soft breasts press against my chest, her pert nipples pressing into me, until she's seated on me.

With the anal plug in place, she's impossibly tight, and it takes all my control to let her control the movement, because I want to slam her against me.

Slowly, she rises. Those swollen lips are parted, and there's awe in her eyes as she grinds against me. My arms wrap around her back, holding her close as I revel in the sensations of her wickedly tight channel working my cock. Her nails score my back as my hips rise to meet hers.

With one hand, I grip her hair and position her head so I can claim that open mouth. It's the kiss that does us in. Our tongues tangle, warring at the same tempo as our hips. The movement is both erotic and soulful.

Her lips brush against my jaw and my cheek as she rides me, and her breath caresses my ear.

"Close," she grunts. "So close."

And I kiss her again, rocking up into her as she grinds down on me and her walls close in, convulsing and shuddering. My release pulses out as she collapses around me.

Her skin is damp and glistening. I hold her tight, us both sitting upright, her legs straddling mine, her heartbeat pounding against my chest.

The dark king-size bed calls to me, and with a groan, I stand, lifting her with me. I almost crash to the floor as I pull my leg over the chaise. She giggles as her head lolls against my shoulder.

With one hand, I tug back the silky comforter, exposing silk sheets, and lay her down. I search for the vibrator remote and dial it to the lowest vibration. Her eyes widen, and I grin.

My cock twitches, coming back to life. I move to the side of the bed. She understands my desire and takes me in her hand, then her mouth. God, she feels fucking divine. She's so good at this.

Once I'm fully ready, I climb onto the bed, between her legs, and thrust inside her. The dull vibration from the plug in her ass is every bit as fantastic as I expected. Her hips gyrate below me, and I press up into her core, balls deep. I have to hold myself above her, on my forearms. She's still as I rock into her. The sensations threaten to overwhelm. She looks up at me, eyes wide, and I lose any semblance of control. I'm kissing her, claiming her breasts, her mouth, her entire body. The orgasm that rips through my body blows my mind. Her screams are the only things that keep me blanketed to reality and chained to our bed.

Her eyelids flutter closed, and she drifts to sleep as I lie plastered on her spent form. With great effort, I get up and run hot water over a washcloth and clean her, providing aftercare. When I remove the plug, she squirms and wakes. A soft smile plays across her lips, and she stretches languidly. My muscles are the most relaxed I think they've ever been, and I slide across the silk to her side, pulling her into my arms. With one quick tug, the comforter falls around us, cocooning us in silky, blissful warmth.

"Do you do this a lot?" Her question comes across as slow and relaxed, but there's a weight to the words.

I don't do this a lot. After my divorce, before Cassandra died, sure. I had women over. No relationship to speak of, but I had an active sex life. Cassie's death hit me like a freight train. The unexpected upended my world. And then Sophia came to live with me, and I vowed to be a better father. As her only living parent, I had to change.

I let work consume me. Until the day I received that fateful phone call. And I had to pick up Sophia from school and tell her she wouldn't see her mother again. She didn't come to me for comfort. It was like I was a stranger delivering horrific news to a family relative I saw once every month or two.

I still relive the moment sometimes. The shock on Sophia's face. The slow crumbling and the denial, followed by tears. Her shoulders caved in, and her head bowed, and her shoulders convulsed as she sobbed. I sat there for minutes, watching her, wanting to hold her but unsure if I should.

"Do you have this arrangement with a lot of women?" Ava rolls onto her side, aligning her naked body against mine, skin against skin. She balls her hand into a fist and rests it on my chest, then her chin rests on that. The space between us offers a view of her breasts, pressed softly against me. Under this light, those bewitching eyes take me in.

I blink to pull myself back from the tangent my mind traversed, one so different from hers.

"I haven't used this room in years, if that's what you're asking." I've never paid someone for sex before either, at least if you don't count a massage parlor that offered happy endings that some of my fraternity brothers dragged me to. But I won't tell her that, because I'd prefer we not reference the financial component of our relationship. I reach up and curl a piece of her silky black hair around my finger. Her bangs crowd her eyebrows, and on a whim, I brush my hand across her forehead. I pause, holding those bangs away. She's truly beautiful.

She drops her head to my chest, and the fisted hand loosens as her arm drapes across me. This is more intimacy than I planned with her, but my muscles are spent, and I have no desire to get out of this bed.

"What about you?" I leave the question open, so she can answer it however she likes.

"No. I mean, you know about me, right?"

I do, and I don't. So, I prod. "Know what about you?"

Her chest expands as she inhales. My fingers comb through her hair.

"I was an addict." She lifts her head and looks me in the eye. "I am an addict." Her shoulders flinch, and she lowers her head back down. "I had a relationship after rehab, and it didn't go well. I'm better off focusing on, well, me."

I had an old military friend who went through rehab. I remember some of it. Relationships are frowned on during the rehab phase. But Ava founded the center Mark's been funding for what seems like forever. I assumed she'd been clean for a long time.

"How long have you been sober?"

"Ten years. Eight months. Three days."

"You're coming up on eleven years." How many of those years was she in a relationship? "Do you still have cravings?"

"No." Her chest expands again on a deep inhale. "And yes. But I will not relapse. I don't ever want to go back to... that."

"And what is that?"

"Sticking needles in my neck. Homelessness. The worst you can imagine. It got bad."

My fingers continue toying with her hair, and I occasionally scratch her scalp the way Sophia used to like for me to do when she was little. My eyelids are heavy, and I let them close.

"You're probably second guessing letting me near Sophia."

My eyes pop open. I squeeze her, prompting her to raise her head and look at me.

"I have zero regrets bringing you into our home. From what I can tell, you've been good with Sophia." I brush my thumb across her cheek. It's my turn for some honesty. "If anything, I feel guilty for having you live here. For uprooting your life." *For treating you like a prostitute.* I look off to the corner of the room where leather restraints hang from a hook. Having her here has been more beneficial for me. It's a sexual release I've craved. And as things at work have intensified, it's been liberating knowing someone was with Sophia. I love seeing her with Sophia. She's good with her. "I can only thank you."

She rolls away from me, onto her side, and pulls one pillow under her head. I roll in her direction, so I'm on my side, next to her. My fingers comb along her arms, over the web of tattoos.

"You've got less than two weeks remaining. When your time is up, will you go to Norway?" She'll have the money.

"Norway?"

"You said you wanted to go there." I want to know more about her. How she plans on spending her money, what she plans on doing, and I want to know about every single tattoo covering her sensuous body.

"I won't blow it on travel. I'm playing around with ideas. Researching real estate options."

"For a home?"

"No. To expand Buena Vida. I'm also working with our financial advisors. I'd like to ensure we don't need to go to your uncle every year for additional funding. And with your sizable contribution, I feel pretty confident I can do that."

"You're a part of Mark's annual giving campaign. To my knowledge, he's incredibly proud of the work you do."

"Hmm. He believes in our mission." She kicks her leg back, and her calf slides over my lower leg. Her breathing regulates into a mellow rhythm, and I breathe her in. Her scent is musky, her skin soft. She's a walking contradiction. Her tattoos and piercings render a hard edge, but those gargantuan chocolate eyes and mass of silky hair render her a fantasy. She's been through hell and not only survived but thrived. It's easy to see why my uncle is so besotted with her and would recommend her for Sophia. She bears the strength and wisdom of scars.

I will lie here for a few minutes, soaking her in. It's been so long since I lay like this, holding someone, lulled into a blissful state of warmth and relaxation. Just a few more minutes, and then I'll get up and go to my bedroom.

CHAPTER 24

Ava

"Fuck!"

My eyes snap open at the angry sound. I blink and rub my eyes. The room is dark and there are flickering golden lights along the wall. Smooth silk cocoons my body.

"Ava? Are you down here?" Sophia's voice is distant.

"We overslept. It's almost ten." Jack's pants are on but unzipped, and he's pulling on his white dress shirt. "There's no fucking light in here. No alarm."

"Dad?" Sophia's voice sounds farther away, like she's headed in the opposite direction.

I'm completely nude. The black lingerie I wore last night is in a pile on the floor. Jack flicks overhead lights on, and bright light washes over the room, forcing me to shelter my eyes.

"Here," I say, one hand over my eyes as I attempt to move to my clothes. "You sneak out. She'll think you went to work early. I'll get dressed and meet her."

"Sneak out? How?" He's fumbling with the buttons on his shirt, and from what I can tell, he's not making any progress. He's acting like a teenager about to get busted for having a girl in his room. If I wasn't for a veil of grogginess, I'd probably laugh.

"She's about to go outside. When she does, just run up the stairs." It's not rocket science. "She thinks this room is storage, right?"

He glances at me, and there's panic splayed across his facial expressions. I wave a hand at him as I bend down and scoop up the lingerie. If I remember correctly, he destroyed the thong, so there's no point in trying to put anything back on.

"My bedroom's close by. I'll sneak down the hall and jump in the shower. When she comes around, I'll tell her I went out for a walk... what time did you say it is?"

"Ten!" he practically yells.

Yeah, this story has some holes. But she's going to want to believe us, and that'll work in our favor. These are things I know from experience.

Jack presses his ear to the door.

"I thought this was a soundproof room. How are we hearing her?"

"Clearly, it's not," he snaps.

He opens the door and peeks his head out.

"She's headed down to the pool."

"Go!" I hiss.

And he's gone. The door clicks closed behind him.

The bed is rumpled, and the used plug sits on a glass plate on a shelf. This place needs to be cleaned, but there's no time now. I mimic Jack, crack the door, view the empty hall, and take off, running naked as a jaybird down the hall to my bedroom.

Thankfully, the covers on my bed are pulled back, as I had been lying there reading, waiting to see if Jack stopped by. I rush into the bathroom. The stage of dressing I've accomplished by the time Sophia finds me will determine the story I weave.

After the quickest shower of my life, I get dressed, pulling on workout leggings and a jog bra. In the mirror, I spot hickeys across my boobs and abs. *Fuck.* I pull on a long sleeve black sweater. It's a light summer sweater that shouldn't look suspect.

My phone vibrates on my bedside table. It's charging. I ignore the phone and dig out socks. I'll put on running shoes. If I pull back my hair into a low knot, Sophia may not notice my hair is wet. I can tell her I went for a long walk and lost track of time. It's something I would do, so I think it's believable. I can even tell her I stopped for coffee and ran into someone I know.

Without my phone and watch, the morning just slipped away. As I tie the laces on my shoes, I run through my concocted story, and it strikes me as solid. All that experience making up excuses is paying off. Lying must come naturally to some people, and by some people, I mean me.

My phone vibrates again, and I debate answering. My story for Sophia is better if I don't have my phone in hand. I'll leave it.

I scan the back yard, searching for Sophia. Where'd she go?

And then I see her in the back corner of the yard. She's leaning over the fence, talking to someone. Based on the crew cut, she must be talking to Fisher. I can't get to the side yard from here without her seeing me, unless I go upstairs and out the garage, but she'd still see me on the side path.

My phone vibrates again. That's weird.

I could pick up my phone and claim I went on that walk and came straight in to get my phone. That she and I must have crossed paths. That works.

I grab my phone and head outside. I'm through the sliding doors for the back patio as the screen unlocks.

PATRICK

Call me

Curiosity kicks in, and I press the message app. Forty-two messages.

"There you are," Sophia calls. I glance up, holding my index finger to her.

"Yeah, I went for a walk this morning and lost track of time. Left my phone home..." I scroll through the messages and the tips of my fingers grow cold.

PATRICK

We have an issue. I need you to call me.

PATRICK

Don't do anything stupid. Will you call me?

PATRICK

Call me.

PATRICK

I'm coming to you. Stay where you are.

The messages are more of the same. Short and demanding. But there's no information. What the hell happened?

I click to my voicemails. There are multiple messages from Buena Vida and a couple of messages from Reid, which isn't unusual, but all these other messages are. My heart rate spikes, and my breath becomes shallow. What the hell happened?

I press the most recent message from Buena Vida and hold the phone to my ear.

"Want to go paddleboarding? Did you eat breakfast?" Sophia asks.

I hold my index finger to my lips, asking for her silence so I can hear.

"Ava, this is Juliette. I'm calling you from Buena Vida. I've been here overseeing the police investigation. They said you aren't answering phone calls. I know this must be difficult for you, but I need you to call me."

She ends the call. What is difficult? What the hell happened at the center?

My feet move in the house's direction. I need my pocketbook and keys. I press the next message and listen as I speed walk.

"Is everything okay?" Sophia trails behind me.

"I don't know. No."

I press Patrick's name on my phone as I sling my pocketbook over my shoulder and snag my keys off my desk. I get his voicemail and hang up.

There's a police investigation. Something happened at Buena Vida. It has to be drugs. There was a drug bust or something.

I scroll through my missed calls, looking at all the missed calls from unknown numbers. Fuck. Well, if I need a lawyer, at least I can afford one now.

I charge up the stairs, forgetting about the messages. Every fiber in my being pulses, my instincts telling me I need to get to Buena Vida as fast as possible. Rush hour is over, so I should be able to get there fast.

My fist slams the square button on the wall of the garage for the fourth bay, where my car has been parked for weeks. The garage door cranks open. Fisher passes by in the driveway.

"I've got to go."

"I can get someone to drive you."

I shake my head as I open my car door and throw my pocketbook on the passenger seat.

"No, thanks. I'll be fine."

I jump in my car, not giving him time to argue. I actually do believe Sophia needs every bit of security Jack is throwing her way, but they have basically locked me in their house, out of sight of the media or anyone who might look for a way to access Sophia.

My tires squeal as I hit reverse, probably because he has some slick, shiny garage floor surface. I curse at the obnoxious noise.

Sophia stands near the garage bay beside Fisher. I roll down my passenger window and shout, "Something happened at the center. I'll be back later."

I press the accelerator. Wind whips from the open passenger window, and I raise it. Speeding through the neighborhood, I scan the sidewalks for any children or animals. The moment I pass through the security gate at the neighborhood entrance, I pick my phone up and dial Patrick.

Again with the voicemail. *Where the fuck is he?*

I dial Juliette. Voicemail.

Fuck. What the hell is going on?

I speed through the side streets on my way to the freeway. I press the voicemail tab.

The first in the list is from an unknown number.

"Hello," a robotic voice states. "Your auto warranty—"

I end the call and click the next message.

A horn blasts, and I lift my head and shoot the fucker the bird. Slow damn driver.

"Avaaaaaa. Baby. Where are you?" I would recognize the deep tone and the slurred words anywhere. It's Reid. *Dammit.* He sounds drunk. Music plays in the background. I lift the phone to read the time of the message. "You're too good for me. But you know that, don't you? You're smart to stay away. You... you were always the smart one. Knew I'd fuck up again. Yep. So damn smart, you are. Never returned my calls. Nope. Not youuuu. You're smart. My smart baby. My smart girl." Another voice pipes in, "Hey, Reid. Whatcha' doing, man?" And the call disconnects.

The call is from three this morning. I play the message again. This time I recognize the song playing in the background. It's an old song from the seventies called "Summer Breeze." What the hell, Reid? Are you hanging out with potheads?

I press the voicemail icon again, searching for more messages from Reid.

My phone lights up in my hand, and I answer immediately.

"Hello?"

"Ava. Honey. How are you?"

"Juliette? What the hell is going on?"

The entrance to the freeway is up ahead. There's one intersection before the on-ramp. The car in front of me is going slow, and I swerve to pass it so I can beat the yellow light.

"You don't know?"

"Know what?"

"What a clusterfuck. Reid OD'd. When they called 911, cops came. Three of our residents were getting high with him—"

Crash! My windshield crumbles. Glass flies everywhere. A force hits my chest. I spin. Metal crunches. And blackness falls.

CHAPTER 25

JACK

With one last look in the mirror, I head down the back staircase that leads to the garage. I never oversleep. I never sleep late. Falling asleep in a darkened room ranks as a colossal mistake. I missed two meetings this morning. Sophia could have caught us. Sleeping late fucked my entire schedule. Like some juvenile teen, I lied to my assistant, telling her I wasn't feeling well. I haven't spit out a lie like that since seventh grade when I needed to avoid a quiz on some unread chapters from *Lord of the Flies*.

And Ryan asked to meet after lunch. He doesn't request a meeting unless it's important. He doesn't want to risk being overheard, and given the crap with the yacht, worry gnaws at my gut.

In the back yard, Sophia sits in a chair beneath a tree reading a book. There's no sign of Ava. Did she find her? Did we get busted? I double-check my phone, and there's no warning text from Ava. Of course, this whole idea of getting busted is borderline ludicrous. I'm a grown adult. Sophia is fifteen years old. If I choose to sleep with a woman in my home, I can. Still, my sex life isn't something my fifteen-year-old needs to be aware of. I'm sure she'd prefer to think of me as asexual.

With a coffee in hand, I gaze at her. She's the picture of innocence, her legs curled up under her in a flowery sundress. She glances up and sees me. I lift my mug to her in greeting, and she closes her book. I head outside onto the deck to greet her over the balcony.

"Morning."

"Where have you been?" Her hand is shielding her eyes as she looks up at the house. "I couldn't find you."

"Sorry, sweetheart. I had a breakfast meeting. Ah, I'm going to be heading out to the range soon. You want to come with me?"

"Yeah, let me change."

"Okay. We'll leave in thirty?"

I head back to my office to check email while I wait for her. An alert comes across my phone that Ryan's helicopter has landed and he's in transit to the shooting range. I power down my computer, double-check my desk is in order, and close the office door. A woman from the cleaning service lowers her eyes as she passes me, and her presence reminds me there's an extra room to clean today.

I shoot a quick text off to my house manager letting her know that the private room needs to be cleaned by someone who will exercise the utmost discretion.

"Sophia?" I call.

"Yeah, Dad. I'm ready." She closes her bedroom door behind her. It's a habit of hers she started recently, and I'm not fond of it. But her phone remains in my office, untouched, so it's not like she's doing something with friends that she's trying to keep hidden.

In the garage, we both climb into my Range Rover. As I start the car, I glance sideways as she buckles her seatbelt. The garage door opens.

"Do you want to drive?" She has her permit, but we haven't left the house much since the incident. She needs to get in hours driving before she gets her license.

"That's okay," she says. "Maybe I'll drive home."

As I'm backing out of the garage, I notice the fourth spot, where Ava's Subaru was parked, is vacant.

"Did you see Ava this morning?"

"Yeah. Something was wrong with her."

With as much nonchalance as I can muster, I ask, "What do you mean?"

In the rearview, I see Fisher pull out of the garage, following me in the black SUV Ryan insisted they needed on the property.

"I don't know. She forgot her phone this morning when she went on a walk, and she got some bad news of some sort. Something to do with Buena Vida, the place she works."

"Huh."

I check back in my rearview and count two Arrow employees in the car behind us.

"She drove herself?"

"Yes, Dad." There is a lot of indignation in her tone that is borderline inappropriate. "You don't own her."

My grip on the steering wheel tightens, and I focus on driving. Sophia changes the station, and we settle into a silent drive. It's not about owning her. It's about her safety, but I will not drill safety into Sophia's head when she still refuses to see friends and possesses a newfound interest in self-defense.

The range isn't far from my home, and when we arrive, we beat Ryan. There's an instructor on site who has some free time, and he agrees to work with Sophia. After she gets started, I back away and keep a lookout for Ryan. The two Arrow security guys hover within fifty feet of Sophia, scanning the grounds. The lunch crowd trickles in, and all the faces are familiar.

Ryan arrives, and I head out to the parking lot to greet him.

"Hey. I've got a spot reserved on the front range."

He nods and opens the back of his truck where he lifts two gun cases. My guns are already in place in my hutch, as I have an arrangement with the facility.

Rapid-fire artillery sounds on the range. The loud booms offer excellent cover, but it also makes hearing more difficult. Ryan guides us near his two employees, who are standing near a fence and far away from any other person.

"Did you know Ava went back to Buena Vida this morning?"

"No."

"Shouldn't you know?" Ryan might be a friend, but I'm paying Arrow a ton of money to have the best security money can buy.

"Well, I'm sure Fisher knows." When we're a few feet away from the men, Ryan asks Fisher, "Ms. Amara left today?"

"Yes, sir." Fisher answers. "I offered to have someone drive her, but she declined."

Of course she did.

I lean closer to Ryan so he can hear me above the booming artillery. "Can you confirm she went to Buena Vida?"

"Sure. We have a tracking device on her car, and we can locate her phone. But she knows about both devices. Are we not trusting her?" His eyebrows narrow.

I don't answer him. I trust her as much as I trust anyone, but I'd like to be certain after last night that she's going where she says she is. That she didn't freak out and decide she needed space. Waking up together was a disconcerting experience. I spent the morning flustered and frustrated. Maybe it troubled her for other reasons.

"I'll track her." Fisher gets out his phone and taps away.

Ryan bends his head and says, "Just so you know, everything I'm hearing from my sister about that center of hers is positive. I've been out there a few times. She's doing good things for people. For the first time, I think Indie might kick her addiction, and a lot of it has to do with that place."

"What do you mean?" My uncle is a big believer in Buena Vida. It's his only non-business-related charity that I'm aware of.

"They just...they have a great support structure. Clean, safe, affordable housing. Group and individual therapy. According to Indie, there's no judgment. If you choose one of the drugs available to help addicts, they offer it for free. Religion or no religion, the choice is yours. Indie says they don't believe in one size fits all. You know, Indie's working for a greenhouse. They helped her get that job."

"So, you're saying I should trust her?"

His mouth opens in a strange smile. He cocks his head then rubs a hand over his face. "All I am saying is that the center is a good place. We'll keep an eye on her and make sure your family is safe."

I give one quick nod. No one is around us, and we're far enough back from the range we can talk easily. The Arrow guys will ensure no one approaches behind us.

"You needed to meet?"

"Your boat is loaded and headed to Mexico."

"That fast?"

"Yep. Went out to sea last night. International waters. Three different boats docked to it and unloaded."

"Did you see where the boats originated?"

"Not through customs. These were fishing boats. But high end. Our current bet is they loaded at someone's private dock."

"Why not just load the boat directly?"

"We're thinking it's a precaution. Maybe whoever owns the docking facility wants to minimize risk. Our cameras on the back of the boat captured the boat names, and we're tracking down ownership."

"Any Sullivan employees?"

"Not that we've picked up on camera. But someone from your company loaded up those boxes and shipped them out."

"Yeah, but they didn't necessarily know where they were going. If the order came through as a wholesale order, with a delivery to a domestic address, there would be no reason for suspicion. From our end, the deal would look clean."

"We've got one guy in the crew. He says it's a full load. Silencers, assault rifles, bump stocks, grenade launchers. Mix of parts."

"Has he got any idea what's going to be returned?"

"Communication with him is limited, but he doesn't think the crew is the brains."

"I read in the news there's been a spate of violence between the cartels the last couple of weeks. You think that's why he's pushing this order?"

"It's conceivable. What other international locations do you sell to?"

"International is about thirty percent of our business. You know as well as I do that there are some countries we aren't supposed to sell to, so we sell to distributors who might sell to those countries." That's one thing I do for the CIA. I tell them who is unofficially buying the guns. But Ryan doesn't know that. No one knows that. I'm not looking to stop the sales. After all, if they don't buy our guns, they'll buy from someone else. But information has value, and I look at it as my national duty to share that information. If anyone from the NRA found out, they'd crucify me or, well, more precisely, Sullivan Arms. The NRA is a staunch believer in privacy and minimal oversight. "Why?"

"Just putting all the pieces together."

"You asked about the senator. I gave that some thought. He's wealthy in his own right. Other than supporting his donors, I don't think he'd be involved in this mess."

"There are records of him attending an elicit club. There are theories he might work to keep some photos or other information from coming out."

"He's divorced. Why would he care?"

"Well, there are rumors about him and underage girls. And boys."

"Because of the club in Houston?" He gives the slightest jerk of the head in confirmation. "That's ridiculous. I'm a member of that club. Rumors abound. Don't know if you've seen him recently, but he's an old man."

"Just communicating what I've heard."

"Yeah, and they also say Hillary ran a sex ring below a pizza shop."

"My sources aren't social media."

He's standing firm, even though I find it to be ridiculous. There must be a reason. "You think this all comes back to human trafficking?"

"We'll see what returns on your boat. My connections with your op suspect drugs. Border patrol is tightening. Small-time guys are still trying to get through in vehicles. But there are theories the major cartels have found other ways in. At least based on the volumes we're seeing stateside."

"Heroin?"

"Could be. But that's not the current big-ticket item. Fentanyl. Pills."

"DEA heavily involved?"

"To a limited capacity. Not sure if you read about it, but there was a spate of DEA officers caught aiding the smugglers."

I tug on my jaw, considering all of this. Drugs and guns. Intertwined in ways we don't like to think about. "How involved is Arrow in all this? Is the government using contractors?"

"You know they like to, sometimes."

Yes, I do. If laws are broken or things go haywire, better for minimal connection.

"We were just read in last week to a tangential UC op. But, man, I gotta tell you, there's no way more people aren't involved at your company. Probably within the government. We'll see what comes back, but running guns through high-end yachts...as you know, that's a well-funded operation. These aren't small-time players."

Ryan pulls his phone out of his pocket. He's wearing cargo pants and boots. With his shades on and his short sleeve button-down, he's the spitting image of a former military guy. There's something about the way his facial muscles freeze as he reads his phone that sets me on edge.

"It appears Ava didn't make it to Buena Vida this morning." He slides his phone into his back pocket and gestures to Fisher.

"What the—"

"She's been admitted to a hospital. She was in a car wreck."

The tree line fades. The gunshots merge into a void. My focus centers in on my reflection in Ryan's sunglasses.

"Is she—" My lungs contract. My mouth opens. Nothing comes out.

Cassie died in a car crash. What are the chances?

CHAPTER 26

JACK

Ava lies in a hospital bed on wheels with her eyes closed. The faded blue hospital gown pales her skin. A white plastic hospital bracelet rests on her wrist. Her stack of shiny bracelets is gone.

A tall, broad shouldered, well-dressed Black man sits in a chair beside her hospital bed. He looks up when the nurse rolls back the ER privacy curtain.

"Ms. Amara has another visitor," the nurse tells him.

He stands and holds out his hand. I sense from the way he's looking at me, he knows who I am. His grip on my hand is firm. "Patrick Smith."

"Ava's mentioned you. Jack Sullivan." Per my sources, this man is also my uncle's boyfriend. Secret boyfriend.

A hint of a smile plays across his lips. "Ava's mentioned you, too."

Again, this is something I know. She told him about our agreement. He returns to his seat by her head.

"How is she?" She's not on an IV. They haven't assigned her a room. These are good signs.

"She's lucky, is what she is." His gaze falls on her. "She didn't break anything. Doesn't seem to have any internal bleeding. She's going to be sore."

Bruising shows on her face, below her eyes and near her nose.

"Her car is totaled." I repeat the phrase that has been boomeranging in my head nonstop ever since Arrow relayed the information before we arrived. Police towed it from the scene.

"Yeah, but it doesn't take much for them to consider an old car like that totaled." Patrick's dismissive statement riles me. She could have been killed.

"You work with her?" I've seen his name before on information about the center. My uncle has been sending me Buena Vida's information for years. It's one of many nonprofits I donate to.

"I do," he says, leaning back in his chair. He fixes a steady gaze on me, like he's sizing me up. "She's my dearest friend."

I step to the end of her bed and drop my gaze to the light blue blanket covering her feet. The weight of his gaze confirms that he doesn't approve of our arrangement, or of me. I don't blame him.

Her eyelids flutter open, and her hand goes to her temple.

"Hey," Patrick says. "Head still hurt?"

"Not as bad." Those sad, brown eyes focus on me, and I take in the bloodshot quality. She could have died.

"When can I leave?" Her question is directed to Patrick.

"They want you to stay tonight for observation."

"No," she moans. "I don't want to stay here. I'm fine."

"You have a concussion," he says.

"You can come back to the house." Patrick and Ava look at me. I sense Fisher behind me.

"She needs to be under observation," Patrick says.

"I can have a nurse at the house before we get home. A doctor too, if we need one. There's no need for her to stay here for observation."

I hate hospitals. If she has to stay here, we'll find a hospital with a private suite available, but based on what I'm hearing, she needs rest. No one rests in a hospital.

"I want to go home," Ava says. She looks completely despondent.

"I don't think it's a good idea for you to be alone. You can come home with me," Patrick offers.

Ava closes her eyelids and turns her head away from Patrick. She doesn't want to come home with me. The realization reverberates within me. I can't blame her, given how I've treated her. I rub my sternum, seeking relief from the pang reverberating within.

"Where do you live?" I ask Patrick.

"Los Angeles." His chin juts out. "Malibu. Just moved from West Hollywood. She hasn't seen my new place."

Certainly a nice place to recover, but too far away.

"Your muscles must be sore." I lean closer to Ava and reach down and touch her wrist. "Stay with us. We can get you home quickly and with the least amount of discomfort."

Patrick's gaze meets mine. *Please don't fight me on this.* I will not accept any other scenario. I can't. I possess a visceral need to keep watch over her. I could have lost her. In one second, that wreck could have taken her. Patrick blinks and slowly nods. I think he reads me well.

"He's probably right," Patrick says to Ava.

"Won't you need to be at the center?" Ava's question sounds like a plea.

"I'll be back and forth. I have to be in LA two days from now." His gaze drifts to me. "Personal obligation."

"I have to plan the funeral." Ava plants her palm against her cheek.

"Funeral?" I ask.

"A resident at the center passed away last night," Patrick offers.

"He was more than a resident, and you know it." Ava moves her hand. A lone tear leaks out of the side of her right eye. Then another. And another. My chest throbs.

"He's being cremated. You have time," Patrick says.

Sophia mentioned Ava received bad news from the center. Someone she was close to died. I have been in a similar place. Only I didn't crash my car. But I had a daughter. I had no choice but to rise above it all.

I locate Fisher behind me, across the hall. I motion for him to join us.

"We will be leaving and transporting Ms. Amara back to my home. Can you check with a nurse and find out what we should do to transport her most comfortably?"

This is outside the scope of his responsibilities, but he nods. In addition to making her comfortable, he will ensure we are safe. I pull out my phone and send a text to my house manager.

Ms. Amara has been in an accident. She will recover at my San Diego property. Please arrange for a twenty-four-hour nurse to be in the house. Also, have a doctor on standby. Ask what kinds of foods a person recovering from an automobile accident should have and get Chef on it.

JANET - HOUSE

Yes, sir.

"Everything's ready. Are we waiting on papers for her to be released?"

Patrick stands and smooths down his pressed Armani dress shirt. I recognize his shirt because it's exactly like one my uncle gave me last year.

"I'll go see if I can find her doctor," Patrick says.

With him gone, I move to the head of Ava's bed. There's a silver guardrail along the edge of the bed, and I lean against it, peering down at her. I so much want to dry her tears.

"I'll be fine at home," she sniffs.

"There's no way in hell you are going back to your home."

Surprise flashes in those eyes. I've been reining in surging emotions because of the stranger next to her, but there's a war raging within me, and my mind struggles to quell the explosions. "You are coming back with me. I'll take care of you."

"Jack..."

"Do you have any idea how it felt to hear you were in a car accident? Do I need to remind you that my wife died in a car crash? That my first thought was that the same people who killed her went after you? Do you have any idea the hell I endured until I learned you survived?" She blinks, and I cover her icy hand with mine. "Let me take care of you."

There is no tenderness in my words because I am on the brink of losing control over a whirlwind of emotions I don't fully comprehend. There is no room for negotiation.

Hours later when we finally arrive at my house, my nerves are beyond frayed. Ava's exhausted, but the doctor explained it's an expected side effect from the pain medication they have given her.

I fling the car door open and scoop her up in my arms.

"I can walk." I ignore her and charge inside to the stairs.

One by one, I climb the stairs, my thighs burning as I reach the top. She rests her head against my chest, and as a true testament to her being slightly out of it, she doesn't notice where we are until I'm laying her down on my bed.

"What?" she asks, pushing up on one arm. I ignore her, go to the far side of the bed, pull back the covers, and return to move her.

"Why? Is this...?"

"My room. The entire floor is a suite. If a nurse needs to be nearby, she can stay in the small bedroom at the front of the house. I'll show you around tomorrow."

I press a button, and a mechanical whir sounds as the shades hidden in the ceiling fall, blocking the sun and the floor-to-ceiling view of the ocean. Low, dim lights cast a golden haze along the walls.

"If you want to listen to music, here's a control. There are sound machine options. Rain, waves, birds. Anything you want."

She rests back on the pillow and brushes her forehead. She's wearing a sweatshirt and sweatpants that Patrick purchased from the hotel gift shop. We tossed the clothes she wore earlier this morning. They were covered in glass and blood.

"I'll bring you some clothes. Do you have any requests?"

"For you to stop this. You are freaking me out." That's rich, given she freaked me out this morning.

"Are you hungry?"

"What is Sophia going to think of me staying here?"

I stare at her for a minute. I hadn't given that one second of thought. In a flash, the answer comes to me. "This is the best room in the house. She'll understand."

"The guest room downstairs is plenty nice."

"There's a soaking tub up here. You'll need that." I sigh. She needs to rest. "The tub downstairs isn't as easy for you to access. And the nurse will have private quarters. This is the best place for your recuperation. Food requests?"

She shakes her head, and her eyelids droop. She's tired, and so am I. As I exit the room, I tap a button to kill the auto movement lights.

"Jack?"

I pause. "Yes?"

"I know you feel this innate need to take care of Sophia, but you don't need to take care of me. I'm a big girl. I can take care of myself."

She's correct, of course. But my muscles tremble. My hands have been frozen all day. My eyes feel like someone is holding my eyelids stretched open. Taking charge is the only way I know to calm the inner turmoil. To find assurance that she is and will be okay.

The entire drive to the hospital, visions of Cassandra laid out on the stretcher flashed. She was dead on arrival, and they aren't particularly careful with dead bodies. I insisted on seeing her because I couldn't believe it. It was all too sudden.

I rest against the wall and breathe in deeply. This isn't about me. It's about Ava. She lost someone today.

"Who was he?" I shove my hands in my pockets. My eyes adjust to the darkness, and I can barely make out her shape beneath the comforter. "The person who died."

"My ex," she says. "Reid."

My fingers curl into my palms. "What happened?"

"He relapsed." She rolls on her side, her back to me. "Sometimes that happens. There's no rhyme or reason." He must have been staying at her facility. "He called me last night. But I didn't have my phone."

Dammit. She's going to feel so much guilt. That's something I know far too much about.

"How did Patrick learn you were at the hospital?"

"I called him." That's what I suspected. Dammit, Ava.

"You called Patrick, and not me?" For all she knew, I was down the street. He lives in Los Angeles.

"He's my..." Her voice becomes dimmer, and she mumbles the rest of her sentence, something about him being her closest friend. On one hand, controlled fury bubbles beneath the surface at her choice. On the other hand, I completely understand her reasoning. Regardless, rational reasons do not quell frustration and anger. But what I'm feeling doesn't matter. She suffered a concussion. Her body took a violent beating. She needs to rest.

"Go to sleep. We'll talk later."

CHAPTER 27

Ava

My eyesight slowly adjusts to the unfamiliar bedroom. A fan spins above, and the soft breeze cools my skin. My leg glides across silk sheets, and the twinge of muscular pain reminds me of the accident. My fault.

Thank god the person I hit is okay. Although he's probably feeling as sore as I am today. The sound of metal crunching and tires squealing is ever present, puncturing the quiet. A deep, heavy sadness reverberates through me.

Over the years, countless friends and connections have relapsed. Logically, my brain accepts relapses are a risk of addiction, and I am not at fault. I wasn't there. I wasn't in the room with him. And if I had been there to try to stop him, he would have found a way. That was Reid's journey. I need to be thankful that it has not been, as yet, my journey. There but for the grace of god go I... and all that.

But he was reaching out. I didn't answer his calls. I wasn't there when he needed me. Why? Self-preservation? God, that possibility sucks. But my inner therapist's voice consoles me. I've been through too much to do anything other than prioritize self-preservation. I loved Reid, but I love myself more. And that's okay. Choosing my mental health over Reid was the right choice. And being his crutch wasn't an option. Addiction doesn't work like that.

Telling myself that doesn't alleviate any of the down emotions. The sadness. The hopelessness. I thought I'd talked him through it. I thought I gave him the tools he needed. God, I was so wrong. So fucking wrong.

The bed I am in is enormous. Instead of two sets of pillows at the head, there are three sets. The middle pillow is untouched, but the far-left pillow, by the edge of the bed, is indented. Someone slept with me last night. Jack? A nurse?

I push my palms against the mattress, and my ribs contract as I rise. The pain elicits a moan, and I keel over. My head throbs. My body feels like a monster slammed it against a wall repeatedly. Or someone took his boot and kicked my ribcage over and over and then my face for good measure.

To my left, a small folding table sits with a silver tray. An entire beverage service including an orange juice carafe, water, silver containers with lids I would guess contain coffee, cream and sugar, and two blue pills are on a small silver circular dish. With a shaky hand, I lift the handwritten note.

Ava,

Text me when you wake. A nurse is outside the bedroom. You told the hospital you didn't need a pain prescription, but these pills are nonaddictive and will ease your discomfort.

There is a remote control on the bedside table. It controls the shades.

Jack

My thumb brushes over the handwritten note. So thoughtful. And kind. I set the note down and push off the bed. The moment I stand, a dim glow of lights along the perimeter of the room flick on. Motion-activated. Fancy.

When I return from the bathroom, I press a button, and all around the room, shades rise. I squint into the bright light. The ocean glistens under a mid-day sun.

Midday. Damn. The hospital must have given me something to sleep. I haven't had a bad experience with medication, but given my history, it's unnerving. Someone set up an entire beverage service while I slept. I must have been comatose.

A deep baritone reverberates through the cracked bedroom door. "Is she up yet?"

A woman's voice I don't recognize answers. "I believe so. I think I heard her moving around, but I've been giving her some time."

"Do they have you stationed out here?"

I can't hear the woman's response, but I move to the door to greet my friend.

"Patrick?"

"Hey, there she is." He reaches for me, his thumb lightly touching my cheek. "Whoa. Those black eyes have really set in."

"I look like I've been in the boxing ring," I joke, stating the obvious. My bruising pattern is strange, but I tried not to fixate on it when I went to the bathroom. Dark scabs pepper my forehead.

"Are you just getting up now?"

A middle-aged woman in scrubs comes to the doorway.

"I'm Felicity. I'm a registered nurse. I'm here should you need anything. How are you feeling?"

"Sore. But okay."

She looks me over, studying me. "Are you hungry?"

My stomach rumbles. "Yes."

"I'll go down and get you some breakfast."

"Oh, you don't need—"

"There's a chef awaiting my instructions." Felicity smiles. "I'll have him whip up something healthy and that will be okay on your stomach. Is there anything you don't like?"

"I'm not a picky eater."

"Great. I believe there's coffee and hot tea set up, but will the two of you need anything else?"

"You're a nurse, not a waitress." What the hell does Jack have her doing?

She smiles. "It's fine. He's paying me well. And besides, getting you fed is important. We'll see how you respond to eating. I think you're going to be absolutely fine, but it's probably a good idea to take the elevator today and not the stairs."

Patrick places his enormous hand on my shoulder and steers me back into the bedroom as he thanks Felicity and assures her he'll get me settled with coffee and water.

He moves me to a set of chairs that face the ocean, and I obediently sit.

"Patrick, this is insane."

He chuckles. "This is the way the Sullivans do things. This is their world. We're just in it. Enjoy it while you can."

He brings over two cups of coffee in dainty white porcelain cups and saucers. The warm coffee soothes my throat.

"You let them medicate me."

There's not an ounce of apology in Patrick's expression. "How are you feeling today?"

I'm sore as hell, both physically and mentally. But he can tell that by the fact I'm moving around like an octogenarian.

"Did the police file charges?"

Sometimes when people overdose, they could've been saved, and we stock Naloxone in all the units for that purpose. Sometimes, though, their friends are too high or too scared to help.

"You talking about you or the folks who just got kicked out?"

I frown over the rim of my coffee cup. I didn't think about me.

"You have a ticket for running a red light. What the hell were you thinking?" He shakes his head. "As for the others, not to my knowledge."

"Who was with him?"

Patrick shrugs. "Two women, and a man not in our program. I don't have much information."

I stare at my friend, trying to figure out if he really doesn't have much information or if this is some sort of protective thing. "Police will obviously try to figure out where the heroin came from. I don't think they had much on them."

Patrick tried to warn me about Reid. He told me he wasn't stable, and I shouldn't let him back into our center. I didn't listen. But Patrick's a good enough friend he won't state the obvious. Not today, when it's clear as hell this is all my fault. Reid's death, the others...the person at the intersection. *Fuck.*

We sit, sipping coffee from dainty saucers and watching the occasional bursts of white against the navy backdrop. I'm wearing a mauve satin pajama set that I definitely do not own but that mysteriously fits me perfectly, sipping coffee from fine china, while comfortably perched before an astounding, wide open ocean view. Low-level nausea stirs in my belly.

"Ava, you're up." Sophia's bright, cheerful tone has me turning too quickly, a sharp pain lights my neck, and I grimace.

"Patrick, can you set this table up in front of her?" Jack holds both a tray with a silver lid and a small folding table. Sophia also has her hands full with a serving tray.

"Guys, I'm not an invalid."

Sophia laughs. "Get used to it. Dad is all about taking care of those he cares about. Trust me. I had every meal in bed my first two weeks home."

She's smiling, but a dagger of guilt strikes when I think about the reasons she was under a physician's care. It's very different from my situation. She was innocent. I'm not. And, while all this is very sweet, it's completely unnecessary.

"There are egg whites and toast. Some fresh fruit. Sliced banana. I can get you anything else, but Felicity was aiming to take it easy on your stomach for this first meal."

He lifts the silver lid, and my mouth waters. God, I really am starving. Scrambled egg whites don't usually have an aroma, but sprinkled with salt and pepper and possibly an additional spice, they smell divine. I take a large bite and close my eyes, reveling in buttery goodness.

"I'll come back up to check on you later. Take it easy today. Felicity is going to check you over, but she thinks she won't be needed."

"She won't. I'm fine," I mumble through a mouthful of food.

Jack's expression softens. It's almost a smile. "I've got a meeting. I'll be back. Sophia, why don't you come in and visit with Ava after her friend Patrick leaves? Give them some time together."

"She can stay. I'm not gonna be here long. I'm heading back home today," Patrick says.

Sophia ignores Patrick and leans over me, giving me a hug. It's awkward because I'm holding a fork and there's basically a tray table in my lap.

"I'm glad you're okay." With her lips near my ear, she adds, "You scared us."

Jack stands at the doorway, holding the door, waiting for Sophia. My eyes must have widened into saucers, and his brow furrows, the way it does when he doesn't understand. He didn't hear her. But what she said doesn't really mean anything. She doesn't know anything. She just means they were all worried about me. I would never want to scare anyone, but a warmth blossoms knowing that someone did worry about me. And not just a single person.

Patrick, Sophia, and Jack. They all care.

Patrick has a wide smile, and he sits back holding his coffee with one pinky swung out, absolutely entertained.

As soon as the door closes, he says, "A financial arrangement, my ass."

I roll my eyes and continue shoving food into my face. After I've eaten, I have an overwhelming desire to shower and put on clean clothes that are my clothes and not something a grandmother would wear.

Patrick and I take the elevator to the main floor, and he steps out, hugging me goodbye and promising he'll call later. Then I continue down to the basement level and my bedroom, because riding a glass elevator with an ocean view is completely normal and standard procedure.

The guest bedroom has been cleaned and straightened. Not a single item is out of place. That's par for the course in this house. I push open the closet door and freeze. It's empty. Even my suitcase is missing.

I return to the elevator, my slippered feet gliding over smooth marble. On the main floor, I exit and head to Jack's office. He may be in a meeting, but he can press mute. I lightly rap on his office door, twisting the knob before he responds. He's in a meeting with two other men in suits. Jack rises and asks them to step out and give him a minute.

"Is everything okay?" He pulls the door closed, and his hands immediately fall to my shoulders.

"My clothes."

"What's wrong?"

"They aren't in my closet."

"You went downstairs?" He towers over me in my slippers, and it's as if he's lording over me.

"I took the elevator," I defend. "But where are—"

"I told you I was moving you upstairs."

"Into your room?" He's insane.

"It's safer. Don't fight me on this."

"Sophia will suspect something. I think she might already." I can't believe he's doing this. It's insane.

He blinks.

"We'll talk later." And with that, he opens his office door, ushers me out, invites the men in, and closes the door to hide inside.

CHAPTER 28

Jack

The obscured moonlight over the water carries an eerie quality tonight. The sand curls between my toes. On the corner of the stone wall bordering my property, a black video camera rotates. I flick my fingers in the direction, fairly certain someone is sitting in the security room watching. There's an earpiece in my ear. I don't need to hold the phone to my mouth, but as a precaution, I do. If anyone is nearby attempting to listen in, the device should muffle my words.

The wind whistles, and the palms sway and bend. The sand whipping my ankles burns.

"The boat's fully loaded in Mexico." Ryan's update is expected. But worry gnaws. My fear is this will be an observational operation. We'll learn from it, but this will not lead us to the source. Some undercover operations can last years.

"Same crew?"

"Mostly."

"Can you tell what the cargo is?"

"Drugs. Packages in plastic wrap. Could be heroin. Fentanyl.

Unless one breaks open, can't be certain. Some of it's packed in crates. There are clay statues too. I'd bet drugs are packed inside. Maybe they were originally packed to go through customs, and they got a ride on this alternate ship."

"DEA is aware?"

"All appropriate parties are in the loop."

"Is there a plan to bust them?" Coast Guard could approach them as soon as they hit US waters. But I could see how it would be helpful to observe their unloading procedure.

"Powers that be are currently debating the best approach."

Up at the house, the bedroom lights on the third floor flicker on. It's late. Sophia and Ava must have finished watching their television show.

"They might keep this operation going for a while," Ryan says.

I close my eyes and breathe in deeply. That's exactly what I don't want to hear.

"Jack, you there?"

"I don't mind if they take their time on the drug piece of this, but I need to get information on my end. I need a list of the involved parties from Sullivan Arms."

"You know, it's looking more and more like your family's company is a small piece in a much bigger chess game."

Fuck. "Any girls on the boat?"

"No."

"That's good." Human trafficking had been my fear because of how they treated Sophia.

"Just because they aren't on this boat doesn't mean it's not going on."

"I know. They'll be cautious with this shipment." It remains unnerving that Victor trusted I me.

"That's the reason the feds may let this shipment run its course. Build trust."

Right. I've been a CIA informant for over fifteen years, and sometimes I swear they collect information for the sake of filling a library. Nothing ever seems to happen. But then, sometimes, an order comes through and plenty happens. There's nothing more I can do.

"How's Indie?"

Ryan fills me in on his sister. She's living at the center, and she told him that a shadow had fallen over the entire complex since Reid's death. But Ryan believes the incident has helped fortify Indie's determination to remain clean. We disconnect, and I head inside.

I pause at Sophia's bedroom door on my way upstairs, but her shower is running, so I continue up the stairs.

A dark shadow passes outside. My hand falls to my waist and a phantom holster. It's been months, and I'm still not used to having a full security detail.

Upstairs, I pass through the suite. There's a library in the space where I relocated Ava's office. She seems to enjoy working from up here, although Sophia has now identified the library as one more room she needs to modernize. Decorating has never been my thing, but it's keeping Sophia's mind occupied, so I'll let her have at it.

The master suite has his and her bathroom and closet ensembles. The light pours from Ava's bathroom. I head into my bathroom and prepare for bed.

When I climb into the bed, Ava is lying back on a pillow. The bruises on her face are changing color, a deep purple immediately below one eye and a musty yellow on the perimeter. She's wearing an old threadbare gray t-shirt, even though there's a drawer full of silky chemises and nightgowns in her closet.

"Done with work?" she asks.

"Yeah."

"You work a lot." She rolls onto her side. Her palms are together, as if she's praying, resting on the pillow. Her bracelets clink from the movement, and a sliver of moonlight reflects off the silver. I reach over and toy with a charm hanging from one of the bracelets.

Her statement hits like an accusation, but cognitively I'm aware it's only because it's the old, rehashed argument between Cassandra and me. An argument that went on and on for years until she no longer cared enough to fight.

"Ryan and I were talking."

"He's a good friend of yours, isn't he?"

"He is." Of course, I'm probably one of his biggest clients and a silent investor in his firm, but he's one of the few in my life who I trust would be there for me even without the financial benefits.

"Do you go out there to talk to him so no one can hear?" My gaze flits from the ceiling to her and back to the ceiling. Cassandra would have assumed I was talking to a woman and using Ryan as cover. But Ava has a different perspective. "Who are you scared of?"

Now I roll onto my side and mirror her position with my hands. There's a pillow between us.

"Why am I here, Jack? Are you really so scared that you think the ground floor of your home, with a state-of-the-art security system and men patrolling the grounds, isn't safe?"

Why the hell do I have her here? It's a fair question, one I've avoided considering.

"I would have assumed it's for sex, but you haven't touched me in days."

"You're hurt. You were in an accident." Does she think I'm a monster?

"I know." Her lips curve up on the ends. She's not wearing any makeup at all, and as always, I'm struck by her raw beauty. Those enormous eyes are like a portal into a caring soul. She's seen the worst in humanity and she's dedicating her life to helping others climb out of hell. "And you've taken phenomenal care of me." She reaches across the bed, like she wants to touch me, but the distance between us is too great. "But I'm all right."

"You got lucky." Ryan's team sent me photos of her car. She's so damn lucky she walked away from that wreck. My throat tightens, and I force myself to swallow.

"But why am I here? In your bed?"

God, she probably thinks I'm some twisted, sick perv. And I suppose, maybe I am.

"Jack, just say it. Whatever you're thinking. Whatever you want. I'm only here for another week."

Christ. I close my eyes and exhale loudly. "I already told you. When you were in that wreck, I relived Cassie's death."

"And me... sleeping here... makes you feel like I'm safe."

It's not a question. She says it like she's completing my thought. I slowly nod and open my eyes, expecting to see judgment, like she thinks I'm being ridiculous. But there's none. Only warmth. Maybe fondness.

"Was Cassandra murdered?"

"Not officially."

"What does that mean?"

"The person who hit her car died. But his wife no longer lives in the US. And his medical records show he had terminal cancer."

"You've been following up on them?"

"After Sophia was abducted, I asked Ryan to look into the case again. She lives in Barbados with more money than a police officer would have earned from his life insurance."

"Ryan is working on tracing those funds?"

"He'll figure it out. It's a slow process."

She squirms, sliding closer on the silk sheets. This time, she reaches me, and she lightly caresses my cheek and along the ridge of my jaw. "My accident wasn't because of those people."

"I know. I watched the video from the intersection. Your accident was your fault."

Her nose scrunches. "You watched?" She shakes her head, and I can practically hear her telling herself I overreached. "But you still don't feel that it's not related." She taps my head. "Up here, you know it's not." She presses my sternum. "But here, that's not what you feel?"

"If I could, I would take you... and Sophia... and ship you off where no one could find you. Not until this is all over."

"Will it ever be over? Will you ever feel safe?"

I can't bear to look into her questioning eyes, so I close my eyelids. I swallow. "It's not about my safety." It's the people I care about. Hell, they could kill me tomorrow, and I wouldn't give a damn. Except Sophia needs me. She has one parent. And Ava... I can't explain why I feel so protective of her. Or drawn to her. From the moment I laid eyes on her, I wanted her. By anyone's standards, my plan for claiming her was unconventional. But I thought one month would be sufficient. More than sufficient.

"You can't be responsible for the whole world, Jack."

Oh, but I am. She can't understand. I can't tell her everything. The same way I couldn't tell Cassie.

Her palm flattens against my cheek, and she inches forward. My heartrate increases, beat by beat, as the frisson of energy courses between us. Her full, soft lips press against mine, and her nose brushes my nose, playfully. I reach beneath the covers for her hip and find smooth, bare skin and the coarse strip of what I assume is a thong. She's sore and bruised. This won't go anywhere but touching her feels right.

"Tell me about Reid." I had Ryan pull information on him. His rap sheet includes charges for possession of narcotics and dealing narcotics. He should've been in prison, but his family obtained an excellent lawyer. They also paid for multiple rehabilitation programs. What I don't understand is Ava's connection to him. "Is he the one who got you hooked on drugs?"

"No." She rests her head on the pillow beside mine. Her hands resume the praying pose, but I don't remove my hand from her. I crave her warmth. "We had friends in common. The wrong kinds of friends."

"Tell me your story, Ava."

"What do you mean?"

"I'm not perfect either, Ava. I've done awful things. You can open up to me, and I won't judge." My head sinks too deeply in the pillow, and I readjust. "I want to know how a girl from a middle-class family in a top twenty-five university ended up addicted to heroin."

"Someone's done some research." She smiles at me. And god, I want to kiss her, but my need to understand is greater than anything physical. Her smile disappears and her eyes glaze over. "I wish I could say that someone other than me is responsible. Or, you know, sometimes you meet people who were abused or had shitty childhoods or something where you just totally get why they needed an escape. But that wasn't me." Her long eyelashes flutter once, twice, and then her lips curl ever so slightly. It's a sad expression, but the kind of sad that has worn its place into her soul and she's adjusted to it. She's moved on. What she's sharing is something she has accepted. "No, my motto was 'born to be wild.' Rage against the machine. Try it all. Live and let die. My friends...the ones I clung to freshman year... they were similar. I didn't really set out to try heroin, but the first time they offered it, I was some combination of drunk and stoned. I figured sure. Why not?" This time, when those eyes look up at me, they are glassy, and her bottom lip quivers. "I did awful things."

"Me too."

Her head tilts, and it's clear she doesn't understand. But whatever she has done, it's not as bad as what I've done. What I do. What I will do. Maybe that's the answer. My inexplicable attraction to her. She and I have both made regrettable choices.

"Your uncle loves you. Whatever choices you made, he still loves you."

"Does your family?"

The slow shake of her head combined with the way her upper teeth sink into her lower lip tell me all I need to know.

"Patrick is my family now. And, well, I suppose your uncle is my extended family."

Uncle Mark and Patrick. Secret lovers. "Patrick is Uncle Mark's partner...or boyfriend."

"You know?" she asks.

I smile at her surprise.

"Pieced it together recently. Patrick was an addict too?"

"He was. Your uncle saved us both. Paid for our rehab."

And given what my uncle told me about Ava, that's probably one reason he keeps Patrick a secret. What won't look good for the CEO of a company doesn't look good for the chairman of the board either.

"Did you ever do fentanyl?"

"No. Back then, it wasn't common. Good thing, because I probably would have died. Why?"

"Just curious. Do you come in contact with many fentanyl addicts?"

Her brow wrinkles in thought. "Not too many. But, you understand, fentanyl can be laced in anything. Heroin, for example. It's scary because it's so easy to overdose. Why?" She reaches out and touches my arm. "I don't think Sophia–"

"I know. It's something else."

"Something else you're working on?"

I want to tell her everything. Explain what's going on. The secrets we keep weigh heavily. Hell, mine destroyed my marriage. And why? For what purpose? I let out a sigh and rub my eyes.

"What awful things have you done?"

I open my eyes and study the woman inches from me.

"They can't be nearly as awful as you think, Jack. Getting it off your chest, sharing with someone who you know has done worse, who won't judge, as you said, can be a relief. Whatever it is still haunts you."

I roll onto my back and stare at the ceiling. "If I tell you, it could put you in danger." It's why I never told Cassie. I just never realized what conclusions she would draw on her own. The human imagination, when crossed with insecurity, can do significant damage.

"I won't tell anyone. You can trust me." The tips of her fingers caress the stubble along my jaw, and I lean into her touch. "Getting it off your chest helps in ways you can't even imagine. I promise, you will get no judgment from me."

Is that the real reason I never told my wife? Because I feared her judgment? Maybe so. She hated violence. She wouldn't have understood.

I let out a sigh and throw caution aside. "I'm not active in the group now, but when I was younger, in my late twenties and early thirties, I did things. For an organization." There's no need to tell her who. "I was perfect for the role. An American businessman from a prominent family. Well known in any country I entered. But I'm also a skilled sniper. Among the best."

"Did you do it for money?"

I look into eyes completely free of judgment, but she blinks and it's almost as if she's scolding herself. "I mean, sorry. How did it make you feel?"

If visions of my victims didn't weigh me down, I'd laugh at her attempting to play therapist. "I did it for our country. I took out dangerous individuals. People who could do great harm." Or so I was told. God, I hope the intel was accurate.

"I should have never asked if you did it for money. You don't need money, and you wouldn't kill for it. You are too good of a man. That's why it weighs so heavily on you. You are a good person. And even if someone told you it needed to be done, those deaths weigh on you. I'm glad you told me. You shouldn't have to shoulder that alone. And it doesn't make you less of a man. You are still a good person."

My eyes burn, and I close them. My chest burns and my throat clenches. "I lied to Cassandra. About what I was doing. Sometimes. That's how she... why she decided I was cheating. I'd go on extended trips. Traveled all the time. I could have told her the truth, but I didn't. Maybe I didn't trust her to forgive me."

"She loved you. She would have still loved you, had she known."

"No." I shake my head. "She loved peace. She didn't want..." She didn't even let me have guns in the house. The CEO of a gun manufacturer didn't have guns in his house. "Every time there was a mass shooting, she would ask me if my guns were used."

"That's not fair. You can't be held responsible for what someone does with your product."

"Legally, that's true. Doesn't mean it doesn't weigh on me. Sad thing is, it weighed on me more when I first started in this industry. Now, I hear about a mass shooting, and I just..." What do I do? Wait to see if I get an alert from our PR department.

"You are a beautiful person with a beautiful heart. A heart so big and so full that you care for everyone in your life. You protect them and love them in all the ways you know how. And your family business is something you were born into. Cassandra might not have liked it, but she had to have understood. I think you could have told her everything, and she would have still loved you. You're a difficult man not to love."

I press my lips to the top of her hand, directly above all her stacked bracelets. She's the one with a strong, gorgeous heart. I've treated her like a prostitute, and yet she's cared for my daughter and is lying here caring for me. I held money over her head for sex and admitted I am a killer, and those enormous eyes are filled with warm emotion.

"You of all people should hate me."

"No. I don't. And I also don't believe in 'shoulds' and emotions. Emotions do not depend on logic. Emotions come from within, and our task is to understand them. I promise you, there is no hate in my heart." Her tongue licks her lower lip, and the moonlight reflects on watery eyes. "Not for you."

She scoots closer to me, and her fingers travel down my chest. Her light touch awakens every fiber, and as she travels lower, I warn, "Ava. You're injured."

"I'm not that injured." She dips below my waistband, and I tip my head back, swallowing a moan as her fingers wrap around my erection.

"Lie on your back," she whispers.

I do as she asks, and she gets onto her knees and tugs on my pajama pants, moving the comforter down as she removes my clothes.

We shouldn't be doing this, but her tongue licks up my shaft and circles my tip. Those big, dark eyes watch me closely as her mouth takes me. It's so fucking erotic I almost lose control right there. The warmth, the suction, the intimacy.

Her mouth eradicates thought. Her sensual tongue renders bliss. But my principles fight for the forefront. I should give her this. I should worship her.

"Get on your back," I force out. "Let me do this for you."

With a pop, her mouth abandons my strained erection. Her swollen lips glisten as she rises and lifts the hem of her nightgown over her head. The pale skin on her full breasts glows in the moonlight. Mesmerized, I watch as she positions her core over me, sandwiching my cock between her folds, and glides back and forth. It's the sexiest movement I've ever seen in my life.

She pauses and reaches between us, positioning my tip just right, and ever so slowly, she takes me. Careful not to hurt her, I let her lead, let her sink down over me.

"God, you feel good, Ava. So good."

The tips of her fingers press against my chest. Her head tips back. Emotions overflow. I want this. I want her. Every day. Every night.

Her hips undulate, and she angles her body, positioning herself so with each thrust of her hips, my pelvis rubs her sensitive spot. She uses my body like she would a toy. And I will always let her use me. Any way she wants.

I am hers.

CHAPTER 29

Ava

"Will Dad be home for dinner?" Sophia enters my makeshift office and pulls me away from an email from Reid's mother. She has requested his remains and plans to hold a memorial service back in Ohio. I emailed almost a week ago, and when I heard nothing, had begun preparations for a service here. But the email Reid had for his mother is one she doesn't use often. They fell out of touch. Addiction rips relationships to shreds.

The people too. Logically, I know I am not responsible for Reid's death. But reason and emotion do not align. Not with this. I didn't return his calls. I wasn't there to watch over him.

"Ava?" Sophia's question pulls me back to the room.

"Yeah. Sorry. He said he would. He'll probably be back after his lunch meeting."

She smiles, and her wavy, loose skirt bounces as she flaunts to the sofa. She pulls her legs up under her and places a throw pillow in her lap.

I barely saw him this morning. He woke before the sun rose for a vigorous workout, then showered and jumped on calls with the East Coast and who knows where else around the world, all before my brain had processed daylight. I wish I'd thought to ask him what exactly he wanted me to say to his daughter about us, if anything, because the way she's staring at me right now has me feeling uneasy.

"Are you and my dad seeing each other?" All my inner working stop functioning. "You know, he was really sad after he and mom divorced." That must have been so hard on her, because I'd bet money she observed Jack closely, and he didn't communicate with her at all.

"What was that like for you?"

She rolls her eyes at me and shakes her head like I'm the child and she's the parent. "You can't stop being a therapist, can you?"

I shrug. "I'm genuinely interested in hearing what it was like for you. My parents are still married but fought like crazy, and I hated it. What goes on impacts the kids, whether the parents want it to or not."

She falls back against the sofa, and her blue, childlike eyes judge me. I sit straighter, hoping I pass whatever mental litmus test she's conducting.

"My parents fought too. I think it's better they got divorced. They cheated on each other. It was a mess." She scrunches her lips and looks at me with guarded caution, like she's not sure she should have shared.

"That sucks."

"Are you going to think less of my dad because he cheated on my mom?"

"Honey, I am not one to judge. Ever." She gives a slight nod. "How did you find out?"

"What?"

"About your parents. Cheating on each other," I clarify. My guess is that the experience could not have been pleasant.

"I overheard my mom telling a friend on the phone. I think she was talking to Aunt Alex about it."

"Alex? Ryan's wife?" She nods again. "Relationships can be complicated."

Sophia sucks on her lower lip, processing my statement. She swallows, and when her gaze lifts, it's clear she's decided it doesn't matter. "I think whoever she was talking to was angry at her. And she was defensive. She said he had cheated on her for years." She rests her head on the back of the sofa and closes her eyes. "I saw her kiss Wayne. Once. That's why I was listening in on her phone conversation."

"Have you ever told anyone? About your parents cheating."

"No," she answers immediately.

"Why?"

"Because it wouldn't look right. People would judge. And gossip."

"Did your mother not like gossip?"

"She hated it." She raises her gaze to me. "Don't you?"

"Everyone hates gossip, I suppose. But it's important to realize that sometimes we need to talk about things. Get things off our chest, you know? There's research that shows that talking about our emotions helps. Things can get bottled up, and they hurt when they are locked inside us, like a million knives, you know?"

"Or weighted stones."

"Right. There's no wrong feeling. Talking about those feelings... it's some of the best therapy there is."

"Which is why you're a therapist?"

"Well, I'm not really a practicing therapist." She squints. "I don't think I'm the best at it. My preference is to help others by providing them a safe and productive environment to transition back to the real world." I think of Reid, and one of those heavy weights Sophia mentioned bores into me. "When someone is in a bad place, it sucks." My eyes glisten as the truth of my words circulates. "But then there's the recovery. And that sucks because, you know, there are all kinds of emotions and cravings and regrets and wishes, and they steamroll, and you have to figure out how to deal with all of that blending and mixing and hurting." My hands roll together, visually playing it out.

"And then there's the transition back to real life. That's hard because you run into people who have expectations, and you don't know what they know about what you've been through, and you don't know if they're judging or what they are thinking about you, and the reality is a lot of the times they probably aren't even thinking about you at all, but you don't know that. And transitioning back is like starting over. Yeah, you might know how to walk and eat, but there's a lot of other stuff to learn all over again."

I look at Sophia, knowing she's been putting off her transition, and I remind myself her transition will be a very different experience from mine. "Transitions are tough. No matter what or who or why. It's a day-by-day, and sometimes hour-by-hour kind of thing. And I prefer to help people navigate the transition."

"But not with therapy?"

"Sometimes with therapy. But for those coming out of rehabilitation, there are some basic needs that really need to be met. A safe place to live, food."

"The basics in Maslow's hierarchy." She uses the pillow in her lap like a drum. "We learned about it in school."

"Exactly."

"Before I met you, when Dad told me about you, he said you'd been through trauma." Those blue eyes glisten in the hazy morning light. "That you'd been raped too."

That's something that's not exactly on my resume. I've never known what Mark told his nephew that made him willing to introduce me to his daughter. But none of that matters.

"I have been."

"What was that like?"

Jesus, Sophia, what was it like for you?

"Honestly, I don't remember a lot. At the time, I was addicted to heroin. I needed heroin so badly I would do anything for it, and I put myself in precarious situations." I had sex for drugs and money, but those are things Sophia doesn't need to know. "When I was strung out, like really strung out, a group of men raped me. I only remember little snippets. I might not know at all, except they also beat me, and I ended up in the hospital."

"That's like me."

I almost miss what she said, she's speaking so low. I get up and join her on the couch.

"Not the craving. Not that." She blinks, and there's a faraway look. "But I just see little flash frames. Like photographs of it happening. It's blurry, and the edges of the photo are dark."

"You were high when they raped you?" I place my hand over hers where she's gripping her knees to her body. "It's probably a good thing. You don't have to—"

"How is that a good thing? I don't remember all the men...or their faces." She looks at me like I've lost my mind. "I don't even remember losing my virginity." Her lips quiver, and tears spill over and pour down her cheeks.

"Oh, honey. You're still a virgin."

"Don't..." She looks up at me with a mix of anger and sadness that tears at me. "Don't lie."

"What is a virgin, Sophia? A woman with a bit of skin that hasn't been broken? Do you realize how many women rupture their hymen with tampons years before they have sex? Or while riding a horse, or hell, doing anything? The way I define virginity is when a woman willingly chooses to have sex with someone else. You didn't willingly have sex with those men."

Jesus. Men? *How many men Sophia?*

"They removed the choice from your hands. And when you choose to have sex with someone, it will be meaningful for both of you. And you will remember it. They didn't take that away."

She buries her head in the pillow, and her shoulders shake. I wrap my arm around her and wait. Moments pass, and her shoulders still. She lifts her head and sniffles.

"Lauren's coming over today."

That's fantastic. She's refused to see any of her friends. But I merely squeeze her shoulder and wait. She has more to unload.

"She's going to know I'm not a virgin. And she's going to ask me what sex is like."

"Oh, honey. You know, you don't have to tell her anything you don't want to."

"We tell each other everything."

"But I honestly can't imagine she will ask that. I would expect her to just be happy to see you again." Her tearful eyes tell me I am naïve. "But if she asks, a perfectly acceptable answer is that you aren't ready to talk about it, or that you don't want to talk about it."

"Not with Lauren."

There are a number of ways I could deal with this, but I sit back, giving her space.

"At school, before the end of last year, there were two girls who had sex. Everyone knew. I mean, every single student knew. Within like a week. And now, everyone knows I had sex."

Shit. She's right. The news coverage didn't shy away from covering the facts. And when her accused rapist was killed in prison, they rehashed everything.

"Everyone knows you were abducted and horrible things happened. There's a difference."

She leans her head back on the sofa and places her palms over her face. "I liked it."

I lean forward again, straining to hear her.

"I liked it. You're not supposed to like being raped."

"Honey, you mean what they did felt good?"

Her lips scrunch together, and she curls over her knees, crossing her arms and burying her face against them.

"Honey, it might have been them, it might have been the drugs. Heroin loosens your inhibitions. And women, well, we're equipped with body parts that enjoy stimulation. But, honey, Sophia, I can't stress this enough. Your body reacted in one way. But it was still rape. They violated you. And there is no reason to feel guilty for how your body responded."

"You said no emotion is wrong."

"And that's true. Guilt is probably a very natural and understandable emotion. But that doesn't mean you deserve to feel guilty. Now, what happened to me? One could argue I made choices that put me in a dangerous place. One could argue I even deserved what happened to me. Some would argue that, but some would argue I am not at fault. But let me tell you, Sophia. In no rational world was your abduction or rape your fault. None of it. Sick men injected you with drugs. Horrible men raped you against your will. None of that was your fault."

"I hate them." She raises her tear-streaked face.

"I hate them, too."

And Jesus, it all becomes clear. She's afraid of telling her friends she remembers it felt good. The thing is, it was probably the drugs more than the sick bastard fucking her.

By the end of our session, she's pulled herself together. I think she's prepared to tell her best friend she doesn't want to talk about it, but I still can't imagine her friend will ask. But I can't convince her of that. Sometimes we build up others' reactions in our minds, and the only solution is to face the fear.

She pauses at the doorway before leaving. "You never answered my question."

"Which question?" My eyes sting from the emotion that welled up while holding Sophia, wishing so much that I could take her pain away.

"Are you and my dad seeing each other?"

My head shakes back and forth and my lips scrunch together. I don't have an answer. I should. This is my fault. I should have discussed this with Jack.

She nods and heads down the hall. I close my eyelids, knowing deep down that I just fucked up. So, I call my best friend.

"Hey, you. Back in la-la land?" Patrick chuckles, and that familiar, deep, rhythmic sound lightens the weight against my chest.

"So, Sophia suspects...or hell, she knows something is going on with her dad and me."

"How're you feeling about that?"

"Not too happy. She's got so much shit going on, and she's dealing with so fucking much. This whole situation is so fucked up."

"There's a lot fucking wrong with that fucking shit." He's joking.

"I'm not joking," I blurt.

"Your abundant use of expletives makes that abundantly clear. Look, I don't know what to tell you. Dating a Sullivan is some fucked up shit. My recommendation is that you complete your contract, return home, live your life, and do your damnedest to forget about all of them."

That response doesn't sound like Patrick at all. "What's going on?"

"Just another day in la- la land."

Shit. We've been down this path before. "Patrick. What did Mark do?"

"Oh. He didn't do anything. Unless you count choosing to go through chemotherapy in Houston, away from his life partner. Because, you know, god forbid one of those self-righteous right-wing nut jobs see him with a Black gay man."

"Mark has cancer?"

"He does. And he's... he won't even let me get near him as a friend. Even though he has straight men around him all the time. Says everyone will know."

"That's not fair. I wouldn't know you're gay just from looking at you."

"Bullshit." He sounds so resigned. And broken. What a fucking day.

"Fine. I'd suspect you might be gay. But only because of your muscles and because you dress... you know."

"I dress to show off the goods. You can say it. It's fine. But I know how to tone it down."

"Does Jack know?"

"Mark doesn't want anyone to worry. Planning to keep it private. He's such a stubborn motherfucker."

"Should I tell Jack? I think he'd want to know."

"Sure. Tell him. I don't like the idea of Mark going through chemo alone. No one should."

"Jack knows about you and Mark."

There's a long pause.

"And?"

"He's fine with it."

"See? This is what I'm talking about. The people he cares about won't give a damn that he's gay."

I think about Sophia and the fear she's built up in her head. For very different reasons, admittedly, but fear is fear. And it's all kinds of powerful.

"Patrick?"

"Hmmm?"

"I love you."

"Love you, too, sweetie pie."

"I'm gonna tell Jack."

"Mark's gonna be madder than hell at me. But yeah, you tell him. His family needs to know. He's stage two liver. His outlook isn't horrible, but his family should be there for him."

CHAPTER 30

Jack

PATRICIA JONES

Pahjeev asked to move the conference call to 9 tonight. Normally, I wouldn't ask you, but I think his assistant messed up when she agreed to 6.

I rub my eyes and let the frustration roll off me. This is a call I want to be on. The CIA will want me to be on this call. Exhaustion rolls off me in waves, as does frustration. I've been up since five. A nonstop day of back-to-back meetings.

This call won't actually happen at nine. Our India counterparts, like those from several other countries, have a different view on meeting start times. When you're in person, it's less noticeable as there can be snacks and small talk. When you're waiting online, especially when it's late at night or early in the morning, it is infuriating.

. . .

Reschedule for another day.

I think about Pahjeev. He won't be pleased. He's considering spending a considerable amount with us. In industry speak, this deal will move a lot of iron.

Tell him I have a prior family commitment.

PATRICIA JONES

Will do.

After I shut everything down, I close the door and check my watch. Six p.m. It feels like I'm working a half day. I promised myself I wouldn't fall into the work trench again. Sophia needs me, and she is my highest priority. She is my reason.

I need to root out the corruption in our family company. And do what I can to keep her world safe. Especially since I failed so massively with her mother. But after Cassandra's death, I stood at her grave and promised I would be there for Sophia, and that requires being present.

Sophia's laughter floats down the hall, through the kitchen. I stop near the foyer, blinking to confirm what I see. There's a young girl in the kitchen with Sophia. They are rolling out dough. Flour is everywhere, on the counter and the floor, and there's a smudge on the tip of Sophia's nose.

"Oh, hey, Dad," Sophia says. Her friend turns, and I recognize her.

"Lauren, it's good to see you."

"You too, Mr. Sullivan."

"Dad, Lauren and I are making homemade pizzas. You want some?"

"Um, sure."

"It'll probably be about thirty minutes—"

"Or more," Lauren butts in. "We keep messing up."

"I'm pretty sure Chef has balls of dough in the fridge."

"Those are our back-up. We want to try this recipe we saw on TikTok. Oh, and Lauren's going to stay over tonight. Is that okay?"

"Absolutely." My chest lightens. Sophia acting like herself, with a friend, has the same effect of a dose of pure oxygen. I've been holding my breath, wanting her to return to normal, and it's finally happening.

"Dad, we'll call you when it's ready." And that's my cue that my presence isn't wanted. Another piece of normalcy. *Thank god.*

"Okay. You two have fun."

I pause, just taking it in. Their heads bent, whispering. Their smiles. The familiar outfits of flip-flops, shorts and oversized sweatshirts are the same they've worn every summer since she moved in with me.

"Dad." Sophia's eyes bulge. She swooshes me with her hand, gesturing for me to go.

I obediently head to the stairs that will take me down and outside, in search of Ava.

When I find her, she is curled up on a lounge chair by the pool with a light throw over her legs and a phone in her hand.

"What're you doing?" I ask as I approach her.

She's got sunglasses on, but they are pushed up on her head, and they've captured the bulk of her bangs, effectively pulling them off her face. Her fading bruises aren't quite as jarring in the evening sun, which is another good thing to see. She's recovering too.

"Reading. You're done with work early."

"Yeah." I gesture to the house. "Got kicked out so I came to find you."

I sit down on the lounge chair closest to Ava and rest my arms on my legs. She lowers her sunglasses and sets her phone down. I haven't seen her all day, and without a second thought, I lean forward and press my lips to hers, then return to my seat.

"Up there... that was pretty amazing to see."

"It's a good step forward."

"Uncle Mark was right. You're a miracle worker."

"Not really." She plays with one of the charms dangling on her wrist, rubbing her finger over it, back and forth.

"There's no room for debate. You've been here less than a month, and... she's back."

"Jack." Her tone is serious, and she sits up, letting her feet fall to the ground. "It's good, yes, that she's reached out to a friend." She holds up her index finger. "One friend. But she's still got a lot to work through."

"Yes, but you did this."

"No." She shakes her head solemnly. "She did this. And she's still got a lot more to work through. Trauma is tricky like that. When I go, she's going to need to see a therapist. A real therapist."

I don't disagree with what she's saying about Sophia needing a therapist, but what I get stuck on is our deadline. This coming weekend technically marks the end of our arrangement.

"I've been wanting to talk to you about that."

"Jack, therapy will not hurt her. It will help her heal."

I hold up my palm, stopping her. "I agree. That's not..." I brush my fingers through my hair and glance up at the house. "I still want to see you. And not because we have a financial arrangement, but because I want to see you."

I can't imagine not seeing her. The need to have her in my life is visceral, and that need arose out of nowhere, but it's there and it's undeniable.

Her unpolished toes wriggle back and forth. She's got silver rings on two small toes, and the silver glistens in the light. She's not saying anything. If she doesn't want to see me, if it was always just about the agreement, then now's as good of a time as any to learn that. I raise my gaze.

She lifts her sunglasses onto her head and reaches for my hand. This could be a therapist's way of breaking bad news.

"How would that work, exactly? I can't live here."

"Why not?"

"Jack. Come on. I have a business. People depend on that business."

"You've been doing fine handling everything remotely."

"Jack." She says my name similarly to how Sophia says Dad. "I'd like to keep seeing you."

Relief overwhelms me, and I reach for her, scooping her up and setting her on my lap. Her arm wraps around my shoulders. She's sitting taller than me now, and I rest my head below her chin, just needing to be near her.

"So, it's not just sex?"

I can't blame her for thinking that. But it's... "Ava, it's not just sex. When you first walked into our house, I wanted you."

"That's just sex."

"I'm drawn to you. But yes, seeing you with my daughter, opening up to you, having you in my life... it's not just sex." I can count on one hand the people who are close to me, and in less than a month, she finagled her way onto the top of my list. Last night, I told her things I never shared with my wife.

"Sophia can see us." She squirms to get up off my lap, and I clasp my arms around her.

"So?"

Her heartbeat thuds beneath my ear, and my grip around her tightens, breathing in her scent. We'll figure it out. I want her in my life, and with my schedule and Sophia at home, that would be a hell of a lot easier if she lives with me. But I get I need to earn that. And maybe we both need to back it up and take things slowly to be sure of our relationship.

The last person I wanted around me all the time, in my bed at night and in the morning, was Cassandra. In hindsight, I bulldozed her into doing what I wanted. There were too many unsaid things between Cassandra and me, but intuitively I know many of our issues stemmed from me preventing Cassandra from growing on her own. And perhaps I wasn't mature enough to address our issues.

Ava's fingers trace my jaw, and I lean into her touch, lifting her palm to my lips and pressing against her skin. Her touch does wonders for me. She soothes the jagged edges in my chest. As if I needed another sign that I've got it bad for her.

"What exactly did you tell Sophia about us?" There's an edge to her question.

I release her hand and try to remember. I was more or less in a crazed state after the accident. Another car accident just hit... too close.

"I didn't, really. She just knows. She's a smart kid."

"You didn't talk to her?"

"No. It's not her business." I pause and take in those addictive eyes. "But if you want me to talk to her, I will."

"She asked me if we were together, and I denied it. I didn't know what to say. That's not good. We need to be on the same page about what we are and what we tell her."

I shrug. What does it matter? She's not upset about it. She's happy with her friend right now.

"We're dating. Right?" I look to Ava for clarification. It's not what I wanted when this started. But it's what I want now, and it feels like what we're doing. What we're talking about doing.

"I'd like to date you. But Sophia deserves for us to discuss this with her. To explain. Maybe not everything, but she deserves to be treated like the young adult she is. I know you want to see her as a kid, but she's transitioning. And you help her do that by treating her with the respect she deserves."

"Okay. That makes sense. Maybe tomorrow, after Lauren leaves, we can talk to her? Together?" I stretch and place my lips on her lower jaw.

This feels like our first relationship discussion. And I like it. We're not yelling. It feels mature. Maybe that's something I didn't have in my first marriage either.

Ava squirms, situating herself so she can look at me directly. I brace. Maybe my perception is off.

"I spoke to Patrick earlier today."

"How's he doing?"

"He's..." She tilts her head, and her eyebrows angle over her nose, like she's thinking. "Your uncle has cancer. Patrick's worried."

"Are you sure?"

"Yes. He's doing chemo at home." She exhales, and she does it in a way that exudes frustration. "In Houston."

"Where else would he be?"

"Los Angeles. With Patrick." She says it like it's obvious. My uncle has never opened up to me about his sexuality. When Arrow confirmed what I suppose I'd always suspected, I chose to go along pretending. If he wants to keep that part of his life private, that's his business. He's so fixated on what others think that I doubt I could change his mind. But he shouldn't be alone.

My brother lives near Houston, but he doesn't see Mark often. He's also in the throes of a nasty divorce, and between his notorious son and the explosion of his marriage, he's overwhelmed.

"I'll go visit him."

"You will?" There's hope in her tone, a sincere caring that has me pulling her back against me.

"Yeah. I will. The company jet can take me out tomorrow." I'll surprise him. Take him off guard and see how much he's willing to share. "He should know he's not alone."

Her phone rings, and Patrick's face shines in the circle on the screen. She gets off my lap, and I move to head inside.

"I'll go check on the girls. See if they need any help. Make sure nothing's burning."

She smiles, letting me know she heard me while she talks with Patrick, and I head inside, giving a quick nod to one of the security men traversing the perimeter of the yard.

I enter the house through the basement level and approach the bar, ready to pour myself a glass of bourbon. But I pause, second-guessing myself. Should I be drinking in front of Ava? It hasn't seemed to cause her any problems, but is it inconsiderate? I should probably have another conversation with her about it.

"Dad." Sophia's voice surprises me, and my gaze meets her in the mirror over the bar.

"Sophia, what's wrong?" Her cheeks are flushed, and her eyes are glossy. "Is Lauren–"

"You are with Ava." Her expression is difficult to read.

"Well, yes, you know that."

"No, Dad, I didn't know that. I suspected it, and I asked you."

"Sophia..." I hold my hands out, trying to think through my conversations with her. "You acted like you knew."

"Lauren asked me if something was going on with you two, and I told her no. I believed you. I believed Ava."

She lets out a loud sigh mixed with anger and disappointment. Just like her mother. An overwhelming wave of exhaustion pours over me.

She charges up the stairs, and the way she does it, hands balled in fists, energy pumping through each thigh, is so much like Cassandra that it takes me seconds to gather myself.

"Wait, Sophia."

"No, Dad. Just..." She pauses halfway up the flight of stairs. "I'd like to eat alone with Lauren tonight. Just...I can't believe you."

I launch onto the stairs, rushing to catch up to her.

"Dad." She pounds up the stairs. "Stay."

Her flip-flops clap against the marble, the sound growing fainter as she moves farther away. Jesus, how did I screw this one up?

CHAPTER 31

Jack

My uncle's penthouse offers sweeping views of Houston and across the Gulf of Mexico. Over the years, I've only been here a handful of times. He has another traditional home outside of Houston, but I don't think he visits that property often.

I decided to go ahead and fly out. My logic was that maybe with some time and space Sophia would calm down. When I return, I'll talk to her. Then Ava and I will talk to her together. I don't get where the anger is coming from, but with space, she'll calm down and accept it. She likes Ava. It shouldn't be an issue.

The doorman downstairs greets me like he knows me. He addresses me by name and doesn't pick up the phone to announce me until after directing me to the penthouse elevator. A male nurse with thick, short, black hair meets me in the foyer. He wears scrubs and black orthopedic looking tennis shoes and a gold chain necklace that glints in the light.

"Good morning, Jack. Let me go see if Mark is ready for you."

"Thank you."

He slips behind two imposing dark walnut doors. He must have been the one who answered the doorman's call.

A low classical melody plays through the foyer. Uncle Mark loves both classical and jazz, but classical music in the home strikes me as formal, even for someone like Mark Sullivan.

The door cracks open, and the nurse slips out.

"You can go in now. If you wouldn't mind, please slip off your shoes? We're keeping his room as sterile as possible."

"Of course." He turns to go. "Ah, is he going to be okay?"

"We are optimistic regarding his treatment plan." That is meaningless to me. "We caught the cancer early."

I narrow my eyes and stand taller. "Is that what he told you to say to me?"

The nurse smiles, and I get the sense I amuse him. He never gave me his name, but he knows who I am. He crosses his arms and stands with his legs spread in a defiant stance.

"Today's not a particularly good day for a visit. But since you're here, he's agreed to see you. He finished a chemo round earlier this morning. At this moment, he's well on his way to getting good and stoned. If you want to have a coherent conversation with him, you should go in now."

Right. I toe off my shoes and twist the knob. I can feel the man's gaze on my back and glance over my shoulder. His arms remain crossed, and he looks like he has something to say.

"Is there something else?"

"No. I'll be right out here if you need me."

The plush maroon carpet in the bedroom fits snugly beneath the door. Heavy drapes block most of the sunlight, leaving only inches of window unblocked. The bright yellow light shining through the narrow gaps provide the only source of light. It takes a moment for my sight to adjust to the dimly lit room.

"Don't just stand there. Come in." There's a false bravado to his tone, or perhaps that's how I choose to interpret his feeble voice.

My vision adjusts to the dim light. Uncle Mark sits propped up in a large wingback chair with a furry throw over his legs. I choose a chair near his throne. He's wearing what looks like deep purple silk pajamas, and I can't help but think the only thing he's missing is an ascot, or a silk scarf to wrap around his throat and tuck in neatly at the top of his pajamas. There's an ashtray on the small table to his left, along with a gold circular trash can.

The walls of his bedroom are dark. I can't discern the hue, but there's definitely texture. An ornate golden four-poster bed reigns supreme in the room. Enormous museum-worthy canvases hang on the walls. I'm not an art guy, but they look expensive. All are hunting scenes from hundreds of years ago, from back when they hunted with crossbows.

"Jack, I'd rather you didn't see me like this."

"Like what? In silk pajamas? You're looking pretty good to me, old man."

"Hush your tongue." His eyelids close and slowly raise. He swallows.

"Do you need some water?"

"It's right here." He gestures to his side table. There's a gold tray with a crystal glass and carafe. "I'm not an invalid. If I need it, I'll get it." He folds his hands in his lap over the fur throw. "To what do I owe this visit?"

"Wanted to check on you. Heard a rumor you were under the weather."

"I'll be fine. If it gets serious, I'll let you know." He closes his eyelids. I sit back in the chair.

"I hope you know you can lean on me. We're family. You don't need to go through this alone."

"You're like the son I never had." His eyes are closed, and his voice is scratchy. He should drink some water. "I'm very proud of you. So proud. I've had my worries, but you've done well."

I'm not sure what to say to this. I'm fully aware he's stoned, maybe too stoned to be fully aware of what he's saying, but this is the first time he's ever said anything like this to me. My eyes sting as unfamiliar emotions surge.

"Working with Victor. Smart. Good business." From his perspective, Victor is just one of several distributors.

"Have you spoken to him?"

"Oh, he's really pleased. Said good things about you. Likes you a lot more than Wayne. I always wanted you to take over, you know. That's what your dad wanted. It might have looked like I didn't want that, but it's always been my goal. But I had to have other options. Raise others who could take your place. You can never be sure of one. That's like putting all your money in one stock. Diversity. Take aim at the pack, to be sure of one. That's how you do it." His eyelids are half-closed, and his index finger gestures as he rambles.

The room pivots. I clinch the armrests for stability.

"And you worried me, you know. Sometimes I thought you might... I blamed that damn boarding school Justin sent you to. Naval Academy not any better." He lifts one wrinkled, bony hand a few inches and lowers it. "But it all worked out. Even if the government got their hooks into you for a bit there. Sniper. Who would've thought?"

My body temperature plummets. I lean forward in my chair, closer to him, to better hear his muffled words.

"You know, I never meant to bring a heroin addict into your lives. I handpicked her, thinking she wasn't your type. I thought you liked blue-eyed blondes. Ava, she's Cassandra's opposite." He exhales loudly through thin, pale lips.

The room's temperature is low, and my fingers are chilled. In the deep recesses of my mind, an inner voice tells me to turn my phone on, to record this conversation. But I can't seem to move.

"If you hadn't found those listening devices, I would've never had to hire her. But she's been useful. Helped Sophia. She'll be ready to go back to school. I know you were worried about that. Pat's probably right. She is good at what she does. But now you want to date her?" Two bony fingers rub his temple, but his eyes remain closed, almost like he's sleep talking. "Told you...it won't work. I mean, I like her. I do. But she's strong willed. She'll want more. And how do you explain to Sophia...Trust me, there are plenty of women. The contract ends this weekend. She's been paid." His droopy eyelids close. "Let her go."

"You hired Ava?" He's unloaded a lot, but that's all my shocked brain centers on.

"So did you."

"Does she report back to you?"

"Don't get mad, Jack. I need to know what's going on with you. Before I let you take over my company, I have to be sure." Did Ava listen in on my conversations? Thank god Ryan and I met at a gun range for most of our debriefings. I am numb. Void of emotion. "Wayne... that was unfortunate business. Who could've known he'd snap like that?"

Alex told me that Wayne had said they had promised him the CEO role, but I'd assumed that was because of the role he played in our company. But now...

"Did you hire Wayne to kidnap Sophia?"

"What?" His eyelids flutter, then fall closed. "No. I would never. I mean, I knew about Cassie and him. Everybody did. But no. He was just a backup. Who could've ever predicted he'd come up with that cockamamie scheme? Insanity. I just... underestimated him." Shockwaves rock through my body. My lips are numb. I can barely swallow. But, somehow, my training kicks in.

"But you..." I close my eyes and breathe in. "The deal with Victor. You structured it and he executed it?"

"International. That's where the growth..." His voice fades.

"How many other deals out there are structured like the Morales deal?"

His head lolls to one side and his lips vibrate as he exhales and inhales, his mouth ajar. He's asleep.

Holy. Shit. What have you done, Uncle Mark? What kinds of deals have you been structuring, and for how long, and why? Does he even realize what's going on? We're smuggling drugs into the US. He's always been about growth but, drugs? And Ava? She not only took money from me, but she also took money from him. She spied on me. For money. It's all for money. She wants money. That's probably what my uncle wants too. He justifies it as growth, but the underlying reason for growth is money. Everything comes back to good old-fashioned greed.

And I am once again the fool.

CHAPTER 32

Ava

"Dad's not getting back until later tonight," Sophia says. "But you probably already know that." She continues on her way down the side path, pausing at the gate.

One of the security men appears at the corner of the house.

"You going for a walk?"

"Yep." The gate clicks behind her.

"Want company?"

"No, thanks."

She turns right onto the beach and the armed security man, someone whose face I recognize but whose name I don't know, quickens his pace down the path. He barely gives me a second glance before passing through the gate.

It's not like Sophia to turn down a companion for a beach walk. She's pissed at me. I can't blame her. But I'll wait for her dad to return before addressing the issues. He's convinced she just needs time, and to some degree, he's probably right. But I hate feeling like a heel for lying to her. I hate what I've done here, and while hating myself is an emotion I'm completely familiar with, it's been a long time since I've had to suffer through it.

I spent part of the day working and part of the day buying a car with my insurance money. I'd been tempted to ask Jack what he thought, but then I feared he'd take over the endeavor. Maybe even try to buy me a car himself, so I leaned on Patrick.

Jack left early in the morning on his private jet to visit Mark. I haven't heard from him, but Sophia presumably has, so I assume the trip went well. Jack told me Sophia's unhappy, but said that she'd come around. Knowing Jack, he texted her to tell him he'd be home late. He'd probably see text as safer than a phone call, where the conversation might become unpleasant.

In this situation, we're both at fault. We shouldn't have lied to Sophia. But she's his daughter, and he's got to take the lead on discussing this with her. If she really doesn't want him dating me, then I need to leave as soon as possible. The thought hurts more than it should, which doesn't entirely make sense. Up until yesterday, I assumed I'd be moving out. I never expected for this to grow into more. I moved into this house as a favor to Mark and to help Sophia. The last thing I want is to drive a wedge between Jack and his daughter. I won't let it happen.

I head upstairs to the bedroom. To Jack's bedroom. It would be smart to move back into my apartment so we can see how we are together under normal circumstances. But, if things go well, and Sophia accepts us, I wouldn't mind living here. Hell, who wouldn't mind living here? And I enjoy seeing Jack each evening. It's not just sex. I like sleeping beside him, knowing he's there. What's between us feels real and mature. How it started feels immaterial, other than my self-hatred.

It's a crazy thought. Me having a relationship with a man like Jack Sullivan. *A relationship.* I'm still trying to wrap my head around how far we've come in less than a month's time. That first day, he glared at me like I was scum, and he'd throw his shoe away if my skin so much as touched the bottom of it. And now, he wants to keep seeing me. He cares about me. And I know it wasn't smart. Sometimes I'm just not smart. But I care about him. I've fallen for him. Hard and fast. It's an overwhelming thought. And unnerving.

I can't throw myself into a relationship the way some women can. I have to keep the ground firmly under my feet. My priorities need to be clear. I can't risk putting myself into a situation where I become broken, because broken for me is destroyed. I have a demon constantly tapping my shoulder. That call isn't as strong as it was my first year, or two, or three, but it's there.

All those group therapy sessions and coaches and words of advice over the years swirl in my head. I must use caution in a relationship. Relationships themselves can become a substitute for addiction. It's a slippery slope.

Reid was my one relationship since achieving sobriety. I stepped away from our relationship before sliding back down with Reid, but at what cost to Reid? Rationally, I know our relationship didn't drive him to drugs. Addiction fueled his cravings. But I'll go to the grave with guilt. I didn't return his calls. I wasn't there to help him during his final attempt to transition.

And now, here I am, entering another relationship. It's not with an addict. It won't bear the same risks. But when it ends, how will I handle it? Will I hurt so much I no longer care and I choose escape? Will I become another Reid? The fear might be irrational, but damn if it isn't real. It doesn't help that we are already off to a faulty start with Sophia angry at us. Why didn't we just talk to her?

The lights are off upstairs, and I don't bother turning the hall light on as the moonlight through the windows lights the way. My hand falls to the lever doorknob of the master bedroom door. A chill runs up my spine, and I glance behind me, but there's no one up here. Who would be? Emotional turmoil generates an overactive imagination. That's what it's got to be. This house is beyond safe.

I push the bedroom door open, leaving it wide, and step into the shadows, intent on reaching the bathroom and closet. I'll get ready for bed and read while I wait for Jack.

The clink of ice against glass slows me. I pause, searching the heavily shadowed room.

Jack sits in one of the high-back chairs. Instead of facing the ocean, like it normally does, he's turned it, facing inward. There's a crystal bottle on the small side table. His tie is half undone, loose around his chest over his unbuttoned collar. Several buttons on the dress shirt are undone, exposing his chest haphazardly. The sleeves of his dress shirt are rolled midway up his forearm, and his suitcoat is nowhere to be seen. In one hand, he holds a glass of amber liquid.

"Jack. I didn't know you'd returned."

The ice clinks against the glass. In the dark shadows, I can't see his eyes, but I sense he's in a foul mood. It's in the way he holds that glass, the stern scowl. Something is very wrong.

"Is everything okay?"

If he needs me, I should go to him. With care, I step to him, hand out to touch him, approaching almost as if he's a wild animal.

"How much did he pay you?" The harsh tone is unfamiliar, and it stops me, frozen before him like a servant approaching her master. "More or less than me?"

I blink, processing his words. How drunk is he?

"How often do you report back to him?" He snaps his fingers. "You're the one listening device Arrow can't find in a sweep."

"What—" He's not making any sense, but he's not slurring words.

"Don't worry. I won't try to get the money back. Your suitcase is packed."

Movement startles me. Fisher stands in the doorway. Silent. As always, he's wearing a gun holster. His hands rest on his waist. Goosebumps rise. This is insane.

"Jack, I don't have any idea what you're talking about."

"Ava. Save it. Don't make a scene. Just go."

"Jack, I'm confused. I have no idea what you're talking about. Report back to who?"

"You need to leave."

"Jack." I point at myself and raise my voice because he isn't listening. "I don't understand."

"Get. Out."

"No. This is ludicrous. Are you drunk?"

He gets up and walks to the window. He stretches one arm against the floor-to-ceiling glass, his back to me. The ice clinks against the glass as his other hand swirls the contents over and over.

"How much did he pay you?"

"He..." I pause, thinking back to the beginning of all of this. "You are the only person who paid me."

"Once a whore, always a whore." His words slice.

My inner self spills out onto the floor, and my brain shuts off all other thoughts. His statement hits like a thousand kicks to the ribs.

"I should've never brought you into this house. Into my home. Anywhere near my daughter. Get. Out."

"Jack." I approach him tentatively, and the tips of my fingers brush his starched shirt. He swings around and his arm bumps me backward.

"Get. Out!" Veins bulge in his throat and brow.

His arm rises. I cower. Glass shatters into a thousand pieces on the wall behind me.

I can't breathe. Fisher steps up behind me, loops an arm around my shoulders, and forcefully removes me from the premises.

CHAPTER 33

JACK

"All okay?"

My blood alternates between ice cold and blistering. My head throbs. The numbness in my chest holds a permanence to it. Anger, fury? My mind has settled into a meditative trance. The bright flash of white, the rolling waves crest and crash, luring me away from absolute madness.

"Fisher told me he escorted Ava off the property and out of your neighborhood last night. He revoked her pass with the front guards." Ryan's on speakerphone.

A rustling noise crosses the line, and I empty my glass with one long swallow. If I had more energy, I would hurl the phone across the room.

"Today? Is that still what you want?"

"Ava Amara is not allowed on the property. Under any circumstance."

Ryan has questions but I don't have to answer.

"Everything we discussed yesterday is underway. But we haven't linked–"

"And you probably won't. He's a master. We'll talk later."

After leaving my uncle, it hit me like a freight train that he'd been fully aware of not only my impending arrival, but other things he shouldn't have known. The government reference. She told him I worked for the government. My deepest secret. The one thing I'd never shared with anyone, not even my wife, and she told him. She told him everything. Either she was listening in behind closed doors or there are more listening devices. Living here, she could plant them anywhere she liked. So, I called Ryan, filled him in, asked him to look closely at all of my uncle's correspondence and financial dealings. And I asked him to do another deep sweep of my home.

Fucking money-hungry bitch.

So far, we haven't found any additional devices. Anything regarding Victor Morales, my loving uncle derived from the source. Ava clearly told him I wanted a relationship after the contract ended. She told him I was on my way to visit him. And... proving I meant nothing to her, she told him about my prior government work. That one really infuriates me. Thank god I didn't tell her everything.

"When we meet next, let's discuss the new project. In detail."

The current joint task force operation, dubbed Operation MexTex, has essentially been hijacked by the government entities involved. They are extremely interested in this distribution avenue and are debating at what point they'll pull the trigger and end it. They could continue the op for eternity.

So, I told Ryan I want to splinter the UC project. My goal is to uncover every deal Mark Sullivan orchestrated behind the scenes, and I want a list of all involved. Whether it's a government contact or an employee of mine, I want their names on a list. And I will systematically work to build a case against them.

"Dad, what are you doing?"

My head pounds and my stomach roils, remnants of the physical abuse I wrought last night. I can't remember the last time I drank that much. I woke up feeling like death and couldn't bear to pick up my phone. I asked Fisher to contact my assistant and have her clear my schedule for the day. It's not in his job description, but they can charge me extra.

"Working."

She crosses her arms and looks at me like she's calling bullshit. Then she leaves. I should talk to her, but my head isn't in the right space. I need to get out of the house, so I head out to the beach. I kick off my shoes at the end of the path and let my bare feet sink into the sand, all the way to the water's edge, where I sit.

One positive outcome of all of this is that when I do talk to Sophia, I'll have good news to tell her. Ava and I are done. She's gone. Never to re-enter our lives again.

CHAPTER 34

JACK

"Dad? I don't think I've ever seen you sit in the sand before. Are you okay?"

"I'm fine. Thinking."

"You've been sitting out here for an hour."

Sophia sits down beside me. She picks up a small stick and draws in the sand. She's probably been looking for Ava. Fuck. I should've gone straight to Sophia this morning. Talked with her. Given her the good news. I've been so wrapped up in my shit that once again I am being a shit dad. Just in a new shitty way.

"Ava left."

"She texted me. Said goodbye and wanted me to know she would be there for me if I ever needed her."

"Did she, now?" What happened to Sophia being mad about Ava? Arrow will need to block her number. And see if there's any way to block emails too. All communications should be blocked. "Did she say anything else?"

"Nope."

A child twenty feet away squeals in delight as the surf laps her calves. I remember those days.

"Dad?"

I return my attention to Sophia. "Yeah?"

"Did you send her away because I was angry about you dating her?"

"No." I close my eyes, then open them and stare out across the ocean.

"Are you lying to me?"

"No." I can't bring myself to talk to Sophia. I want her to walk away. My thoughts are blocked, and there's no way I will deal with this well right now.

"I don't believe you." She stands and moves in front of me, hands balled into tiny fists. The water laps her ankles, over her shoes. She yells, "Liar!"

"You will not speak to me like that, young lady." I am practically growling.

She glares right back at me, and I should stand military style and tower over her, but the energy to do so is absent.

"Or what?" She stomps her left foot and leans forward. "You gonna take away my phone? Cut back on my TV time?"

Jesus, she is really pushing it. My palm plants on the sand and I push up, rising to my full height. She's done it now.

"You can't tell me what to do."

"Oh. Yes. I. Can." Anger vibrates through my core. I don't trust myself to touch her, so my hands remain clenched at my waist.

"No. You. Can't." She shakes her head and stomps off like a petulant child.

Jesus fucking Christ. Why isn't Cassie here to deal with this? I pace back and forth on the beach long after the click of the gate wafts through the wind. Fisher hovers near the edge of the property, presumably watching me.

"Watch Sophia," I snarl.

He doesn't hear, so I charge up the beach. I didn't hire security for my safety. He backs away from the gate as I approach. He'd better back away. I won't put a hand on my daughter, but I'd love nothing more than to throw a fist at someone.

My hand falls on the gate, and all that anger evaporates. A heart-wrenching sound carries through the air. I scan the back yard and crumble inside. Sophia sits bent over in a pool chair, arms wrapped around her knees, head down, bawling. *Fuck me.*

I join her on the chair. There's a part of me that wants to pull her onto my lap, just like I used to do when she was little. But she's no longer little. She's not an adult either. She's somewhere in between. But I'm going to lose her if I don't figure out how to bridge the gap.

"Sophia. Sweetheart. The last thing I wanted to do was hurt you."

She sniffs and rubs her nose on her knee, then wipes her knee with her hand. Tears continue to freefall, and my insides detonate.

"I don't know what to say. Or what to do. But I love you more than anything, and I want to figure it out. I'm so sorry your mom isn't here. She'd know what to say."

"Dad." There's so much exasperation in the way she draws out my name it's borderline humorous. "Sometimes saying something is the best you can do." The skin below her eyes is puffy and tinged pink. Her lips curl together like she's going to cry again, and a few tears escape. "Saying something is better than saying nothing."

"I'm not great at communicating." That's something a couples counselor once told me.

"That's probably true. But I still hear you. Most of the time."

"You hear me, huh?"

She exhales, scoots next to me, and wipes her nose on the edge of my shirt. Then she gives me a sheepish smile. "And I love you. When I was little, I kind of held you up to superhero status. You could do no wrong. But now I see you as, well, human. I don't expect you to know what to say all the time. But I expect you to fucking speak."

"Hey." I scrunch my eyebrows and scowl. "Language."

She smirks. "Dad, my perception of you has evolved. And for the better. Instead of the superhero, I see my dad. Someone who loves me more than anything." Her voice cracks, and I wrap an arm around her, pulling her into my side. "But your perception of me needs to evolve. I'm not a little girl. And I'm definitely not innocent."

"You'll always be my little girl."

She pushes back, out of my hold, and stares at me. "No, Dad. I'm almost sixteen. You should be able to tell me when you're dating someone. You don't need to try to protect me from every little thing. It's bad enough I can't go on the beach without security following me."

"I had no business dating Ava. She was here for you."

"I don't care about that. What I care about is you lying to me. Trying to protect me from what? Like I don't get that you might date someone? I don't need that kind of protection."

I'm not certain I agree with her, and I stare down at my palms. God, I wish Cassie was here. "I wish I could be more for you."

"Dad, I don't need you to be more." She lets out a sigh and twists on the lounge chair, crossing her legs, facing me. "I know it wasn't easy when Mom died. But you stepped up. You've been there for me. I mean, yeah, you're not perfect. But I've decided there are degrees of imperfection."

"Oh, you have, have you?"

"Yeah." She nods. "Mr. Killington?" My gut clenches at that bastard's name coming out of her mouth. "Unacceptable. He's over here, in the really bad person area." She gestures far out to the right. "And then there's you. You can be moody and a little obsessed with work. And you lied to me. You lied to Mom. You guys didn't think I knew, but I did. Those aren't good things, but you've been there for me. I think you've always done your best. And that's acceptable, right?" Those precious blue eyes look at me like this is such a simple thing. "You always said that. If I do my best, you don't care what grade I get. As long as I do my best."

"I appreciate you letting me off the hook so easily, but there's a difference between grades and parenting."

She reaches out and squeezes my forearm. "I still love you."

I scoop her up and pull her against me. She lays her head on my shoulder, and we sit there like that for a long time.

"For the record, I never cheated on your mother. I know she thought that, but she was mistaken."

"Why didn't you tell me?"

"By the time I found out you knew about everything, your mother was dead. I didn't want to blacken her image in any way. But there were other issues with our marriage."

"Was that so hard to say?" She lifts her head and looks at me in a way that lightens the weight crushing down on me. I kiss the top of her head, and she rests her head back on my shoulder. "What happened with you and Ava? Am I the reason you ended things?"

"No." She remains squeezed against me, but I shift and lift her chin so she looks at me. "No. I was telling you the truth. You are not the reason. But she and I are over."

"Why?"

"Ironically enough," I huff, "she lied to me." Sophia lays her head back against me. Ava stirs raw painful emotions. I want her far away from us. But if Sophia forgives her, that might be hard to ensure. "How do you feel about her lying?" *How much am I going to have to tell you?*

"I think that what you think... and feel... is most important."

Damn, that's a therapist's response if I've ever heard one. "Therapy really worked on you, huh?"

"What do you feel?" She nudges me. "Dad, you can tell me."

What do I feel? So, my teenage daughter wants to play therapist. "I'm livid. Furious. We had... I'm angrier at Ava than I was when your mother told me she'd had an affair. Does that even make sense?" I risk a glance at my daughter.

My verbal vomit was more than I should've shared with my daughter. But she wants communication. "I blame myself for your mother's affair. Too absorbed in work. Too many excuses that didn't make sense. But this... it's all on Ava."

I'm so fucking furious at Ava. Way more than I was with Cassie. Maybe that's because I was responsible for Cassie's betrayal. And I did absolutely nothing to deserve Ava's betrayal.

Greed brings out the worst in people, but I gave Ava so much money, she should have been immune to greed. Maybe it hurts more when someone hurts you and it's not something you deserve.

I deserved Cassie's betrayal. I did that to her and to us. But everything with Ava was fresh and new. Maybe we didn't start off in the most orthodox manner, but I did nothing to deserve this bullshit. I let her near my daughter, and she betrayed me. Us.

"Dad, I know you loved Mom. You cared for her deeply. But maybe there's a difference between loving someone and being in love with someone." I side-eye my daughter. Is she assuming I wasn't in love with her mother? Because I absolutely was. I battled my family to be with Cassandra. "I mean, I don't know. I've never been in love. But it seems like that's true."

"You're a teenager."

She smiles up at me. "But Dad, you fell in love with Ava. I might be a teen, but even I could see it. Lauren saw it. Ava loves you, Dad. She knows all the bad things about you, and she still loves you."

I exhale. Everything is so simple to Sophia. "I'm not sure you're old enough for me to be having this conversation with."

"You treat me like an adult, I behave like an adult. You treat me like a kid, I behave like a kid."

"Did Ava teach you that?" In how many ways am I going to regret trusting my uncle and bringing his recommendation into our home?

"No. It was in one of Mom's parenting books. It sat on the shelf near her computer."

"And you read it?"

"I wanted to see where she came up with her punishments."

"She punished you?"

"Not really. Time outs when I was little. She didn't believe in saying no 'just because.' We discussed real-life consequences. She always wanted me to understand the why, so I could decide how to act based on the life consequences, not based on whether I'd get in trouble if caught."

"She was a good mom, wasn't she?"

"The best."

I squeeze her tighter into my side. God, I love this kid. "I'm sorry you lost her."

"Me too."

"Sophia, Ava can't be trusted. I don't want to go into details, because some things are between adults."

"Did she cheat on you?"

"No." I had her locked in my house. It's not like she had the chance. "But it's important that you not speak to her. I need for you to trust me on this. Can you be okay with that? Can we put her behind us?"

Sophia's lips purse. Those blue eyes, replicas of her mother's, run all over my face. Probably taking in the fact that I haven't shaved. My sunglasses hide what are no doubt bloodshot eyes.

"She hurt you, didn't she?"

"Yes, she did." The admission offsets the numbness, replaced by a sharp stab. She fucking crushed me. My uncle too, but I can't say I'm shocked by Uncle Mark. He's always put Sullivan Arms ahead of anything and everyone. I just hadn't realized the man was morally bankrupt.

"Okay, Dad." The weight of Sophia's head against my shoulder soothes me.

I refuse to taint her view of Ava by laying the ugly truth out there. Telling her that Ava took money from me in exchange for sex. That she took some sort of payment from my uncle to spy on me. Arrow is combing the financials now to sate my curiosity. We may never find it. The payment could show up as a donation to Nueva Vida. The fact of the matter is, we can't trust Ava. But I don't want to ruin Sophia's trust in humanity. She cared for Ava.

Somehow, we'll get through this.

CHAPTER 35

One week later

Ava

For the first time in my life, I'm not restricted by money. Here I am, reviewing a realtor's report on a new apartment building that hit the market less than twenty-four hours ago. I can actually afford to buy the building at the asking price, tear it down, and build exactly what I want. The building location is perfect for Nueva Vida because of its proximity to our existing campus. That this is even an option for me, that I'm in the negotiation seat on this commercial property, is surreal.

Surreal describes the entire last month. It's like someone plucked me out of my one-bedroom apartment in a shitty part of town and dropped me into a stunning ocean-side mansion and said you get to experience all of this, but only for a very little while. But do not fret, you will not turn back into a pumpkin. Your bank account overflows, and you may buy anything you wish for.

It's not like I can be mad at Jack. He was quite clear. One month. Sure, it ended a few days early. And yes, he opened the door to more, and I almost let myself buy into the possibilities. I almost hurdled the fear and went for it. You'd think I'd know better after the life I've lived. There was never a real possibility that would be my life. That a man like Jackson Sullivan would fall for someone like me and want her by his side.

I considered returning the payment. Rejecting his money would soothe my pain. Show him I'm not the whore he claimed. But I am the whore. I accepted his ridiculously large payment so I could do good for other people. If I return the money, my ego gets soothed, but the center will take a colossal hit. And it would mean I wasted this past month.

I need to forget about the Sullivans. Forget I ever agreed to that crazy situation. Forget I ever got to know the infamous Jackson Sullivan and his abducted daughter. Forget about his twisted little sex room and his payment plans for women he wants. Forget I ever agreed to it. Forget I sold myself, once again, something I promised myself I'd never do. But hey, wouldn't a lot of people do what I did if they found themselves in my shoes? I couldn't really say that when I'd gotten strung out on drugs. But last month, that life. I'm not the only one who would make that choice. I am not horrible or evil.

The problem is, I can reiterate that to myself all I want, but there's a deadness inside me that isn't healthy. I've hit rock bottom before, and I'm not close to it right now. But getting out of bed in the morning is tough. Everything should be great. I'm looking at expanding Nueva Vida and really putting it on the map, and yet there's no excitement. No drive to come to the office. At night, I eat and go to sleep. I've been craving a drink... just a nice glass of red wine to curb some of the pain. But I haven't done it. I won't go there. Still, the cravings are undeniably stronger, and that's not good. And this is exactly why I never should have opened up to him or risked falling for him.

Last month, I got off my workout schedule. Those walks on the beach and paddleboarding didn't deliver the sweat or endorphins of a grueling workout. That's what I need to do. Get back into a stringent workout routine. Pump those endorphins the healthy way. Get my body and mind out of this cloud of funk. Unfortunately, my deflated self has zero desire to enter a gym. Maybe a long walk tonight will kickstart my improvement. Tomorrow, I'll dig in and work my ass off.

There's a knock on my office door that pulls me out of my internal pep talk.

"Hey, do you have a minute?"

Ryan Wolfgang's sister, Indigo, stands in the doorway. I have seen little of her since she came to live at Nueva Vida, but I've asked about her more than once to have an answer for Ryan if he asked me how she's doing. Does she have a message for me? That's an absurd thought. If Jack wanted to talk, he'd call. Or text.

"Sure. Come on in."

"I got a job." She beams, and a little part of me twists. It's the stupid part of me. Of course her visit has nothing to do with Jack.

"That's great. Where?" Jobs for felons are challenging to acquire, but Indigo is lucky. Her brother hired a good lawyer, and they expunged her possession charges.

"A call center. It's for a bank." She shrugs and steps closer. "It's a lot more interesting than I thought it would be. The training alone lasts for a month." Her eyes widen as if a month is an incredibly lengthy amount of time. "There's so much to learn."

"That sounds great. Truly impressive. How are you doing otherwise?"

Her gaze drops to the floor. She knows what I'm asking, what everyone in this place is asking. It's a loaded question because it dredges up thoughts of before, when everything was anything but okay.

"I'm okay. It's only really bad at night. When I'm busy during the day, I can... I'm good."

"Have you been working out?"

"Meh." She wobbles her head back and forth and offers a sheepish smile. "Some."

We endorse all rehabilitation strategies. Faith-based, non-faith based, drug assisted... we don't care, as long as it works for the individual. But one overriding principle we promote is physical exercise, both cardio and weights. But it's hard to do it when you feel like shit, even if it's one natural way of finding a path to better. And I, of all people, know this.

"I'm actually not in a great place right now."

Her face instantly morphs into one of genuine concern, and she slips into one of my office chairs. She says nothing, but looks expectantly up at me, leaving the floor open for me to say more. She'd be a good therapist or coach.

"Would you like to maybe grab dinner and go for a long walk tonight? I haven't been great about getting exercise, and I need to get back into it."

"Absolutely. That would be great." She glances at her wrist. "I'm working from ten to six today, but they never keep me late. Want me to come by here when I'm done?"

"Yeah." This is good.

"Well, I came by to tell you I'll be paying the full rent next month. That call center job actually pays really well. Sixty-eight thousand a year. So, I can pay rent. And I'll probably start looking for an apartment of my own, you know, once I get my feet on the ground."

"That's great, Indigo."

"Indie. Everyone calls me Indie. Um, I don't want to be overly confident, but I'm sort of thinking I'll be out of here within sixty days."

"That's great." Having a good-paying job is an important component of transition success. She's also got her brother backing her. Sometimes worry percolates when someone tells me they are moving on, but there's no worry for her. She's got a supportive family and a good job.

My phone rings, and Patrick's name flashes on the screen.

"I'll get out of here and let you get that. See you later. Probably around six thirty or seven? Depends on traffic. You know, the bus can be off schedule too."

I give her a thumbs up sign and answer the phone.

"Hey, hey, hey." Patrick's deep rumble eases some of my discomfort. I lean back in my chair and spin it around so I'm staring out my window at the dingy stucco wall of the nearby building.

"Hey."

"Now, that does not sound like my cheery Ava."

"I'm fine."

"Uh-huh. Still no word from Jack?"

"I told you. He kicked me out. I keep thinking about his belief that someone paid me, and the only logical conclusion I can come to is Mark. Does that make sense to you?"

"Well, you agreed to go over there partially out of loyalty to Mark. But he didn't offer you money... Jack did."

I hold in my sigh. There's no point in going 'round and 'round about this. I tried calling Jack, and he blocked my number. After deciding there had to be some massive misunderstanding, I drove back, only to be treated like scum at the neighborhood gates. It's possible he's a narcissistic sociopath. He got what he wanted from me and gaslighted me, making up some bullshit reason for kicking me to the curb.

Only, that doesn't make sense either. None of his other actions fit. But it's just as well. It's not like he and I were really going to work out. That was some kind of bizarre, surreal fantasy that the sooner I release the better. He always saw me as a piece of trash, and it was always going to end.

"How are you doing?" Patrick's all-serious, and I get it.

"Am I about to break down? Relapse?"

"I didn't—"

"No. It's okay. I'm good. Really. I love my life and what I'm doing too much to do anything stupid. You don't need to worry."

"Good to hear. But that's not what I meant either."

"Patrick." I close my eyes, seeking strength. "We're supposed to accept the things we can't change. He's blocked my number. He's got twenty-four-hour security around him in a gated community. None of this makes any sense, but he obviously doesn't want to talk about it. What the hell am I supposed to do? Hang out on his beach? Wait for him or Sophia to come out like some stalker?" And the stalker option wouldn't even work. His security would spot me. Not that I've given it a lot of thought.

"So, he cut you off?"

"Completely. If you could have seen him, Patrick... he was so cold." It was a different Jack than I'd ever seen before. Maybe he has multiple personality disorder.

"He cut Mark off too."

"Really? Even though he's going through chemo?"

"Yeah. Mark asked me if I'd spoken to you. I don't know what's going on. But Jack knew about your past, right?"

"Yeah. Why?"

"Some things Mark was saying didn't quite make sense. But he's stoned half the time these days. And I'm so mad at him for sitting his ass in Houston that I haven't pushed him. But we'll get through it. We always do. Our relationship is a series of ups and downs. But what about you? What are you going to do?"

"What can I do? That night, I was so shocked. None of it makes sense. He acted like I took money from someone, yet he's the one I took money from. Do you think he has multiple personality disorder?"

Patrick's laughter through the line has me pulling the phone away and rubbing my forehead. I sound ridiculous. My brain is just trying to make sense of this, and I need to let it go.

"Sorry. Damn, Ava. You and I are definitely different. You go off with a mental diagnosis. If I was in your shoes, I'd be thinking Mark found some nineteen-year-old stud."

"Thanks for putting that into my stream of consciousness. Jeez."

Maybe he did find some hottie on that trip to Houston. But that doesn't seem like Jack. There is something else going on. Or he has multiple personality disorder.

"I will grant you that his theory that someone else paid you to have sex with him is crackers."

"No. I don't think that's what he was saying. I think he's worried I was giving information to someone else, but who? I never left the house. And when I did, he had security trailing me."

"Huh." Patrick sounds thoughtful, but this is all stuff we've been over. Only the first of many times Patrick and I went over everything I couldn't stop crying. The tears are dried up, replaced by profound sadness and frustration. "Like he thought you were reporting back to someone?"

"Yeah, I guess."

"And he's mad at Mark too. Do you still wear that bracelet Mark gave you?"

"Yeah."

"Did you find it odd when he gave that to you?"

"Geez, thanks."

"No, I mean he didn't have me shop for it. Did you find that odd?"

"I didn't think about it." The bracelet in question clinks against the other bands on my arms. I don't always wear it, as charms aren't really my style, but I've been wearing it daily since all the bullshit erupted.

"Can you do me a favor?"

"Yeah." Patrick confuses me. Where is he going with this?

"Can you take it off and put it in a metal file cabinet? Just keep it there until I arrive tomorrow. Don't say anything right now. Just take it off and put it in the back of a metal file cabinet." Frissons of fear light my skin.

"Patrick, you're not—"

"Shush. Just do it. Don't say another word about it. I'll be there tomorrow. Tell me when you've taken it off and locked it away. Preferably in an office other than yours."

We have a storage room filled with tall metal file cabinets. A local business donated them years ago when they were renovating. I set the phone down and unclick the silver latch. The bracelet is heavy. Nausea stirs as I lock it away in the tall cabinet, nestled in the back of the bottom drawer. I lock the storage room door, and it's not until I'm back in my office that I speak.

"It's locked away. You think he put something on that bracelet?"

"It's one theory. Would explain some of his ramblings. And Jack thinking he paid you. I'll be there tomorrow. I mean, maybe I've been watching too much spy shit."

My mind races forward. "Even if Mark did something like that, I'd never be able to convince Jack that's what happened."

"Sure you would. You'd show him the bracelet."

"I can't get near him. I've tried. Remember?" It's a long shot, and a pointless one. But it would help me understand what the hell happened.

"When you get home, I need you to go through your closet."

"Why? If he's got some listening device or something in there, I wouldn't recognize it."

"That's not why. I've got another idea. Something that's going to help both of us. Do you have any gowns?"

"What?"

"I don't know why I asked. First things first, we've got some shopping to do. I'm scheduling us a private appointment at Gambucci."

"I can't afford that place."

"How much did you say he paid you?"

I let out a sigh. "I'm not using that money on clothes."

"Well, never fear. I've got Mark's black card. And I can promise you... he'll never notice."

CHAPTER 36

JACK

From the back corner of the room, I watch the parade of tuxes and gowns enter the banquet. The wire taped beneath my dress shirt itches, but this isn't my first rodeo, and I won't be scratching. Ryan and I stand around a small round cocktail table.

Turns out Ryan is the perfect plus one. Ryan, or Wolf as we called him back in the day, intimidates like none other with ice-blue eyes and a scowl that growls "stay away." If it weren't for Ryan's intimidation, men who knew my father and who do business in some capacity with Sullivan Arms would surround me.

The annual banquet tonight is the biggest of the year, and I'll be one of the dutiful men donating ten million dollars and receiving special mention and a gaudy golden jacket as a token of appreciation. My donation will serve as a notice to the entire industry that Sullivan Arms plays for the team.

But that's not why I'm wearing a wire, and it's not why I'm present at this function I have grown to abhor. Tonight is all about completing my list.

Victor told me last week that Senator Talbot appreciates all I am doing. Given Victor turned out to be in bed with my uncle, the FBI and other assorted groups have a keen interest in hearing exactly what the United States senator has to say about my illegal smuggling operation. As do I.

Personally, after decades in the CIA, my hunch is this effort will be wasted. Someone doesn't rise to the level of senator by documenting illegal activities verbally or in writing. At best, he'll incite greater interest in his activities through a vague reference. Maybe he'll drop another name. At worst, I'll spend thirty minutes locked in a boring conversation.

Arrow is in attendance and is monitoring every single person Sullivan Arms' employees interact with during the event. Phone and email records are a more efficient way of discerning connections, but guards might be down tonight with all the alcohol flowing.

Outside, Fisher and a team of four additional Arrow employees wait. I'm hardly the only person present with personal security. There are plenty of high-powered politicians and executives here. In theory, no one is allowed to possess any weapons inside the banquet, but they're using the honor system tonight. I'm armed, and so is Ryan. Based on the bulges on hips beneath dress coats, I'd estimate a good portion of the men tonight are armed. No telling how many supportive spouses have minuscule pistols inside their clutches. Conceal and carry enthusiasts crowd this banquet.

There's a jazz band set up in the far corner. Waitstaff roam the crowd offering champagne and hors d'oeuvres. All the men are decked in black and white coattails, or what my father used to call penguin suits. And the women are cloaked in sequins or velvet and shimmering with diamonds. An enormous ice sculpture glimmers in the center of the room, and there are full-service bars set up in three locations around the perimeter.

I would normally arrive toward the end of cocktail hour, but on the off chance the influential senator wishes to catch me alone before dinner, here I stand.

Ryan sets his drink down and tilts his head to me.

"This is going to get interesting," he says.

I scan the entrance, assuming he's talking about a recent arrival. He's getting updates from his team through an earpiece. But a sinking awareness hits.

"Mark showed, didn't he?"

He's reached out many times. I'm not sure exactly what he expected to come out of his truth bomb. The smuggling venture wasn't called off, so it's clear he doesn't know about the UC op. Whatever Ava told him about my prior work with a government entity must have been conveyed as past tense, which would make sense since that's essentially what I told her.

My hope is that he slips up and we gather enough evidence to connect him to the smuggling operation. Right now, we have nothing other than one unrecorded conversation. There was a time when I would have tried to protect him out of a sense of family obligation. That time has passed.

Several of the men in the room turn to the double doors. Ava Amara, in a full length, curve-hugging black gown enters with her hand in the crook of Patrick's arm. Diamonds glitter in her ears. A thin layer of black gauze covers her chest and down her arms in skintight sleeves. The gown reeks of sophistication and glamor.

Every cell in my body awakens. Patrick bends and says something to her. She points toward a bar along the wall. He puts his hand on her lower back, and yes, he's a gay man, but I grit my teeth to control a surge of possessive, irrational anger.

"Told you." Ryan smirks and swirls the bourbon in his glass.

"Patrick sells magazine space for several gun industry publications. It makes sense he's here. But why is Ava here?"

She's absolutely stunning. She swept her unruly black hair up into an intricate design, away from her face and off her neck. To look at her, you'd never know her past. Any onlooker would expect she is an up-and-coming socialite, or possibly a wealthy wife. A tuxedoed man approaches her at the bar, no doubt having spotted the absence of a wedding ring.

How deep into this is she? I'd love to get Ryan's point of view on this, but I can't bring myself to ask, knowing an entire team of feds listens to every single word I say.

Patrick sees me from across the room and raises his glass in a distant salute. I do the same. Dread circulates through hardened veins when he leads Ava to me.

Fuck it. This operation aims to catch a senator, but we'll be catching two small fish instead. No part of me wants to be the one who captures Ava. I'm angry and pissed and a world of other things, but I don't want to be the one to send her to prison. At least she's well-funded and can hire a dream defense team.

"Patrick," I say as they approach. "Ava."

Gone is the drastic eyeliner and the ten earrings lining each lobe. A stream of diamonds cascades elegantly from each lobe. Blood red lipstick glistens on her full lips. If I had to guess, I'd say a makeup artist applied her makeup with the goal of highlighting those enormous eyes. Those dark orbs hit like a bludgeon to my chest.

She'll do anything for money.

It's a reminder I hold on to.

"You remember Ryan?"

"Yes, I do." She offers her hand. She painted her nails a neutral color, and several thin tennis bracelets on her wrist sparkle. Did she buy herself diamonds with my money? "Indie and I have been spending time together. She's become my walking partner. She's doing really well."

"She told me. It's nice of you to spend time with her. She's had trouble making friends. I mean, the good kind of friends."

I glare at Ryan and wonder if he's lost his mind. How on Earth is he okay with his sister spending time with her? He's fully aware if she says anything incriminating she's going to be hauled off to prison, possibly tonight.

"If you have a minute, Patrick and I would like to talk privately with you."

They really want to do this?

"There's a private room down the hallway. We have time before the dinner hour starts," Patrick offers.

Ava believes she can deceive me. And when she weaves her lies, there's going to be an entire team listening.

There's no way out of this. And I shouldn't be wanting one. My goal is to catch all the players behind this scheme. Might as well start with the most obvious ones.

Ava saunters down the hallway, and my gaze locks on the sensuous sway of her hips and the seductive curves of her backside. The soles of her sky-high black heels flash red. She's spent money on this outfit. She wouldn't wear the clothes I bought her, but she knows how to glam it up. The vixen can play any role she desires.

The body-hugging gown begs for someone to pull the gown up to her waist and demand she grip something while she gets fucked hard from behind. Judging from the absence of panty lines, she's either not wearing any or she's got on one of her barely there, easily ripped thongs.

"Should we close the doors?" Ava asks.

She's led us to a small room not far from the coat closet, although this is Houston, so the coat closet isn't a popular destination. Someone mans the room because, Houston or not, you never know when a woman absolutely must wear her mink stole. The young tuxedo nods as I enter the empty room Ava has selected.

"What is this about?"

Ryan positions himself near the doorway, his body angled so he can scan the hallway and monitor Patrick and Ava.

The two look between each other, silently communicating the way old friends do. Down the hall, I hear an unmistakable, familiar, deep, Texan genteel twang.

What the hell? I charge toward the familiar voice, ready to

confront him. Is playing along like everything's fine the role that twisted man thinks I'll play for the sake of the company?

"No. You're not going anywhere." Patrick grips my arm, and it takes every ounce of control to refrain from going for his throat. "You owe it to her to hear her out."

So, that's the plan. She's going to try to convince me of her innocence?

"We found this." Ava opens her clutch and shows us a silver bracelet. "I would have called you to tell you, but you blocked my number. I could have gone to Ryan, but I needed to do this face to face."

"Do what?" I say at the same time Ryan says, "Let me see."

"It's a charm bracelet," I tell Ryan. It's immaterial. A diversion.

"And there's a listening device. You can see it right here." She bypasses me and hands it to Ryan. It's a bracelet I've seen often. One charm is cracked open.

"You wore that bracelet everywhere." Along with a stack of gaudy, cheap bracelets, she wore the out-of-place charm bracelet.

"I didn't tell your uncle anything. At least not anything you wouldn't be okay with me sharing. And he didn't pay me." She grits her teeth like that little fact makes all the difference.

"You brought listening devices into my home? And you think somehow I'm going to be okay with it because He. Didn't. Pay. You?" My voice rises, and Ryan shuts the door. "I cared about you." This woman makes me want to rip my hair out. "Like a fool, I trusted you. A woman I hired. I trusted. And you... you!"

"I what, Jack? What the hell did I do?" The vein in her forehead pulses, and she clenches those perfectly manicured hands into fists at her sides. "Your Uncle Mark asked how you're doing. He cares. Why the hell is telling him how you're doing problematic? I never told him anything you wouldn't tell him yourself."

Ryan's hand falls to my shoulder, and he tugs me back. I whip around to face him. I rail against her, but it's not like I would actually give in to the desire to throttle the conniving bitch.

"She might not have known." He grits his teeth, and his lips barely move, but I hear him. And the truth filters in. It glimmers in Ryan's hand as he examines it on his palm. Separated from her stack of trash, the bracelet looks expensive. It's probably worth more than the car she was driving. That should have told me something.

"Mark gave that bracelet to her. She didn't know." Patrick's expression is cold. He addresses Ryan. "Check the opened Eiffel Tower pendant."

"Did you disable it?" Ryan asks.

Patrick shakes his head. Ryan's hands fumble with the charm.

"You didn't know?" I ask.

Her eyes grow impossibly wide, and she shakes her head. "I didn't know. And yes, he asked me to keep an eye out on you, but only to let him know if I had concerns. If I thought you weren't in a good place to run the company. That was it. He didn't pay me. I went to meet with you as a favor to him because he's Patrick's partner and because he's our principal investor."

I hear the truth in her words. My mind slowly processes it all. We could never find a payment to her. All of her bracelets glimmered in the moonlight on the bedside table the night I opened up to her.

"Mark may have a surveillance team watching all of you," Ryan says. "With enough money, anything is possible. I'd bet he listens in on Patrick's phone calls at a bare minimum."

Patrick's lips purse. He's completely still.

"I needed for you to know the truth." Ava's soft tone draws me back to her. I so readily believed she deceived me. "I couldn't let you think I would do that to you."

Her gaze falls to the ground, and she moves to Patrick's side, returning her hand to the crook of his arm. She has said what she needed to say, and she's ready to leave. I am numb.

Ryan's hand goes to his ear, a sign of something coming through in his earpiece.

"Time to mingle. Senator Talbot has arrived."

My mind whirls over this new information. She didn't deceive me. I am a fool, but not in the manner I believed.

"Can I give you a ride home, after the banquet?" I need to process this. Zero emotions are surfacing, but my gut tells me I can't end things like this. I said hurtful things to her. "We need to talk, but I have... there's more going on here."

Ryan's ice-blue gaze directs me to fall in line. It's game time.

"I need to... after this is over?" It's an incoherent request, but I'm rattled, and my brain short circuits. If I didn't have a team of men outside and a wire strapped to my chest, I'd say screw it, and haul her back to my house to deal with this. But no, I have a list to complete. Tonight is important.

"You don't owe me anything. We don't need to speak later." Her voice shakes, and those enormous eyes glisten. Stirring sensations chip away at the numbness that had set up residence.

"Please?"

Ryan opens the door and glances at his wrist. Seconds pass.

"There's nothing else to say."

"Ava. Please. I have plenty I need to say to you."

Those dark eyes hesitate, but she gives me a brief nod, and I'm out the door.

When I glance over my shoulder, Ava's arm is on Patrick's, and he's still frozen. I wonder what else he's pieced together from this, but the hum of voices rises, and if I'm going to stand a chance of catching the senator's attention before he's seated at a table of twelve, I need to move.

As I walk, the gaping wound in my chest eases. The fog of rage that has clouded my thinking lifts. We round the corner, and I slow as my uncle shakes Senator Talbot's hand.

The man orchestrated illegal deals to ensure we continued to increase sales. The growth of our family company trumped all. What about the senator? Is power his reason? Or are these two simply acquaintances? There's only one way to find out.

Let's get this done.

I paste on a cordial smile and stride toward the two men, leaving Ryan to fend for himself. Uncle Mark greets me with a familiar expression. It's the same expression he used when I presented at my first board meeting as CEO.

Pride seeps from my uncle's pores. He believes he successfully groomed me into a cutthroat business titan. A man who sold his soul for company dividends. He doesn't comprehend how his accusations about Ava gutted me. Or maybe he does. Maybe she served a purpose when I didn't care for her, but once I did, her presence in my life became disadvantageous to the company. It's clear he keeps Patrick, his so-called partner, a secret from the public and his family.

"Jack," the titan says. "Good to see you." With a slight twist, he addresses the senator. "My nephew is receiving an award tonight." Then, with expert maneuvering, his commanding attention is back on me. "Jack, I believe you know Senator Talbot."

"Jack, good to see you again." The man's sweaty palm presses against mine in a slimy shake, and I cover my cringe. *Just get through this.*

CHAPTER 37

JACK

"Would you like a cigarette? There's a smoking area outside, and I'd like to take a break before we're trapped inside." The charismatic senator projects confidence, gesturing for me to proceed without hearing my answer.

"Certainly," I answer, although he's not really giving me a choice.

With his hand on my shoulder, the senator guides us out of the hotel lobby, as if we're the best of friends. His snakeskin cowboy boots tip-tap on the marble as we head outside into the night. Only in the south do men pair cowboy boots with tuxedos, and I suspect this man at my side wants to remind all the attendees he's a hardcore Texan.

Outside the hotel, we wordlessly weave through a battalion of drivers and security officers until we reach the narrow path that runs to the side of the building. Gold stands holding red velvet rope mark the area where smokers can dispose of ash and cigarettes.

The senator offers me a cigarette, and I accept, even though I hate the things. But I suppose it's all part of building his trust. I haven't smoked a cigarette since seventh grade, and back then, on my one experimental try, I coughed and my eyes watered. If my novice smoking status rears its head again, my cover will be blown.

He offers a lighter, and I wave it away.

"No, thanks. Actually, I don't smoke." He raises an eyebrow. "I didn't want to turn down the chance for some time to talk."

With a wide smile he drops his lighter back into his inside coat pocket, but he holds on to the unlit cigarette.

"I can't stand the things either. But they are a nice excuse to leave the crowd. Wish we'd thought to pick up a glass of bourbon before we came out here, though."

"I can get you a glass."

"Nah. We'll be quick. Don't have much time before the dinner bell. Mark talks a lot about you. A whole lot. He loves you something fierce."

"That's good to hear." I keep my expression as neutral as possible while my fingers dent the unlit cigarette.

"I'd like to get to know you better. Would love to have you sometime at my family place. Do you like quail hunting?"

"I like all kinds of hunting." There are people, mostly men, nearby, but none within listening range. If he's going to say anything that will make wearing this wire worthwhile, this is the place. "Last time I went quail hunting was years ago. In Idaho. But I'm always game. And you know, if you're ever in San Diego, I'd love to have you over."

"Will do. I'll get my assistant to get on scheduling something. You know, I've heard all about your mega yacht. I'd love to go out on that sometime."

"Name the time and place." My CIA training kicks in, and I strike a comfortable pose, look him in the eye, and do a casual smile, all the while controlling the urge to scratch the hell out of my jaw. "Just recently docked back in San Diego."

"Is that right?"

"Yep. Got back, I believe... yesterday." The ship unloaded approximately five hundred pounds of cocaine, four hundred pounds of fentanyl, and fifty pounds of heroin. The DEA made the call to follow the shipment and not bust them at the private harbor. I haven't heard an update since, but ballpark math on drugs that were smuggled in is close to twenty-five million dollars. The DEA suspects this was a conservative run, and they'll transport more as they gain confidence in my ship. Current theory is the Morales Cartel operates a fleet of ships with different owners to avoid drawing attention from any country.

"Nice. Since it's not quail season, let's take advantage of your yacht first, then we'll have you out to the family place in Arizona."

"I'd love that."

He tosses his unlit cigarette into the trash. "Let's go get that bourbon."

Damn it. Nothing. We got nothing. I told them this entire effort would be fruitless.

Back in the lobby, suits and gowns immediately flock to the senator. He shoots me with his hand, thumb to index finger, and says, "Talk soon, son."

Politicians are a unique breed, but that man is as slimy as they come.

With that part of the night behind me, I stride into the banquet hall to search for Ava. Ryan sees me and meets me ten feet inside the ice sculpture room.

"You okay with switching seats with Ava?"

We can't really talk here, but I'd prefer her seated with me at my table. Then as soon as I receive the blasted award, she and I can escape. I've got a lot of explaining to do.

"No problem. She's back in the far-right corner."

I survey the room and locate her. Patrick's head bows low, and the two of them appear to be having an intense conversation.

"Anything good out there?" Ryan asks.

"No. More of the same." I'm so sick of barely moving forward.

"You look pissed."

"Not even enough to get a wiretap."

Men like the senator don't go down easily. They're slippery like eels. I'm just so damn tired of playing this slow game. This hunt has gone on too long. I feel like I've been tracking wolves for years with absolutely nothing to show for it. They're thriving and, the worst part is they've been flourishing in my neck of the woods.

Ava and Patrick step out of the banquet room through a side door. I tap Ryan and jerk my head.

"I'm going after her."

"I'll stay here. If you head outside, remember Fisher and his team are out there. Just don't go anywhere they can't follow."

"Yes, sir." If my nerves were settled, I'd salute him in jest. The nerves could be a side effect from actually being wired, from having everything I say tonight recorded, or from the thrill of a hunt. Even a boring hunt with a nothing five-second conversation with a US senator stimulates.

But right now, this undercover op has the feel of a multi-year, multi-agency effort. That's exactly what I don't want. My contact promised me they wouldn't let the drugs onto the street. Said they just need to get a better understanding of the players in a newly identified drug ring. They didn't want to bust them on my yacht, as it would close that tracking avenue. All the guns we sold to Mexico... well, they're out there. Probably being used to kill Mexican law officers in the decades-long drug war. We can't stop that. But we sure as hell can prevent the siphoning of drugs onto American streets. Or will the desire to build a concrete legal case against as many participants as possible win out?

Ava trails Patrick. He's charging out of the building.

"Ava," I call, and a few heads turn my direction, but not hers.

I catch up to her and she calls, "Patrick."

He turns around, and my gaze fixates on the tears streaming down the big man's face.

"I gotta get outta here. You got her?" he asks, and I nod in the affirmative.

With a protective surge, I sidle up to Ava, claiming her with my arm around her lower back.

"Everything okay?" Obviously, it's not, at least not with Patrick, but she's back by my side, so in my world, one of the most important parts has righted. Operation bullshit be damned, she's important to me. And Sophia.

Ava's glossy, painted red lips turn down on the ends. Her brow crinkles. A line forms between her eyebrows, and I lower my lips to it. She places her hand on my chest, and her touch over the crisp white shirt soothes me. God, I missed her so much more than I realized.

"Patrick is leaving Mark. I think this time, it's for real. They've broken up before, but I think this is going to stick." My thumb caresses her smooth cheek. She's thoughtful, and the concern for her friend is touching. "I've tried so many times to get him to leave Mark. I've always said he deserves more." Those irresistible eyes flash up to mine, seeking understanding.

"But he wouldn't listen?"

She shakes her head with an emotional heaviness.

"It can be hard when a man loves someone," I say. "Hard to get them to listen to reason."

"It was pretty easy for your uncle to persuade you."

And there it is. She's right to be angry with me. "When you've been betrayed by people you love, it becomes easy to believe a loved one will betray you."

She twists in my arms, and her body presses against me. My hands fall to her waist, and I hold her there.

"I would never betray someone I love." She fixes me with a heartfelt stare, simultaneously accusatory and possibly promising.

"I know that now. You're one of the good ones."

"The money you paid me, I only used it for the center."

The pad of my thumb lightly brushes the diamonds circling her wrist.

"Gifts from your uncle's Black card via Patrick. They aren't real, but they are expensive."

"Money well spent."

"Patrick spent it. He spent a lot of money getting me glammed up so I would fit in."

"Ava, it doesn't matter what you wear. You're better, stronger than anyone else in this room. You're stunning. His money wasn't wasted. But it wasn't necessary. You could have walked in here with your combat boots and any outfit you own, and I would have wanted you by my side."

"I would have spent time with you, slept with you, done everything with you, without the money."

"And I only paid you as an attempt to keep you at arm's length. The moment I first saw you, thick eyeliner, an armory of silver, and clad in black, I was drawn to you. I couldn't figure it out. My reaction to you was a puzzle. On a base level, my reaction terrified me, because the last thing I need is to fall for someone. I thought with you in my home I would see your flaws. The attraction would fizzle."

"Jack." She drops her arms and shifts back, putting distance between us. Those large brown eyes are glassy and reflect the golden overhead light. "I just... I don't fit in your world. I care about you, and I'm glad you know the truth, but I can't..." She glances over her shoulder, through the open door into the cocktail banquet room. "This isn't me. Those people? If Patrick didn't spend a small fortune, these people, they would all see it."

"How can you say that? You're the most beautiful woman in the room, inside and out."

"I only fit in tonight because Patrick dressed me. If it wasn't for these mesh sleeves, they would all be staring at my arms." A winding mix of tropical and wildflowers cover her arms in arresting sleeves. The dress covers her in such a way that the designs show, but one might assume the tattoos are the gown's designs. "You need—"

"Don't you tell me what I need. Ava, I need you."

"It crushed me to think that you thought I was just one more person who would hurt you. But... Jack. This. Your world..." She's struggling for the words, but she doesn't need them, because I have them.

"My world needs you."

I link my fingers through hers. She might think this banquet room means something to me, but she couldn't be farther from the truth.

"Let's go." I need to get her out of here. I need to show her I love her in the only way I really know how.

"Don't you need to... you're on the program."

"I've done what I need to do here."

The dining room hall doors have opened, and attendees filter through, searching for their tables. I lead Ava in the opposite direction. I text Fisher, letting him know we're ready to leave.

"Where are you going?" Uncle Mark blocks the exit. "You can't leave."

"We can. And we are." I move to skirt around him. He presses his shoulder into mine and leans so his lips are inches from my ear.

"You don't give a shit, do you? It was all an act."

I haven't been acting with him. I've been avoiding his calls. "Excuse me?"

"You walk out of here, how will it look to the industry?"

"I don't care." I stare back at the man who played father figure for so much of my life. A virtual stranger.

"You don't, do you? You'd willingly be seen with a woman like her, and not give a damn if it hurts your reputation or the company." Fury illuminates his expression. He's off kilter. Awareness flashes. He might break, and I'm wearing a wire.

"I'm glad you understand. The company would never be my highest priority. Unlike you, I would never hide my true self for the sake of a business. And that right there is why you lost Patrick." The glare he gives me would shoot bullets if loaded. "And as for the company, I'm cleaning shop."

"What do you mean?" He grits the words out, leaning so close his breath heats the side of my face.

"What do you think I mean?" I hold my breath, waiting.

"If you think you're closing down the international partnerships I have worked damn hard to cultivate, you are out of your mind."

"Plural? Which partnerships do I need to leave alone?"

He scowls, but he doesn't speak.

My grip on Ava's hand tightens, and I move to bypass Mark. If anything will make him break, it's bypassing him and moving on.

He pushes hard against my shoulder, keeping me in place. Through gritted teeth he says, "There's a group of feds monitoring this site. We thought it was typical government overreach. Watching the NRA." His eyes narrow. "Are you working with them?"

No, the automatic lie thanks to years of training is on the tip of my tongue. But I hold it back, willing him to break. I raise one eyebrow and put on what I hope is one smug fucking expression.

His gaze falls to my chest, and his fingers rip my tuxedo shirt, sending buttons scattering across the marble floor. "Don't look surprised. I've ripped many in my time."

His fingers lift my undershirt, and his face transforms the second he spots the thin wire.

"First Patrick, and now you." In the last week, I have questioned if my uncle were a sociopath. But his pale skin and sad eyes hold too much emotion. He's simply a misguided man with warped priorities and a weak moral foundation. "I gave you so much."

"I know you believe that." It's all I can say.

He disregards me, and his focus falls to Ava. "And you. I've given you your life."

She's silent. Which doesn't seem to work for Mark Sullivan. He raises his hand, and I block him.

"Don't."

He peers around me to glare at Ava. "I'll get Patrick back."

"No, I don't think you will." She holds her chin up, and in her elegant gown and glittering diamonds, she looks like a queen censuring a peasant.

Mark's face contorts into one of blood-soaked rage.

A few stray tuxedoes and gowns gather nearby.

My hand wraps around my uncle's frail wrist, and I discreetly speak into his ear. "People are watching."

It's the magical phrase for Uncle. He straightens his coat and glances down at my torn shirt.

"Don't leave like that. The media is outside."

He leaves through the front of the hotel. And I curse, because he's right. I text Fisher and ask if I can borrow his tuxedo shirt. He's about my size.

It takes several minutes for an inconspicuous change to occur. As we're exiting the hotel, one of my uncle's assistants comes out of nowhere.

"Mr. Sullivan?" A young woman wearing a black business suit instead of a gown approaches. I recognize her from my uncle's office staff. He's brought her along to some of our meetings.

"Yes."

"I understand you need to leave. We've adjusted the program schedule. If you can just come and receive your award? Please?"

There's a desperation to her, and if I were to bet, my uncle has threatened her with the fear of god's wrath... or rather, his wrath. Ava's fingers press against my forearm.

"You might as well."

"I'm not supposed to tell you, but in addition to the golden jacket, you're receiving the NRA Businessman of the Year award. It's an enormous honor."

I let out a loud sigh. If I have to do this, I will.

"You're sitting at my table." I look into Ava's eyes, questioning. I'm only doing this if she remains by my side. Fuck my uncle and every other person in this room.

"If you're sure." She's tentative, but I'm not.

I brush my lips across hers, and a seismic shift occurs within. I love this woman. Passionately in love.

"I've never been more sure of anything in my life."

Thirty minutes later, we're finally done. After curt apologies and excuses to our dinner table, we exit the ballroom.

As expected, the media hover outside the hotel on the street. Cameras flash.

"Mr. Sullivan, may we ask who your guest is tonight?"

Ryan and I arrived by the side entrance and escaped the circus earlier. I briefly check my phone for an update on where to procure our ride.

"Certainly. Her name is Ava Amara, and she is my girlfriend." Ava's eyelids flutter, most likely shocked from the explosion of bright white flashes. "Hopefully more, very soon."

Adding that last bit goes against every bit of my nature. I do not share with the media. But if there is any doubt about my intentions, or where I think Ava can fit into my world, there's nothing quite like announcing it to the media.

"How long have you two been together?"

"How did you meet?"

"Does she live in San Diego with you?"

I hold up my hand and say, "No more questions."

They'll be hounding our press department, but that's a matter for tomorrow.

With her hand locked in mine, I guide Ava to Fisher and our awaiting limousine. He's parked to the side, since other vehicles blocked his ability to approach the front entrance.

A green dot on the stucco pillar sets me on alert. Across the street, there's a building. I scan the top, searching.

The green dot floats closer.

"Get down," I yell.

A poof of dust floats behind my head on stucco.

All around us, men raise their guns.

"Shooter. Three o'clock," a man shouts as I sling the back door open and shove Ava into the safety of the car.

She clutches my arm. "Wait. Where are you going?"

"To find the shooter."

"What? No." Her eyes are wide. Scared.

Ryan runs up with several men at his back.

"Sniper. He's going to be running," I tell him.

Police sirens pollute the air. Blue lights flash. On the street, cars are at a standstill, possibly barricaded in. No one is getting out of here in a vehicle.

"He was aiming at you," Ryan says.

"Keep her safe," I tell Fisher.

"No, wait. Why you? Let someone else go after him." There is panic in those eyes, and I gently release her hold on me with my focus peeled on the front of the opposing building.

"Ava. This has to end. If we don't catch this guy, it may never end." And I'm done. I want evidence that will lead to convictions. We didn't get enough from my uncle and nothing from the senator. I tap the window and close the door. "Take care of her," I reiterate to Fisher.

Ryan and I cross the front of the limo, headed straight to the building. Given their proximity, the FBI are already in the mix.

"This is a shit show. By now, he's off the roof. He'll be in disguise. It's the only way out of this," I say to Ryan.

"Copy that," he responds.

Shooting at an NRA event is complete madness. Technically, guns aren't allowed, but these people love their guns. There's no way the wealthy patrons' security doesn't have guns, and most of the attendees are proud conceal and carry members. Plus, in Texas, it's legal to conceal and carry pretty much anywhere you please.

A gun goes off behind us. We crouch. Scan. A drunken man yells, "Yahoo." Another man says, "You dumbass. You just hit a car."

Sirens flood the street.

I tap Ryan on the shoulder, inching forward. One of the FBI agents looks our way as we cross onto the sidewalk. He's moving to stop us when he recognizes Ryan. He nods and turns his attention back to a police officer.

I tap Ryan and jerk my head in the agent's direction. "Make sure they're looking for uniforms. They shouldn't let any cops off the block until we've confirmed identity."

Ryan nods and steps back to speak to the FBI agent. The building across the street is flanked by one building, and one narrow alley behind the building. Blue lights flash in the alley. It's an office building with multiple business signs in the window. The windows in the office building are all dark.

If I were a sniper, I would either enter the building from the back or from the adjacent building. The building next door houses a twenty-four-hour Medic Aid. Several medical professionals in scrubs huddle outside, watching the pandemonium on the street.

A police officer yells at them, "Go back inside. We have an active shooter."

The glass doors behind them open, and a man in scrubs exits. He looks like he's going to approach the group. I recognize him. Black choppy hair. Navy scrubs. The other women wear teal. His eyes flash.

It's the nurse. From Uncle Mark's apartment. I leap forward, and he takes off running. Only, he's shorter than I am. And within fifteen feet, I reach him, airborne, tackling him to the ground.

CHAPTER 38

Ava

"Shots fired at NRA Annual Awards Banquet. The shooter is in custody. Sources say the shooter may have been targeting Senator Talbot, who was in the area. Stay tuned as we get more updates."

I'm snuggled beneath a blanket on a black leather sofa in Jack's Houston penthouse. Uncontrollable shivers have wracked me for the last hour. Jack noticed and insisted we leave. The FBI reluctantly agreed. If he hadn't already been working with them, if he had just been a random person shot at in the crowd and who tackled the suspected shooter, I'm not sure they would have let us leave.

The television set is on, and Jack is on the phone, pacing the floor at the end of the room. Fisher is in the kitchen, also on the phone. He's wearing a holster, and I can't seem to stop staring at it. The man is always armed, but he hasn't tried to hide it since the shooting earlier tonight.

The shooting. Holy fuck.

My phone sits out, and I keep waiting for Patrick to call. But he hasn't. My bet is he's on a plane headed back to Los Angeles, and he's completely unaware of the chaos he left behind.

Indie saw the news. She texted, checking on me. I tried on my fancy outfit for her before flying first class with Patrick to Houston. So, she knew I was at the event. She told me that TMZ and a few other sites posted pics of me and Jack. She said everyone is wondering if the eligible billionaire has been snagged. I haven't looked. To be honest, it's disturbing to me that there was a shooting and Jack's dating status is a headline topic. Of course, no one died, so why would they care? If it hadn't been an NRA event, and if the senator wasn't present, it probably wouldn't even have made national news.

The thing is, I don't remember seeing the senator around us at all. But once the first shot fired, the scene devolved into mayhem. He could have been six feet away and I wouldn't have noticed.

Jack leaves the room, phone still tucked to his ear.

He called Sophia from the car. She'd been blissfully unaware, hanging out with Lauren and another girlfriend. He put her on speakerphone, and said, "Hey, there's also someone with me who wants to say hello."

"Ava?" she squealed.

"Hey, girl."

"I knew Dad would get his head out of his ass."

"Sophia." He reprimanded her with his tone, but the smile on his face said otherwise.

"You didn't lie, did you? Or if you did, you had a reason, right?"

"I didn't lie."

"I knew it! Are you guys coming home tonight?"

"I don't think we can." Jack told her. "But tomorrow we should be back."

His phone beeped with an incoming call.

"Don't leave the house tonight, okay?"

"Yes, Dad." I could practically see her rolling her eyes.

"I'll see you soon, Sophia." It's all I could get in before Jack clicked over for another call.

He's been on endless calls since.

Jack enters the den with Ryan at his side. Both men wear stern expressions. The sofa sinks from Jack's weight, and he pulls me up against him.

"Still cold?" he asks.

"It's shock and adrenaline," Ryan says.

He takes a chair across from us. Fisher joins us, sitting in the chair opposite Ryan.

"The surveillance team is in place. But I have to warn you, what we discover might not be admissible in court."

"I don't care. Some people within Sullivan Arms are involved. This time, I'm not looking for admissible in court. My cover's blown. I'm no longer useful to the operation. It's time to get the dirty players out of my company." Jack speaks to Ryan, but I follow every word. Fisher taps away on his phone.

"Just setting expectations. There's a good chance any involved will panic in the coming days and slip up. Especially now that Mark Sullivan has been detained."

Jack doesn't look like he agrees with Ryan. He confirms my suspicion when he says, "I doubt many of the low-level players know he's involved."

"Maybe. But the drug bust earlier today led to a warrant for Victor Morales' arrest, and thirty minutes ago they picked up Phillip Moore," Ryan says.

"Phillip Moore?" Jack asks Ryan. He nods, confirming he heard him correctly. "Strong case against him?"

"Unsure. But there are a lot of phone calls between one guy at the drug bust today and Moore. It's only a matter of time before we locate the financial trail. Only one undercover DEA agent was exposed during the bust. Not a bad day."

"Is it over?" I ask. The serious countenances clash with what they're saying.

"My part is." He brushes his lips across the top of my head. "My dear uncle screwed up royally when he came after me. With my cover blown, the DEA's hand was forced, and they had to go ahead and pull the plug on a different op. It all hit the fan tonight. I wore that wire to catch a senator. Didn't catch him, but I'd still call it a win." His thumb brushes back and forth against my arm, but his attention centers on the other two men in the room. I lay my head on his shoulder. "Smuggling contraband? That'll never be over. But my involvement, that's ending."

There's a niggling part of me that keeps telling me this isn't real and that I don't belong with someone like Jack. But the larger part of me is so shaken by what happened tonight, I can't question the future. Jackson Sullivan is a good man, and I care about him. No, I more than care about him. I love him. I love his daughter, and I love that she's excited at the prospect of seeing me again. This man is dealing with a shitstorm, and yet he is still concerned about me. He cares about me. Whether or not I deserve it, he cares.

"One agent leaked the guy you tackled is talking. And he hasn't asked for a lawyer."

"Thank fuck." Jack lets out a deep sigh. "They have to be all over him while he's detained. I don't trust Senator Talbot, or whoever else is in on this, won't pull strings to end a potential witness."

"Let's hope they learned from Killington's case," Ryan says.

The one guy who could have locked away Killington for smuggling ended up committing suicide his first night in jail. But, given the guards were conveniently sleeping, no one believes it was suicide. Killington is still going to jail, but for planning Sophia's abduction. Jack's pissed because he should face a life sentence, and instead he'll be out in ten or fifteen years, possibly earlier on good behavior.

"Have you heard anything about the case against my uncle? I keep thinking about what he said to me, and I could see it winning a search warrant, but it's not enough to convict."

"Sounds like he picked the wrong lover to play sniper. If he's spilling his guts, maybe he's sharing something good. Guy isn't trained at all."

"Well, he did miss," Jack says with a cocky smirk.

I remember that he himself is a sniper, and I gather the expressions traded between Jack and Ryan are some sort of brotherly macho display.

Ryan grins. "Apparently, he told them where to find records and videos Mark used for blackmail. I know you're close to him, but I don't think his lawyers will get him out of this."

I sit up straighter, not positive I am following the line of conversation. "Wait? Mark's lover?"

Jack brushes my hair behind my ear. "Apparently, the guy I thought was a nurse is his live-in lover. In Houston."

"He had someone in Houston?" All those times Patrick told me he wouldn't risk being seen as a gay man in Texas. Was that all a lie? Was Patrick the other man?

"I don't know how serious they were. You saw him. I'd guess he's early twenties. I can't imagine he's been with my uncle for long."

Holy shit. "Well, I guess on the bright side, there's no risk of Patrick going back to him now."

Jack presses his lips to my temple then maneuvers me back against his shoulder. "I'd say that's a safe bet."

"You need anything else?" Ryan asks.

"We're good," Jack says. "You two go get some sleep."

"Will do. You've got two security guys out in the hall. Shift change at zero-seven-hundred."

"And full staff back in San Diego?" Jack asks Fisher, but he says it for confirmation, like he's already fully aware of status.

"Full staff plus two. We'll revisit in a week," Fisher answers. "I don't want to take any chances."

"Thank you," Jack says. The two men exchange a pointed gaze.

Jack appreciates anyone who keeps his daughter safe, and as head of his security detail, he places a tremendous amount of trust and respect at Fisher's feet. It's something I suspect Fisher doesn't take lightly.

"Indie has been in touch," I tell Ryan as we walk them to the penthouse door. "She knows you're here and safe."

He nods. He's got whisper-light blue eyes, and his facial muscles hardly ever move. Most of the time, I consider Ryan to be unreadable, but when he says, "Thank you," I hear his sincerity. I'm not sure what history lies behind the man and his sister, but addiction casts a shadow. I'm glad Indie and Ryan seem to be out from under it.

After closing the door on the two men, Jack clicks the lock and drops his forehead to mine.

"Finally. It's just you and me."

CHAPTER 39

Five weeks later

Ava

"Dad, really? You're going to make me hold a sign?" The placard shows her name and grade. Patricia, his assistant, created it.

"He's not going to post it anywhere. But it's what all the cool dads do. Don't deny him."

Jack glances back at me and does a full-on eye roll. He has a teenage daughter, therefore he's familiar with the eye roll, but I've never seen him attempt one. And he screws it up epically. I laugh, but Sophia doesn't seem to notice, as she's fussing with her hair in her handheld mirror.

The doorbell rings. It's the first day of her junior year of high school. She doesn't yet have her license, but several of her friends do, and she's hitching a ride with Lauren. She begged her dad to please keep the security on the down low, so while they are present, they remain unseen. Fisher parked farther up the street, ready to discreetly follow her to school. Once she's on school grounds, Jack grudgingly agreed she'd be safe, but only because her ridiculously expensive private school is secure.

The investigation into Senator Talbot is still underway. The current team isn't optimistic they will find prosecutable evidence, although no one seems to doubt his involvement. At least, no one in law enforcement. Public opinion is divided along party lines.

Mark Sullivan has been charged, but he's hired a legal dream team, and it could easily be a year before his trial. Even if convicted, Jack's positive he'll convince the judge he should serve time under house arrest, given his current battle with cancer.

They found plenty of evidence against three Sullivan Arms' employees, and those employees are currently held without bail awaiting trial. There's a list of additional participants, and the federal government is leading the charge on prosecution.

Jack, for his part, has moved out of day-to-day operations and will continue in an advisory capacity on the company's board of directors. He plans to get more involved with Arrow Tactical Security and says he'd like to spend his time exploring technology that he knows will help the good guys.

As I open the front door, a bright beam of sunlight blinds me. I squint, and a wave of nausea rolls through me.

"Ava, are you okay?" Lauren asks.

"I'm fine." Lightheadedness blends with the nausea, and I grip the knob for stability. "Why'd you come to the front?"

Lauren always enters from the side of the house. She's been a staple here over the last month, along with one other girl and a guy who comes around every so often. Both are classmates, neighbors, and apparently good friends of Sophia's.

Lauren leans forward, speaking in a hushed tone. "It's easier. Don't tell Mr. Sullivan. If I drive up the side of the house, I have to reverse."

"Yeah, let's not mention that to him." He's nervous enough about her driving off with a new driver. I'm sort of shocked Sophia pulled it off, but he's so relieved and thankful she's moving forward with her life, he's liable to give her anything she asks for. Anything other than laying off on security.

Another wave of nausea hits me, and this time bile rises.

"They're in the kitchen." I point, even though she totally knows where it is, and rush for the nearby guest bath.

"Are you okay?"

"Something's not sitting right in my stomach." I reach the toilet just in time, and my morning coffee floods the bowl. The coffee didn't smell right this morning. The milk must have been bad.

There's a quick hard rap on the door. "Ava? Are you okay?"

My fingers tremble. The nausea bubbles up, and I lean forward as another round of bile surfaces. I breathe hard, and tears sting my eyes as I struggle to gain equilibrium.

"Yeah… just not feeling good."

"Sophia's about to go."

"Okay. Take photos."

Sophia's voice mingles with Jack's and Lauren's through the door as they all discuss my retreat for the bathroom. My forehead is damp. It might be a stomach bug.

I've been living here with Jack and Sophia since returning to San Diego from Houston. But things have changed. I drive to Nueva Vida three days a week. The Arrow security team keeps trackers on my car, in my purse, and in my jewelry.

I keep telling Jack that it's unnecessary. Sure, there were a handful of photographs of the two of us in circulation, but he's not a movie star. People simply don't care that much, and I keep telling him that no one is going to associate me with him. He doesn't need to worry someone will snatch me up for ransom.

His argument is that if anyone wants to target him, they'll watch the house and him, and it won't take an observer long at all before they recognize I am important to him. It's hard to argue against his points, because he thrust himself into the public eye when he offered that obscenely high reward for information leading to Sophia's kidnapping. The two of them will have to live with the repercussions of that decision for a long time.

I could probably push back more than I have. I haven't done so, because truthfully, I feel loved when he makes a big fuss. No one's ever made a big fuss about my safety before. In high school, I rebelled, and my parents did nothing. I can't exactly blame my parents for all of my choices, but now that someone is constantly showing how much he cares, I love it. There's a peace I haven't felt before. It's as if all the pieces of my life have fallen into place. I'm now in a mutually loving and supportive relationship, and it's more empowering than I could have ever imagined.

Of course, none of that helps with how sick I'm feeling. I sit on my butt with my head against the wall, near the toilet but not so close I'm looking down into it. The cool marble floor soothes my hot skin. My body hates me.

Rap. Rap.

"You okay?"

"Yeah. I'm starting to feel better."

"Can I come in?"

"Yeah."

Jack peeks in. I'm sure I'm quite the sight, sprawled on the floor, resting against the wall. I must look like a drunk binger.

"It's getting better. I just... I'm gonna sit here for a little bit, just in case."

He nods and pulls the door closed. I envision the climb upstairs and wonder if I can make it without another surge of nausea. Or I could take the elevator, but the thought of rising in the glass case stirs my stomach. No. The elevator holds no appeal.

There's a soft rap, the knob twists, and the door opens. Jack kneels by my feet, and I hold out my hand.

"Don't come near me. If this is contagious, you don't want it."

He cocks his head at me and smirks. He's wearing a t-shirt and shorts instead of his usual suit, off his usual workday schedule on account of it being the first day of school. Casual is a good look on him, and he wears it more regularly.

"After what we did last night, if you're contagious, do you think there's any way I'm not getting it?"

Well, that is true. Last night, Sophia went to bed early, on account of the first day of school, and Jack and I... well, we went into the locked room in the basement, and we explored new toys. We don't use that room frequently, as more often than not we retire to Jack's bedroom, but when we do, I really enjoy it.

In his palm, he holds a blue velvet ring box. Jack is the most generous man I've ever met. He's always buying me things, or rather, having the house manager buy me things. He bought a ton of bright, colorful clothes but then realized I just don't like clothes that scream *look at me* and filled my side of the closet with tons of black and monotone shades of white and gray. And the jewelry... he likes to give jewelry. But right now, as subtle waves of nausea roll, it's not a great time to give me yet another set of earrings or a silver stacking ring.

I breathe deeply to further quell the nausea. I should tell him now's not a good time, but that feels rude. His gifts are sweet. The last thing I want is to make him feel unappreciated. Sometimes I think he's overcompensating, trying to make up for how he treated me at the beginning. One day he'll understand he doesn't need to do that. When I told him I don't judge and don't harbor grievances, I meant it. I've just done too much shit in my time to hold much against anyone else. And I love him.

"Ava... it's early, but you need to know how I feel about you and where I want this to go." I open my mouth as he flips the lid, exposing a classic diamond solitaire. "This is my mother's ring. It's probably not your style, but it can be a placeholder until we go shopping."

"Your mother's?" Confusion overwhelms the nausea. "What?"

"Ava, I love you. I was drawn to you from the moment I laid eyes on you. You are the strongest woman I've ever known. You climbed out of a hellhole and built a new life not only for yourself, but for others. I've never known anyone so selfless, so logical and rational.

When I watch you with Sophia, when I listen to the two of you talk, my heart swells with so much love. It's more than I knew I could feel. I can't imagine a life without you, and more than that, I don't want to. Please say you will spend the rest of your life with me, as my wife."

Little black spots dot my peripheral vision. My heart bursts, but my brain struggles. He's proposing when I am kneeling by a toilet. And it all crystalizes.

"You think I'm pregnant. That's not what this is."

One of his hands clasps my ankle, and he edges toward me as his other hand lifts the sparkly ring closer.

"No."

"Don't lie to me, Jack." I soften my words with a smile. The man can really be too sweet.

"Yes." He taps the top of my nose with his finger, amusement playing across his face. "But here's the thing. I want to marry you whether or not you're pregnant. If you are, I'll be thrilled."

"You have an almost sixteen-year-old daughter."

"And I missed so much of her childhood. This will be my chance to do it over. The right way. To be a better father. If you're pregnant and want to keep the baby. And if you're not and want a baby, we can try. And if you don't want kids..." He lifts his shoulders, and his gaze drops as if he's having an entire conversation with himself in his head. "If you don't want kids, that's okay. We have Sophia. I want you. You are what I want."

"But you're proposing because you think I'm pregnant." That's not what I want. That's not what any woman wants.

"Yes, I think you might be pregnant. But..." he squeezes my ankle until I lift my gaze and look him in the eye, "I always felt like Cassie questioned if I would have asked her if she didn't get pregnant. Maybe she did, maybe she didn't. My parents definitely didn't help. Now that I look back on it, neither did my uncle. All of that combined put a lot of pressure on Cassie and me... Look, I don't want to risk any of that hanging over us. I want you in my life. End of story.

New baby or not." My throat tightens, and the room blurs. "Do you hear me?"

I nod as an errant tear escapes. He reaches out and gently wipes it away with his thumb.

"I hear you. I want to spend my life with you. But... I'm probably not pregnant. That's probably not what this is. Given my age and... I've been on the pill for years."

Years ago, I had a hormonal IUD, but then my insurance policy changed and I had to switch to the pill, which isn't as effective, but it wasn't a huge concern. For years I pretty much only took them to help with cramping.

He lifts my ring finger.

"Is that a yes? Will you marry me?"

"Yes." More tears fall, and cool gold slides across my finger, sticking at my knuckle, but with a wiggle, continues down to the base. I hold my hand up, and it's truly the most elegant and beautiful piece of jewelry I've ever seen. It's nothing like me. But I don't want to ever take it off. Ever.

"I love you, Ava."

"Love you, too." He pulls me onto his lap, and I tuck my head below his chin. "I need to go brush my teeth."

"Oh, Ava. God, I love you."

He somehow rises with me in his arms. His knees creak, and I can't stifle the giggle.

"You should not be lifting me."

"Just watch me."

EPILOGUE

Six Years Later

Jack

The back lawn has transformed into party central. We are hosting a catered lunch to celebrate two big family events.

Ava believes the lunch is strictly a graduation lunch for Sophia. My baby girl graduated from UCLA and has been accepted into the FBI graduate program. She'll be heading to Quantico in two short weeks. To be honest, I'm not thrilled, but she's determined to dedicate her career to locking up criminals. With any luck, she'll be an analyst.

I still don't know everything she endured when she was abducted, and as her father, I probably don't want to know. I'm so damn proud of her, though, for fighting through the dark and finding her way to better days.

Sophia believes this lunch is strictly a graduation lunch for Ava. My wife completed her Ph.D. in Experimental Psychology from

UCSD. She completed the rigorous program while continuing to oversee Nueva Vida and giving birth to our son, Justin, named after my father.

My uncle passed away two months before Justin was born. He died disgraced, under state penal custody, and alone. He begged for Ava to convince Patrick to reach out to him. Patrick blocked his number and returned all mail. To our knowledge, Patrick never spoke with him after his arrest.

Patrick waves to me from outside. He's carrying a bag loaded with wrapped presents. I exit the house and greet our friend.

"This looks amazing, Jack. I didn't know you had this in you." He's complimenting me on the party aesthetic. Bubble machines hidden in bushes send a whirl of bubbles over the swimming pool, and profuse flower and balloon arrangements are scattered everywhere. This is what money buys.

"I don't have this in me. Janet did it all. Well, she hired an event planner."

"I want that name. This is stunning."

Patrick no longer lives in Los Angeles. He moved to San Diego to take a more active role in Nueva Vida and to be closer to Ava. About a year after he and Mark split, he met a fantastic guy who we all love.

"Where's Joey?"

Patrick glances at his watch. "He'll be here. His shift doesn't end until one."

Joey is a police officer with the SDPD. For a few years there, I worried he'd convince Sophia to join the police force. I'm not entirely sure the FBI is safer than the police force, but she's making her choices.

Ava and I have our hands full with our son. She was pregnant on the day I proposed, but it wasn't a healthy pregnancy, and she miscarried. It was an emotional time for us, but we made it through with open, honest communication. The kind Ava specializes in. And a little over two years later, she delivered our healthy son at the age of forty-one.

I am bracing myself for that first day of kindergarten when some parents are half my age, but that's fine. Chances are I'll be much wiser than the younger parents. For one thing, work no longer rules my life. Supporting my wife and being a dad are my top priorities by miles.

"Look at these cakes. Holy...!" Patrick sets his shopping bag down and pulls out his phone to snap photos.

One cake says Congratulations Sophia and the other reads Congratulations Dr. Amara. Yes, Ava kept her name. She said she needed to maintain her identity. I'll give her anything she wants, and most definitely everything she needs.

"How many people are coming?"

"Janet handles the details. I'm not sure."

I glance around at the tables and chairs. An acoustic guitar player Ava and Sophia like is setting up in a corner. Guests will arrive in about thirty minutes, but Ava and Sophia should arrive any minute. Patrick and I will surprise them.

Sophia thinks she's getting Ava out of the house for this setup, and Ava thinks she's getting Sophia out of the way for the party. It's truly the most ingenious plan I've ever had.

Ryan and Alexandria round the path to the back yard.

We have a valet service out front, and they will handle parking cars and instructing guests to come along the side of the house to the back. Arrow Security has a staff monitoring video and a few discreetly placed employees along the beachfront and at the front of the property.

"This is amazing," Alex gushes.

Ryan flew his helicopter down from Santa Barbara so they could join us. They didn't bring their kids since Alex says parties like this are more enjoyable without them in tow, but Ryan confided that their kids don't do adult parties too well. They're a couple of years older than Justin, but I definitely understand.

"You've done a great job," he says.

"Puh-leaze," Patrick says, his grin wide.

"Hey, even for hiring someone, this is impressive," Ryan counters.

I give Alex a hug, and as I do, I see my family come around the side path.

Justin sits on his mother's hip, but his legs are kicking back and forth, eager to get down and check out the balloons and bubbles and probably climb on all the tables. He's four, and I could swear his sister was much calmer at age four, but maybe it's a case of rose-colored glasses.

Sophia lights up, clearly enchanted by the flowers and balloons. I used all her favorite colors, since my wife's favorite colors remain what I consider non-colors. Our back yard is an explosion of dark and light pink, blues and greens.

Fisher trails them along the path but stops and finds an out of the way location near the back of the house. He meets my gaze, and we nod at each other. He's been the head of our home security team for six years. We discussed having someone follow Sophia to Quantico, but Fisher convinced me that would be unnecessary. We agreed that once she completes the program, depending on where she's assigned, we may send a security detail. I sent one to UCLA, but they remained largely on the periphery.

Fisher will be leaving our services. Against my advice, he's joining the CIA. But with his military experience and ongoing work with Arrow, he'll be an asset for them. I'm not entirely sure what he will be doing for them. The only reason I'm aware is that one of my contacts within the organization reached out to me as his employer when they were considering him. His official reason for leaving Arrow is that he is changing careers and entering corporate America's concrete jungle.

Several of Sophia's friends arrive at the same time my wife sees the cakes.

"You." It's all she says. She sets down Justin, and he takes off. I go to my gorgeous wife and accept the kiss she wants to give me.

"I'm so proud of you."

She constantly amazes me. Today she's wearing a sleeveless white dress. She no longer worries over her tattoos. The tattoos cover most scars, but there's one nasty scar from an infection site that remains visible. I've told her over and over that her scars bear witness to her strength. It took a long time, but she finally heard me.

An expose about her history, her heroin addiction, homelessness, and her rehabilitation success came out not too long after I announced to the world she was mine. Letters poured in from all over the country from others inspired by her experience. Nueva Vida has grown and flourished, and Ava has consulted with three other nonprofits to build similar facilities in their states.

She says to this day that she doesn't know why she's one of the lucky ones. She claims anyone can relapse and the statistics prove that not everyone survives addiction. But she's got an inner strength and conviction. She says she takes it day by day and takes nothing for granted. But there's a light within her. I once suspected her darkness drew me in. But now, I believe on that first day when she entered my home, her inner light called to my soul. I didn't listen at first, but now, she's my guiding siren.

"Did you really think I wouldn't celebrate your achievement too?"

"But Sophia," she hisses, and I shut her up by claiming her full, soft, kissable lips.

And that's when we hear the splash.

He can swim, so there's no panic, but now he's wet, and guests are arriving.

Hands linked, Ava and I stroll over to the pool. Justin bobs up and gives us a sheepish grin.

"Justin, what did we say about getting close to the pool?"

"But the balloons," he whines.

"Justin," I say, bending down to take his hand and haul him out of the pool. "What did—"

"I not listen."

Water pools at his feet, and smiling, Ava takes his hand. "Let's go get you cleaned up."

"Oh no. You are the guest of honor. I got it."

His small hand wraps around two of my fingers.

"I'll get him—"

I loop an arm around my wife, letting my hand drop to her ass and giving her one firm squeeze that shuts her up. "I've got him."

"But—," she tries to argue.

"I've got everything. Now, go celebrate. And as soon as I get the little terror dressed, we'll be down to celebrate. And tonight," I dip my head close to her ear, "we'll have a private celebration."

A flush of color lights her cheeks, and god, I love that blush. My wife doesn't blush often, but when she thinks about our secret room among the company of others, she does. She places the tips of her fingers to her lips and blows me a kiss as she walks away, going to greet our guests. But she gives me that little smile, and those deep brown eyes glint with amusement and love, and yeah, she hears me.

The End

Sophia's story, many years later, is up next in *Cloak of Red.*

In the past, he was paid to protect me. Now, he's being paid to marry me.

One Fake Marriage and an Easy Op.

That was the plan.

They were never supposed to fall in love.

CIA legend Damien Fisher has a stellar reputation. As an undercover operative, love isn't something he sees as a possibility. It's not even something he wants.

. . .

Sophia Sullivan started her career as an FBI analyst, but the CIA won her over with the promise of fieldwork. After being abducted as a teen by men who wanted to play her billionaire father, she's dedicating her career to taking down criminal enterprises.

They never expected to work together. When she was a teen, he was her bodyguard.

It's supposed to be an easy op, simply build a rapport with the wife of a man suspected of working with a Colombian cartel.

But the easy op transforms into a cross-agency endeavor. Secrets from the past unfurl. And lines blur when the physical relationship becomes all too real. In the end, it's not just their mission on the line. It's also their hearts and lives.

How far will she go to unravel the truth?
How far will he go to protect her?

FROM THE AUTHOR...AKA IZZY

If you enjoyed the story, I hope you'll take a moment to leave a review. Five-star reviews truly do sell books, bringing me closer to the day when I might be able to do this full time. So I'm deeply grateful for them.

In case you are curious...

Better to See You is technically the first in the Arrow Series, but the Arrow series is a spin-off from the Twisted Vines series, which spun-off from the Haven Island series.

Sophia's story, many years later, is up next in *Cloak of Red.*

At the age of 15, I was abducted by men who played me like a pawn.

Their mistake?

They let me live.

ALSO BY ISABEL JOLIE

Arrow Tactical Security Series

Better to See You (Wolf and Alexandria)

Sure of One (Jack and Ava)

Cloak of Red (Sophia and Fisher)

Stolen Beauty (Knox and Sage)

Savage Beauty (Max and Sloane)

Sinful Beauty (Tristan and Lucia)

Gilded Saint (Sam and Willow)

Scarlet Angel (Nick and Scarlet)

Prophet (Dorian and Caroline) - Releasing June 12th

The Twisted Vines Series

Crushed (Erik and Vivi)

Breathe (Kairi and David)

Savor (Trevor and Stella)

Haven Island Series

Rogue Wave (Tate and Luna)

Adrift (Gabe and Poppy)

First Light (Logan and Cali)

The West Side Series

Blurred Lines (Jackson and Anna)

Trust Me (Sam Duke and Olivia)

Finding Delilah (Delilah and Mason)

Forgetting Him (Jason and Maggie)

Chasing Frost (Chase and Sadie)

Misplaced Mistletoe (Ashton aka Dr. Bobby and Nora)

Standalone Romances

How to Survive a Holiday Fling (Oliver Duke and Kate)

Always Sunny (Ian Duke and Sandra)

The Romantics (Harrison and Zuri)

NOTES & GRATITUDE

Sure of One was so much fun to write and research. Some of the books I read when formulating ideas for this book include *The Big Fix* by Tracey Helton Mitchell. Her memoir of life after heroin greatly inspired Ava's strength. Also, *Gunfight* by Ryan Busse was incredibly informative and thought-provoking. But, I suppose most importantly, Busse offered a view into life as a gun runner and manufacturer. One podcast that I routinely listen to is FBI Retired Case File Review. It's so great to hear retired agents talking about successful cases and operations and it's a great resource for ideas.

Also...there's the sex room. I had a beta reader comment "no one with a child would ever have a sex room in their home." Oh contraire, my friend! There's a reality TV show about a charming British dame in her, I'd guess early-to-mid sixties, who goes around to people's homes and designs sex rooms. If you haven't seen it, definitely check it out. I think it only lasted one season, but it's fanfuckingtastic. It's HGTV for sex rooms. She interviews the couple (or multiples), finds out what they want (sort of) and then they go away and she designs the room and fills it with furniture and toys galore. Then - just like HGTV - they get that open-the-door reveal moment. There's some full-on construction that's done too. Which there should be - the show is titled "How to Build a Sex Room" and it's on Netflix. Go watch it. It's funny, informative and you will want to talk about it with your friends.

Anyway, inspiration for Jack's playroom came from this show, and the idea he'd hire a designer (which, let's be real...Christian Grey absolutely hired someone and said..."surprise me").

As always, heart-felt thanks and appreciation goes out to my beta and ARC readers, to my editor, Lori Whitwam, and my proofreader, Karen Cimms for all her special care and attention. Most especially, **thank you**, dear reader, for reading. Thank you, thank you, thank you!

ABOUT THE AUTHOR

Isabel Jolie, aka Izzy, lives on a lake, loves dogs of all stripes, and if she's not working, she can be found reading, often with a glass of wine. In prior lives, Izzy worked in marketing and advertising, in a variety of industries, such as financial services, entertainment, and technology. In this life, she loves daydreaming and writing contemporary romances with real, flawed characters with inner strength.

Sign-up for Izzy's newsletter to keep up-to-date on new releases, promotions and giveaways. (**Pro-tip** - She offers a free book on her home page...just scroll down after arriving at her site.)

Buy ebooks and signed paperbacks direct from Isabel at www.isabeljoliebooks.com

Want to say hi? Email her through her website or reply to her newsletter...she loves to hear from readers.